PRAISE FOR *THE SHADOW BOX*

"*The Shadow Box* is Luanne Rice at her dazzling best. Filled with dark family secrets and wells of deep emotion, this novel will stick with you long after you've finished reading."

—Harlan Coben, #1 *New York Times* bestselling author of *Run Away*

"As always, Luanne Rice gives us characters so real they feel like family and families so flawed they give us chills. Shocking, compassionate, and told with the unerring eye of a true and gifted observer, *The Shadow Box* will keep you turning the pages long past your bedtime."

—Tami Hoag, #1 *New York Times* bestselling author of *The Boy*

"A clever protagonist in extreme danger pitted against a cruel and powerful circle made the stakes in *The Shadow Box* so high I could barely stop reading for a drink of water. Luanne Rice creates a thrillingly compelling tale of common cruelty, high ambition, and the courage it takes to oppose them. Well done!"

—Barbara O'Neal, *Wall Street Journal* and *USA Today* bestselling author of *When We Believed in Mermaids*

"Every family has secrets, but in Luanne Rice's clever thriller, *The Shadow Box*, the truth won't set you free—it will put you in a shallow grave . . . particularly if you live in the posh Connecticut enclave of Catamount Bluffs, where corruption, kidnapping, and murder are only a few of the community's hidden sins."

—Lee Goldberg, #1 *New York Times* bestselling author

PRAISE FOR *LAST DAY*

"Lovely, lyrical—and lethal. Luanne Rice turns her talents in a new direction and succeeds completely."

—Lee Child, #1 *New York Times* bestselling author

"Luanne Rice is the master of small towns with big secrets. With a deft touch, she draws us into a picture-postcard New England village, behind the closed doors of a well-loved home with its beautiful gardens and perfect family, only to expose the truths within. Surprising, powerful, a total page-turner."

—Lisa Scottoline, *New York Times* bestselling author of *Someone Knows*

"In *Last Day*, Luanne Rice shows once again her unique gift for portraying the emotional landscape of a family. By adding a riveting thread of suspense, she proves beyond the shadow of a doubt that love and murder make brilliant bedfellows."

—Tess Gerritsen, *New York Times* bestselling author of *The Shape of Night*

"*Last Day*, by Luanne Rice, shines with its brilliant plot about four women friends, their families and loves, and, shockingly, a murder. Rice's writing is flawless and fast—her characters are like the women I have coffee with—and the desire, violence, and betrayals shock me and remind me of Liane Moriarty's *Big Little Lies*."

—Nancy Thayer, *New York Times* bestselling author of *Surfside Sisters*

"A dark family history. A deeply flawed marriage. The complicated tangle of the ties that bind. Luanne Rice writes with authenticity and empathy, unflinchingly exploring her characters and diving into the shadowy spaces where they hide their secrets. Like all great stories, *Last Day* is a compulsive, twisting mystery dwelling inside a searing portrait of what drives us, as riveting as it is human and true."

—Lisa Unger, *New York Times* bestselling author of
The Stranger Inside

"A brutal murder, a failed marriage, secret lovers, and enough suspects to fill a room. The truth lies somewhere between betrayal and love. A compelling mystery you won't put down or solve until the final pages."

—Robert Dugoni, *New York Times* and Amazon Charts bestselling author of the Tracy Crosswhite series

"I've long loved Luanne Rice for her trademark elegant style and her deep understanding of familial relationships, and she brings these superpowers with her as she delves into suspense. *Last Day* is a true page-turner, peopled by characters I care deeply about, with an ending I never saw coming."

—Joshilyn Jackson, *New York Times* and *USA Today* bestselling author of *Never Have I Ever*

"In a family drama that is as suspenseful as it is empathetic, Rice again displays her ability to portray female friendship and the pain of loss."

—*Booklist* (starred review)

"Rice keeps the reader guessing as she gradually doles out long-hidden family secrets. Fans of intense family dramas will be rewarded."

—*Publishers Weekly*

"Strong love overcomes pain in this latest from Rice, which combines suspense with stories of survivors, sisterhood, best friends, and small communities shaken by violence or death."

—*Library Journal*

"A riveting story of a seaside community shaken by a violent crime and a tragic loss."

—*Brooklyn Digest*

"From the exquisite opening, through twists and torment, this domestic thriller weaves an irresistible story of family and friends, trust and betrayal, love and murder."

—*Suspense Magazine*

"Luanne Rice's opening pages of *Last Day* illustrate elegant writing at its finest. Twist after twist is guaranteed to keep readers guessing all the way to the surprises in the final pages . . . a sheer pleasure to read. Rice, the author of more than thirty books, is a master at writing descriptions and portraying story settings, a skill other writers admire and strive to acquire."

—*New York Journal of Books*

"The themes of love, loss, sisterly devotion, betrayals, and family ties are skillfully interwoven. [Rice] provides just enough intriguing detail to make the reader want to learn more . . . She once again doesn't disappoint in this novel."

—*LymeLine.com*

"*Last Day* by Luanne Rice is a gripping psychological suspense story. It starts out with an intensity from page one that never lets up."

—*Crimespree Magazine*

"If you're a fan of Shari Lapena or Ruth Ware, order this book and get ready to be sucked in. It's one of the best books of the year so far."

—*GQ Magazine*

THE
SHADOW
BOX

OTHER TITLES BY LUANNE RICE

THE
SHADOW
BOX

LUANNE
RICE

THOMAS & MERCER

Published by Thomas & Mercer, Seattle

www.apub.com

Amazon, the Amazon logo, and Thomas & Mercer are trademarks of Amazon.com, Inc., or its affiliates.

ISBN-13: 9781542025188 (hardcover)
ISBN-10: 1542025184 (hardcover)

ISBN-13: 9781542009553 (paperback)
ISBN-10: 1542009553 (paperback)

Cover design by Shasti O'Leary Soudant

Printed in the United States of America

First edition

For Maureen and
Olivier Onorato

THE ATTACK

1

CLAIRE

I died, and I relive my death hourly. Although my absence from the world remains constant, the method changes each time. Could it be that I was strangled, staring past the mask into emotionless eyes as he crushed my larynx with his thumbs? Or was it this rope knotted around my neck? I try to grab onto memories, but they slip away like waves and the receding tide.

Nothing is clear, but I feel blood trickling from my head, and I think, yes, he threw me across the garage in a sudden fit of rage, cracking my skull against the Range Rover's right rear bumper, shocked and sorry for what he did.

I wonder, Did he try to revive me? Or had he come to kill me, plotting it out in his meticulous way? Had he come armed with his knife, maybe Ford's baseball bat, timed my arrival, and patiently waited for me to walk into the garage with my beachcombing treasures? Friday, the start of Memorial Day weekend, and I was feeling so happy.

Am I dead? Am I dreaming this? What time is it? Are people showing up for my opening? My best friend manages the gallery. Does she realize yet that I'm not coming? Will she send help? A thought shimmers through my mind: I was warned, and I didn't listen. My mind is dull, and my mouth is dry; my face and hands are crusted with blood. The sound of my head being smashed rings in my ears. I hear myself crying.

There is a line tied around my neck, chafing the skin raw. I can barely breathe; I try to claw it away. The knot is too tight, and my fingers barely work—my hands are covered with shallow cuts. I see the knife waving, jabbing my hands as I hold them up to block the thrusts. But he didn't stab me. My wrist is raw, not from knife wounds, but from where he yanked my gold watch, a wedding present, over my hand.

I'm still in the drafty old carriage house we use as our garage. The concrete is solid beneath me, and I taste my own blood: signs that I'm still alive. Beside me on the floor are two lengths of splintered wood. My throat is on fire from the rope's pressure. My fingernails break as I struggle to loosen the knot. I pass out on the hard floor. When I come to, I feel cold. Was I out for a minute or an hour or all day and night, and did I die? I try again to tug the line from my neck—that must mean I'm not dead. The knot refuses to give.

Still on the ground, lying on my back, I stretch my legs and flex my feet. My limbs work. Slowly I pull myself up by the car's bumper; I lean on the rear door, leaving bloody handprints. My palms and fingers and the insides of my wrists are covered with small, almost superficial cuts.

An image fills my mind: a knife slashing the air but barely touching me, me punching and slapping and ducking, him laughing. Yes, it's coming back now. He wore a black mask. He dangled my watch in front of me, a taunt that seemed to mean something to him but not to me.

"Let me see your face!" I screamed as I fought him.

My attacker wore black leather gloves and blue coveralls, the kind mechanics wear, and the mask. So he planned it. It wasn't a bout of sudden rage. He came ready for this. He hid his face and hands, so he couldn't be recognized. But it was his body, tall and lean, and nothing could hide that from me.

My husband is Griffin Chase, the state's attorney for Easterly County, Connecticut, and a candidate in November's gubernatorial election. Smart money says he will be the next governor, and there is a lot of money, a fortune, in his war chest: he has big donors, and he has made promises to all of them.

He studies the cases he prosecutes. He tells me what the husbands did wrong and that he would never make those mistakes. Griffin convicts violent offenders. He sends the abusers, the batterers, the stalkers, and the murderers to prison, and then comes home for dinner and tells me they are his teachers. He admires women killers too, including a local mother of two he successfully prosecuted for murdering her best friend.

John Marcus, a murderer he put away for life last October, had stabbed his wife forty-seven times. He was caught because he had accidently cut himself when his hand slipped down the bloody blade and his DNA had mixed with hers.

"I can't think of anything more horrible than being stabbed," I'd said to Griffin. "Even just *seeing* the knife, it would be pure terror, knowing what he was about to do with it."

Now the memories flood in—clear, no longer a dream. Of course, he wouldn't stab me, because prosecuting John Marcus had taught him what not to do. But he must have remembered what I'd said about the dread of a knife. Leaning against the car now, I could still see the blade thrusting, glinting in the cool daylight streaming through the window, nicking my palm, the insides of my wrists, but nothing more, never going deep. Terrifying me would give him pleasure.

After he shoved me and I hit my head on the car bumper, he quickly tied the rope around my neck.

"Griffin, take off the mask," I said while I could still talk, before the noose tightened. Did he want my death to look like suicide? Or would he remove my body after I was dead? Stash me in his boat, take me out into the Atlantic, past Block Island, where the trenches were so deep a person would never be found?

He threw the rope upward once, twice. It took him three times to toss it over the rafter, but then he began to pull, and I could hear the line inching and scraping the rough wooden crossbar overhead. He was strong, his body taut—athletic and lean.

My neck stretched as he pulled on the line, my lungs bursting with air I couldn't exhale. I rose onto my toes, up and up. I grabbed the rope circled around my neck and tried to loosen the grip. The insides of my eyelids turned purple and flashed with pinprick stars. *Breathe, breathe, breathe,* I thought, hearing the gasps and gurgles coming from my throat. I tried to keep my feet from leaving the ground, but they did, and I thrashed and scissor kicked the air. I passed out.

Through the fog of near death, I thought I heard a scream outside, a high-pitched wail, primal and wild. Is that why he left me there before he had finished killing me? Had the sound scared him off? Or had the noise come from my own throat? Had my attacker run into the kitchen, hidden in the house? Or slipped out the garage door and escaped along the beach path? He must have thought I was dead or would soon die.

I look up at the garage ceiling. One rafter is damaged, part of it lying on the floor next to me. I realize it broke under my weight, and my eyes fill with tears. This old carriage house was built around 1900, at the same time Griffin's great-grandfather, governor of Connecticut, the first Chase man to hold political office, constructed the "cottage"— growing up, I would have called it a mansion. We live at the edge of the sea, and countless nor'easters and hurricanes have battered this place. We've been meaning to reinforce the building for years. The rafter gave way, and I tumbled to the floor and lived. This weathered old structure saved my life.

My left ankle is bruised and swollen, and my legs are stiff. Will I make it through my backyard, over the stone bridge, into the marsh, and from there into the pines, the deep woods, to the safe place my father and I built together? It is a long way. Will my blood leave a trail for Griffin to follow? The state police have a canine unit. Griffin will make sure his minions send the cadaver dogs after me.

When will I be missed? I have until they first notice I am gone to get where I need to go. My whole body is shaking. Will I make it? What if the police find me first? They belong to Griffin. My husband rules law enforcement in Connecticut. He was already a man of power, and the backing he has for his run for governor gives him even more. The secret I keep could ruin his career. And once it gets out, his campaign will end, and the men who support him will be furious.

I think about the letter I received, and the warning it contained. Why didn't I listen?

My hands hurt. I picture the knife again, and my knees feel like jelly.

Using the garage walls for support, I stagger to a shelf at the back and take down a can of animal repellent—a foul-smelling powdered mixture of fox, bobcat, and cougar urine that I bought by mail order. It is intended to keep deer away from gardens, dogs away from borders. The smell of predators will raise their hackles, send fear through their blood. My woodsman father taught me the potion has another use: when spread in the wild, rather than repelling, it will attract the species of animals that excreted the urine.

Ever since my father's death, we have stayed connected in spirit, through the myth of a mountain lion said to live deep in the woods nearby. Perhaps that big cat is a ghost, just like my father, just like members of the Nehantic and Pequot tribes who lived here before us. But I have seen and tracked large paw prints, collected tufts of coarse yellow fur for my work, and I have seen his shadow. Could that have been the caterwaul I heard just as I was supposed to die?

The smell of the mixture will throw off the dogs. They will be intrigued by the possibility of a wild animal; they will sniff along the boundary line I will create. They will not cross it, and they will forget about their quarry—me. My father's lessons along with years of loving the forest, observing the behavior of its inhabitants, will help me escape.

I find a beach towel in the cupboard and use it to put pressure on my head wound. The blood soaks through—I am shocked by the amount because there is already a pool on the floor. How much have I lost?

I feel weak, and I bobble the tin. Some urine powder falls to the floor. I try to wipe it up, but the putrid stench nearly makes me vomit. When the search dogs get here, they will growl and back away from this corner; they will be on guard before they even begin.

I start to walk and trip on the rope around my neck. If I can't untie the knot, I can at least cut through it. I look around the Range Rover for the knife my attacker used, but it's not here. He must have taken it.

Garden clippers hang on a rusty nail; I use them for pruning roses and hydrangeas. The handles fit my hand, but it hurts to maneuver them. Do I have the dexterity to snip the line instead of my artery? I nick the skin, but victory—the rope falls to the floor. This effort has taken all my energy, so I sit down and hope I'll be able to stand again before the police arrive.

Griffin's police departments throughout eastern Connecticut will investigate my disappearance with the full force of his office behind them. Suspicion will fall on violent criminals he sent to prison—he will make sure of that. People will assume someone wanted revenge. Detectives will investigate every recently released convict. They will question the families of prisoners still incarcerated.

My husband will hold a news conference and say that the police will catch whoever harmed me, abducted me, or killed me and removed my body, and he very personally will prosecute that person, get justice for me. The tragedy will burnish his image: public servant, grieving husband. I will become a hashtag: #JusticeForClaire.

But he, someone on his force, or one of his political backers with too much to lose will find and murder me first.

Terrified and half-dead, I choke on a sob. I had loved my husband more than anyone, this man who now wanted me dead. I am dizzy, can barely stand. I think, for half a minute, of going to my studio behind the house, grabbing the letter. But why? I ignored it when it mattered most, when it could have saved me. Let it stay in its hiding place. If I die, if I never return, it will be a record of what happened.

It is time for me to set off on a journey that will be short in distance, endless in effort. Maybe I'm delirious, just coming back from having been deprived of oxygen, but I sense that big cat padding silently in the woods ahead of me—my destination—and I walk cautiously. Fear is the gift.

It's how I will stay alert and alive.

2

CONOR

Conor Reid arrived at the Woodward-Lathrop Gallery at four forty-five, fifteen minutes before Claire Beaudry Chase's opening was scheduled to start. His girlfriend, Kate Woodward, owned the gallery in the center of Black Hall, and his sister-in-law, Jackie Reid, managed it. Kate was flying a private charter and wouldn't be back in time. Conor had promised he would show up to celebrate their friend Claire.

Conor was a detective with the Connecticut State Police and had just finished interviewing witnesses to a hit-and-run on the Baldwin Bridge. A speeding black pickup had clipped a Subaru, smashing it into the guardrail. There were no fatalities, but the car's driver had gone to the hospital with a head injury. No one had gotten the truck's license number.

It was the Friday of Memorial Day weekend, and the madhouse of summer on the shoreline was just starting.

"Hey, you made it," Jackie said, walking over to give Conor a hug. She was married to his older brother, Tom—his first marriage, her second. Conor had liked Jackie and her two daughters right away. Tom was a coast guard officer, often at sea on patrol, and Conor saw how happy Tom was to come home to her.

"Looks like you're expecting a big crowd," Conor said, glancing at the bar and catering table, loaded with bottles of wine and platters of cheese and bread and smoked salmon.

"We are," she said. "Everyone's excited to see Claire's new installation, but I think we'll also get a lot of people curious to meet the candidate. Judging from the calls I've gotten, I expect more political than arts reporters. Do you think Griffin will win? Be our next governor?"

"Seems he has a good chance," Conor said. He had worked with Griffin Chase on many cases. Chase played hard and knew what it took to come out on top.

People began streaming through the door. From being with Kate, Conor knew that there were three types of people who attended art openings in Black Hall: true collectors who intended to buy, serious art lovers who were there to appreciate the work, and people who came for the free food and wine.

On the bar table were plastic glasses and bottles of red and white wine, both from southeastern Connecticut vineyards. Someone had calligraphed a card for the wine: *Courtesy of Griffin Chase. Smart,* Conor thought: showing that he supported Connecticut businesses.

"Come on," Jackie said. "Take a walk around with me; check out the work."

"Sure," Conor said. He had never been that interested in art; Kate had taught him pretty much everything he knew. Kate was a huge fan of Claire. What she did couldn't exactly be called paintings, collages, or sculptures, but it had aspects of each. She made shadow boxes, driftwood frames filled with objects from nature, especially the beach.

"Who buys these?" Conor asked.

"Claire has devoted collectors," Jackie said. "One actually commissioned her to do a private piece for him and his wife."

"Which one is that?" Conor asked.

"She's not putting it in the show. It's back in her studio," Jackie said. "She told me it's 'guarding her secrets.'"

"What secrets?" Conor asked, but Jackie just shook her head. He felt a ripple that sometimes signaled the start of a case, but he figured he was overreacting.

He saw Jackie glance at her watch.

"It's nearly five, and she's still not here," Jackie said.

"Maybe she wants to make an entrance," he said.

"No, she said she was coming early, to autograph a few catalogs for clients who can't make it. Let me check on her."

Jackie stepped away and made a call from her cell phone. Conor took the opportunity to grab some cheese and crackers and survey the room. He would never enter this gallery without thinking of Beth Lathrop, Kate's sister. He and Kate had gotten close while he was investigating Beth's murder.

Beth used to run the place; after her murder, Kate had hired Jackie. Conor knew it was hard for Kate to come here; it wasn't easy for him, either: the building was haunted by violence and tragedy, but it had been in the Woodward family for three generations, and Kate would never let it go. Conor couldn't help feeling that Jackie was helping Kate keep it in the family, partly for Beth's daughter, Samantha.

"No luck," Jackie said, walking over to him.

Conor didn't reply, distracted by one of Claire's shadow boxes. It was about twelve-by-sixteen inches, bordered by a driftwood frame, and filled with mussel- and clamshells, moonstones, exoskeletons, sea glass, crab claws, and carapaces. It also contained what looked like the skeleton of a human hand and was titled *Fingerbone*.

"That hand," Conor said.

"I know, creepy, right?" Jackie said. He felt the ripple again and sensed her watching for his reaction.

"Reminds me of something," he said, not wanting to say too much, wondering whether she had heard what Claire told him at dinner on Monday.

"Ellen?" Jackie asked—proving to Conor that she had heard enough. She was referring to Ellen Fielding, a school friend of Jackie, Claire, and Griffin's, who had died twenty-five years ago.

Griffin's official state car pulled up in front of the gallery. He stepped out, projecting the confidence and power that everyone in the court system was so familiar with. He wore custom-made suits and Hermès ties, and Conor had heard one corrections officer say he could put his kid through college on Griffin's tie budget alone.

"Look who's here," Jackie said and headed for the door.

Conor hung back, watching. Griffin had grown up as a rich kid in tragic circumstances. He had lost his parents young. His college girlfriend had died just after graduation. His PR spin was that the losses had given him tremendous compassion and that he was devoting himself to justice for others, that as state's attorney he cared personally about the victims whose cases he prosecuted. A murdered child's family had said he was "the most caring man in the world," leading one newspaper to dub him the "Prince of Caring." The moniker had stuck. It played well politically and was featured in many of his campaign ads.

Conor watched Jackie greet him, usher him into the show.

"The show looks great," Conor heard Griffin say.

"Roberta Smith from the *New York Times* came for an early look, and *Smithsonian Magazine* wants to do a profile on her," Jackie said.

"Fantastic," Griffin said. "Have you heard from Mike Bouchard yet?"

"From *Connecticut Weekly*? Yes," Jackie said. "We spoke on the phone, and he wants to meet Claire here tonight. I take it someone from your election committee arranged for the interview?"

The room was getting crowded. Conor leaned against the wall and watched Griffin examine *Fingerbone*: hundreds of fine silver wires attached to the outer edges of the rough wooden frame caught the light, creating the illusion of water. A gold coin that appeared to be ancient and authentic lay at the bottom, beneath the skeletal hand.

Conor stared, watching Griffin's reaction. Was it his imagination, or was the prosecutor rattled?

"I'm buying this," Griffin said to Jackie, gesturing at the shadow box.

"It's very compelling," Jackie said, "but you don't have to buy it! I'm sure Claire would give it to you."

"I insist," Griffin said, the charm gone from his voice. "I don't want the gallery to lose its commission." He took out his checkbook, and Conor watched him scrawl the amount and a signature. Conor wondered if he was thinking about Beth. Griffin had successfully prosecuted her killer; he might be aware that Sam had inherited her mother's share of the gallery and that profits would help pay for her college education.

"Well, thank you," Jackie said to Griffin. She put a red dot on *Fingerbone* to let everyone know it was sold.

"I'm going to call her right now—see where she is and tell her I have a surprise for her," Griffin said. He pulled out his phone and dialed.

"Sweetheart," he said. "Where are you? We're waiting for you—are you okay?" He disconnected. "Voice mail," Conor heard him say.

"She must be on her way," Jackie said. Then, as if noticing the worry in his eyes, "What is it?"

"Nothing," Griffin said. Then, "She's been anxious lately."

"It's normal," Jackie said. "Preshow butterflies."

"Hmm, you might be right," Griffin said, but he didn't sound as if he believed it.

The space was packed; Conor watched Griffin take *Fingerbone* down from the wall. That struck Conor as weird; it was customary to leave works hanging for the entire duration of an exhibition, and being married to an artist, Griffin should have known that.

Griffin was halfway out the door when a throng of people surrounded him. Conor watched the way he smiled, shook hands with them, made easy conversation, spoke of being proud of his wife. One was a reporter and had his notepad out. Conor wondered if that was Mike Bouchard. Griffin was animated, full of passion, looking like someone born to run for governor.

Then Griffin slipped away, the shadow box under his arm. Conor watched him open the trunk of his car, put *Fingerbone* inside. Conor felt that ripple again.

3

CLAIRE

Griffin and I go back forever. My crush on him began in eighth grade. He was a lanky boy, a graceful athlete, a high-velocity soccer and tennis player who made the crowd gasp as he kicked the goal or nailed the point. He had sharp cheekbones and deep-set green eyes—sensitive eyes that would occasionally catch mine and make me feel he wanted to ask me something. I'd lie awake at night and wonder what the question could possibly be.

He always dated cool girls from the country club or beach club. They went to private schools, drove sports cars, and wore cashmere sweaters tied around their shoulders. Griffin and I would sometimes play in the same round-robin tennis match or see each other at a beach bonfire, but that was about it.

One foggy night, the summer between our junior and senior years in high school, he and a bunch of country club boys showed up at the Hubbard's Point sandy parking lot. There was a cooler in Jimmy Hale's trunk, and Griffin and I reached for a beer at the same time. Griffin's knuckles brushed mine. "Hi," he said. "Hi," I said. His eyes had that question in them, but I felt so shy, I looked away. Nothing happened for a long time after that, till after college.

Griffin went to Wesleyan, and so did Ellen Fielding, a girl from our town. When they began to date, no one was surprised. She was from Griffin's old-money world and lived in a sea captain's house on Main Street. Although she didn't have to worry about paying for college or buying books, each summer she waitressed with Jackie and me at the Black Hall Inn. Her family thought it would be character building. She worked as hard as we did and made us laugh with her dead-on imitations of the drunken chef and lecherous manager. She always wore a heavy gold bracelet with what looked like an ancient gold coin dangling from it. She told me it had been her grandmother's.

That summer before senior year, when Griffin picked her up after her shift, I tried not to look at him—I was afraid Ellen, or even worse, Griffin, would see that my attraction to him made me want to explode. But sometimes I couldn't avoid saying hi when I walked past his car, a vintage MGB, British racing green. He would be sitting there with the top down, engine running, watching me with those serious eyes. And then Ellen would come out, and they'd drive away.

I went to RISD—the Rhode Island School of Design—and fell in love with the world of art and artists. I dated a sculptor who etched transcripts of his therapy sessions into polished steel, then a performance artist who channeled Orpheus and visited the underworld onstage. But I still dreamed of Griffin.

He and Ellen broke up right after graduation. Instead of going to London for July, as planned, she moved back home with her parents. He began showing up at the Inn, after my shift was done, even though she no longer worked there. "Ellen changed, Claire. She went away on spring break, and nothing has been the same," he said.

"Why?"

"I have no idea. She won't talk about what happened, and she knows she can tell me anything. Now she doesn't even want to see me."

"I'm sorry," I said.

"Yeah," he said. "The worst part is, I'm positive something bad happened down there. Did she mention anything to you?"

"No, like what?"

"Not sure," he said. "You sure she didn't say anything?"

"Positive," I said.

Jackie and I had gotten to know Ellen at the Inn, and we cared about her. I felt guilty, getting close to Griffin, so Jackie was the one to approach her, to find out how she was doing. She had gone to Cancún with family friends for a beach vacation, a last blast before college graduation. She asked Jackie, "Do you believe in evil?"

"What was she talking about?" I asked.

"I have no idea. She just stared at me. Claire, her eyes were hollow."

"God, poor Ellen," I said.

Griffin was devastated, and I became his confidante. At first that's all it was—a boy with a broken heart and the girl who consoled him. But that began to change, and I couldn't believe it. We were from the same town, but from completely different worlds.

I lived at Hubbard's Point—a magical beach area that time forgot. Small shingled cottages, built in the 1920s and '30s by working-class families, were perched on a rock ledge at the edge of Long Island Sound. The weather-beaten cottages had window boxes, spilling over with geraniums and petunias, and brightly colored shutters with seahorse and sailboat cutouts.

Hubbard's Point families had cookouts together. Friends as kids became friends for life, just like Jackie and me. Every Fourth of July there was a clambake and a kids' bike parade. Movies were shown on Sunday and Thursday nights on the half-moon beach, and everyone would bring beach chairs and watch classics on a screen so wind rippled it might well have been a canvas sail. At the end of the beach was a secret path, winding through the woods to a hidden cove. I could have found my way along it blindfolded.

Griffin grew up at the other end of that narrow trail, in a posh enclave called Catamount Bluff, with only four properties on a private road. The Chases' house—the one in which we now live—was built on the headland by his paternal great-grandfather, Dexter Chase. He had founded Parthenon Insurance—the biggest insurance company in Hartford—before running for governor and holding that office for two terms. His son, Griffin's grandfather, had been a three-term senator representing Connecticut. Griffin's father had been a lawyer—in-house council for Parthenon. They used *summer* as a verb—they *summered* at Catamount Bluff. When I asked Griffin about his mother, he said, "You don't want to know."

I am an only child, unconditionally loved by my parents; we "went to the beach" when school got out in June. My mother was an art teacher in public school, my father an environmental studies professor at Easterly College. He taught me everything I know about the woods, and she encouraged me to paint what I saw. When I was nine, she died in a car accident; she lost control in an ice storm, crashed into a tree, and was killed instantly.

The shock and sorrow paralyzed my father and me. We turned to nature. After school and work and on weekends, we trudged the woods, climbed the rock face between Hubbard's Point and Catamount Bluff. Members of the Pequot tribe had lived in these woodlands. A burial ground sat atop one boulder-strewn hill. My father told me to always treat this land as sacred.

He taught me how to blaze a trail—to notice rocks, trees, a broken branch and use these landmarks to orient myself and not get lost. At night he showed me Polaris and taught me to navigate by the stars. Late that summer we built a cabin at the edge of the marsh on the far side of the hilltop, in almost-impenetrable woods. One night we stayed there and heard an eerie, blood-chilling cry.

There was an enduring myth that mountain lions, their woodland habitat displaced by farms in northern Connecticut, had been driven south through the greenways of open space and conservation land to the river valley. The name *Catamount Bluff*, given to the land in the 1800s, was testament to the legend's long history. My father and I scanned the ledges and rock shelves. We searched for tracks, remains of white-tailed deer, any sign that mountain lions lived here.

He died of an aneurysm when I was twenty. His brother's family in Damariscotta, Maine, would have taken me in, but my sorrow was too great to accept help, to try to join another family. I dropped out of college. The cabin reminded me of my dad and became my refuge. I felt his presence there. At night I would look for the North Star and know he was with me. I began to build shadow boxes of things I found nearby: lichens, pebbles, dried seaweed, mussel shells, the bones of mice in owl pellets.

That August night, the summer after Griffin's graduation, when the Perseid meteor shower was due to peak, he called to ask me to meet him at the cove—a rocky inlet halfway between Hubbard's Point and Catamount Bluff.

I figured he meant a group of us would be getting together. "Should I invite Jackie?" I asked.

"No, Claire," he said, his voice filled with magic. "Just you. I want to watch shooting stars with you. Is that okay?"

"Yes," I said.

"Meet you there," he said.

I ran through the forest path from the Hubbard's Point end, almost breathless knowing he was on the way from his house—to meet *me*. I couldn't believe it. Halfway there I slowed down and peered up a steep hill, thick with scrub oaks, white pines, bayberry, and winterberry. Deep in those woods were the Pequot graves, and beyond them was my cabin.

He was waiting at the cove. When I saw the blanket he had spread above the tide line, and knew we were going to be together on it, my knees felt weak. We were isolated from any town or houses, with nothing but hundreds of acres of granite ledges and woods and marsh and salt water surrounding us. In the dark of the new moon, the sky blazed with stars.

His dark-brown hair tumbled into his eyes. A white streak slashed across his left temple—shocking, considering he was only twenty-one. His eyes were emerald green in the starlight, with the same questioning look as ever.

"What is it?" I asked, laughing nervously. "I feel as if you're wondering something."

"I am," he said. "I always have been. I've felt it forever, that you're my best friend. And more."

"We've hardly ever talked," I said.

"Not with words," he said, and he leaned back on one elbow.

He pulled me down on the blanket. This time when he looked at me, the question was gone from his eyes. I heard waves hitting the rocks, splashing against the sand. He rolled toward me, slid his arms around me. He pressed his body against mine and kissed me. Our first kiss: tender, then rough. I could practically feel the waves beneath us, lifting us, as if the sand had turned into the sea.

I touched his face, ran my fingers down his neck; his pulse was seismic under my fingertips, just like mine. There was a strange abrasive sound coming from the water, but I was too excited to pay attention.

"Do you hear that?" he asked.

The sound was crisp: scritch-scritch, like rough sandpaper on wood.

"What is it?" I asked.

"I don't know. But then again, who cares?" he asked.

He pulled my body back toward his, hard, kissed me again, his hand running down my side. He hooked his thumb into the waistband of my jeans. I wanted him to keep going, but now I couldn't stop hearing the noise.

Now it sounded more like clicking and seemed to be coming from the tidal pools. With a new moon, tides were extreme, and this was dead low, with rocks and ledges that would normally be underwater exposed. I pushed myself off the blanket and walked toward the rocks.

"Claire," Griffin called. "Be careful."

Starlight caught the white edges of the small waves, the glossy black tendrils of kelp, and illuminated a swarm of rock crabs completely covering a lumpy object in the shallow tidal pool. The crabs moved as if they were one entity instead of thousands of individuals, summoned from rock crevices by whatever was rotting beneath them. Their claws click-click-clicked.

I thought it must be a dead fish, a big one, maybe a striper. Or even a seal—they lived here over the winter, into the spring. *Please don't let it be a seal,* I thought. Or any other marine mammal. Not a dolphin, not a baby whale. The smell of decay was overpowering.

I stomped my feet on the wet rocks as I approached, to scare the crabs away, and I saw what was underneath. Bones gleamed white. Long brown hair was matted like seaweed. A glint of gold shone from the half-devoured left wrist. There were still shreds of flesh on the upper arms, but the wrists and hands had been stripped bare. They were skeleton hands; the finger bones were long, skinny, and curved.

I screamed. It was Ellen Fielding.

I lunged toward those crabs, brushing and kicking them away, to get them off Ellen's body. They scattered, then covered her again.

"Claire," Griffin said, yanking me away from Ellen's corpse. I sobbed, staring at the gold bracelet around that horror of a wrist, the ancient gold coin dangling from thick links, given to Ellen by her grandmother.

Griffin wanted us both to go to his house and call the police from there, but I refused to leave. I didn't want her to be alone. The tide could come in and sweep everything away, take what was left of her body out to sea. I sat in the wet sand guarding her. Starlight glinted on the crabs' black-green shells, their pincers tearing her apart.

Eventually Griffin arrived with a Black Hall police officer. The cop crouched beside the body, then called for a forensic team and the police boat. Soon the boat came around the point, searchlights sweeping the cove.

"What's that for?" Griffin asked.

"She might have been on a boat," the cop said. "It could have sunk, and there could be someone else out there, needing help."

"This didn't happen tonight," I heard myself say. "The crabs have already ripped her apart!"

The policeman was young, not much older than us. I'd seen him around town—directing traffic during the Midsummer's Festival, after the concerts on the church lawn, writing speeding tickets on Route 156.

"I'm Officer Markham," he said. "What's your name?"

"Claire Beaudry," I said.

Griffin stood beside me, put his arm around my shoulders. I'd gotten cold sitting there on the damp beach, and I shivered against his warm body.

"Why are you two here tonight?" Officer Markham asked. "Kind of dark, late for beach time."

"We wanted to see the meteor shower," Griffin said.

"How did you come to find the body?"

"Claire did," Griffin said.

"I heard the crabs," I said.

"Well," the officer said. "We're going to have to identify the victim. Give me your phone numbers in case we need to talk to you some more."

My heart was racing hard. My lips tingled and my hands felt numb. I waited for Griffin to tell him it was Ellen, but he was silent. Was it possible he hadn't recognized the bracelet?

"I know who it is," I said finally, because Griffin didn't speak.

"Who?" Officer Markham asked.

"Ellen Fielding," I said.

Griffin drew a sharp breath, as if he were shocked.

"Oh God, oh God," Griffin said, his head in his hands, pacing in a circle. "She did it."

"Did what?" the cop asked.

"Suicide," he said. "She was so depressed."

"You knew her?" the cop asked.

"We both did," Griffin said. I waited for him to add that he had dated her, but Officer Markham just asked for our numbers and said we could go, that a detective might get in touch with further questions.

After that, Griffin walked me home through the dark woods. I shivered the whole way. Right by the overgrown trail to my cabin, there was a break in the canopy of branches overhead, and suddenly it filled with shooting stars.

"Look," Griffin said, pointing up. We stared for a few seconds. "Finally—what we came here for. The Perseids."

"They're for . . ." I began to say *for Ellen*.

"They're for us, so we'll never forget this night," he said, his voice catching.

"Something beautiful," I whispered. "After something so terrible."

Over the next few days, the police investigated. As Officer Markham had said, a detective questioned me about finding Ellen's body, about whether we had noticed any changes in her mood or knew of anyone who might want to harm her. Tucker Morgan, the state police commissioner, was a friend of Wade Lockwood—Griffin's Catamount Bluff neighbor and surrogate father—and did the questioning himself. With Wade present. Over lunch at the yacht club.

After the coroner made his examination, there was an inquest. The toxicology tests came back negative—so Ellen hadn't overdosed. She had a fractured skull. Had it happened in a fall? Or had someone attacked her?

Rumors began right away: whatever had happened in Cancún had pushed her to the brink, and she had drowned herself. Or she had gotten involved with something illegal, dangerous enough to get her killed. But Commissioner Morgan chose not to pursue those leads. Wade convinced him that the idea that someone had followed Ellen north, murdered her, and left her body on the beach was too far fetched. She had slipped on the rocks, that was that.

My interlude with Griffin lasted all that August: fire, passion, and wild fascination with each other. The reality of finding Ellen's body was traumatic; at first it pulled us together, but eventually it drove us apart. We both wanted to stop thinking about that night.

Griffin went to Yale Law School. I considered returning to RISD, but instead, I just kept making art on my own. In the following years, we each married other people. Even though I tried, I couldn't stop thinking of Griffin. I hated myself, but I would feel his body when Nate, my first husband, was holding me. Later, Griffin told me it had been the same for him with Margot, his first wife. Those years of longing, while we were apart, made our need and desire for each other almost unbearable. I didn't have children, but he and Margot had twin sons, Ford and Alexander.

Griffin became a prosecutor, eventually rising to his current position as state's attorney for Easterly County, second only to the chief state's attorney. After Margot had been to her fifth or sixth rehab, they divorced, and he got custody of their sons. She moved to New Hampshire, where she had grown up. She never saw the boys. Griffin had to keep them going, to somehow make them believe their mother still loved them, even though she never visited or asked them to visit her. At least, that's what he told me.

By the time he and I ran into each other at a cocktail party in Black Hall, I was separated from Nate, a man I loved and cared about but wasn't in love with. Nate begged me to come back, but by then I was involved with Griffin and went through with the divorce anyway. Griffin's sons, forever traumatized by their mother's abdication, weren't ready for a stepmother.

There is power in dangerous love. You can be so focused on the forbidden nature of it, justifying your choices to the world—me falling in love with Griffin while still legally married to Nate, Griffin giving me all his attention instead of trying to find a workable custody agreement with Margot, instead of doting on his devastated sons—that you miss the fact you're completely wrong for each other.

Ellen's death never left me. It informed my work, led me deeply into nature's darkness, the terrible beauty of it echoed in every shadow box I created. Griffin said it inspired him to go to law school, to become a prosecutor, plumb the pain and dark side of life—and in doing so, honor Ellen.

That was a lie.

Ellen was buried in Heronwood Cemetery. The rumors that she had been the victim of a violent crime faded away. Perhaps she had slipped and fallen on the rocks, died of a terrible accident. Or, as was more commonly thought, she had killed herself.

I, too, believed it was suicide at first but not any longer. I am positive it was homicide, just as I am sure that Griffin took me to the cove that night so I would find her body.

And I know because he all but confessed that he killed her.

I can picture us, Griffin and me, in our kitchen at Catamount Bluff. Late at night, him coming home after a meeting of the Last Monday Club, black tie loosened, dinner jacket slung over his shoulder. I'd said something "wrong"—it doesn't matter what; asking about the weather could be "wrong" if he wasn't in the mood for the question. His face looming into mine, his green eyes turning black—literally black—and him saying, "Do you want what happened to Ellen to happen to you?"

He said things like that to me all the time. He'd say it about other murder victims, whose killers he prosecuted. "The defendant was pushed too far, Claire, just like you push me too far. I have to do my job and send him to prison, but that doesn't mean I can't understand why he did it. He takes it and takes it until he can't anymore. And then she dies."

"Like Ellen?" I asked. "Did she push you too far?"

That was my fatal question.

Now that I am about to go missing, Griffin will appear on every local TV station, frantic with love and worry for me. The state police will drag rivers and salt ponds and the inshore waters of Long Island Sound, send divers into lakes and reservoirs, scour rock quarries and ledges and hills of glacial moraine. They will question my friends and ex-husband, neighbors, fellow artists and naturalists. Griffin will let them read my notebooks—the ones I left unhidden—look through my computer files, examine the cell phone I left in my SUV when I was struck.

There will be blood evidence, and the forensic team will analyze it. Buckets from my head wound, drops from the halfhearted slashes. Oh, that knife—I keep seeing my attacker wave it. I thought it was going to pierce my heart, so I tried to dodge it. The tip pricked my forearms and the palms of my hand—but he kept pulling it away, never let the full blade slash me.

Griffin would never have killed me with a knife.

Too messy, too much evidence left behind.

The night the jury convicted John Marcus, Griffin and I were in our kitchen, just the two of us, about to have dinner. It was a chilly October evening, cold enough to leave frost on our Halloween pumpkin. The kitchen was cozy. I had made roast chicken. He had brought home a bottle of Veuve Clicquot, so we could toast his victory. People were already talking about a run for higher office.

I lifted my glass. He was carving the chicken.

Right there next to our white marble island, he raised the knife above his head, lunged toward me, and I flinched so hard I dropped my champagne glass and it shattered on the floor.

"Jesus, it was a joke!" he said. "You make me feel like a criminal when you get scared like that."

"Then don't come at me with a knife."

"When I come after you with a knife, Claire, you'll know it."

I felt the blood drain from my face.

"Don't worry, I would never stab you," he said, his voice perfectly calm. "Why do you think the jury came back in two hours? Because he was an idiot, he made so many mistakes. He was practically begging

27

to be caught. You have to be smart. You can't leave DNA. But Claire? I feel like it right now. That glass was Baccarat crystal. It belonged to my grandmother."

You know? I can't say he didn't warn me.

Then I think of the letter and tear up because I didn't listen.

How far will I be able to walk?

He won't stop until he finds me. And when he does, he will make sure I never return home.

The entire state of Connecticut will ache for his loss.

Griffin got away with Ellen, but he won't get away with me.

It's time for me to leave. I force myself off the floor a second time. My legs barely work; I stumble through the side door. I know to walk on the ledge to avoid leaving footprints, to brush the ground behind me with a pine bough, to head for the deepest part of the woods.

I will hide in the wild, where I feel safest. My feet know their way along this path. I am making my way northeast, but I curve around, and before I circle back to resume my intended route, I cover rocks and tree trunks with the animal mixture. The scent will throw the dogs off my trail.

I will make sure Griffin is caught. I will let everyone know the light is a lie, that darkness is his only truth.

I'll do it for myself, and I'll do it for Ellen. I say her name as I walk, and I talk to my father. "Dad, help me. Help us, me and Ellen. Get me to the cabin." I swear I feel my father lifting me up, carrying me through the woods, and suddenly my refuge is in sight.

4

CONOR

"She still hasn't shown up," Jackie said to Conor. "It's her own opening, and she's not here."

He looked at his watch; it was five thirty.

"Half an hour late," he said.

"That's not like her, not at all," Jackie said.

Nate Browning, Claire's first husband, began walking toward them. A Yale professor, he had been in the local paper lately for doing whale research in Alaska. Three women were right behind him, all dressed expensively in an art world way.

"I am not up for this," Jackie said under her breath. "The Catamount Bluff social circle."

"What?" Conor asked.

"Claire's neighbors. Leonora Lockwood, Sloane Hawke, and Abigail Coffin."

Conor recognized Leonora, a grande dame married to Wade Lockwood, a generous donor to charities that benefited the police. She was regal, in her late seventies, dressed in a bold green-and-yellow-print caftan with gold bangles on tan arms, long white hair pulled up in a French twist, and wrinkles she wore proudly. It was well known in law enforcement circles that she and Wade were political donors and honorary parents to Griffin.

"Where's Claire?" Leonora asked, glancing around.

"I'm not sure," Jackie said, exchanging a quick look with Conor.

"She should be here, greeting her public!" Leonora said. "And Griffin's, too, for that matter. They want to meet our state's next first lady."

"I'm sure she'll walk in any minute," Nate said. He was about five foot nine, rumpled, with a comfortable and expanding belly. Needing a haircut and a beard trim, he was the opposite of fastidious Griffin.

"What do you think of her new work?" Leonora asked Nate, and the group began to discuss it.

Conor watched Griffin, across the room and deep in conversation with Eli Dean, the owner of West Wind Marina. Many people in town kept their boats there. When Conor saw Griffin put his head in his hands, he walked over.

"What's wrong?" he asked, standing between Griffin and Eli.

"Claire told me this morning she was going to row to Gull Island, to clear her head before the show," Griffin said.

"But I just told him she wasn't at the boatyard at all," Eli said. "I was working on dock two most of the day, and that pretty little rowing dory of hers never moved."

"When did you talk to her last?" Conor asked Griffin.

"This morning," Griffin said. "After breakfast."

"Hey, listen," Eli said. "It's hot in the sun, out of the wind, today; she probably just didn't feel like taking the boat out in the heat."

"Seventy-five degrees," Griffin said. "Seems pretty perfect to me." He took a deep breath. "Look, I'm worried."

"What can I do?" Conor asked.

"I'm going home to see if she's there," Griffin said.

That ripple Conor had felt when he'd first walked into the gallery got stronger.

"I'll follow you," Conor said. And he and Griffin Chase hurried to their cars.

5

JEANNE

Late that afternoon, the easternmost part of Long Island Sound was unusually calm and gleamed amber in the declining sunlight. Jeanne and Bart Dunham were sailing northwest from Block Island on *Arcturus*, their Tartan 36, barely speaking because Bart had had too much to drink at the Oar and Jeanne had thought they should wait till morning before heading back home to Essex, Connecticut.

Jeanne stood at the helm steering while Bart stretched out in the cockpit. The sails were up, but the boat was motoring. There wasn't a bit of wind. She had brought them through Watch Hill Passage—shoal waters, hair raising at the best of times—past Fishers Island, then Race Rock, then the mouth of the Thames River.

There wasn't a lot of boat traffic—it was early in the season, but she and Bart were retired, and they wanted to get a start on summer. They were considering the idea of selling their house, sailing to Fort Lauderdale, and living aboard *Arcturus*. These short trips were test runs. She gave Bart a disgusted look. He had failed the test.

She had seen the cross-Sound ferries pass each other, coming and going between New London and Orient Point. She took care in the shipping lanes, where tugs and barges plied Long Island Sound. The tide was with them after the long day on the water, and she couldn't wait to get home, throw Bart into bed, and take a shower.

"How you doin', hon?" Bart asked.

"Fine," she said, the word clipped.

"No problems in this weather!" he said. "Don't know what you were so bent out of shape about. Put 'er on autopilot, and come over here, sweetheart." He held out his arms. "Is this the life or what?"

She ignored him, peering west, focusing on the glowing water ahead.

"Okay, then," he said. "You don't love me anymore."

"What's that?" she asked, distracted by a disturbance just ahead.

"Where, baby?"

"Right there," she said, pointing. "Something swimming around."

Bart lifted himself onto one elbow and peered west, into the lowering sun. "Fish or whatever. A school of bluefish, feeding."

"Not a school, just one fin. Oh my God, a shark?"

The boat slipped along the golden surface, a wake rippling out behind. The sails luffed and snapped.

"What the hell's it doing?" she asked.

"Swimmin', what sharks do best," Bart said. "Hey, look at all this oil—did it kill a seal?"

Changing water temperatures had attracted a seal population to southern New England. Seals were the favored meal of sharks. Jeanne slowed down as they approached. The water glistened with an oil slick; maybe Bart was right, and a shark had killed a seal. And then she realized it wasn't a fin at all but a small furry creature.

She steered toward the animal.

It wasn't a seal.

It was a tiny dog, frantically paddling, trying to climb onto a slab of white fiberglass. In the seconds it took Jeanne to grab the boat hook, her heart began to pound. She could almost see a shark rising up, snatching the dog before she could get to it.

But that didn't happen; she reached overboard, snagged the pup's bright-pink collar with one swipe of the hook, and pulled the Yorkshire terrier into the cockpit. The dog was barely larger than Jeanne's hand. The small silver tag dangling from her collar was engraved *Maggie*. Jeanne held Maggie tight to her chest, felt her shivering uncontrollably.

"She's absolutely adorable," Jeanne said.

"Must've fallen overboard," Bart said.

"It's okay, Maggie. You're okay, girl," Jeanne said. As she clutched the dog, sliding her under her fleece to warm her, she scanned in all directions to see if there was a boat searching for her.

"What's this oil from?" Bart asked, staring into the water.

The slick Jeanne had previously thought was seal blubber ran in a winding current, a river through the sea, and now she saw that it contained shards of wood and a section of white fiberglass charred black at the edges. Fragments of blue Styrofoam insulation swept by, an empty bottle of Polar lime seltzer, two red personal flotation devices with a boat's name stenciled on: *Sallie B.*

"Oh my God!" Jeanne said. "We know that boat!"

"Seen her a million times. She's from West Wind," Bart said.

"Looks like she caught fire," Jeanne said, watching a soot-stained green cushion float past. She scanned the horizon for smoke, for a vessel still smoldering.

R 22—the red bell buoy marking Allen's Reef—swung in the current a hundred yards south. The bell tolled with the movement of the waves, but beneath the mournful sound, she heard a voice—very weak, calling for help.

Jeanne placed Maggie at her feet and steered toward the buoy. Bart stumbled below, lifted the mike, and called the coast guard. Jeanne heard him give the operator their GPS coordinates.

"A boat sank out here," he said. "The *Sallie B.* And someone's alive. We can hear them, over by R 22. We're going there now."

Jeanne sped up, and as they approached, she saw a man clinging to the red metal structure that rose tall in the water, swinging wildly in the tide, the clapper banging with each wave. She didn't know his name, but she recognized him—one of the many local skippers that greeted each other as they passed in the channel. She'd often seen a woman and two children in the cockpit with him. Knowing who he was, wondering what had happened to his family, made it even worse, and she choked on a sob.

6

CONOR

The road to Catamount Bluff was unmarked and unpaved and meandered along the western edge of a protected seven-hundred-acre forest and nature preserve. A security guard was stationed at the head of the road. Conor Reid recognized him as Terry Brooks, an off-duty Black Hall police officer. It wasn't uncommon for town cops to moonlight as private security for exclusive compounds along the shoreline. Conor waved as he passed.

His Ford Interceptor took the ruts with no problem as he followed Griffin Chase. They passed three mailboxes; the houses to which they belonged were hidden behind hedges. This was the kind of old-money place where they didn't bother with fancy gates or even a paved road.

The road ended at the Chases' house. Conor drove into the turnaround in front of a large silver-shingled house, on the bluff above the rocky beach, Long Island Sound sparkling into the distance. Conor was surprised to see Ben Markham, a uniformed Black Hall cop, standing by the front door.

He paused a moment before getting out of the car, watching Griffin speak to Markham. There was obvious familiarity between them. Markham had been called to testify in some of Griffin's trials; plus, as a local cop, he would do regular patrols here and possibly pick up shifts as a guard, just like Brooks.

The Chases' rambling old house sat on acres of direct waterfront—property worth more than the average prosecutor and an artist could afford—but everyone knew Griffin came from a family fortune. Conor figured this had to be one of the most expensive pieces of real estate in the state.

Conor walked from the vehicle toward the two men and exchanged a nod with Markham.

"I just called Ben and asked him to meet us here," Griffin explained.

"Got it," Conor said. He hadn't heard the call over his police radio and realized Griffin had used his cell phone.

"Claire has been really nervous," Griffin said. "Jackie says it's just jitters, but I don't know. She's had something on her mind this last week, but she wouldn't miss her show for anything."

"You think something happened to her?" Markham said, frowning at the house.

"I'm sure she's fine," Griffin said. "But let's find her. We'll start in her studio."

He led them around the side of the house, through an arch in a privet hedge, to a solid post-and-beam barn built at the edge of the bluff. It looked new in comparison with the hundred-or-so-year-old house. Griffin unlocked the door, and Markham and Conor followed him inside. Conor made a quick scan of the structure. It had an open floor plan, north-facing windows, an easel, a worktable, a daybed, and bookshelves. The space smelled of oil paint, turpentine, and the beach.

"She designed it herself," Griffin said. "And I had it built for her."

The space had no interior walls—there was nowhere to hide.

"She's not here," Conor said.

Griffin nodded, and he was already out the door, Markham at his side. Conor walked a few steps behind them, his eyes on the house. French doors and tall windows faced the sea. The doors were closed, glass panes unbroken. Griffin had his key out and opened a kitchen door. Conor looked around the vast room—nearly every wall and surface was white.

He saw a Viking stove, an industrial-size refrigerator, and racks of copper pots hanging above a large island topped with white marble. There were dirty dishes and two half-empty coffee mugs in the farmhouse-style sink.

"You said you had breakfast together?" Conor asked.

"Yes," Griffin said.

"What time did you leave?"

"About seven forty-five. I had a pretrial conference at nine."

"And Claire planned to go rowing?"

"Yes, she was getting her things together when I left."

"Would she leave here without doing the dishes?"

Griffin gave him a surprised look. Conor hadn't intended to offend him, making a comment about Claire's housekeeping, but he wanted to establish a timeline.

"She might have," Griffin said. "When she gets inspired, she can lose track of real-world stuff."

"Inspired? As in her art?" Conor asked.

"Yes. Going down to the dock is part of it. She collects sea things to use in her work. For her, taking a walk or going for a row is as much making art as actually creating her pieces. It grounds her. And she's needed that, especially lately. I have no idea what's going on with her. She's been, I don't know . . . distracted lately."

Conor thought back to Monday night, when Claire had unexpectedly dropped in on Tom and Jackie's family dinner. He had seen something of her state of mind, but he didn't mention it now.

Conor walked slowly around the kitchen. He noticed a dark wooden block made for holding knives on the marble countertop. It was marked *Sabatier*. One slot was empty.

"What's usually here?" he asked, pointing.

Griffin stared. "A carving knife, I think."

"Could it be anywhere else?" Conor asked.

"The dishwasher?" Griffin asked and opened it. It was empty. "Sometimes the cleaning lady puts things in the wrong place. The pantry or the utility drawer." He rummaged through both, but there was no sign of a Sabatier carving knife.

"Where next?" Markham asked.

"Upstairs," Griffin said. "The bedroom."

Markham and Griffin disappeared down a hallway, but Conor didn't follow. He smelled something that didn't belong here. It didn't necessarily signal something dead, but it raised the hair on the back of his neck.

He checked the small bathroom off the kitchen, but it was pristine. No, the odor was coming through a door he hadn't noticed before—at the end of a short breezeway, cracked slightly open. He used his foot to inch the door open wider and stepped into an old building that seemed to serve as the garage.

Conor had walked in on death before, and he instantly knew this wasn't it. The smell was strong, that of an animal marking its territory. He found the source, a spill of rancid-smelling granules, at the foot of a tall row of shelves filled with garden supplies. It smelled as if an animal had sprayed urine. Did the Chases have cats? Had a skunk or raccoon gotten inside?

The garage—more of a barn or old carriage house—sagged slightly. It was old and bore the brunt of a century of coastal storms. Conor looked up at splintery rafters; a sheet of plywood had been laid between two and served as a makeshift platform to hold oars, sail bags, and an unrigged mast. The garage had room for three cars; a black Range Rover was parked in one space, and the other two were empty. The barn-style doors were closed, but late-day light streamed in through two sets of windows.

He glanced into the vehicle—it looked clean and empty, no sign of Claire. He circled around back, to the side closest to the wall and saw the blood: rust-colored smears on the concrete floor, the right doors of the Range Rover, and its right rear bumper—a coagulating pool just beside the tire.

He continued around front and found two broken pieces of two-by-four pine on the floor. A long white line—the kind used on boats—lay twisted beside them. One end was red with blood that looked fresher than the brownish splotches. The middle of the rope was cut clean through—no frayed edges. He tilted his head back, saw where the rafter had broken. He crouched down to examine the broken wood. Caught in the splinters were white fibers, as if the rope had snagged there. A blue-and-white-striped towel, soaked in blood, was crumpled under the vehicle.

There had been a violent assault; that much was clear. Griffin had said Claire was distracted. Had she walked into the garage, where a perpetrator was lying in wait, and not seen the attack coming? She had lost a lot of blood. He made a quick search for a knife, but he didn't find one.

Conor heard voices coming through the kitchen. He walked toward them, again opened the door with his foot. He hadn't touched one surface since arriving at the house. Griffin and Markham were about to enter the garage, but Conor stopped them. Griffin looked pale.

"You're right," Conor said. "Something happened."

"Did you find her? I want to see her," Griffin said. He tried to rush past, but Conor grabbed his shoulders.

"She's not here, Griffin," Conor said. "But there's a lot of blood."

Griffin touched the marble counter, then crouched down, as if his legs had gone out from under him. Markham leaned down to support Griffin.

"Ben, call this in," Conor said to Markham.

Markham took his radio from its holster and called the state police dispatcher.

"Are you okay?" Conor asked Griffin, watching his reaction very carefully.

"No," Griffin said, his voice barely a whisper.

Conor waited for a few seconds, then helped Griffin get to his feet. Griffin was beloved by the people of Connecticut, had the devotion of almost every cop Conor knew. His wife was missing, and he gave every appearance of being in shock. Conor saw him take his cell phone out of his pocket and turn his back and step away to make a call. That wasn't unusual—not at all. But Conor had a strange feeling and couldn't help wondering who was on the other end.

40

7

TOM

The *Sallie B* was named after Sallie Benson: a forty-two-year-old interior designer and the wife of Dan Benson, mother of Gwen and Charlie, and owner of Maggie the Yorkie. So far, only Dan and the dog had been found alive. US Coast Guard Commander Tom Reid was in the midst of a search and rescue (SAR) operation for Sallie, Gwen, and Charlie.

From the moment the Benson family members were reported missing, USCG vessels and aircraft had been deployed and SAR controllers had begun amassing data to create models to aid in the search. They analyzed factors such as debris from the vessel, tide, currents, air temperature, sea surface temperature, and wind speed and direction. They coordinated information offered to investigators by Jeanne and Bart Dunham and the very brief discussion with Dan Benson. He was in shock from his injuries and had been taken to Easterly Hospital.

A simulator wizard spit out computational algorithms to approximate drift and to aid in the development of the grid search pattern. The last known location of the *Sallie B*—a forty-two-foot Loring cabin cruiser—caused particular challenges because it was close to the spot where Long Island Sound met Fishers Island Sound, flowed into Block

Island Sound, and from there into the Atlantic Ocean, creating a much larger search area. And now it was night.

Sunset occurred at 8:40 p.m. By that time, thirty minutes ago, the SAR had been underway for two hours. Tom was aboard the 270-foot USCG Cutter *Nehantic*. Joining the search were two rescue boats—measuring 45 feet each—from Coast Guard Station Port Twigg, Rhode Island, an HC-144 fixed-wing aircraft, and an MH-60 Jayhawk helicopter out of Air Station Cape Cod.

Although the day had been warm—with a high of 76 degrees, warmer than average for the end of May—the temperature at 9:10 p.m. had dipped to 59 degrees. The surface temperature of the water was 51.1 degrees. In those conditions, a person could survive for thirty to sixty minutes. Less if badly injured, very old, or very young.

Gwen was nine and Charlie was seven.

From what Tom had seen of the debris and heard about the USCG investigator's short interview with Dan Benson, there had been a catastrophic explosion on board the *Sallie B*. Except for fragments of the hull and some personal items found floating nearby, the boat had sunk over a deep reef running perpendicular to the current, where the sea bottom rose sharply from 131 feet to 52 feet.

Dan Benson had hauled himself onto the base of bell buoy R 22 and was currently at Easterly Hospital being treated for hypothermia, second- and third-degree burns on his hands and forearms, and a punctured lung. He had been sedated, rushed into surgery to repair his lung. According to USCG Lieutenant Commander Alicia Gauthier, who had talked to the victim two hours earlier, Benson had been inconsolable—*hysterical* was the word Gauthier used—crying for his children, begging that they be found.

"What about Sallie?" Tom asked.

"He didn't mention her," Gauthier said. "Only the children."

"Did you question him about that?" Tom asked, wondering exactly what Benson had seen, whether he had witnessed his wife dead or dying but not his children.

"He could barely talk. All I could get out of him was that Sallie had gone below to fix supper," Gauthier said. "The kids had been playing in some kind of raft on deck. Sounded like a toy boat. Yellow. And he said they were wearing life jackets—family policy out on the water."

"So they were on deck with him?"

"Near him. In the toy boat. Tom, what if they both got thrown clear, along with him?"

"It's awfully cold out here," Tom said, scanning the sea. "Thanks, Alicia."

Tom wondered if the explosion had occurred when Sallie had been below. Had the propane stove malfunctioned? Had something on the burner caught fire? Or had fuel leaked into the bilge, ignited by a spark?

Searchlights illuminated the ocean and sky. What if Sallie and the children, like Dan and the dog, had escaped the flames? Even if they had, it would be unlikely that they could survive the cold water and night air. Some personal floatation devices had whistles and waterproof flashlights attached. It would be hard to see through the brightness of the searchlights, difficult to hear over the drone of ship and aircraft engines, but Tom knew every officer on the search was keeping a sharp lookout.

Tom's cell phone buzzed. He glanced at the screen. The call was from his stepdaughter Hunter Tyrone. Inspired by Tom's younger brother, Conor, she had joined the Connecticut State Police and was an eager rookie. Tom hit the default message button: Can't talk now. Two seconds later she texted back: Emergency. Pick up!

She rang again, and this time he answered.

"Hunter, what is it?" he asked.

"Are you on SAR for the Benson family?"

"Yes, which is why I can't talk now."

"Tom, I'm at the hospital with Jake." Her partner on the state police force. "Detective Miano is here too."

"Jen, yeah?" Tom asked. Jen Miano had been Conor's partner for a few years.

"She just finished talking to the dad—he's out of surgery—and she's going to call coast guard command, but I know how long it can take for information to get to you guys, so I wanted to make sure you heard it right away."

"What's she going to tell us?"

"First, that Dan said 'they got her.' He kept repeating it."

"What does that mean?" Tom asked. "Was he talking about Sallie?"

"I don't know. He was out of it. Detective Miano will ask him more when he's awake. But listen, Tom—the kids might have made it. Dan said they were playing in the little boat, and he saw it floating away— intact—when he surfaced after the blast."

"That was a toy raft," Tom said. "I've already heard about it from our investigator."

"No, it *wasn't* a toy. He said the kids sometimes played in it, but it was an actual life raft. They could be alive. It's completely possible."

"Wow. Thanks, Hunter," Tom said, hanging up fast. Then he radioed the rest of the fleet, and the SAR throttled up, taking on a whole new energy. The search was on for a small yellow boat with the two Benson children aboard.

FIVE DAYS
EARLIER

8

CLAIRE

On Sunday morning I got up just before dawn. Griffin slept beside me, and I moved carefully, so I wouldn't wake him. I turned on the coffee maker in the kitchen, then grabbed my red Patagonia fleece and walked outside. The air was chilly, the sun still below the horizon, the eastern sky starting to glow deep, clear blue.

Instead of taking the path through the woods, I climbed down rickety steps onto the beach. I walked the tide line, soothed by the sound of waves hitting the shore. As the sun rose, I began to collect shells and sea glass. Moonstones gleamed in the wet sand. They rattled as I filled my pockets. Walking the beach had always been my comfort and inspiration.

During a blizzard last December, an entire tree washed ashore. It had been uprooted by the wind, left here on our beach. Wind and waves had stripped off the bark, and what remained was a magnificent bone-white relic. With each subsequent storm, the branches and root system broke apart a little more. I always wondered where the tree had come from and stopped to look at it. Twigs and broken branches glistened in the early light; I picked up some of the smallest to add to my other treasures.

When I got to the cove, I couldn't help going straight to the spot where I'd found Ellen Fielding's body twenty-five years ago. I'd been coming here lately, pulled by a powerful force. Ellen and I had so much in common. We had both seen the other side of Griffin, the one he kept hidden from everyone else. I wondered if Margot had seen it too. I figured she had.

I used to place flowers in the pool where Ellen's body had lain, but they seemed too pretty, too frivolous. So I'd started leaving pebbles, moonstones, and wishing rocks—smooth round stones perfectly encircled by a contrasting ring. I crouched down now, placed a handful of offerings just under the water's shallow surface. It was as if no time had passed at all; I remembered the sound of the crabs. While I was there, I collected some empty crab shells and claws—no longer glossy, just dry and brittle, bleached a pale orange-red by sea and sun.

"I'm almost there, Ellen," I whispered. "You've helped me get to this point. But I promise I will come back no matter what. I'm going to leave him. And I'm going to tell."

"Who are you talking to?" Griffin asked. I jumped—so startled that I practically tumbled into the tide pool. He was standing right behind me. I hadn't even heard him approach.

"What are you doing up so early?" I asked, my heart racing.

"Good morning to you too," he said. He held out his hand to help me up. "I heard you leave, and I figured you'd be beachcombing. Less than a week till your show. You fiddling around on some last-minute shadow box things?"

"Yes," I said. "There's one I haven't quite finished."

"Well, it's Sunday, my only day off, and I was hoping we could go out in the boat," he said. "It's a photo opportunity. The *Shoreline Gazette* is sending a photographer—you know, Chase family outing, humanize the candidate."

"Everyone already loves you, Griffin," I said. Could he read my true feelings? The idea of having to play the role of smiling wife, standing at his side during the election, shook me to the core.

"You'll come out on the boat?" he asked.

"Of course," I said, because *of course* was always the right thing to say to Griffin. "Should we have breakfast first? And let me put the stuff I collected in my studio."

"Claire, what are you doing with dead shellfish?" he asked, noticing a pile of crab carapaces I'd placed on the rock ledge. "You want your work to sell, don't you? Collectors aren't going to buy if it smells like rot." He smashed his foot down on the fragile shells.

I steeled myself, pretending not to care. At one time I would have reacted, but I had learned. There was another way.

"You'll thank me," he said. "When you walk into the gallery on Friday and people aren't holding their noses. Right?"

"Right," I said.

One of Griffin's favorite moves was to hurt and insult me, then make me say I agreed-understood-admired him for having my best interests at heart. There was no point in fighting it.

"Why do you come here anyway?" he asked.

"I love the beach," I said.

"I'm not talking about the *beach*," he said. "I'm talking about this cove. It's full of traumatic memories for both of us."

"Oh, Griffin," I said. "Remember that night when you walked me home, toward Hubbard's Point, and you said the night was about us, that we should remember it for our kiss and for the shooting stars?"

He stared at me. Did he realize I was mocking him? This moment could go either way; I tensed, ready for the blowup. But he decided to let me stroke his ego. "You're right," he said. "That night was our beginning."

"It was," I said. I looked into his sea-green eyes and tried to remember how I had felt on the blanket, waiting for his kiss. He was still the handsomest man I knew. His gaze was penetrating—in his cases, he looked straight into the defendants, saw who they were, and used his knowledge to convict them. When he focused those eyes on me, I felt he could see into my soul. I had always felt that way.

"When I first walked up just now," Griffin said, "I heard you say something."

"I don't remember," I said, thinking: *I'm going to leave him. And I'm going to tell what I know.* "Talking to myself, I guess."

I waited for him to challenge me, but he didn't. He just stood there looking at me. Then he broke into a big smile.

"Let's go back and have breakfast," he said, his smile widening. "I really want to get out on the water—it's going to be a perfect day."

We started walking. When I was young, I thought that living at Catamount Bluff would be the luckiest, most wonderful thing that could ever happen. I would look at the big house where the road ended at the sea and imagine the people who lived there. The naive girl I used to be had pictured Griffin and his friends in blue blazers, girls in summer dresses, gin and tonics on silver trays, and all the happiness and confidence and goodness that must come from the ease of that life.

Six years ago, we got married just down the road, in a small ceremony at the Lockwoods' house. Alexander and Ford were Griffin's best men. Our only guests were Leonora and Wade, Jackie and Tom. I wore a dove-gray dress and a wreath of flowers in my hair. Griffin wore khaki pants and a white linen shirt. He held my hand when we stood in front of Enid Drake, justice of the peace, and kissed me in the middle of the ceremony, before she pronounced us husband and wife.

"A little impatient, are we?" Enid asked, smiling.

Griffin ignored her, just smiled and kissed me again before Enid could resume the ceremony.

We were a lightning storm together—but without the thunder, no fighting, nothing but electricity. I had felt insane desire for him that summer after college, tried to bury it during the years I was with Nate, and was overtaken again, from the minute we reconnected at that Black Hall cocktail party.

When I walked home from the cove that day, my jacket pockets were full of beach finds. Griffin headed into the house through the kitchen door, and I ducked through the hedge to my studio. I took a deep breath—this was my true home, far more than the big house. It calmed me to come in here.

My collections were organized in baskets and pottery bowls—different ones for mussel shells, quahog shells, periwinkles and moon shells, green sea glass, brown sea glass, interesting bits of seaweed, and driftwood. I emptied my pockets, putting every object where it belonged. The sea-scoured twigs went directly onto my worktable—I would be incorporating them into my last piece.

I spent a few extra moments staring at a large basket. It was full of crustacean shells, both lobster and crab. I could still hear the sound of Griffin's angry heel smashing the ones I had collected this morning.

What had made him this way? That question never stopped running through my head, because the answer was so terrible. Another question was, Why had I stayed so long? The weight of his anger reverberated, and I knew I would use the sound and the feeling it had caused in my chest to complete my project.

I checked to make sure the letter was exactly where I had left it. It had arrived the week before, and I had been debating what to do about it. Written on expensive blue English stationery, monogrammed *EC*, it had come out of nowhere from a woman I had met only once. I left it in its hiding place, deciding I would deal with it after my opening.

When I walked into our big, sterile pure-white kitchen, Griffin was sitting at the table reading the *Shoreline Gazette*. He was getting ready to start a trial, prosecuting Gary Jackson, a middle school teacher, for sexually assaulting two female students. There were articles nearly every day. I opened the refrigerator, took out bacon, eggs, and a perfectly ripe cantaloupe.

I refilled his coffee cup and poured one for myself. While the bacon was frying, I set the melon on the counter. Griffin had had the kitchen redone after we got married. He told me the plans the late May day we moved in. We had returned from our honeymoon in Italy early because he had had to get back for a trial. He carried me over the threshold and made the announcement.

"Say goodbye to this old kitchen, Claire," he had said. "I'm having a new one built for you," he said.

"But I love this one!" I said. It was cozy and beachy, nothing fancy about it: Butcher block counters had been well used. The porcelain sink dated back seventy years or more, an oak ice chest was being used as a liquor cabinet, and black-and-white Chase family photos hung on the beadboard walls.

"There are plenty of memories I want to wipe out," he said.

"Really?" I asked, feeling compassion. I'd thought he had a good upbringing—perhaps not as close to his family as I was to mine—but happy and well loved. "You don't talk about your childhood much."

"There's not much to say," he said. "I'd rather live in the present. Erase my parents, erase Margot."

I stayed quiet, listening.

"She sat there," he said, pointing at the window seat I had already pegged as a wonderful reading nook. "And that was her bar." He gestured at the oak chest. "She was never far from it."

"That must have been painful," I said.

"Her drinking? Yes, you could say that."

"We can make this our own," I said gently. "Change small things." I didn't want to impose myself on this home that had been in his family for generations, but I supposed we could get new curtains, paint the cabinets.

He didn't reply. He spread out plans on the counter. I felt a little shocked—he had already had them drawn up?

"The overall plan is by David Masterson of Chester Architects—he is the absolute best in New England. You're going to love it."

"Oh, Griffin . . . I love the comfiness of *this* kitchen. You don't have to spend money to make me happy—the opposite. I just want us to be together. I'm going to cook everything you love, right here. We can fish off the beach, grill the bluefish and stripers we catch. I want to plant a vegetable garden too." I glanced across the room at the lovely old enameled stove; I couldn't wait to use it.

"I've hired Sallie Benson to do the design," Griffin said, as if he hadn't heard me. "David gives her his top recommendation, says she did the interior at the Pemberley Inn, as well as some very important properties in Watch Hill and Newport. She has a fantastic vision." He paused. "Her husband's an acquaintance of mine."

I had heard of Sallie Benson and knew she had a great reputation, but I felt stung by the idea that someone else was going to redesign the kitchen I already loved and felt at home in. I couldn't stop glancing at the window seat.

"Griffin," I began—he was the crush of my teenage years, the love of my life, the most passionate man I'd ever been with. "You're all I need. Not a fancy kitchen. Besides, if there's a big renovation, we'll have workmen in our house for who knows how long. We're newlyweds, and I just want to be alone with you. We . . ."

The look on his face stopped me.

This was the first time it happened. It would be far from the last, but I will remember this moment until I die. It was as if I had thrown a switch. My loving husband who had constantly said he adored me, felt blessed to be with me, loved me to death, transformed into someone I had never seen. His eyes glared straight into me, and they changed color from pale green to pure black.

"You shame me," he said. "Instead of accepting my gift, you shove it down my throat. Do you know how much that hurts me?" His face darkened and twisted. He took a step closer to me. I saw his shoulders tense, his hands form fists, but his black eyes were what terrified me.

"Griffin," I said, panicking and leaning back because I thought he was going to hit me. And here it came: my first apology. Heartfelt, at the time. "I'm so sorry if I said the wrong thing. I didn't mean to hurt you."

"But you *did* hurt me."

My eyes filled with tears—both because I was scared and because I had obviously touched a tender spot in Griffin. I always thought of him as so tough to do the job he did; he was sensitive to me, to the victims whose cases he prosecuted, but I never thought of him as being so vulnerable. Thin skinned. "I'm sorry," I whispered again.

"I don't want to hit you," he said. "And because of that, I need you to be out of my sight. I go out or you do. Your choice. I need time alone."

I turned into an ice sculpture, frozen in shock. Without waiting for me to reply, he walked out of the house. I heard the car start and drive away. I was stunned. And terrified.

I couldn't stop thinking about those gleaming-black raging eyes. How do green eyes turn black? Was it my imagination? A trick of the morning light? I had just seen my husband turn into a monster.

But the longer he was gone that day, the more my emotions shifted. I told myself I must have been wrong. Eyes could not change color—I had imagined it. And had I heard him correctly? Griffin would never threaten me. Not the man I'd loved so long.

I found myself thinking of how he had said I'd hurt him. I wondered, What could I have said differently? Was it my tone? I looked at the kitchen plans. He had wanted to surprise me, thought I would be delighted. I began to convince myself that no wonder he was hurt by my reaction: I had not appreciated the gift. I had dismissed his effort, not been thankful that he wanted to spend so much money on a kitchen to make me happy.

When he came back, he was his old self. He brought me a bouquet of sunflowers from Grey Gables Farm. He wrapped me in his arms and kissed me. I shivered with relief at his touch, at the sight of his green eyes. He tilted his head back and smiled.

"I never wanted to hurt you," I said.

"I believe you," he said. "I know you didn't mean it."

"If you want a new kitchen, it's fine. It's great," I said.

"Claire, that means the world to me. I love you to pieces."

"I love you too," I said, and then he led me upstairs, into our bedroom with an entire wall of windows looking out to sea.

I told myself I was not "the abused woman type"—as if there were such a thing. I was strong, could take care of myself, and I could handle anyone's pain and carry it for them. But abuse, though it can seem to happen all at once, is cumulative. I was like a lobster in a pot of cold water, the temperature being raised bit by bit before I realized I was in danger. Every apology I made to Griffin chipped away at my soul, brought me closer to being boiled alive, because I gave up a little more of myself. And a little more. And a little more.

Griffin wound up working very closely with Sallie Benson to create the kitchen we had now. Many people would find it beautiful. It was featured in *Luxury Coastline Magazine*. As much as Griffin wanted me to love the kitchen, I couldn't. I hated it. It was all white marble, white tiles, white wainscoting, stainless steel appliances, and cookware fit for a professional chef. Every surface was smooth and sleek—and sterile. And it reminded me of the first time I saw his eyes turn black.

The funny thing was, in spite of what I considered an ice-cold color scheme, Sallie was warm. When she finished the job and came over to drop off a bouquet of all-white flowers, she beamed at me and gave me a hug.

"You were wonderful to work for," she said.

"I was? I was hardly here. Griffin oversaw everything."

"Oh, Claire. You're a brilliant artist, and I was worried I wouldn't be up to your standards. But Griffin told me you checked in after I left each day and that you loved the progress. It was so encouraging."

"I'm glad," I said, even though I had mostly removed myself, found it hard to praise a room I couldn't imagine myself living in.

"He's such a sweetheart, and he's so in love with you. That really, oh gosh, it moves me. I go into a lot of houses and see a lot of marriages, and Claire, yours is inspiring."

I couldn't even respond to that. Two months of being married to Griffin and I had started thinking of leaving. It was a tug-of-war, ruled by his moods. When he was loving, I was positive that was the *real* Griffin and that things between us would get better. But when he was angry, I shut down, became depressed. I'd wonder—is *this* the real Griffin? And often, on those nights, I would dream of Ellen. I hadn't yet started thinking he killed her, but if he treated me this way, he may have started with her.

"I was intimidated by you being an artist," Sallie had said. "I don't need to tell you that you can add color touches in here—you'll make it your own, and it will be beautiful!"

"Thank you, Sallie," I said.

A few days later, Sloane and Edward Hawke came to dinner, and Griffin's delight in showing off the kitchen seemed to captivate Edward. Within a week, they had signed a contract with Sallie Benson. When the work was done, the Hawkes had all the Catamount Bluff neighbors over for cocktails—Wade and Leonora Lockwood, Neil and Abigail Coffin, and Griffin and me.

"Here's to Sallie!" Sloane said, raising her glass.

"Dan certainly married up," Neil said, laughing.

"Sure as hell did," Wade said. "Never thought he'd wind up with a gal like that."

I saw Leonora shoot Wade a sharp look and wondered what it meant.

"Well, she did a great job and we're happy," Edward said, putting his arm around Sloane, and we all clinked glasses.

I found myself thinking about that toast to Sallie while I cut up the melon for Griffin's breakfast after our ugly dawn beach encounter. I used an expensive French paring knife, from a set chosen by Sallie because she thought a dark wood knife block would make a stunning contrast to the white marble counter.

"Are there any articles about the trial?" I asked Griffin. He was still at the table, reading the paper.

"Of course," he said. "It's going to make jury selection tricky. I don't know who's leaking what we have for evidence, but someone is. Right here—an unnamed source saying we have a student's underwear with Jackson's DNA on them."

"That's too bad," I said.

His silence made the sound of my knife slicing through cantaloupe and clicking on the counter sound like it was happening in an echo chamber.

"Too bad?" he asked.

"Yes," I said. "I know how closely you guard your facts, and you don't want the jury pool hearing . . ."

"It's a little more than *too bad*, Claire," he said. "Do you know what Jackson did to those girls? I could sit here right now and tell you the specifics, you want to hear them? I need an impartial jury. I can't afford to lose a big case right in the midst of my campaign."

"Of course," I said. "I know."

"Of *course*. You *know*," he said in a mimicking voice, pushing his chair back, then slapping the newspaper down on the table. "If you knew the things men do to women, you'd fall apart."

"I'm sure I would," I said. My tone indicated I had something on my mind.

He stood up and exhaled hard, taking one step toward me.

"You know, it really bothered me to see you kneeling at the cove. As if you were worshipping Ellen like a goddess."

"Far from it," I said. "She was as human as I am."

"Why now? Why are you torturing me with her now? Don't I have enough on my mind?"

"I don't think I'm torturing you," I said, keeping my voice steady.

"You act as if I had something to do with her death. And that insults me. Believe me, I know the syndrome. A couple grows apart, and suddenly the husband is vilified. My office receives a hundred calls a year from women saying their husbands committed terrible crimes. They think he's the Marshfield serial killer or a trucker murdering women on I-95. You're such a cliché."

"I still hear the sound of those crabs eating her flesh," I said.

"So do I," he said. "And the difference between you and me is that I loved her. She was my college girlfriend. Do you know what it was like for me to see her like that? I lost her when she went to Cancún."

"Who did she go with?" I asked.

"What's the difference?" he asked. "It was half my lifetime ago."

And half of what would have been hers, I thought. I caught him gazing at me, almost dispassionately, as if taking my measure.

"You know, Claire," he said. "I don't need this swirling around right now."

"What do you mean?"

"Rumors. Innuendo."

"I don't know what you're talking about."

"People hinting that I had something to do with what happened to Ellen," he said.

"Who is hinting about that?" I asked.

He didn't quite answer but went on, "I am in the middle of a campaign. I expect my wife and friends to protect my reputation, not cast doubts."

58

"What friends aren't protecting you?" I asked.

He stopped talking, just gave me a long curious stare; again, I had the feeling he was assessing me.

"Breakfast is almost ready," I said.

"I'm not hungry anymore," he said.

"Okay."

"It's clear you don't appreciate me or my work," he continued. "Nate, the great scientist and environmentalist—you admire him even though you couldn't wait to leave him and marry me. But your actual, current, working-his-fingers-to-the-bone husband, who only wants justice for two girls Jackson raped with a pipe wrench—you don't care, it makes no difference to you. You can only think of Ellen."

Interesting, his choice of words: *fingers-to-the-bone.*

At one time I would have turned myself inside out, saying I was sorry for giving him the wrong idea. By that Sunday morning, I was past apologies. Even so, I had to play my part, at least a little, to get what I wanted out of this week.

"Griffin, I admire you so much," I said without inflection, just as if I were reading a script. "You care so deeply about your cases, all the victims. You're just so amazing, so caring."

"Other people think that," he said. "You don't."

He filled his travel mug with coffee, then turned to look at me. "Maybe while I'm on the boat, you can reflect on what I said."

"I thought I was going with you," I said. "And the boys."

"No," he said. "I really think it would be to your benefit to give some thought about being more protective of your husband, instead of undermining him."

Outside, tires crunched on the driveway.

Griffin checked his watch. "Seven fifteen, and they're right on time."

We both walked to the door, saw his two sons getting out of Ford's black Porsche. They house-sat in a guest cottage on the estate of one of Griffin's biggest political donors. It was thirty miles away, so they'd gotten up very early to get here.

Although they were twins, only Ford looked like Griffin. At twenty-one, he had his father's height and build, the same cockiness, the same white streak in his dark hair. Alexander was taller but fair like Margot, less athletic, and sensitive. They walked into the kitchen dressed to go out on the boat: khaki shorts, polo shirts, ball caps. Alexander's was from the Hawthorne Yacht Club; Ford's was his college baseball team's, worn backward.

"Well, you two are up with the sun!" Griffin said, smiling as if we hadn't been fighting at all. He opened his arms, and both boys hugged him. "Isn't this great!"

"You mentioned sailing, Dad," Ford said. "Are we still on for that? And a photo op for the campaign?"

"Absolutely, we absolutely are on," Griffin said.

"Hi, Claire," Alexander said.

"Good morning," I said. "Looks like a great day to be on the water."

"It does, doesn't it?" Griffin asked, then gestured toward me and said sweetly, "It's too bad Claire isn't feeling up to joining us."

"Are you okay?" Alexander asked.

"I'm fine," I said.

"She's just tired out," Griffin said. "A bundle of nerves, getting ready for her exhibition. She'll be the toast of the town once everyone sees her latest work. We're proud of her, aren't we, guys?"

Ford gravitated toward the stove. Although I had turned off the burner, the bacon was still sizzling in the skillet.

"Did you hear me?" Griffin asked. "Are you proud of your stepmother?"

"Griffin," I said, "that's okay."

"I asked a question," Griffin said.

"Definitely," Alexander said quickly. "Your stuff is so cool, Claire."

"Thank you," I said, smiling at him. Out of the corner of my eye, I saw Ford use the spatula to take a slice of bacon out of the pan. He blew on it to cool it off, then bit it in half, crunching away. Griffin glared at him.

"I know the three of you will have a great time sailing," I said, feeling the air fill with electricity.

"I never thought I could do it," Griffin said. "Never."

"What, Dad?" Ford asked.

"Raise a couple of animals."

"Griffin—" I said.

Griffin crossed the kitchen in two steps and slapped the cap off Ford's head; it landed in the bacon grease. "Eating straight out of the pan. Wearing caps in the house." He turned toward Alexander, but he was already holding his yacht club cap in his hands. His face was pure white. The reaction seemed to please Griffin. He clapped Alexander on the shoulder.

"Let's go," Griffin said. "I want to catch the tide."

"Should Alexander and I follow you in my car?" Ford asked.

"Alexander will ride with me. Why don't you go home and try to get the bacon grease out of your hat? Try soaking it."

"But Dad . . . ," Ford said. Where Alexander had gone pale, Ford's face had turned crimson.

"See you later. We'll all meet at the yacht club for an early dinner," Griffin said. Then he and Alexander walked into the garage, and I heard the barn doors swing open and Griffin's car start up.

"Ford," I began, walking toward him. He stood with his back to me, trying to fork his cap out of the skillet. "Just leave it. I'll take care of it."

"No, he said I have to," Ford said. He wouldn't turn around. I put my hand on his back, and I felt his shoulders quaking. We just stood there for a long time. The sound of Griffin's car receded. Waves broke on the shore. Gulls cried as they flew over the house. After a while, Ford shook my hand away. I didn't want to leave him, but I knew he couldn't stand for me to see his tears.

I left the house and returned to my studio. I thought about crab claws and those bare twigs, of the shadow box I was about to make, of how it would be titled *Fingerbone* and dedicated to my husband.

Looking back, I wonder if Griffin was giving me one last chance by telling me to think about protecting instead of undermining him. Or had he already made up his mind that I was a liability and set his plan in motion?

Even though he'd pretended not to hear what I'd said at the tidal pool that morning, we both knew I'd been talking to Ellen and that I'd told her I was going to leave. But my leaving might raise too many questions, trigger "rumors and innuendo," and he couldn't let that happen.

ONE DAY LATER

9

CONOR

On Saturday morning, the forensics team was still processing the Chase house, and Conor Reid drove toward the scene. Everything had changed: they now knew the DNA belonged to Claire. It appeared the rope had been used to hang her from the rafter, that it had snapped under her weight. Blood loss from the fall was possible, but the amount, and the pattern on and around the car, suggested to Conor that she had been beaten, possibly stabbed.

So far, Griffin Chase was the last person known to have seen Claire on Friday morning, at approximately 7:45. She hadn't shown up at the dock as planned, and she never arrived at the gallery. The crime scene had been discovered by Conor, Griffin, and Ben Markham at about 5:30 p.m., and the forensic team began their work an hour later. That provided an approximate ten-hour window for when the attack could have taken place.

From blood in the garage, especially the still-not-fully-coagulated pool beside the right rear tire, the time frame was narrowed to two hours—the medical examiner estimated she had been assaulted no earlier than 3:30 p.m.

Ralph Perry, another off-duty Black Hall cop, was parked at the head of the private road that led into Catamount Bluff, and he waved as Conor approached. Conor rolled down his window, and Perry did the same.

"How's it going?" Conor asked.

"Busy morning. You know, people wanting to gawk. It's even juicier for them because it's a rich family. That plus the usual trespassers trying to sneak onto the private beach. I just tell 'em how to get to the state park."

Conor nodded and drove through. He saw the Major Crime Squad van outside the Chases' house. Investigators walked between the van and garage wearing gloves and protective shoe coverings.

Catamount Bluff was bordered on one side by Long Island Sound and three sides by marsh and five hundred acres of deep coastal forest. The four families that had founded the Bluff in the late 1800s had decreed that the wildland be preserved from development. One section had been logged in 1906, and the ponds were a source of ice in winter. Period maps showed an abandoned icehouse as well as a series of caves in the rock ledge bordering one of the salt marshes.

Other than the cart path to the icehouse, the woods were inaccessible to vehicles—and pretty much any human encroachment. Conor would have expected the Bluff residents to create trails for hiking or to reach hunting and fishing grounds, but the deeds stipulated that the land remain forever wild.

Aside from the Chase house, there were three others that shared the private road, and the occupants were being questioned. The old icehouse, next to Lockwood Pond and close to the main road, had been checked, and no sign of Claire had been found. There were some beer cans and bags of fast food refuse in a corner, indicating that someone had used it at one point—possibly a party spot for kids.

Search dogs had been brought in last night, but they lost Claire's trail on the dirt track just fifteen yards east of the Chases' house.

Someone could have hidden a vehicle there, where Claire wouldn't have seen it. After ambushing her, the suspect could have loaded her inside and driven away with her.

In fact, there were signs that several vehicles had parked in that spot over time. When told there were tire impressions of trucks and various makes and models of cars, Chase had said it was where workmen parked and also guests from when he and Claire held parties.

Flowers bloomed all around the house. The beds looked well tended. Conor wondered if the Chases had a gardener or whether Claire took care of them herself. He couldn't imagine Griffin doing it, working in the soil.

Maybe a landscape crew had made the recent tire tracks. Or perhaps it was Claire's attacker. Had she been abducted? Or had he taken her body away? Although the tire tracks were photographed by investigators and impressions were taken, it was impossible to determine which were most recent. Conor needed a list of all tradespeople known to work on the Chases' property.

Conor spotted Trooper Peggy McCabe standing by the front door. They waved at each other; he had worked with McCabe before, after Beth Lathrop's murder, when McCabe was a town cop. She was local, born and raised in Black Hall. He made a mental note to ask her if she knew the Chases.

Last night detectives had questioned the Coffins and Lockwoods. The Hawkes had been out, and Conor intended to drop by to interview them today.

All four families were friendly—in fact, they had all gathered at the Coffin home just two weeks earlier for the annual Catamount Association meeting. Cocktails and hors d'oeuvres had been served. It was also a private campaign rally, with the neighbors toasting Griffin's run for governor and writing big checks.

All day yesterday, Neil Coffin had been at work in Hartford, where he was an insurance executive; Abigail owned a yoga studio in town and had taught a class that started at three p.m. She hadn't seen Claire at any point during the day, and she didn't return home until six thirty, after dropping into Claire's opening. Like the Chases and Hawkes, Neil Coffin was in his midforties, Abigail a couple of years younger.

Wade and Leonora Lockwood, a couple in their late seventies, had left their house in separate cars but at the same time: five p.m. Wade went to meet some friends at a club he belonged to, and Leonora drove into town to attend Claire's opening.

They hadn't seen Claire all day, hadn't noticed any vehicles other than a FedEx truck driving toward the Chase home—as they were leaving their driveway. Wade reported the time as 5:00 p.m. sharp. He had been in the navy, fought in the Vietnam War, then returned to his family home on Catamount Bluff to settle down. He had inherited land and buildings on the gritty Easterly waterfront. Over time, he had developed many warehouses for commercial use and luxury condos.

Leonora thought she might have seen Claire drive past around noon, but she couldn't be sure whether Claire was leaving Catamount or returning, and she wasn't positive it hadn't actually been the day before. Wade had expressed displeasure over his wife's inaccuracy.

Conor had not seen a FedEx box outside the house when he had arrived there last night. He had called their dispatcher in Norwich, and she'd told him that nothing had been delivered. A pickup had been scheduled by Claire—she was a frequent customer, often shipping work to collectors—but the driver had not found a package.

As Conor walked down the road to meet with the Hawkes, he heard blues music coming from their house. Catamount Bluff seemed so sedate and buttoned up, Conor welcomed the sound. Two Mercedes sedans and a catering truck were parked in the circular driveway. The house seemed a mirror image of the Chases': shingled, sprawling, over a century old, worth a fortune. Conor rang the front bell, and a minute later, a man answered the door.

"Mr. Hawke?" Conor asked.

"No," he said. "I'm just breaking down the party—they're out back. Come on, I'll show you."

Except for art on the walls, the house's decor was pure white, similar to the Chases' kitchen: white walls, furniture, rugs on the hardwood floors. In stark contrast, abstract paintings, in shades of red and pink, covered the walls. A tripod by a picture window held a telescope, and Conor noted it was pointed toward the Chases' house.

Glass doors opened onto a pool, turquoise and sparkling in the sun. Tables and chairs had been set up, and a crew was folding them, packing them onto dollies. A couple stood by the bar, pulling down lengths of red, white, and blue bunting. The woman turned, spotted Conor, and said something to the man. She was thin and blonde, rings on her fingers and bracelets on her wrists, wearing a dress the same raspberry shade as some of the paintings inside. Conor approached the couple.

"Hi, did you call? Are you from the police?" she asked.

"Yes," he said. "I'm Detective Reid. Mrs. Hawke?"

"Sloane, please. And this is my husband, Edward." They all shook hands. Both looked solemn. He was tall with brown hair, muscular but turning soft around the middle; he wore faded red shorts and an untucked starched white dress shirt; the breast pocket bore a small embroidered crest: a dark bird with outstretched wings, talons clutching a banner. He had seen it before.

"We want to help however we can," Edward said.

"Claire would never run away," Sloane said, shaking her head. "Never. If that's what you're thinking."

"Why would I think that?" Conor asked.

"All marriages have problems," she said, looking downward. "Lawyers don't always appreciate what it's like to take in the world and turn it into art."

"She means me," Edward said.

"You're a lawyer?" Conor asked.

He nodded. "Yeah, corporate law. My office is in Easterly."

Conor found his gaze pulled back to the insignia on Edward's shirt pocket. He was pretty sure he'd seen the same one on Griffin Chase's shirts.

"And in case you haven't guessed, Sloane's an artist," Edward said. "She painted those masterpieces in the living room."

"What happened to Claire?" Sloane asked, brushing off her husband's compliment. "I can't stand not knowing."

"Two tragedies on the same day," Edward said.

"He means Sallie Benson. The boat explosion," Sloane said.

Conor's antenna went up. The Benson case belonged to Conor's old partner, and Jen had told him what Dan Benson had said: "They got her." Hours later, when the anesthesia had worn off, he claimed not to remember saying that and said Sallie had been upset and maybe her carelessness had caused the explosion.

Two local women affected by violence on the same day seemed like an awfully big coincidence. Could there be a connection between whatever had happened to both women?

"Do you know Sallie Benson?" he asked.

Sloane didn't reply. Edward stared at the ground.

"Yes," Sloane said. "We know her."

"Are you close friends with both women?" Conor asked.

"Ironically, Claire and Griffin introduced us to Sallie," Edward said. "She did some decorating work for us." His eyes were red rimmed, and Conor sensed him holding back emotion. "But Claire, yes—we are very good friends with both her and Griffin."

"Is that right, Mrs. Hawke?" Conor asked.

"Definitely," Sloane said, her eyes filling with tears. "I hardly know Sallie, but Claire is one of my closest friends. We support each other's work. When things are bad, we're always there for each other." She broke down, couldn't go on.

"Can you tell me what you mean, 'when things are bad'?" Conor asked.

Sloane stared down, her shoulders shaking hard, clearly trying not to let him see her cry.

Edward put his arm around Sloane. "Claire's had a rough time with Griffin's boys. Well, Ford anyway. He resents having a stepmother, and he can be a real prick to her. To everyone, frankly. He moved out. Alexander, too, although he and Claire get along much better."

"Well, they were too old to be living at home anyway," Sloane said, sniffling. "At least they're being productive now."

"If house-sitting can be considered 'productive,'" Edward said. "Well, I suppose they get paid for it."

"What does Ford do that bothers Claire?" Conor asked.

"He's confrontational," Sloane said. "He came down to her studio two days ago while I was there with her and said awful things. He'd been drinking."

"What did he say?"

"I barely remember," Sloane said.

"Anything would help," Conor said.

She cleared her throat. "Dumb stuff about her not belonging here, that the property had been in his family. That she'd married his father right after his mother went away because she wanted the money. As if she ever . . ."

"So what can we do for you?" Edward asked abruptly, interrupting his wife. "I don't mean to be rude. It's just that we're very upset. We always have a Memorial Day party. This year it was going to double as a fundraiser for Griffin, but with Claire missing, we decided to cancel."

"Did either of you see Claire yesterday?" Conor asked, and he watched them shake their heads in unison.

"No," Edward said, sliding a glance at his wife. "I was at the office, and Sloane was running around, shopping for the party."

"All day?" Conor asked.

"Lots to do for the party," she said, glancing at Edward. "Got to keep up appearances, you know?"

"Appearances?" Conor asked. She didn't reply. "When were you home?" he asked.

"Well, I left here midmorning, came back for lunch and a swim, then headed out again. I went to Claire's opening with Leonora and Abigail. I spotted you at the gallery. I actually saw you leave with Griffin. I guess that's when you came here and found . . . she was gone, right?"

"Did you see Claire at any time while you were home?" Conor asked, leaving her question unanswered.

"No," she said. "And it breaks my heart. I thought about running over after lunch, just to give her a hug and moral support for her show. But I figured she might be busy getting ready or with some last-minute touches on this one particular piece. It had special meaning to her, and she wanted to hold on to it longer than the others."

"Which piece was it?" Conor asked.

"*Fingerbone,*" Sloane said. "Kind of disturbing."

Conor nodded, picturing the skeleton hand. "Do you know why it meant so much to her?"

"She said it was inspired by something she saw when she was young."

"Okay," Conor said, remembering what Claire had asked him at dinner Monday night.

"Anyway," Sloane said, frowning. "I didn't go to her house. Everything might have been different if I had."

"Yeah, you might have been bludgeoned or stabbed and strung up too," Edward said. He looked at Conor. "I know, you're wondering how I know, none of that is public knowledge. Griffin told me what you found in the garage. All the blood. It's horrific."

"She has to be alive," Sloane said, her eyes filling with tears.

"Yes, we have to hope," Edward said. Again, Conor was struck by the emotion in his face. "Is there anything else?"

"That's all for now," Conor said. He started to turn away, then stopped. "Just one more thing, completely separate. That insignia," he said, pointing at Edward's shirt pocket.

"Oh, that," Sloane said. "It's his secret society."

Edward's arm tightened around her shoulders. "It's the crest for a men's club I belong to. Sloane thinks women should be allowed to join."

"The Last Monday Club. Actually, Claire and I just think it's silly," Sloane said.

"So Griffin's a member too?" Conor asked.

Edward gave Sloane an angry glance and didn't reply; chastened, Sloane stood stiffly and gave a single, brisk nod.

"How about Dan Benson?"

Neither of them replied. Conor thanked them and walked away. It had struck him when Sloane had mentioned the small-world connections all around that Edward had interrupted her, effectively cutting her off. Even more noteworthy had been the way Edward had clearly not wanted Sloane to tell him that Griffin belonged to the same men's club. The secret society.

He would look into the Last Monday Club, including whether Dan Benson was a member. And he would talk to Ford Chase, find out how badly he resented Claire for moving into his family home at Catamount Bluff.

10

TOM

The USCG search for survivors of the *Sallie B* had been going on for fourteen hours. No one had been found, and no debris had been sighted since yesterday. Tom had been up all night. He felt himself flagging, but all he had to do was think of Gwen, nine, and Charlie, seven, to sharpen up. He stood on the bridge of *Nehantic* and drank black coffee.

Sallie Benson's body had been recovered from the wreck. She had been trapped in the galley and badly burned in the blast. Divers had searched for the children, found no sign of them. They did, however, discover a large hole blown through the floorboards, indicating the explosion had come from the bilge.

Dan was at Easterly Hospital recovering from surgery. A length of the boat's aluminum trim, turned into an arrow by the blast, had hit his chest. It had just missed his heart, punctured a lung. By all reports, he was frantic about his family. Tom knew that both Conor and Jen considered his changing statements about what happened to be suspicious—first saying "they got her," then claiming that Sallie's negligence had blown up the boat. Tom wasn't sure where the investigation stood, but he assumed that until the explosion was ruled an accident, Dan himself was a suspect.

Computer models showed that if the children had made it into the water in the small yellow life raft, they would be drifting toward or past Block Island. At that point, they would be in the open Atlantic Ocean, a far more treacherous proposition considering that the next landfall was Portugal.

Tom studied the chart. The computer factored in every possible environmental factor and wanted to send him south-southeast—and that rang a huge bell. It had done the same thing on a previous SAR, for two young girls whose voyage had started off roughly five miles from the site where the *Sallie B* sank.

If he had followed directions, he would have missed the children entirely—they would have been presumed lost at sea. But he had accounted for the possibility that they might somehow have steered themselves to safety, and he had checked unlikely rock outcroppings. That's when he had found them on Morgan Island.

Tom took a deep breath. He ordered *Nehantic*'s officer of the deck to change course. The day was so bright and the water so calm that the sea was a mirror. It was time to look at Morgan Island. It had saved two sisters' lives once—why not Gwen and Charlie now? But the radio squawked, and he heard the Jayhawk pilot calling in, saying they had just spotted a yellow raft on the far side of the Block Island windmills. It appeared that no one was aboard.

Nehantic was the ship closest to that location, so Tom ordered another course change, and they steamed full speed toward the reported position. The helicopter hovered above, at enough altitude to avoid swamping the small craft.

Tom had the same concern about the large wake caused by his 270-foot cutter, so he deployed a rigid inflatable boat. Seaman Ricardo Cardoso steered the RIB toward the yellow raft; Tom stood on the starboard side, ready to lean over and grab a line when they approached. His heart was racing, but it crashed as soon as they came broadside. The pilot was right: the raft was empty.

Tom turned toward Seaman Cardoso and started to shake his head when he heard what sounded like a bird. It squeaked once, twice. He leaned farther over the side of the USCG inflatable and saw her. A little girl was lying on her side in the shadow of the raft's hull, pressed so tightly against it that she might have been part of the boat. There was no sign of the boy.

The raft was small. Tom was afraid his weight could cause it to capsize, so he balanced himself by holding the inflatable's rail, lowered himself dead center in the raft. He knelt beside the girl—slight, white-blonde, wearing bright-yellow shorts and an orange PFD over a pale-yellow shirt. At first, he didn't see her breathing, and he thought the worst, but then he saw the pulse in her neck beating fast.

"Gwen?" he asked. "My name is Tom. I'm a coast guard officer, and I'm here to take you home."

She didn't speak or turn toward him, but he heard that bird sound coming from her mouth—tiny peeps. He lifted her into his arms, smelled smoke from the explosion, saw that her eyebrows had been singed and her eyelashes burned off. His chest tightened at the thought of what Hunter had told him: that Dan said Sallie had done this on purpose.

Cardoso leaned over the rail, and Tom handed Gwen into his arms. The raft was barely four feet long and obviously empty. Charlie wasn't there. Tom would radio the Jayhawk and the rest of the fleet, and he knew they would focus their search for Charlie in this area.

When Tom climbed into the RIB, he went to Gwen and tried to meet her gaze. Her eyes were open, but she seemed to be staring at a point far off in the distance. "Gwen?" he said again. "You're okay. We're taking you home. Gwen, can you tell me about your brother? Where's Charlie?"

A tremor shook her body so hard that he thought she was having a seizure. After a moment it subsided, but she still wouldn't, or couldn't, meet Tom's eyes, and she didn't answer him. But the squeaks didn't stop—they kept going over and over, almost as if they were her breath, almost as if they told her she was still alive.

Tom took off his personal flotation device and uniform shirt. Even though Gwen was so small she swam in them, he buttoned and buckled them tight around her to keep her warm and safe. He held her tight while the Jayhawk lowered the rescue basket.

He climbed into the basket with her and shielded her with his body as the winch roared and hoisted them up. He held his hands over her ears, so the booming sound of the rotors wouldn't scare her, and he didn't let her go until he carried her into the chopper's cabin, laid her on the gurney so the medics could take care of her. He took her hand; it was ice cold. She neither squeezed his hand nor pulled away.

She didn't flinch when the medics took her vital signs and pricked her arm with a needle to start an IV. They all spoke to her, making sure to say her name: "Gwen, you're safe now."

"Gwen, do you know where you are?"

"Hey, Gwen. How old are you? Are you nine?"

"Gwen, what's your favorite color?"

But she didn't reply to any of them. She just kept staring off into nothing—or at least nothing that Tom or any of the others could see—peeping like a baby bird, in a language that made sense to no one but Gwen.

Then she said one word: "Mermen."

After that, the tiny sounds resumed.

FOUR DAYS EARLIER

11

SALLIE

Love was truly a series of blunders. That's how Sallie Benson had started to think about it. Even knowing that she was making a mess of her life, she felt powerless to stop. Here she was at West Wind Marina, on a boat two docks over from where she and her husband kept the *Sallie B*, waiting for her true love—a man who wasn't her husband. Dan was at work, their kids were at school, and she was breathless with desire and guilt. She was addicted; she might as well be waiting for her dealer.

Sitting in the cabin of *Elysian*—the sexy sixty-five-foot sportfishing boat that she had been paid to decorate—she wondered for the hundredth time that day what she was doing. She knew everyone at the boatyard, and they knew her. She had parked in her usual spot, next to where her family's boat—named for her, by her husband, a gift for their fifteenth anniversary—was docked.

Then she'd had to walk past dockhands and guys who had worked on the *Sallie B*. She felt their eyes on her, watching as she held her head high and strode down a completely different dock to someone else's yacht. She had said hi to Eli Dean, the yard owner, and she was positive his normally friendly smile had turned into a leer.

She glanced in the mirror in the main salon: she had white-blonde hair—the same color she'd had as a child but now maintained at a price—big blue eyes that, to her, reflected the innocence she felt about the world and those she loved, and a white piqué sundress that revealed the fact she didn't have much of a tan. How had the nice woman she'd always been become someone who committed adultery—and couldn't get enough of it?

She had worked hard to build her business, and she was so grateful she had become the go-to designer for the moneyed set. Even some of the oldest blue-blood families on the shoreline wanted to redo their houses and, lately, yachts, with her signature style. Designing the interior of *Elysian* had come with particular challenges, namely, Edward's wife, Sloane.

Sallie felt very at home here, although, naturally, she had no ownership rights. Every inch of the interior bore Sallie's mark. Edward had insisted on it. Sloane—had there ever been such a boarding school name?—loved bright colors, especially deep shades of pink, and she had cozy inclinations. That was not what Edward wanted.

When Sallie designed the Hawkes' house on Catamount Bluff, she had had to convince Sloane that white was the perfect base color for seaside living. It caught and reflected light sparkling off the water. And many people didn't realize how many variations there were in the white palette—all kinds of shades, with hints of blue or green or yellow or even pink. Depending on your choice, you could warm or cool a room—or do both at the same time. Sallie would have expected that Sloane, as an artist, would understand that.

Benjamin Moore paints made over a hundred shades of white. The names were poetic: cloud white, Chantilly lace, white heron, distant gray, white diamond, dove wing, sea pearl. Sallie loved perhaps their most famous shade—linen white. With hints of pale, almost invisible yellow, it spread warmth through a room and flattered everyone in it.

And why did she love white so much? The answer seemed sacrilegious, waiting on *Elysian* for her lover to arrive, but it was because of her mother. When she was fifteen and her mother was dying of cancer, Sallie had sat beside her hospital bed.

Her father and little sister, Lydia, had gone downstairs to the cafeteria. Mass cards and get-well cards were propped up on the wide windowsill. It was a Catholic hospital, and there was a crucifix and a painting of Mary on the wall above the bed. Sallie had prayed the rosary while her mother slept.

"Sallie," her mother said, taking her hand when she woke up. She gazed at Sallie with loving blue eyes that seemed to be getting cloudier by the minute. "When I get to heaven and it's full of angels, I won't meet anyone better than you."

"I don't want you to leave," Sallie whispered. "Please stay . . ."

"Sweetheart, I would if I could. But that's why we have to stay connected, no matter what. That's why I want you to stay the same as you are now, as smart and kind, so when I look down from the sky, no matter how much time goes by, I will always recognize you. You're my angel, Sallie."

"You're mine, Mom."

Her mother died before her father and sister returned to the room.

Sallie had been wearing her school's summer uniform—a white cotton dress—that day. White was the last color her mother ever saw her wearing. So even now, Sallie gravitated to white and almost always wore it.

And after she graduated from Parsons School of Design, put in her time with a famous New York design firm, and started her own company, she found herself drawn to the beauty of angel-white rooms, the color she had been wearing the day her mother died.

She wanted her mother to be able to see her, to recognize her always, as she watched over her from heaven. She hoped her mother would forgive her for what had started at Catamount Bluff: love and trouble.

That was where she had fallen in love with Edward. It had started slowly, but she had noticed that he would often show up at the house around lunchtime, when Sloane was over at Claire's studio or taking yoga at Abigail Coffin's wellness center in Black Hall.

He would sit at the kitchen table, watching Sallie with such admiration in his eyes. One day he walked right up to her, touched the back of her hand as she held up swatches of fabric for him to examine. Sallie's heart had practically stopped.

She felt overwhelmed—she had never had an affair, never been unfaithful to Dan in spite of how unloved she felt. She had not felt so excited, so wanted by a man, since before Gwen and Charlie were born. She found herself thinking of Edward all the time. She lost sleep fantasizing over what might happen. Lying beside Dan, she could practically feel Edward holding her, kissing her, undressing her.

As time went on, she felt an unspoken agreement with Edward that he would come home for lunch and Sallie would be there. Every day.

The "trouble" part of Sallie's time on Catamount Bluff came in the form of one of Griffin Chase's twin sons. They looked nothing alike, but at first she kept forgetting which was which. After a while she figured it out—Ford was the brash one; Alexander was reserved. Also, Ford was the one who developed a big ridiculous crush on her.

In the beginning, she had thought it was semiadorable, the way he would show up to swim in the Hawkes' pool. He would drive a half hour back to Catamount Bluff from where he housesat near the Rhode Island border and stand by the pool—shirt off, covered with coconut oil—watching her out of the corner of his eye before diving in, leaving a slick of oil on the water's surface.

But when he'd started coming into the kitchen while she was waiting for Edward, helping himself to cold drinks from the refrigerator, reeking of coconut, Sallie began to get annoyed. He would prattle on about his sailing prowess, his college baseball batting average, the way girls were always calling and texting him, how they all seemed so young to him, without substance—he needed a woman he could really talk to.

"An older woman," he actually said one day. "Do you mind if I text you?" he asked.

"Why do you want to?" she asked.

"I don't know, just send you stuff I think you might appreciate. Videos and stuff." He tried to smile. She could see he was holding back strong feelings. "I just want someone who *gets* it."

"Ford, I'm not that person."

"Maybe no one is," he said. "Girls my age don't. My mother bailed, and my stepmother . . ." His mouth twisted, and his eyes were full of pain.

"You're not close to Claire?" she asked.

He snorted, as if he'd never heard anything more absurd.

Sallie felt bad for him, and she wound up giving him her card. His mother had left the boys. It was a terrible thing to do, but Sallie knew there had to be another side of the story. Dan and Griffin had caroused around when they were young, and from what Dan had said, they were lucky they'd gotten away with so much. They were both members of the Last Monday Club now, but Dan kept his distance.

He once said he felt sorry for Margot and for Claire. "Griffin is hell on women," Dan had said. "And I wouldn't want to be his sons. He belittles them. I hope they don't turn out like him." That made Sallie feel even sorrier for Ford, the way he tried to make himself sound important, indispensable to his father.

"My dad's going to be governor," Ford said. "I'm helping with his campaign."

"Really," she said.

"Yeah. Basically, I do oppo research."

"Excuse me?"

"Opposition research. I help look into the guy who's running against him but what a socialist. He doesn't have a chance. My dad's going to sail right through."

"My husband said he's quite a guy," Sallie said.

"Oh yeah? He talks to you about my dad?" Ford asked.

"Yes, they had some adventures when they were young," Sallie said, pausing. Then, "My husband tells me everything. That's the way we are. Very close. No secrets." She was sure that Ford had picked up on the heat between her and Edward, and she thought by talking about Dan, she would throw him off. But by the strange glint in Ford's eye, she realized her statement had somehow set him off—maybe now he was jealous of Dan too.

She regretted giving Ford her card, because he sent texts or emails nearly every day—videos of dumb comedy sketches or his favorite bands. Tell me about the adventures that your husband and my dad had. I wanna tease him, he'd write. For the first couple of weeks she had replied just to be polite, but then she stopped. She knew her silence might hurt him, but she needed him to get the hint.

After Edward hired her to redo *Elysian*, she began to notice Ford showing up at the dock. True, the Chases had a sailboat and a skiff, both kept here at West Wind. Was Ford's being at the marina a coincidence, or was he following her?

Sallie told herself she was being paranoid about Ford. Instead she focused on Edward and began wondering whether they could really have a life together—leave Dan and Sloane and become a couple. The agony of that construct was her love for her children. In her grandparents' day, Catholics didn't divorce. Some of her parents' friends had split up, but fingers were always pointed, someone was always bad, a sinner, whispered about. The kids always paid the price.

If she left Dan, he would fight her for custody. Sallie could never be without her children. Gwen was such a little toughie, the way she raced her bike against all the boys in the neighborhood, could swim from one end of the beach to the other without resting. She did cartwheels and backbends and was in constant motion, all day long, until she was ready to collapse into bed after dinner.

And Charlie. Even at seven, he was still her baby. Sallie loved the way he tried to keep up with Gwen—and how Gwen let him. She took him almost everywhere. Would most big sisters do that? Maybe it would change when they got older, but for now they were an inseparable pair.

Sallie had been like that with her sister, Lydia. She still was; she and Dan had agreed that if anything ever happened to them, Lydia would be the guardian for the kids. Of course, Lydia had agreed.

It made Sallie feel horrible, to be thinking of her kids while she waited for Edward on his boat. She heard her phone buzz, and she grabbed it from her purse.

"Hello," she said, seeing his name on the caller ID.

"Are you at the boat?" he asked.

"Yes," she said. "Everything okay?"

"Yes, and I'm so sorry to be running late. In fact . . ."

She heard it in his voice: he wasn't coming.

"Sallie, I'm so sorry. I thought I'd be there by now, but I'm stuck at work, waiting for a conference call with the other side. They're scrambling to get documents together. Then tonight I have Last Monday Club."

It was Dan's club, too, but he had stopped going in recent months.

"I'd skip it," Edward continued, "but tonight's especially important. We're presenting Griffin with a big campaign contribution. I can stop at the boat between the call and the meeting. Will you wait for me?"

Sallie's heart fell. He wanted her to stay, so they could have sex, and then he'd run out to be with the guys. She made some sort of sound into the phone.

"Okay," he said. "I'll be there as soon as I can."

She hung up and checked the time again. The kids' after-school programs would be letting out in an hour; she'd planned to be in the parking lot to pick up Gwen and Charlie, but now she wouldn't have enough time.

She'd have to call Dan, make up an excuse. She would say she was stuck at a client's—not a total lie—and ask if he could get the kids. He wouldn't care that she was late. He'd take the kids to the tennis courts and then out for an ice cream.

She walked forward, into the owner's cabin. She sat down on the bed, the fluffy comforter sheathed in the pure-white Sferra duvet cover, *Elysian* embroidered in cream-colored silk thread. Edward had told her that Sloane had not spent even one night aboard.

What was she doing? She had never thought this would be her life, yet she had created it. She had brought herself to this point.

She typed a message to Edward on her phone:

Can you tell me what this is? Is it love? It is for me.

She hesitated ten seconds, then hit send.

Tied to the dock, *Elysian* rocked gently on the tide, but she heard a thump and felt the boat jounce. Footsteps sounded on deck, and for a second, she imagined it was Edward. Someone stumbled down the companionway.

Ford Chase bumped into the stateroom door, steadied himself, and walked toward her. He was disheveled, unshaven, with bloodshot eyes full of pain.

"I didn't want you to be here," he said. "I hoped you wouldn't be."

"I'm not sure why you'd care or why it's any of your business," she said, her heart thudding. "The Hawkes are my clients. Just like your father and Claire were."

"I don't believe you," he said, shaking his head. He stepped closer, smelling like alcohol and slurring his words. "That's not why you're here."

"Ford," she said.

"I love you," he said quietly.

"You don't," she said.

"Why are you with Edward? Why him? You don't know him at all. He's a bastard, just like my dad," he said.

"If your dad is so bad, why are you working to help him win office?" she asked, challenging him and hoping the shock would sober him up.

"You think he shouldn't win?" he asked.

"Not if he's a bastard," she said.

Ford just stood there, weaving, staring at her.

"Come on, Ford, you've had too much to drink. Let me drive you home."

"Home? Where's home? I live in someone else's house making sure the pipes don't freeze all winter and the sprinklers work all summer, with my goody-goody brother, while our father lives in our family home with a whore."

"Claire?" she asked, shocked.

"I bet they started up before my mother even left. Cheating to be together, just like you and Edward."

Sallie felt sick.

"Come on," Sallie said. Her tone was gentle, but she was falling apart inside. She stepped toward him and took his arm. "You tell me where you're living, and I'll take you there."

He started to nod, then lurched toward the head, using one hand to steady himself, projectile vomiting all over the sleek white wall and falling to his knees.

Sallie turned away, disgusted by Ford but, even more, devastated by what he had said because his words had rung so true.

12

CLAIRE

With just four days till my opening at the Woodward-Lathrop Gallery, I had jitters. I was most comfortable in nature or in my studio, and being the center of attention made me nervous.

It was six p.m., and Griffin was on his way to the Last Monday Club. He took it very seriously, but Sloane and I secretly laughed about the whole thing. All those men dressing in black tie for their secret society meeting—they got together the last Monday of each month, went hunting and fishing several times a year, and planned how to get one of their own, Griffin, elected governor. We wondered if they had a special handshake.

The group did have a philanthropic side. Each year they chose a local nonprofit, and the members donated $1,000 each. Last year's charity was the Domestic Violence Prevention Center of Southeastern Connecticut. I wondered if Griffin had steered them to it as a private joke. I doubted most of them realized that emotional abuse was as devastating as physical—the scars were just as painful, but they were internal, where people couldn't see. The abusers were so good at it that no one but their partners knew what they were doing. Or at least my husband was.

The size of the Last Monday Club membership never changed—twenty men. As members died, new ones were admitted. It was a morbid truth that death was the only way a man could get in. The new members had to be the same "type"—in other words, rich and connected. They claimed that background didn't matter. Bank accounts did.

But like all organizations, there was a hierarchy within this one. Wade Lockwood was the oldest member and had the most power. Griffin's closeness to Wade, and the fact Wade championed his political future, made Griffin next in line. The Catamount Bluff connection was powerful. Edward Hawke was in the inner circle and so were Neil Coffin and his brother, Max.

I had heard the Catamount men laughing about it one night over brandy on our terrace. They loved the club, partly because the other members were a built-in constituency: men with money and influence, to finance Griffin's campaign and get their friends on board to donate and vote.

Ford and Alexander were in line to join. I had no doubt that as sons of the golden boy, they would be welcomed into the top tier.

I was glad for the night alone. I gazed out the window at our wide lawn sloping to the edge of the bluff, the gracious and impeccably trimmed privet hedges, and a rose garden that had been here since Griffin's great-grandmother had first planted it. It was all so perfect—on the outside. I thought of heading over to see Sloane but remembered that she had said she was taking an early-evening yoga class with Abigail Coffin.

Every man on our road was there, in that closed room on the top floor of the Mohegan Hotel. They didn't even allow women servers. There were waiters and a male chef, none of them members of the society. Once the meal was served, the staff would leave the members to their port and cigars, when the real discussions would begin. The employees were sworn to secrecy—they signed nondisclosure agreements, and not even the members were allowed to repeat what was said in the meetings, least of all to their wives. They were not even supposed to tell who the other members were. But of course, the wives talked—most of us, anyway. Leonora never would.

I felt the urge to get away from Griffin's upper-class domain, his black-tie Monday night, and head to Hubbard's Point. I hurried along the forest path—as always, pausing at the cove where I had found Ellen's body.

I made my way down the steep hill, onto the beach at Hubbard's Point, and my whole body relaxed. Instead of the four mansions on Catamount Road, there were over a hundred small cottages scattered close together on winding roads, with a feeling of fun, joy, and togetherness. Not tuxedo-clad secrets of the rich and infamous. This was my home.

I spotted Jackie walking slowly along the tide line, head down as she looked for beach treasures. We'd been beachcombing these sands from the time we could walk.

"It's you!" she said, hugging me. "The star of the show!"

I tried to smile, but I couldn't.

"What's wrong?" she asked. "Something about the exhibit?"

"I was just thinking of Ellen. I just passed the spot."

"Oh, Ellen," Jackie said.

We walked in silence, the memory of our old friend shimmering between us. I thought of *Fingerbone*, of how angry Griffin would be when he saw it. Protect his reputation? No. His campaign was gathering steam, amassing huge contributions, but it would soon come to a halt.

There was no way I could let a killer, a man who hated women, take office. I would show Griffin my shadow box at the same time I told him I was leaving, and he would know that this was real, that I knew he murdered Ellen. And he would realize that I was ready to tell.

"Hey," Jackie said, pulling me out of those troubled thoughts. "Are you okay?"

"Sort of," I said. Then, "Not really."

"Tell me," Jackie said.

"There's something I have to figure out," I said.

She stared at me with her big, beautiful, kind eyes, and I felt bad for not being ready to confide in her.

"Have you eaten?" she asked after a moment.

"No," I said. "Griffin's out, and I wasn't in the mood to cook."

"Come join us," she said. "Kate and Conor are coming over, and I know she'd love to see you. She's so disappointed she has to fly Friday and will miss your opening."

"Sure," I said. "I'd love to."

I felt a rush of blood in my chest. Conor Reid was a detective. Although I didn't know him well, he had become part of Jackie's family when she married his brother, Tom. He seemed quiet and serious. Could I trust him? Would he listen to me, believe me? Or was he, like many in Connecticut law enforcement, so loyal to Griffin that he'd find a way not to investigate?

The challenge was to find someone I could trust. I wondered if that person might be Conor.

13

CONOR

Conor grabbed every chance to hang out with his brother, Tom, and Jackie, and any time he got with Kate was a bonus. Claire Beaudry Chase had joined them, spur of the moment. They all gathered outside Tom and Jackie's cottage. The charcoal sizzled as Tom flipped the swordfish. Jackie stood beside him, brushing on the marinade. Claire sat at the table, sipping wine and gazing at the water.

The cottage faced west over the beach. Conor and Kate stood slightly apart from the others, holding hands and watching the spectacular red-and-gold sunset. The woods between Hubbard's Point and Catamount Bluff were dark and shadowed.

"Did you walk through the path to get here, Claire?" Conor heard his brother ask. "Or did you drive over?"

"I walked," she said.

"I met her on the beach," Jackie said.

"Well, I'm really glad you joined us," Tom said.

Conor noticed that Claire looked worried, almost shell shocked. She didn't seem like an artist with a big show about to open. Conor had seen similar expressions on the faces of crime victims.

"Dinner's served!" Jackie said after a few minutes. Everyone sat around the wrought iron table. Platters were passed, drinks poured. Kate raised her glass.

"Here's to Claire," she said. "And a great exhibition!"

Everyone clinked glasses. Claire smiled, and her mood seemed to lift slightly, but Conor still saw the heaviness.

"I have a charter to LA that day," Kate said. "Memorial Day weekend and my clients are flying to their house in Malibu. It's killing me to not be able to celebrate at the gallery, but Conor will be there."

"Wouldn't miss it," he said, not letting on that Kate had leaned close in the car on the way over, said that she just *knew* he'd love representing her at the opening, being there for Claire, and in return, she'd promise to attend any police banquet he asked her to. He laughed because he knew Kate realized he'd do anything for her—there didn't have to be a quid pro quo.

After dinner, Tom and Jackie went inside to make coffee and get dessert; Kate followed them into the kitchen to help clean up. Conor was about to follow, but Claire stopped him.

"Have you ever seen eyes change color?" Claire asked.

"Uh," he said. "You mean how babies' eyes are blue when they're born but can change as they get older?"

Claire didn't reply right away. The sun had nearly set, and it was getting almost too dark to see.

"No, not that," Claire said. "Not babies. I mean a grown-up whose eyes change color depending on mood. Have you ever heard of anything like that?"

He felt that familiar shiver run down his spine, a signal that this was important. He stayed silent, the way he did in interrogations, waiting for her to go on. Claire stared at the beach. The sound of waves hitting the shore echoed up the hill.

"It's something I wonder about," she said. "Probably just my imagination. But I wonder, Is it possible for anger to alter a person's eye color?

A person whose green eyes turn black when he gets furious. I mean totally black, in one second. Not bruises on the skin, not shadows under the eyes—the eyes themselves. The irises actually change from green to black." She stared hard at Conor.

"Yes," Conor said. "It does sometimes."

"What kind of person would it happen to?" Claire asked.

"A psychopath," Conor said.

"Has it been documented?" Claire asked. "Have people actually seen it happen?"

Conor could tell by the tension in her voice that she herself had witnessed it. "A famous example is Ted Bundy," Conor said. "One of his only victims to survive said that during the attack, his eyes turned from blue to black. And police interviewers saw it too. The eyes don't actually change color, but the pupils completely dilate from extreme arousal."

"Fueled by rage?" Claire asked.

Conor nodded. "And the desire to inflict pain."

"What can you do about a person like that?" she asked.

"Stay away from him," he said.

"Sometimes that's not so easy," she said. She looked away again, gazing across the crescent bay at the woods between Catamount Bluff and Hubbard's Point. "Have you ever heard of Ellen Fielding?" she asked.

"Of course," he said. "I remember it well. I was a town cop back then, and my partner and I got to the cove right after you and Griffin left."

"So you know," she said. "That Griffin and I knew her. That I found her body."

"Yes, I remember that," he said. "I read your statement at the time." He pictured the gruesome scene: the dead girl who had been in the water for days, her flesh ravaged by marine life, the horrific sight of that massive gold bracelet dangling from her skeletal wrist.

"Do you believe her death was an accident?" she asked.

"That's what the medical examiner ruled," Conor said carefully.

Claire had been staring at him with electricity in her eyes, but now she blinked, and her expression went flat. She looked away. He had the feeling he had let her down. He didn't say that although it wasn't his case, he had been on the scene and it felt personal to him: Ellen was about his age, local, and had died without any explanation.

He had followed up, read the autopsy report. Ellen had sustained blunt force trauma to the head. The shape of her skull fracture indicated that it could have been caused by a fall on the rocks or a blow from a weapon. The findings were inconclusive. Ellen was from a rich family; so was her ex-boyfriend Griffin. Money and influence could do a lot, and he had always wondered if those things had played a role in preventing further investigation.

He wanted to ask Claire more, but just then Kate came out with a mug of coffee for him, and Jackie and Tom followed with bowls of ice cream. Claire thanked Tom and Jackie, said it was great to see everyone but that she wanted to leave for home before it got completely dark. She headed down the stone steps and across the footbridge. Conor watched her run along the tide line. He found himself thinking of what she had said about green eyes turning black. And he wondered why she had fallen silent after he had answered that Ellen's death had been ruled an accident. Did she suspect it had been a homicide?

Conor knew he would take another look at Ellen's case file when he had time.

And he decided that the next time he saw Griffin Chase, he would check to see the color of his eyes.

THREE DAYS
LATER

14

CLAIRE

The cabin was my hospital for the first three days and nights. At the edge of the marsh behind the woods, I felt hidden and safe. I wrapped myself in my old sleeping bag and slept on a bed of pine needles, slipping in and out of dreams. My cuts and bruises stung and ached. At night I heard screams—a rabbit being killed by an owl or the wild cat I'd tried to spot my whole life. In my dreams and delirium, the rabbit was me.

I knew I was being hunted, no differently from the creatures of the night. My attacker wore that black mask, but his size and shape made me positive it was Griffin. During the first twenty-four hours, I heard bloodhounds and knew that Griffin's police had ordered search dogs. Their baying sounded distant; I hoped my concoction would keep them far away.

First thing, I knew I had to get water. There was a spring nearby, at the foot of the granite ledges. I left the cabin at dawn. I carried an empty plastic jug from the cabin, filled it up, and drank straight from the bottle right there by the brook. It took all my effort to trudge back to the cabin, staying in the shadow of the rock face as the sun's first light began to penetrate the woods.

I had no appetite. My head felt as if nails had been driven through my skull, and I had double vision. Did I have a concussion? If I could look in a mirror, would my pupils be different sizes? Maybe my brain was bleeding and I would die of traumatic head injury.

Better than letting Griffin find me.

But I was stubborn, and I had every intention of either surviving or leaving evidence of what had been done to me. The problem was, I couldn't be sure what *had* been done to me. The force of the attack had been so swift and violent and the mask so terrifying. By the time the noose was around my neck, I had passed out once, then twice. Cuts on my hands oozed blood from where he had jabbed me with the knife.

He must have thought the hanging had killed me. Had someone interrupted him, forced him to leave me there? I escaped before he could remove my body. It gave me pleasure to picture his face, the shock when he returned to find me gone. But once he realized he had failed, he would rage and search until he found me.

I knew I needed to eat, to get strong again. In my search for food, I headed toward the beach. It was a longer walk than it was to the spring. I had to skirt the ledges on my way downhill, and I felt nervous because once I got to the cove, I would be close to Catamount Bluff, almost within sight of my house. It was barely dawn, but the last morning stars were still out, and I was able to slowly follow a deer track through a grove of scrub oak and white pine.

At the edge of the rocky uplands, I came upon the burial ground. I passed the sacred place, made my way down the ridge, and crossed the path between Catamount Bluff and Hubbard's Point. For a moment I considered going "home"—to Hubbard's Point, to Jackie and Tom Reid's cottage. But could I trust Tom? Especially since his brother, Conor, as a member of the state police, was closely connected with Griffin.

My instincts told me Conor was good, but those same instincts had allowed me to fall in love with Griffin. I didn't know who to trust.

It was only a few days after I had sat at that picnic table with the Reids that someone tried to kill me. Could Conor have told Griffin that Ellen was still and forever on my mind? Griffin already knew that, but coming from Conor, it could feel like even more of a threat. Had Conor figured out that when I talked about green eyes turning black, I was talking about Griffin? He had told me psychopaths had eyes that did that.

Conor had clearly said that Ellen's death had been ruled an accident. He didn't show any doubt, so I stopped myself from saying more. Griffin demanded loyalty. Every law enforcement agency in the state was rooting for Griffin to win the election. Having a law-and-order governor would benefit and empower them. Conor was part of that group. Tom too.

Before I stepped out of the woods, I broke a low bough off a pine tree. From spending my childhood here and from all my beachcombing treks, I knew every inch of this shore. I took off my shoes, carried the branch as I crossed the sand, and dropped it on the tide line. I stepped very carefully onto the granite ledge, inching my way over the slippery surface to the shallow water.

It was midtide. Sargassum weed, attached to rocks, wafted in and out. I brushed aside clumps of seaweed and in the gray light from the last stars was able to see a colony of blue-black mussels clinging to the rocks. I gathered a handful, cracked them with a loose stone, and ate the sweet shellfish raw.

I knew I needed to return to my cabin before the sun rose, but I had a pilgrimage to make first. The cove was just around the bend. This spot was as sacred to me as the Pequot burial ground—the tidal pool where I had found Ellen. Emotion overtook me. My neck was so bruised from the rope that each sob felt like it was crushing my throat from the inside out.

I crouched beside the pool where Ellen's body had lain. I reached into the water with both hands, splashed it on my wounds. The ocean called to me. Some people are scared of what they can't see in the depths, especially in the dark, but I knew I had to go in. I stripped off my clothes. Dried blood made the fabric of my shirt and jeans stick to my cuts. I winced as I tugged them off, reopening wounds. My father had said nothing was more healing than salt water.

I dived in. The Sound was late-May cold. It felt bracing, and it stung every inch of my body, but just for a minute. I got used to it quickly. The salt buoyed me up. It soothed my bruises, felt like salve on my neck and shoulders. My muscles and joints had seized, like bolts rusted solid, after barely moving for three days; swimming fifteen yards off the beach loosened them and brought me back to life.

By the time I climbed out of the water, the sun was just cresting the horizon. I gazed west, saw lights on in one of the houses at Catamount Bluff: mine. Griffin was up already. I knew I had to move fast. I put on my clothes, tried to ignore the harsh feel of cotton sticking to my salty skin. Then I picked up the branch I had dropped and used the pine needles to brush away my footsteps. I found my shoes and disappeared into the trees.

The woods embraced me every bit as much as the sea had. By the time I reached my cabin, the sky was the deep blue of dawn, and I was so exhausted I could barely make it inside. Thoughts tumbled through my mind: *I should go to the spring and rinse off; I should get more water before the sun is all the way up; I should go to the marsh and try to catch some blue crabs to eat later.*

I lay down just for a moment, but my eyes wouldn't stay open, and for the first time since I'd gotten here, I slept without nightmares.

15

TOM

Seventy-two hours after the *Sallie B* went down, the coast guard called off the search for Charlie. Tom couldn't think of a time he had felt more shattered by the failure of an SAR operation. He'd known from the beginning that finding the Benson children was a long shot. After they rescued Gwen and saw that Charlie wasn't in the yellow raft with her, the search shifted from rescue to recovery.

Both Dan and Gwen were still in the hospital, recovering from their injuries. While Dan had been taken to Easterly, Gwen was at Shoreline General; they were known for their superb pediatric care. Other than the single word Gwen had whispered to Tom, she still hadn't spoken.

The incident was under investigation by both the USCG and the Connecticut State Police. Tom had been tied up on *Nehantic*, then spent two good hours on paperwork detailing the operation.

Last year he had been appointed AIES—adjunct investigator for Easterly Sector, meaning he had to follow up marine incidents. So when he finished at his desk, he headed toward the Hawthorne Shipyard, where Jeanne and Bart Dunham, the couple who had first come upon the wreck, kept their sailboat.

It was Memorial Day, and he hit major traffic on I-95. The weather was beautiful, and with hordes of people heading to beaches and harbors, he doubted he would find the Dunhams there—it was too nice a day not to be sailing. But when he parked in the shipyard lot and asked a rigger where *Arcturus* was docked, he found the boat in her slip and the couple sitting on deck. She was reading a book; he was staring at an iPad.

Still in his USCG uniform khakis, Tom walked down the finger pier, stopped at the stern of the vessel. She was sleek and pretty, well maintained with a white hull and a freshly painted blue cove stripe just below deck level. The couple glanced up as he approached.

"Hello," he said. "I'm Commander Tom Reid from the coast guard. Are you the Dunhams?"

"Yes, Jeanne and Bart," the woman said.

"Are you here about the *Sallie B*?" the man asked.

"I am."

"Come aboard," Bart Dunham said.

Tom stepped from the wooden pier onto *Arcturus*'s deck, ducked under the frame of the white canvas awning that stretched over the cockpit from the cabin to the sailboat's backstay. The Dunhams both stood, and they shook hands with Tom. The day was sunny and warm, but the awning kept the cockpit fairly cool.

"Please sit down," Bart said. "Would you like some iced tea? Or a rum and tonic?"

"Iced tea would be great," he said, and Bart went down below and almost immediately handed up a plastic glass. Tom heard bottles clinking and figured Bart was fixing himself a drink.

The three of them sat in the U-shaped cockpit, on blue-and-white-striped cushions.

"You're not out sailing," Tom said. "There's a good breeze."

"Right now, I never want to sail again," Jeanne said.

"It must have been upsetting," Tom said.

"Oh my God," Jeanne said. "You wouldn't believe. I can still smell fuel and smoke and burning hair. I can't get the taste of it out of the back of my throat. Was that hers? The burning hair?" She shivered.

"We did recover Mrs. Benson's remains," Tom said, leaving out the part that, yes, the smell of incinerated hair and everything else had probably come from her.

"I've been reading about it online," Bart said. Tom noticed the way Jeanne shot him a look. "The daughter's okay?"

"How okay can she be?" Jeanne snapped at Bart. "She was blown out of the water, her mother's dead, her little brother is drowned or worse!" Then, turning to Tom, "Did you know we saw a shark in the area? Good Lord, the boy could have been attacked! Didn't you see our statement?"

"I read it, but there was no mention of a shark."

"That wasn't a shark fin, sweetie, it was the dog," Bart said.

"How would you know? You were half in the bag. I saw what I saw."

Tom made note to add the shark to the report, although he had his doubts—sharks known to attack humans were rare to nonexistent in the part of Long Island Sound where the wreck of the *Sallie B* had been found.

"After a shocking experience," Tom said, "such as the one you went through, memories can be muddled. Sometimes they don't come back for a long time. Is there anything else you saw or heard that you might not have remembered right away?"

"Well, the note," Bart said.

"What note?" Jeanne asked.

"I showed it to you," Bart said.

"You did not! What note?" she asked.

"Just when we got back to the dock and I hosed her off—you know I always do, wash the deck after coming back in," he said, looking at Tom.

"Good for the boat," Tom said.

"Get the salt off," Bart said. "Helps keep the rust away. And I like a clean boat."

"So when you hosed her down . . . ," Tom said, wanting Bart to get back on track.

"Right. I found this scrap of paper stuck to the side of our damn boat, above the waterline. I mean, it had ripped, some of it was gone and the ink was pretty much unreadable. But I could see it was signed 'Love, Sallie.' Like the end of a note."

"Where is it now?" Tom asked. During Dan's second interview with the police, he had said Sallie had been distressed, and her distraction had caused her to make a mistake in the galley, that she had caused the explosion herself. Could she have been upset enough to do it on purpose? Could this be a suicide note?

"I threw it out," Bart said. "It was soggy as hell. Must have stuck to our hull when we motored through the debris. There was a bunch of ash and other rude shit plastered to our port side. I tossed it all in the dumpster." He gestured toward the shipyard.

Tom glanced over. "Where's the dumpster?"

"In that alley between the rigging shed and the big boat building."

Tom nodded.

"It's in a plastic garbage bag along with a couple empties. Don't bust me for not recycling."

"Very funny," Jeanne said.

"Do you know what happened, what caused the fire?" Bart asked. "I mean, I'm reading the news, hitting refresh constantly, but there's nothing."

"Not yet," Tom said.

"Yeah," Bart said. "I thought you might tell us something off the record sort of, considering we were right there. And the part we played, and all."

"It was horrible," Jeanne said, her eyes bright with tears. "The Bensons, we didn't know them, but the boating world is so small, especially around here, at the mouth of the river. We saw them all the time."

"Where?" Tom asked.

"You know, coming and going at West Wind Marina. Or out on the Sound. Just, out having fun. All of them, the four of them," Bart said.

"Sometimes just him," Jeanne said. "With a few guys. You know, friends heading out for some fishing or whatever. She was well known, you know. Once I heard 'Sallie B' was Sallie Benson, I recognized her name right away. A decorator."

"Famous," Bart said. "It's all over the news. She designed half the muckety-mucks' houses on the shoreline." He finished his drink, swirled the melting ice around the bottom of his glass, and took a step toward the companionway. "Can I get you another iced tea?" he asked, glancing at Tom.

"No, thanks," Tom said. "I'll be going now. Thanks for your time. I'm going to call the state police right now, and someone will come by to collect that trash bag with the letter."

"Waste of time. You can't even read it," Bart said.

"It's one big nightmare," Jeanne said. "As if it wasn't bad enough seeing what happened to the people on board a boat we knew, we rescued Maggie, their little dog, and she's probably going to die. It's a miracle she survived at all."

"Yeah, and we're out a couple hundred bucks for a vet bill," Bart said, coming back with a full glass. "Just to find out she'd swallowed sea water. Breathed some into her lungs too." He took a long drink. "Not that it's all about the money, but I wouldn't mind getting reimbursed from Dan Benson. When he's out of the hospital, I mean."

"Bart!" Jeanne said, giving him a sharp look.

Tom nodded. He shook the Dunhams' hands and stepped onto the dock. Then he stopped and turned around.

"What vet did you take her to?" he asked.

"Silver Bay Veterinary Clinic," Jeanne said. "We could tell she was having breathing problems, so we got her there fast. I haven't had the heart to call and see if they've put her to sleep yet. Poor little Maggie."

"We did our best," Bart said, putting his arm around her.

Tom left Jeanne leaning against her husband's shoulder. He took out his cell phone to call Conor and tell him about the bag full of *Arcturus*'s trash. He knew Conor was busy on the Claire Beaudry Chase disappearance, but ever since Tom had been appointed an investigator, his younger brother had become his mentor.

He then called Detective Jen Miano, lead detective on the Benson case, to inform her of the situation. Then he called Conor. He parked his truck at the entry of the alleyway where the dumpster was located, to guard it, on the off chance some refuse truck would come by to pick up the boatyard's trash on the national holiday, and settled back to wait for the police.

16

CONOR

After getting Tom's call, Conor drove to the Hawthorne Marina. He spotted Tom standing by his truck, talking to his stepdaughter Hunter. Hunter wore her Connecticut State Police uniform and hat.

"Hello, Trooper Tyrone," he said as he approached her and Tom.

"Hi," she said, her expression serious.

"What brings you here?" he asked.

"Detective Miano asked for me," she said. "I thought I was going to get the boot for busting protocol and giving Tom a heads-up about the yellow raft instead of letting him get the news from command."

"Yes, that wasn't cool," Conor said, sounding as stern as possible. He made sure not to catch Tom's eye. It was the Reid way, to let law enforcement family in on details of shared investigations.

"I know," Hunter said.

"Good to have you on the case," Conor said.

She nodded. "Thanks a lot. I'm glad to be here." She glanced toward the road and quickly walked away, as if she didn't want to be seen talking to them.

Jen Miano's Ford Interceptor drove into the parking lot, followed by two more state police vehicles. She parked and walked toward Conor and Tom. Dressed in a blue pantsuit, she looked sharp and professional.

"So what's this about a note?" she asked.

"Bart Dunham says he found one stuck to his boat's hull. He said it was signed 'Sallie.'"

"Why didn't he tell us when we questioned him?"

"The shock of it all, I guess. And he likes his rum. In fact, it's in the trash bag with some empties."

"Got it," Jen said. "So we're going dumpster diving?"

"Yes, and glad you brought reinforcements," Conor said, watching personnel suit up in white hazmat suits, booties, and gloves. He glanced at Tom. His brother had been at sea for three days straight and looked it.

Both Reid brothers stayed with Jen, watching the forensics team. They taped off the scene with yellow tape and headed into the alley to start pulling trash bags out of the dumpster.

People walking to and from their boats had seen the police cars and had gathered to find out what was going on. Hunter was stationed outside the line of tape to tell everyone to move along. After a few minutes Tom excused himself and went back to his office.

"So," Jen said, looking at Conor.

"Yeah?"

"This is my case," she said. "And you've got a missing woman to find, so I'm wondering why you're hanging around the boatyard with me."

"I miss you, Jen," he said. "I never see you now that we're not partners."

"Right, that's it," she said.

"Okay, Claire Chase and her husband, Griffin, used Sallie Benson to design their kitchen."

"And?"

"I don't know. It's a coincidence, Sallie and Claire both victims of violent crimes on the same day. And they knew each other," Conor said.

"So someone coordinated attacks on the two women?" Jen asked.

"I'd like to figure out the links," Conor said.

"Well, Dan says that Sallie's responsible for the boat. She was the only one below."

"And what, she did it on purpose?"

"I don't know. We'll see what this note says," Jen said.

"She didn't care that her whole family was on board? Her two kids?"

"I hear you," Jen said. "But we've seen crazier."

"What about him?" Conor asked. "Who's to say he's telling the truth about Sallie being down below? Maybe he did it."

"Blew up his own boat? Again, what about the kids—would he do that to them?" Jen asked. "You think he's a family annihilator?"

Conor thought that over. "What about his initial statement?" he asked.

"When he said 'they got her'?" Jen asked.

"He was doped up," Conor said. "Not thinking or talking straight, didn't know what he was saying. What if he meant 'I got her'? What if he wanted to kill his wife, not the kids?"

"Right," Jen said, nodding. "He could have put both Gwen and Charlie aboard that raft, but something happened to Charlie—he got swept away, fell overboard . . . Dan never intended for that to happen. He didn't want the kids to die."

The puzzle pieces didn't fit. Conor had to believe that if you wanted to kill your wife, an explosion was a particularly tough way to go, especially when you and your children were at risk. And the connection between Sallie and Claire still bothered him.

Just then, one of the hazmat-suited officers walked to the head of the alleyway and waved. Jen started toward him and Conor followed. They ducked under the crime scene tape and saw eleven plastic garbage bags spread out in two rows in front of the dumpster. Two state police officers were standing there.

"It's got to be this one, Detective," Trooper Alan Williams said, pointing at a trash bag, lumpy with discarded bottles.

"Open it up," Jen said, and the tech slit the plastic.

Conor crouched beside her. He saw a banana peel, a melon rind, a chicken carcass, wadded-up paper towels, the remains of several squeezed-out limes, beer cans, and two empty quarts of Mount Gay rum, all covered with coffee grounds.

"And there it is," Jen said. Conor saw it too. The wet paper was wrapped around an empty bottle. One edge was torn off, but he could see the cream-colored paper. The handwriting was faint and blurred.

"Can you make out any words?" Conor asked.

"No," Jen said. "But we'll get the note to the lab right away, and I'll make sure you get a copy. You'll let me know if . . ."

After three years of being her partner, Conor knew what she was about to say.

"Of course," he said. "I'll call you if anything in our investigation points back to yours."

"Shit, Conor," Jen said. "Back together again."

17

TOM

The children's hospital was quiet. It was late afternoon on Memorial Day, and the shifts had just changed. It seemed to Tom Reid that there was pretty much a skeleton staff. On such a pretty day, the first holiday weekend of summer on the Connecticut shoreline, the corridors were quiet and mostly empty.

Tom walked down the gleaming first-floor hallway, carrying a black duffel bag with the USCG insignia on it. He stopped at the nurses' station, said he was planning to visit Gwen Benson, and asked for her room number.

"Are you a relative?" the nurse asked. She was petite with long brown curls. Her name badge said *Mariana Russo, RN*.

"No," he said, showing her his ID.

"Coast guard? We've had the police here, talking to her. Even a reporter from the *Shoreline Gazette* trying to get in."

"Has she said anything?" Tom asked.

"No," Mariana said. "She's completely shut down. We're limiting who goes into her room. She's been through enough of a trauma—having strangers asking questions just adds to it."

"I understand," Tom said. "I don't have any questions for her. I just want to see her. I'm the one who pulled her out of the life raft."

"Oh," Mariana said, looking at him more closely. "It's nice to meet you. From what I've heard, her rescue was a total long shot."

"It was," he said.

Mariana was silent, seeming to consider whether she should allow Tom into Gwen's room or not.

"It might help her to see you," she said. "But I don't know. She got agitated when her father walked into the room. They brought him over from Easterly Hospital to visit her. The mental health staff thinks it's probably because he brings back memories of what happened. Or maybe it was seeing him all bandaged up—kids don't like to see their parents hurt."

Tom nodded, picturing what had been left of the boat, the evidence of explosion. He wondered how much Gwen had seen of the aftermath. He wondered whether she had seen her mother's body, whether she knew that the search for Charlie had been called off.

"Other than her dad, her only visitor has been her aunt," Mariana said. "Her mother's sister, Lydia."

"How many times has her father been here?"

"Twice. Both times she got so upset her doctor thought they should take it slow." She looked at Tom for a few seconds. "I'm going to let you in for a few minutes. But you'll have to leave right away if there's any sign of distress. She made a very high-pitched sound when her father was here."

"I've heard it," Tom said. "When we found her. She was peeping, like a little bird. Nonstop, even after we brought her to the ER."

"Then you know."

"I do," he said, holding tight to the duffel.

They walked into a room directly across from the nurses' station. The curtain had been pulled to shield Gwen from the eyes of people passing in the hallway. Mariana beckoned Tom to follow her.

Gwen lay completely still in bed. The red burn patches on her cheeks, chin, forehead, and where her eyebrows had been looked raw and were covered with salve—it looked as if she had a bad sunburn. The charred ends of her silvery hair had been trimmed away. Her eyes were full of almost unimaginable sadness. Her gaze followed Tom and Mariana as they entered.

"Gwen, you have a visitor," Mariana said.

"Hi, Gwen," Tom said. "Do you remember me?"

Although she didn't speak or nod her head, he saw in her eyes that she recognized him. She seemed very calm. She didn't make a sound.

"I'm very glad to see you," Tom said. And he was. Emotion filled his chest. He remembered picking her up, lifting her into the rescue basket, and holding her hand during the helicopter ride. Mariana had been right—it was beyond a long shot that Gwen had been found at all.

Mariana indicated that he should sit in the chair by Gwen's bed, and he did. He sat silently, gazing at Gwen, and she returned his gaze: a form of communication. A bell sounded from the hall—a patient summoning a nurse. Mariana stayed in the room for another minute. Then, seeming satisfied that Gwen was okay, she quietly left.

"You're such a brave girl," Tom said.

Gwen stared hard into his eyes.

"Finding you was one of the most important moments I have ever had in the coast guard," he said. "It meant so much to all of us, Gwen. Everyone who was searching for you. And now, seeing you here right now, knowing you're getting better—that is the best news we could have."

She closed her eyes. Two big tears rolled down her cheeks. Tom knew she was far from okay.

"I wanted to bring you something," he said. "A book, a game, a stuffed animal—I just wasn't sure what you might like. I asked my wife and stepdaughters, and they had some good ideas. But I started thinking, and then I knew."

Her eyes opened, and she waited for him to tell her.

He unzipped the duffel bag, and he saw her watching him carefully, following his movements. He reached inside, pulled out the tiny dog. She was so small, barely bigger than his hand. He held her toward Gwen, who gasped and reached out her arms.

"Maggie!" Gwen cried.

Tom placed the Yorkshire terrier in Gwen's arms, watched Gwen bury her face in Maggie's fur, kissing the back of her head as Maggie squirmed with joy.

Mariana entered the room, gave Tom a hard look.

"Really?" she asked.

"I picked her up from the vet," he said.

"Dogs aren't allowed in here."

"I figured," he said and grinned. Watching Gwen pet and kiss Maggie, Mariana smiled too.

Tom knew that when Mariana said he had to leave, he would take Maggie home and keep her until Dan and Gwen were discharged. But for now, he just sat beside Gwen's bed, watching the reunion between a girl and her dog, trying to swallow past the lump in his throat.

THREE DAYS
EARLIER

18

CLAIRE

Today I planned to bring the last pieces over to the gallery and help Jackie get ready for Friday. I had finally finished *Fingerbone*. I stood in my studio, doors open to a sea breeze and the sound of breaking waves, and leaned over the shadow box I had constructed to resemble a tidal pool.

I examined the placement of mussel shells, barnacles scraped from granite at low tide, crab claws, fragments of their carapaces, and sun- and sea-bleached twigs—each small section forming a knuckle and bones, fashioned together to look like the grasping hand of a skeleton.

People with no idea about Ellen's death wouldn't understand, but I did, and one other person would, and that was the whole point. There were ways to go about a divorce, but I would take nothing mone- tary from Griffin—not the house or alimony or any material object. I wanted only for him to know that I knew, without any doubt, exactly who he was and what he had done.

I would make sure he dropped his candidacy. Before I left for good, I intended to pull off his mask. And the timing had to be now: next week was a major campaign event, when Senator Stephen Hobbes would publicly endorse Griffin for governor.

"Well, hey there!"

I was so lost in thought that Nate's voice made me jump. He stood in the doorway, then came toward me to give me a hug. He was as rumpled and shaggy as ever, and I fit into his arms so comfortably. We hadn't been able to stay married, but he was the perfect ex-husband, and I would love him forever.

"You're back!" I said. "How were the whales?"

"The humpbacks send their regards," he said. "It was hard leaving them. I'm not sure which I loved more—watching them feed in the Bering Sea or calve in Baja. You should come next time. I kept thinking of you, how inspired you would be."

"Let's do it," I said. I smiled into his twinkling blue eyes.

"Don't tease me," he said, his sun- and wind-weathered face crinkling into a grin. "Griffin will never let you travel with me. I'd never bring you back."

"I'm so glad you're home again," I said. "Why didn't you call to let me know?"

"I figured I'd stop by and surprise you, get an early viewing of your new show." He smiled again. "And it's the middle of the afternoon, so I know Griffin's at court or deposing someone or charming some audience or sweet-talking donors, whatever it is he does."

"You're right," I said. "Today he's taking depositions."

"So, okay if I take a look at the work?"

"Sure," I said, and I was excited to hear what he thought. Nate had always been my favorite early viewer of my work. More than anyone, he understood how I tried to express human life and emotions through elements of nature. He had invited me to speak to his classes at Yale, where he taught about extinctions, psychology, and how the decline of species affected human existence. His nine-month sabbatical had seemed forever—I had really missed him.

"These are beautiful, Claire," he said once he had made the circuit of my studio. "But they're dark."

122

"You see that?" I asked.

"Of course," he said. "I know you. You've captured pain and apprehension. What took you to this place?"

"The way the world is," I said. I left it open for him to interpret: the political landscape, growing fascism, the suffering of refugees, failure to address climate change. If anyone could look into my heart and see my own personal darkness, it was Nate—but just then I wanted to hide it from him.

"The global situation is beyond troubling," he said. "Being on the research ship was a respite, in a sense. I avoided the news as much as possible. But I felt it as soon as we made port." He turned toward *Fingerbone* and shuddered. "This one looks like the end of life on earth. Is that what you intended?"

"Yes," I said, not lying.

Outside, I heard voices coming from the main house. My pulse raced—it was only three thirty, too early for Griffin to be home. Even though he was publicly accepting of my friendship with Nate, privately there was hell to pay whenever he knew I saw him.

"Oh boy," I said.

"The monarch of all he surveys?" Nate asked.

I went to my studio's north-facing window, looked out. Griffin stood on the terrace with Wade Lockwood. At least he wouldn't blow up in front of Wade—or Nate, for that matter. But there was always later. As I watched, I saw Griffin and Wade walk into the house.

"He's home," I said. "He must have seen your car, and I guess he's giving us the chance to catch up."

"Nope," Nate said. "I came by dinghy, beached her at the foot of the bluff. I doubt he knows I'm here. C'mon, let's go. We can go get the bigger boat. I'll spirit you away, take you to Shelter Island for dinner, and regale you with tales of humpbacks."

"Next time," I said, giving him a hurried hug. "Do you mind just . . ."

"Leaving?" Nate asked. "Okay, I get it. But Claire . . ."

I saw the worried look in his eyes. Even though Griffin shone his charm on Nate, my ex-husband was too sensitive not to see what lived below the surface. And there was no doubt Nate was picking up on my anxiety now. The thing was—at that moment, I didn't care whether Griffin saw Nate or not. I just wanted my next encounter with Griffin to follow the script I'd written in my mind.

"I'll get out," Nate said, his expression grave. "But this exhibit . . . it makes me worry for you. You want me to think it's geopolitical."

"It is," I said.

"No, it's not," he said. "It's all you. The darkness is personal. He's a power-hungry asshole, no matter how much you try to protect him, and there's something going on. Tell me, Claire."

"Everything's fine," I said.

"I don't believe you."

"Let's drop it, okay?" I asked, glancing out the window. "Will I see you at the gallery on Friday?"

"Wouldn't miss it," Nate said, giving me one last skeptical, worried glance. Then he left by the seaward door and disappeared down the narrow overgrown path to the beach. After a few minutes I heard his outboard engine start up. I went back to my studio's north window, stared at the house, and waited.

19

SALLIE

Sallie wished she could take a shower and wash yesterday from her body and mind. The memory of waiting for Edward aboard his boat and fending off Ford filled her with feelings of disgust, mainly for herself. She had scheduled a design consultation with a couple who had just bought an antique Georgian house on the Connecticut River, but she canceled. She needed to stay home. She gave Harriet, the nanny, the day off.

She wore her comfiest jeans and the pink *Someone at Black Hall Elementary School Loves Me* T-shirt that Gwen had given her for Mother's Day, just two weeks ago. She sat in the living room on the sofa with Maggie snuggled by her side. She called her sister, Lydia, to ask her to come over, but Lydia was a publisher's rep for children's books, and she was visiting bookstores in New Hampshire and Maine today.

Sallie couldn't shake off the slimy feeling of Ford's hands grabbing her, the sound of rage in his voice, and the smell of his vomit. She felt like running out of the house, but she had nowhere to go. Her most important refuge, Abigail Coffin's yoga center, had turned into a place she now felt unwelcome.

At first, it had been wonderful. Abigail taught deep breathing and talked about *mettā*—the Pali word for *loving-kindness*. While Sallie had always felt compassion for others—her family, friends, and strangers— she had never directed it toward herself.

Feeling semigood about herself was a new skill. It was partly what had led her to Edward, to allowing love—both physical and emo- tional—into her life. After class one evening, Abigail handed her a bottle of water.

"I'm so glad you started coming," Abigail said. "We have to stick together."

"Women, definitely," Sallie said.

"Actually, I meant the Monday Night Sisterhood. Wives of the Last Monday men. Our husbands have their secrets, don't they?" Abigail asked, watching for Sallie's reaction.

"I suppose," Sallie said. "But Dan doesn't go anymore."

"Really?" Abigail asked, frowning. "Why?"

"One day he just stopped," Sallie said. She knew it had something to do with a disagreement with a member, but she didn't want to say that in case it was Abigail's husband.

"No one just *stops*," Abigail said. "It's a lifetime membership. Only twenty at one time—it's an honor to join."

"I suppose," Sallie said.

Abigail backed away, as if Sallie had suddenly turned toxic. Sallie wondered what she had said that was so bad. Abigail disappeared into her office for a few minutes. Sallie heard her voice, muffled on a phone call. When Abigail returned, she was smiling again, as serene as ever.

Abigail, with her long brown hair and big eyes, her yoga body, seemed so able to bounce back from negative feelings. Sallie had never returned after that incident; she still felt hurt by Abigail's reaction to what she had said about Dan leaving the club.

So now Sallie didn't have the yoga studio, and she didn't have Edward. He had never replied to her text about loving him. The truth had been there all along, but she hadn't let herself see it until yesterday on the boat: she was just a mistress to him, nothing more.

She sat immobile on her couch with Maggie, trying to meditate, counting her breaths, letting painful and unwanted thoughts pass through her mind like clouds through a blue sky, until she heard the school bus stop at the end of the driveway.

Maggie woke up, shimmying and barking with joy, and she raced outside as soon as Sallie opened the door. The kids tore off the bus, crouching to hug and pet Maggie on the house steps. Gwen scooped the Yorkie into her arms, letting Maggie kiss her face. Charlie reached up, trying to get his pets in.

"Why are you here instead of work?" Gwen asked, putting Maggie down to hug her mother. Sallie held her tight, rocking her, grabbing Charlie into the family embrace, eyes squeezed shut, afraid she couldn't trust herself to speak and not cry.

"I wanted to be here when you got home from school today," Sallie said, keeping her voice steady.

"Where's Harriet?" Charlie asked, pulling out of the hug and looking around for their nanny.

"I gave her the day off," Sallie said.

"Why?" Gwen asked. "Don't you have meetings?"

Sallie shook her head. "No, not today," she said.

She loved her work, but lately she had hardly been able to concentrate on it. She had used it as an excuse to see Edward. It didn't matter what time of day: if it was early morning, before breakfast, she would say she had to drive to the design center in Boston. If she wanted to leave the house after dinner, she would invent meetings with clients who had to work all day and were only available in the evening. On Saturday afternoons, when Edward's wife, Sloane, was out with friends, she would say she had to go fabric-wallpaper-granite-paint shopping with a customer.

But today she was home.

"I don't like when you have to go to work," Charlie said.

"Neither do I," Gwen said.

"Neither do I," Sallie said. "I'd rather be with you two. What should we do today?"

"The beach!" Charlie said.

"That's a great idea," Sallie said. "What do you think, Gwennie?"

"Sure," she said.

"Grab your bathing suits, and let's go," Sallie said.

They climbed into the white Suburban. The cargo space was full of sample books from Clarence House and Scalamandré: a basket filled with swatches of vintage silk velvet, cashmere velvet, nacré velvet, chiffon velvet, and ciselé velvet, all in shades of white. She had long been obsessed with velvet and usually found it incredibly beautiful and sensual, but right now she felt like throwing it all away.

At the beach club, Sallie and the kids changed into their bathing suits. Maggie raced around, checking out every corner. The snack bar would open for the season in three days, for Memorial Day weekend, but for now the windows were still shuttered. Later, Sallie would take the kids to Paradise snack bar, pick up sandwiches to take home. She would let them eat ice cream in the car, before dinner.

Charlie raced down to the water's edge, Gwen and Maggie right behind him. He was the first one in, diving into a small wave, swimming underwater for a few yards before coming up for air, sputtering and grinning, waving to make sure Sallie saw.

"Great job!" she called. They had spent every Wednesday afternoon throughout winter and spring at swimming lessons. Last summer Charlie had been afraid to put his face in the water. Now he was fearless.

"Mom, can Maggie come in with us?" Gwen asked.

"Sure," Sallie said. "But we'll have to stick close to shore. I'm not sure how well she can swim."

"That's okay. I'll stay with her," Gwen said.

Sallie watched her daughter lift Maggie, hold her against her chest. She walked slowly into the Sound, dipping Maggie's paws in to let her get used to the feel of it. Gwen had been asking for a dog since she was seven; Dan and Sallie had given Maggie to her for her ninth birthday, with an agreement that Gwen would feed and walk and take care of her.

Gwen had embraced the responsibility with all her heart. She walked Maggie twice a day, helped Sallie to train Maggie to sit and come and to fetch a small ball and—knowing the family would be out on their boat a lot this summer—walk the beach, tease the waves along the tide line.

"She needs to know how to swim in case she falls overboard," Gwen had said.

With the way Gwen took care of Maggie, Sallie thought it really unlikely the dog would ever leave the cockpit, get anywhere near the boat rails. She made a note to see if she could find a tiny Yorkie-size life jacket. There might not be time before they went out this weekend, but she and Dan made sure the kids wore PFDs on the boat—why not the dog too?

Now, standing barefoot in the warm sand, Sallie watched Gwen ease Maggie into the water. The two of them paddled around, Maggie obviously overjoyed to be near her favorite person. Charlie dived down to the bottom, came up with a strand of seaweed, held it over his head so Sallie would see. She applauded, and he dived again.

This was her real life—this moment here on the beach with her children was what Sallie lived for. How could she have been so foolish and come so close to throwing it all away? She swore she would make things better with Dan. They were good parents together. And right now, that seemed good enough.

Sallie walked knee-deep into the water. She took a sharp breath— Long Island Sound in late May was still cold. It really didn't warm up until after the Fourth of July, but her kids were water dogs, just as she had been at their age. She dived straight in, swimming underwater as far as she could go.

When she came up for air, her children swam over to her, and the three of them trod water in a small circle, legs kicking and arms moving, with Maggie in the middle. They were all smiling with the sheer joy of one of summer's first swims, of being together. They stayed there for another minute, until Gwen decided it was time for Maggie to get out and warm up, and then they all walked onto the beach, and Sallie tilted her face up toward the sun.

FOUR DAYS
LATER

20

CLAIRE

That night, I saw the mountain lion. Hungry and tired of being in the cabin, I set out for the tidal pool earlier than usual. Blue hazy dusk had given way to darkness, and I had no cell phone, no communication with the world beyond the woods and beach, so I had no way of knowing where Griffin was directing the search. It occurred to me that law enforcement might bring back the dogs I had heard the first day, so I should reinforce my perimeter with the big cat/fox mixture. I spread it on the far side of my usual trail.

I traced a large circle with my cabin at the center, sprinkling the concoction as I went. Once my eyes got used to the dark, the stars shone bright enough to light my way. As long as I stepped carefully, I had no worry about walking in the woods at night. My father and I had done it so often. I kept glancing north, and guided by Polaris, I felt as if I were creating a magic circle that would protect me.

After the perimeter was set, I went swimming in the Sound to wash the smell off me and to soothe my wounds. My bruises were already turning from purple to yellow, the cuts on my hands forming scabs. When I emerged from my swim, I climbed the hill again. I stood at the edge of the burial ground and shivered. I felt as if someone were watching me. I glanced to the southwest—the direction in which the Pequots believed their spirits left their bodies—and thought I saw a glint of light.

I had made my way toward the spring to rinse off and get drinking water when the back of my neck tingled. I felt danger; that most ancient part of the brain that registers sounds and smells we would otherwise ignore lit up. I knew I was being tracked and froze, listening hard. Even on high alert, I heard nothing but normal night sounds: tree frogs peeping in the marsh, a slight breeze ruffling the new leaves.

I slowly turned. I wondered whether I would see Griffin with his knife or one of his police officers with a gun drawn. Instead, not twenty yards away, I saw glowing yellow eyes, the shimmer of a tawny coat. The cougar kept to the thicket that bordered the Pequot cemetery. He was a shadow, liquid gold in the starlight. I stood perfectly still.

"Claire, never turn your back on a big cat," my father had said. "They're stealthy; you'll never hear them coming. And once they decide you're prey, they'll close the distance so swiftly you'll never have time to react."

He told me to make myself look bigger, braver than the cat itself, but for some reason that night in the woods, I forgot everything my father had said—not because I panicked but because the cougar was inside the circle I had made. He was part of my world, part of the magic. Maybe I was still delirious from the attack, but I didn't feel scared.

I stared into the lion's eyes. I knew that he could take me down so easily. He'd swipe me with his curved claws, clamp his fangs around my throat or my skull, kill me in an instant. Was it because I knew what humans could do, what my husband had done, that I felt no fear? Attracted by the potion, he must have smelled his own kind; perhaps he was looking for a mate, or maybe he wanted to claim his territory, fight another male to the death. All I knew was that I was in the presence of the animal that had fed my imagination for so many years.

He knew I wasn't a threat. His gaze held mine for a long minute, then two, then three. My breathing was steady. I knew I should back away, very slowly, but I didn't. I blinked, and in that single second, he was gone. I didn't hear him, but I felt a whisper of air as he left, and I saw the slightest shadow of gold shimmer in the southwest, on the path of the spirits.

After that encounter, I skipped going to the spring that night. I knew he would go there to drink, and I didn't want to test my luck. I had no food in my cabin, no smells to tempt him. I told myself he was a protector sent by my father—he wouldn't attack me, but he might maul anyone who came to harm me. My thinking was probably skewed, but I couldn't let myself admit to even more danger than I already was in.

I climbed into my sleeping bag, but I couldn't close my eyes. The mountain lion had reminded me I had to be vigilant. I had to come up with a plan. I was getting stronger, and I had to get help. The only problem was, I still had no idea whom I could trust.

The constellations moved across the sky; the hours passed by. I drifted off, then heard the cries of an animal, death in the woods. Had the cougar made a kill? Or was I dreaming about the sound of my own voice, screaming for help four days earlier? Or was it a dream of the future, of what Griffin would do if he found me?

I didn't know, and I couldn't go back to sleep.

21

CONOR

Conor and Jen Miano decided to question Dan Benson together. Conor still wondered about a possible connection between the two cases. A word that might have been *Ford* had appeared twice in the note written by Sallie, and he made a note to ask Dan if the family drove one.

It occurred to Conor that he still hadn't questioned Ford Chase. He was Claire's stepson. If Sallie had been referring to him, and not a car, could he be the link between her and Claire?

They arrived at Easterly Hospital in separate cars, and Conor followed Jen through the revolving door. Benson was on the mend and had been moved to a different floor. They spoke to the nurse in charge and went to his room. He lay in bed, upright and watching a talk show on TV.

"Mr. Benson," Jen said. "This is Detective Reid."

"Hello," Benson said. His skin was sallow. He was small and muscular with short graying brown hair. His eyes were open very wide, and Conor thought he looked scared, like a deer in the headlights. He had a gauze bandage above his left eye.

"How are you doing, Mr. Benson?" Conor asked.

"I'm fine," he said.

"You don't look fine. I know you were badly injured."

"Yeah. They say I'm lucky the metal didn't hit my heart," he said. "But it's nothing compared to what Gwen's been through." He swallowed hard, looked toward the window. "And my Charlie, my boy. Where is he?"

"We don't know," Jen said gently.

"We're very sorry that he's still missing," Conor said.

Benson nodded without looking up.

"Can you tell us what happened on Friday?" Conor asked.

"I already told her," Benson said, gesturing at Jen and seeming to slash away tears—but his eyes were dry. He hadn't mentioned Sallie.

"Take us through that day," Conor said. "It was a weekday. Why weren't the kids in school?"

"We wanted to get a jump on Memorial Day weekend," Benson said. "Get out to Block Island before the crowds. Get a good slip at the marina."

"So you planned this early departure?" Jen asked. "Or was it spur of the moment?"

"We planned it. We even wanted to provision the night before."

"Provision? Tell me more," Jen asked. "I'm not a boater."

"You know, buy food, soda, snacks, stuff like that. Head down to the boat and load everything up first thing so we could take off, leave the marina early. Right after breakfast, we thought."

"Who did the grocery shopping?" Conor asked.

"I did. *That* part I did after work Thursday."

"Where?" Conor asked.

"Black Hall Grocer's," Benson said.

"And who did the loading, down at the boat?" Jen asked.

"Me. But not Thursday night. It didn't quite work out that way."

"Then when did you do it?" Jen asked.

"Friday morning. The day we left."

"Mr. Benson, what kind of car do you drive?" Conor asked.

"A BMW."

"Do you have a Ford?"

"No, why?"

"Did Sallie?"

"No, she had a Suburban."

Conor nodded. So if that spidery handwriting in Sallie's letter did say *Ford*, it wasn't about a family car.

"All right," Conor said. "What time did you load the provisions onto your boat?"

"Nine a.m."

"Friday morning, right?"

"Yes, I already said that."

"Did you call the school and tell them the kids wouldn't be there?" Jen asked.

Benson shrugged, winced as if he'd moved the wrong muscle. "Sallie took care of things like that. But, yes, she probably called."

"So you left the dock that morning?" Conor asked.

"No," he said, letting out a big exhale. "It wound up being early afternoon."

"Why is that?" Jen asked. "What was the holdup?"

"Sallie," he said, looking stone faced.

"Why?" Jen asked.

"It started the night before. She said she didn't want to go."

"Did she say why?" Jen asked.

"She didn't feel good. She didn't think she could handle the boat ride and a whole weekend away."

"That must have been frustrating," Conor said.

"Yeah," Benson said.

"She screwed things up?" Conor asked.

"You could put it that way. I finally convinced her to go. I ran out to load up the boat before we all headed to the dock . . ."

"Just you?" Conor asked. "I wonder why that is, considering you were all planning to go down there and take off that morning. Couldn't you have done it all in one trip? The provisioning and getting the family on board the boat?"

"Trust me, when you have little kids, you want to get as much done as you can before they get there—they get impatient, you know? Waiting around while we stow the food, put ice in the icebox, fill the fuel tanks. Trust me, it's not fun. So I did it myself, then went back home to pick everyone up."

"What time did you get home?" Jen asked.

"About ten thirty. We had the kids all set, practically in the car, when Sallie broke down again, said she didn't want to go at all. She started to cry—almost hysterical."

"In front of the kids?" Conor asked.

"No. As usual she had her meltdowns in our bedroom. But they heard, especially Gwen. She knows everything that goes on between us. She gets stomachaches over it, worries we're going to get divorced. But that didn't stop Sallie from deciding to ruin a nice family weekend away."

Jen and Conor let his words hang in the air. He was exhibiting anger instead of grief, striking for a man whose wife had just died.

"Did something physical take place between you two?" Jen asked.

Both Conor and Jen watched his face carefully. He squinted and scratched the bandage on his forehead. It slipped slightly, and Conor saw an incision closed with stitches. Conor knew that Sallie's body was too badly burned for the medical examiner to find signs of assault.

"No!" Benson said. "What do you think I am?"

"We have to ask," Jen said.

"Mr. Benson, do you know Claire Beaudry Chase?" Conor asked.

"Griffin's wife? No."

"But you know Griffin?" Conor already knew the answer, but he wanted to hear what Benson had to say.

"Yeah."

"How?"

"Family friends from way back. And we're in the same club."

"What club's that?"

"Last Monday. But I don't go anymore. It's just a bunch of guys drinking scotch and talking about how to get Griffin into the governor's mansion."

"You don't think he should be governor?" Conor asked.

Benson snorted. "When you know someone since you were kids and you think of all the stupid shit they did, you have a hard time imagining them leading the state. I used to joke with Sallie about it." He paused, as if he'd just heard what he'd said. "I mean, don't get me wrong, Griffin is all right. A little in love with himself, some people would say."

"What kind of stupid kid shit are we talking about?" Jen asked.

Benson tried to laugh again, but now it sounded nervous. "I shouldn't have said anything. Dumb stuff. Like playing pranks, sneaking parents' booze, skipping school. Nothing bad. I'll vote for him."

Conor heard the edge in Benson's voice. There was emotion there, behind the seemingly lighthearted words. Resentment but also fear.

"Do you know his kids? Alexander and Ford?" Conor watched for Benson to react to the names. Was that a slight flinch?

"Not well."

"But you do know them?"

"From around town, seeing them at the boatyard, stuff like that."

"Okay. Now, Sallie did some work for the Chase family. Fixed up a kitchen for them, wasn't it?" Conor asked.

"Yeah, that's right. She did. But I stay out of her business."

"Did she ever say anything about the Chases?" Conor asked.

"No. I figured he was probably a prick to work for, but she never said."

"When will you be able to go home?" Jen asked.

"They're discharging me today," he said.

"That seems soon," Jen said. "Considering what you've been through."

"I'm going stir-crazy in here," he said. "And I have to make plans to bury my wife."

Conor and Jen thanked him for his time, expressed their sympathy again, and left the room.

"What do you think?" Conor asked.

"A lot of anger at Sallie," Jen said. "He didn't even try to hide it."

"Right. He wasn't playing the grieving husband. And he's got some kind of issue with Chase," Conor said. "Enough that it made him stop going to the rich-boy secret society."

"Enough that he'd do something to Claire?" Jen asked.

Conor mentally ran through the Friday morning timeline; Chase had said he last saw Claire after breakfast on Friday, around seven forty-five. Benson had gone to the boat at about nine. What if he had encountered Claire, had some sort of altercation?

"Why's he in such a hurry to get out of the hospital?" Conor asked. "So he can get home and clean up evidence?"

"Search warrant," Jen said. "Coming right up. I need an iced latte. Think they have them in the hospital dining room?"

"Give it a go," Conor said. "I'm heading out. Catch you later."

They said goodbye, and Conor decided to return to the Chases' house on Catamount Bluff, walk through the scene of Claire's disappearance again. And if only to clarify what Sallie might have meant by the word *Ford* in her note, Conor was going to find Ford Chase and ask him some questions.

TWO DAYS EARLIER

22

CLAIRE

Some of my favorite moments in the studio were when Sloane Hawke came over. It was late afternoon, and in honor of the fact summer would unofficially start that weekend, we opened a bottle of rosé. I had delivered most of my exhibition pieces the day before, so the studio was nearly bare. Only one shadow box destined for the show was left. I still hadn't had the chance to show *Fingerbone* to Griffin.

It was a warm, sunny day. The forecast for Memorial Day weekend was looking great, and Sloane was excited about the annual party she and Edward always gave. She was trying out a new caterer this year—instead of the lobster boil and clambake they'd had the last few years, they'd be serving Texas-style barbecue.

"Edward's got a Stetson, and I bought a pair of Lucchese boots when we went to Dallas in April," Sloane said. "It was his idea to get the boots. I love how much he's getting into this party, and he knows I adore it. Usually he doesn't care about the details, but this year it's so different. What do you think that's about?"

"I'm sure he just wants to make you happy," I said.

"That's how it feels," she said, smiling.

"I'm glad," I said, having completely forgotten what it was like to have a husband who wanted to make me happy. I hadn't felt that since my earliest days with Griffin. And with Nate . . .

We sipped our wine and worked in silence. Sloane had stretched and applied gesso to a new canvas, set it up on her easel, and started painting. I was mulling over my next project—inspired by Nate's recent research, I thought I might travel to Tadoussac, a town on the Saint Lawrence River in eastern Quebec, where humpback and beluga whales gathered. Each fall, humpbacks migrated south from Canada, along the eastern seaboard, through the Anegada Passage from the Atlantic Ocean into the Caribbean.

As soon as I moved out, I would be free to follow the whales. My new shadow boxes would reflect migration—the whales' and my own. The studio doors were wide open to Long Island Sound, and a warm breeze blew in. I sat at my drafting table, doing a watercolor of the view.

Maybe I'd want to remember it after I left, or perhaps I was just getting into practice painting salt water in preparation for the whales. All I knew was that divorce wouldn't be a good look for a man running for governor—but Griffin had brought this on himself.

"Oh, look," Sloane said, gazing out the big north window toward the house. "The boys are here."

I glanced out and saw Ford and Alexander standing on the terrace. They seemed to be having an intense conversation. Then Ford shoved Alexander, and he stumbled backward, knocking over a wicker chair. I felt a shock. I had never seen them argue, much less push each other around. I stood up, but before I could hurry to the house to see what was wrong, Ford was at the door of my studio.

"Hey, is the bar open?" he asked, spying the wine.

"What's going on?" I asked. "Is everything okay?"

"Yeah, Alexander's just being holier than thou, as usual," Ford said.

"That sounds boring!" Sloane said, laughing. "Ford, are you going to use our pool today? I know you love it, and it's all set for the party on Saturday."

"Not today, Mrs. Hawke," he said. "I think my days of swimming in your pool are about to be over."

"Well, we love having you use it," she said. "Edward and I need to start swimming more."

"He's probably too busy for that," Ford said. I watched him pace nervously from the open door to the table where I'd put the wine. Sloane and I were using two glasses I'd brought down from the house, but Ford grabbed an empty mason jar I used to soak my brushes, filled it with rosé, and gulped half of it at once.

"You're right about Edward," Sloane said. "He works too hard, just like your dad. Lawyers, you know? All those billable hours."

"I didn't mean busy with work," Ford said. "I meant with Sallie."

"Sallie?" Sloane asked. "Do you mean Sallie Benson?"

"Yep, I do."

"Well, we're done with the redecoration," Sloane said. "She was a great help, especially with the boat, that's for sure, but it's over now."

"No, it's not over," Ford said. He looked pale. He pushed his dark hair back, and I saw the circles under his eyes. He downed the rest of the wine. Through the north window, I saw Alexander coming down the hill.

"What's not?" Sloane asked Ford, smiling.

"Your husband and Sallie," he said.

Alexander walked into the studio, approached his brother.

"Don't," Alexander said, his face in Ford's.

"She needs to know," Ford said.

The two brothers stared at each other. Alexander reached out to grip his twin's shoulders, and there was both tenderness and firmness in the way he held Ford at arm's length, gave a quick shake.

"Know what?" Sloane asked, approaching the boys.

"Ford loves Sallie," Alexander said, staring at Ford with incredible angst in his eyes. "That's why he's doing this. Telling you. It's not his fault; he's just really hurt. Please don't be mad at him."

"Mad at him—at Ford? For what?" Sloane asked.

"For what I'm about to tell you," Ford said. "You need to know about Edward."

"Christ," Alexander said, hand on his brother's shoulder. "Ford, stop it, come on . . ."

"Edward? What are you talking about?" Sloane asked.

"Your husband is sleeping with Sallie," Ford said, wrenching out of Alexander's grip. "They meet on your boat. On *Elysian*. They used to meet at your house, when she was decorating it, when you were at yoga or down here with Claire."

"Ford!" I said, shocked at his drunken idiocy.

"I'm talking to Sloane, not you," he said.

"I don't believe you," Sloane said.

"You *do* believe me, though," Ford said. "When you love someone, you see through them, whether you want to admit it or not. That's how I knew about Sallie. I felt it coming through her skin, that she wanted *him*. You feel that from Edward, don't you? That he's been with someone else? That he wants her?"

I looked at Sloane, saw the flash of despair in her eyes, and realized that Ford's words were registering with her. Sloane turned too quickly, and she knocked her easel and paints over. The canvas went flying. Ford tried to catch it, but it skittered past, sliding across the floor. He stepped toward Sloane, reached out to touch her. She stood facing the wall. She was shaking.

I took Ford's hand to pull him away from Sloane. He yanked it away, enraged. He poked me in the chest with two fingers, glared at me with fury I'd previously only seen in his father's eyes. I felt terrified.

"I'm trying to *help*," he yelled at me. His tone was just like Griffin's. His body tensed, as if he wanted to hit me. I took a step backward and forced myself to stay calm.

"Leave, Ford," I said. "Now."

Alexander caught my eyes and nodded. "She's right, Ford," he said, with the tone of a peacemaker. "Let's go."

"You're always judging me, Claire," Ford said. "Just like you judge Dad. I know all those lies you tell yourself about him, about that other bitch."

"What bitch?" I asked.

"The one in the tide pool," he said. "You want to ruin his chances in the election?"

"Ford, shut up," Alexander said.

He was talking about Ellen; my skin crawled. I saw him glance at my worktable, where I kept my notes for each shadow box. Had he gone through them, read what I had written? I wrote in code, lines of poetry to describe my feelings and the meanings of each piece. Was it possible he had deciphered my words about *Fingerbone*, connected them with Ellen's death?

"What has your father been saying to you?" I asked Ford.

"That elections are lost on rumors," he said.

"What did he tell you about the tide pool?" I asked.

"Nothing! Because there's nothing *to* tell. See? You're so focused on a lie, something that didn't even happen. My brother and I are working our asses off on his campaign. You should be too. He's a great man, Claire."

"She knows that, Ford," Alexander said with a glance at me. "She wants him to win, just like we do. We're all on the same team."

He started easing Ford toward the door. Ford's gaze was on me, full of hatred, as if all his fury needed a single object. He was out of control, drunk on wine and his wild emotions. But he finally gave in to Alexander, let him lead him out of the studio. I was shaking. I couldn't imagine Griffin discussing Ellen with Ford, but maybe I was wrong. I had seen, just now, how alike they were.

When the boys had left, I went to Sloane. I tried to put my arm around her shoulders, but she backed away.

"Sloane, I'm sorry," I said.

"Did you know about Edward and Sallie?" she asked.

"No, I had no idea. It might not even be true."

She turned to me, a blink of hope in her bleary eyes. "Would Ford make it up?"

"I don't know," I said. Griffin was cruel. Although I hadn't seen that explicit tendency in Ford before, his behavior just now showed he was his father's son.

"Maybe he did," she said. "He wasn't making any sense, all that stuff about his father and a tide pool and the election. He sounded insane."

"He did," I said, and I hugged her.

We stood together for a minute, each of us lost in the pain of wondering about truth and lies and love and hurt. And I stared at the sheaf of notes beside *Fingerbone* and realized that Ford had probably read them.

23

SALLIE

Sallie sat at the desk in her home office, listening to sprinklers through her open window. She loved the sound of water—whether at the beach, on the boat, or in the garden—and as sunlight streamed in, she closed her eyes and felt at peace for the first time in weeks. Swimming with her children, making the decision to stop seeing Edward had given her a fresh start.

It was late afternoon. Dan had taken Gwen and Charlie to the tennis court. Many days after work he would play with them—teaching them how to swing the racket, wait for the ball, toss it straight up, and hit through for a strong serve. They enjoyed learning how to keep score, and Charlie thought it was hilarious to keep saying *love*. "Love–fifteen, love–thirty, love–forty!" he'd say to Sallie, running in from the court, sweaty and laughing.

The smell of flowers and freshly mown grass filled her with the joy that summer was about to start. A week away from June, the roses were in bloom. She loved old varieties, English roses from the David Austin catalog. She found their names to be romantic, inspiring: Munstead Wood, Gentle Hermione, Golden Celebration, Scepter'd Isle, and Susan Williams-Ellis.

She had wanted to name Gwen *Susan*, after the beautiful white rose, but instead she had let Dan talk her into naming their daughter after his mother, Gwendolyn. It wasn't that Sallie hadn't liked her mother-in-law—she had, very much. It's just that it was the beginning of her giving in to Dan, just to mollify him—keep him happy and prevent his mood from turning dark for too long.

Her bookcases were full of design books from the Victoria and Albert Museum, Taschen, Rizzoli, stacks of *Architectural Digest* and *Martha Stewart Living* going back fifteen years, and photo albums of every design job she had ever done. She had surrounded herself with beauty—her house, her garden, her books, but especially her children.

Gwen and Charlie reminded her of everything that mattered in life. Watching them play in the waves with Maggie had made her happier than she had been all spring, all winter. She was actually looking forward to the family trip to Block Island. She had phoned the kids' school to let them know they wouldn't be there on Friday.

She would make a bigger effort to enjoy being with Dan. She would try to find love for him again.

Her cell phone rang. It brought her back to reality, away from the dreams of all she planned to do to make life better for her family. A glance at the screen was a punch in the heart: it was Edward's number. He would want to know when they could meet again; she would have to be firm, let him know it was over.

"Hello," she said, steeling herself.

"What the fuck did you do?" Edward asked.

The question shocked her. She had started an email to him but hadn't sent it.

"I didn't do anything," she said. "But I want to talk to you. We can't go on, Edward. It's . . ."

"You've done enough talking," he said. "You told Ford Chase about us, and he told Sloane, and now she wants me to move out."

"Edward, I didn't tell him! He spied on us."

"Bullshit. We were careful."

"He came to your boat two days ago. You and I were supposed to meet, but you were working. And he showed up. He was drunk, and . . ."

"He came aboard *Elysian*? What did he say?"

Sallie hesitated. She had wanted to wipe the slate clean, never think of Ford's words again. "He called me terrible things." She paused. "And he said he loved me."

"*Loved* you? Were you sleeping with him too?"

"Of course not! Edward!"

"I'm going to walk over to the Chases' house right now, and that kid will be lucky if I don't kill him. I swear to God, if he tells anyone else or if you do . . ."

"What, you'll kill me too?"

She waited for him to say *no, I could never do that, I love you*, but he was silent, and she felt as if he'd stabbed her.

"Ford told Sloane right in front of Claire," Edward said. "Now Claire can hold that over me. I feel like . . ."

"Like what?" Sallie asked, afraid of how menacing he sounded—as if he meant Claire harm.

But just then she heard the sound of car doors slamming and of voices. Gwen and Charlie, happy and laughing. Dan talking, then the voice of another man. She craned her neck to see around the corner of the house.

There in the driveway were her husband and children. And a black Porsche 911. As she watched, Ford Chase got out of his car and stood face-to-face with Dan.

Sallie hung up on Edward and ran downstairs.

FIVE DAYS
LATER

24

CONOR

At ten a.m. the Wednesday after Claire disappeared, Conor drove down the long dirt lane to Catamount Bluff. He noticed that the security guard usually posted at the entrance was not at his post. The trees were leafing out, making the woods on either side even denser, harder to see along the trails. This enclave was completely private, no way for a car to get in or out except this road.

He thought back to Friday, to the timeline he had established. If Griffin was telling the truth and he had said goodbye to Claire right after breakfast—and she wasn't reported missing until after five thirty—that gave someone nine hours to lie in wait for her, attack her, and take her or her body away. Based on the freshness of the blood, the window had been narrowed to the middle of the afternoon.

He passed the neighbors' driveways. Coming from the main road, in order, were the Coffins, Lockwoods, Hawkes, and at the dead end atop the bluff, the Chases. They all had security cameras, and police had reviewed the footage, but because of the foliage, nothing more than glimpses of the road were visible. The examiners noted that a FedEx truck had been seen entering and leaving Catamount Bluff.

FedEx had been rolling out a program of installing drive cams in the cab and cargo hold, and both were present, showing no suspicious activity. The truck had been gone over for signs of blood, and none was found. The driver was questioned and cleared. The package he had been sent to pick up had indeed been called in by Claire, and the air bill was stamped with her account number.

Considering no vehicle other than the FedEx truck had been seen—by camera or naked eye—the attacker must have removed Claire one of two ways: either along the trails that ran through conservation land or by boat from the beach. The trails were too narrow to accommodate vehicles, even ATVs.

If Claire was dead, the killer could have dismembered her, scattering body parts through the woods and in the Sound. Or he could have dug a grave prior to Friday, had it ready, and buried Claire somewhere in the forest.

One of Connecticut's most famous cases, best known as the "Wood Chipper Murder," concerned Helle Crafts. Her husband, Richard, had murdered her, put her body through a wood chipper that he had rented and installed on a bridge. The trial was nationally groundbreaking in that it was the first time a prosecutor had achieved a conviction without a body—only fragments of teeth and fingernails.

Investigating Claire's disappearance, police had contacted every heavy equipment rental company in a twenty-five-mile radius around Black Hall. Only two wood chippers had been rented for a period that included that Friday, both by landscapers who had done business with the companies before. The company representatives attributed the small number of rentals to it being a long weekend. Their offices were open just a half day on Saturday and closed both Sunday and Monday. Renters wouldn't want to incur the extra charges.

When Conor got to the Chases' house, he parked in the turnaround and got out of the car. He had called Ford and told him they needed to talk. He had offered to drive to wherever Ford lived, but Ford said he was at the Catamount Bluff house. There was a Porsche and a Mercedes SUV parked in front of the barn where Claire had been attacked. Conor wondered which vehicle was Ford's. He hesitated, glanced toward the woodland trail. He wanted to follow the course the dogs had already searched, look for anything they or the team might have missed. But he wanted to talk to Ford first.

He knocked on the front door and waited. When no one answered, he walked around to the seaward side of the house. He walked up the back steps, peered into the kitchen, rapped on the glass. Still no reply.

Claire's studio was just down the hill toward the Sound, and Conor walked across the lawn, mown grass sticking to his shoes. A large picture window faced north, in the direction of the house, and as he approached he saw shadows moving within the studio. He headed around the whitewashed building and saw that the double doors facing the beach were closed. He knocked hard. No response.

"Police," he called. "Please open the door."

He heard the murmur of voices inside, but then one of the doors slid open on an iron track. A fair-haired young man stood just inside, trying to smile.

"Officer?" he said.

"Detective Reid. Are you Ford?"

"No, his brother, Alexander. We've been expecting you."

"Is Ford here too?"

"Yes, he's inside."

"May I come inside?" Conor asked.

"Of course," Alexander said, casting a nervous look over his shoulder and stepping aside. "Please come in."

Conor entered the large bright space. He immediately noticed a young man lying on a sofa bed across the room, beyond Claire's workbench, a tool chest, and an easel. Alexander led him over.

"Ford?" Alexander said.

"Hi, Detective," Ford said. His hangover was painfully obvious, and he seemed disinclined to move.

"Hi, Ford," Conor said.

"You might as well know, if you haven't already heard, which I'm sure you have, that Claire and I didn't get along," Ford said.

"That true for both of you?" Conor asked, glancing at Alexander.

"My brother likes everyone," Ford said. "That's why you want to talk to me, right? Because you think I'm the bad one and I did it, right?"

"Did you do it?" Conor asked.

"I don't even know what 'it' is," Ford said.

"That's fine," Conor said. "I just want to get an idea about Claire. Why don't you tell me what you think might have happened to her?"

"We want to know that too," Alexander said. "Where is she? Why was so much blood in the garage? It's all over social media that she was probably murdered. But that can't be true."

"Why?" Conor asked.

"She's strong," Alexander said. "Amazing. She would have fought like hell. And she's . . . not here. There's no body. She's not dead. Those people posting on Facebook don't even know her. They're wrong."

"Dad's the state's attorney," Ford said to Alexander. "You don't have to go online to know how the investigation's going. Just ask him."

"What does your father say?" Conor asked.

"That he's going crazy, wondering what happened to her," Ford said. "Wanting her to be okay and come home. That he feels the cops aren't doing enough."

Conor ignored the last part. "Does he think she *can* come home?" he asked.

Ford shrugged. Conor stared at him. The kid was making it sound as if Claire had a choice in the matter.

"What do you think happened to her?" Conor asked again.

"No idea," Ford said.

"Alexander, you said Claire is strong and would have fought back. What makes you say that?" Conor asked.

"If you saw her work, the art she produces and the message in it—statements about the environment, humanity, abuse, even life and death. She cares, and she's out there with what she has to say. She's fierce. She fights against what she considers wrong."

"She doesn't know anything about abuse," Ford said.

"Well, through Dad," Alexander said. "The cases he works on."

"If you're wondering, Claire's not an abused woman," Ford said. "And neither was my mother. Or that other one. Ellen."

"Okay," Conor said. He paused, watching Ford's face for his reaction to the next question. "Who is Ellen?"

"Someone my dad dated in college and Claire's obsessed with. She doesn't like thinking he was with anyone before her. She'd like to forget my dad was married before. To our mom," Ford said.

"Did she talk about Ellen?" Conor asked.

"No," Alexander said. "And I think my brother's wrong about Claire being obsessed with her or anyone. She's an artist, she's curious."

"Let me ask you this, though: Why are you guys here today? In Claire's studio?"

"Because I'm hungover like a motherfucker," Ford said. "I didn't want to drive home drunk last night. And I don't feel like being up at the main house where my Dad might come in."

"Why would that be a problem?" Conor asked.

Ford just stared at the ceiling.

"Our mother left because she'd rather drink than be with him. With us," Alexander said, staring at Ford. "And our dad worries about Ford."

"I'm not an alcoholic," Ford said.

"How do you feel about Claire?" Conor asked.

Ford made a scoffing sound. "I told you, we didn't get along. I didn't want anything bad to happen to her, but it's not making me drink."

"What is, then?" Conor asked, taking note of the fact he had said *didn't* twice—past tense, as if she weren't coming back.

Ford clamped his lips together and his eyes tightly shut. Conor watched waves of pain pass through him. Alexander stared at his brother, brow-furrowed worry on his face. He looked at Conor.

"Someone Ford loved died," Alexander said.

"I'm sorry to hear that," Conor said.

Ford didn't react.

"Can you tell me who?" Conor asked.

"Sallie," Ford mumbled, and he turned toward the wall, perhaps so his brother and Conor wouldn't see his emotion.

Conor's pulse jumped. The mention of *Ford* in Sallie Benson's letter now had context. He was facing the big window, and he spotted a tall young brown-haired woman running across the grass—not from the house but from the direction of the beach path that led to Hubbard's Point. Alexander saw her too and met her at the door. She threw herself into his arms.

"Is Ford okay?" she asked.

"He is," Alexander said, and when he looked at Conor, the young woman's gaze followed.

"Oh," she said, startled. "I didn't know anyone else was here."

"I'm Detective Reid. And you?"

"Emily Coffin," she said. "Alexander's girlfriend. I'm sorry, is this a bad time?"

"Not at all," Conor said.

"He's investigating what happened to our stepmom," Alexander said. He held Emily's hand, and she leaned into his body.

"You're Neil and Abigail's daughter?" Conor asked, trying to keep the neighbors straight.

162

"I'm their niece—I live in Stonington."

"That's how Alexander and she got together," Ford shot over his shoulder. "He and I live in her family's guesthouse. Proximity makes the heart grow fonder."

"We caretake the property when Emily's parents are away," Alexander explained.

"Emily, do you know Claire?" Conor asked.

"Not very well, unfortunately," Emily said. "I'm not here that often. But I really like her—she's always so nice to me. It's horrible. The reporters keep talking about the blood." She gazed expectantly at Conor, as if waiting for him to comment, but he didn't.

"Dad says he'll never go into the garage again," Alexander said.

"I can imagine!" Emily said. "Is the blood still there? I mean not the actual blood but the stains? The stuff you can see with that chemical in the blue light?"

"It'll never go away," Alexander said, putting his arm around her.

Conor noticed Alexander glance over at Ford, but Ford hadn't moved—he was still lying down.

"Ford," Conor said. "When you said 'Sallie,' did you mean Sallie Benson?"

"Yes," Alexander answered for his brother.

"You loved her?"

"Yeah," Ford mumbled. "She was married, older than my mother; I've heard all about it. But none of that mattered."

"When did you last see her?" Conor asked.

"Two days before the explosion," Ford said, sitting up, looking unsteady even though he was on the daybed. "We had a fight. I was a fucking asshole. And she fucking killed herself because . . ." He choked on a sob.

"Because what?" Conor asked, taking note of the fact Ford thought Sallie committed suicide. Or he wanted Conor to think he did.

Ford shook his head and couldn't speak.

"Ford told her husband," Alexander said. "He told Dan, but he didn't do it to be mean—he really loved Sallie. He wanted to be with her, that's the whole thing. He thought if Dan knew, it would be easier for her to leave him. She'd have no choice."

"Were you angry with her?" Conor asked. "When she didn't leave him, when you had the fight?"

"Yes," Ford said. "Because . . . I never even fucking slept with her. She wanted someone else. I mean, not her husband."

"You going to tell me who?" Conor asked.

"Edward," Alexander said.

"Who's that?"

"Edward Hawke," Ford said. "Our neighbor, right next door. I used to swim in their pool. I told Sloane too. His wife, Claire's best friend. I told her right here," Ford said, gesturing around the studio. "Told her Edward was having an affair with Sallie. We had some nice rosé. I drank with the ladies while I told Sloane her husband was cheating on her. Knowing Claire, that shit was probably straight from France. Straight from Provence. She loved stuff like that."

"Stop now," Alexander said. He dropped Emily's hand and went closer to his brother on the sofa bed.

"Claire loved spending Dad's money," Ford said. "It didn't make me want to hurt her—it's just a fact. Sitting here drinking expensive pink wine with Sloane. She was a so-called artist, but how much could she earn from that crap she made? Sallie was the opposite. She never took anything from Dan—she was a successful businesswoman. How could you not admire her?"

"It's been traumatic for Ford," Alexander said. "The whole family is going crazy about Claire—no matter what he says, he's worried too. And then Sallie. You have to understand him, Detective. Our mother left when we were young, and it's never really been right since."

"The sad boys, the lost twins," Emily said, embracing Alexander.

"Sad, not lost," Alexander said, looking over her shoulder at Ford.

"Fucked up, not sad," Ford said. "I'm out of here."

"Better not drive," Conor said.

"Don't worry. I'm going to my old room. Now that Claire's not here, I won't get shit for sleeping in it. Why do you think we live half an hour away on Emily's property? Because Claire didn't want us here." He stumbled out of the studio.

Didn't. Past tense again, Conor thought. As if Ford knew Claire wasn't coming back.

Alexander took a step toward the door, starting to follow his brother, then turned and faced Conor. "He didn't mean it that way."

"What way?" Conor asked.

"Like he's glad Claire's not here," Alexander said.

"He didn't say that!" Emily said.

"I know, but the whole family's being investigated. Right, Detective?" Alexander asked. "Mostly Ford?"

"We have to follow every lead," Conor said.

"Look," Alexander said. "We'll do anything to help you find Claire—even Ford. He's just had too much to drink, and he's wrecked about Sallie, and he's not making sense."

"I understand," Conor said. "Thanks for talking to me, both of you." He nodded at Emily. "If either of you think of anything, just give me a call. Please tell Ford too." He started to hand Alexander his card, but Alexander stepped back, hands at his sides.

"Thanks anyway, but if we think of anything, we'll tell our father," Alexander said, not smiling. "No one wants to find Claire more than he does, and he's the state's attorney."

"That he is," Conor said.

"You know, he is pro police all the way. Investigating my brother could really hurt his chances."

"You mean his chances to become governor?" Conor asked.

"Yes," Alexander said. "My father's a good man. The best there is. And my brother has some issues, but he wouldn't hurt anyone."

"Got it," Conor said.

That was weird, he thought as he walked toward his car. Alexander had floated a little threat his way. Investigate Ford and maybe Griffin won't be so pro police. It rolled off Conor's back but showed how loyal Alexander was to his brother.

Conor stared into the woods that ran east from Catamount Bluff. The trails were overgrown and numerous, but if Claire wasn't taken away by car or boat, they were the only other possible means of escape. With hundreds of acres of forest and marsh to dispose of her body. The extensive search had turned up nothing, but Conor wanted to walk the path himself.

He stopped at the edge of the coastal forest. To the south, there was Long Island Sound and a long strand of sandy beach and rocky pools. North of the woodland, a salt marsh, full of reeds and creeks and poles supporting osprey nests, spread into the distance. He glanced down Catamount Road—an old white-haired man, wearing khakis and a long-sleeved green shirt, spotted Conor and lifted his hand in a feeble wave. Conor had only questioned Wade Lockwood once, right after Claire went missing. But he recognized the eldest resident of Catamount Bluff, and he waved back.

Staring at the thicket and woods, Conor saw no visible paths, only small gaps between trees. Were those deer tracks or paw prints on the sandy ground? Either way, he was going to follow them.

He wasn't a nature guy. He liked the shore but mostly from the porch of a seaside bar. Sometimes he and Kate flew out to Block Island to hike through Rodman's Hollow. His brother, Tom, made his life and living on the ocean—and Kate in the sky—but from the time Conor had become a police officer, he'd gotten used to the highway, shoreline towns, urban and suburban crime scenes. He shouldered his way between two pines, smelled sap, and headed into the dark unknown.

25

CLAIRE

Daylight. I tried to sleep during the day and be up at night when it was safe, but a sound awakened me. Something crashing through the brush. Was that a swear word, a human voice? I lay still in my sleeping bag, clawing myself out of wild dreams, and listened.

Yes, it was a person. No big animal would stalk the woods at this hour, when bright sun was streaming through branches and new leaves. It couldn't be my mountain lion, and I felt a million times more danger than if it were.

I thought: *Griffin.*

The cabin was hidden so deeply—and it was so camouflaged by its weathered boards, with vines growing up the walls—that I wanted to believe he would never see it, no matter how close he passed by.

I started to sit up, but my bones ached. I hadn't eaten much since I had seen the mountain lion—not because I was scared of him, or at least I don't think that was the reason—but because I was so tired. I'd gathered green seaweed—"sea lettuce"—both to eat and to press into my wounds. It contained alginate, known to aid healing. My father had taught me that. Yarrow worked as well, and I had picked some and mixed it with water to make a poultice and pack the worst cuts.

I thought I was getting better, but this extreme exhaustion made me wonder if an infection had seeped in.

The weakness spread from the cuts in my skin into my blood, my bones, my brain. I would tell myself to move a muscle, but nothing would happen. I began to see the mountain lion sitting in the corner of my cabin. At night, where the North Star used to appear in the cracks of the cabin roof, I would see the cougar's eyes. What did it mean that I was no less comforted? My father was the mountain lion, and the mountain lion was my father.

The sound of someone coming through the woods got closer. No animal would be so clumsy, breaking branches and tossing leaves. I imagined Griffin approaching. He was so deft in his legal work—never a wrong word in a brief, never a mistake in court. But in the woods? He loved the water, going out on his boat, but he'd never enjoyed hiking or exploring the woodland with me.

It was true, however, that on that night when he and I had met at the cove twenty-five years ago, not half a mile south of here, he had moved like a jungle cat along the path—but that had been the main trail, not the narrow, meandering, and hard-to-spot deer tracks that crisscrossed the woods and marsh around the cabin.

I had a vision of Griffin on the beach, the night of shooting stars. I tasted his lips. In my dream, I felt the heat of his mouth. His body pressed against mine. Time slipped away and came back.

I thought of the love I had had as a child—the strength it gave me now. And I thought of the day I learned how cruelty in a childhood could create a demon.

It was just one year into our marriage. By then, I had seen the black-eyes phenomenon several times. It always terrified me, and immediately after each bout of rage, I would think of leaving him. Sometimes I would come to this cabin to think. And once I calmed down, once the reverberations of fear passing through my body had subsided, I would decide to stay.

I had already been divorced once—I didn't want to fail in another marriage. I'd tell myself he would never physically hurt me—everyone got angry, and in fact, it was a healthy emotion. With his high-pressure job and the tragedies he encountered at work, he had to let off steam. I'd just have to find a way to tell him venting was fine but he couldn't take his stress out on me.

And almost every time I returned, shaken and full of doubt, he would hold me and tell me he loved me.

"You're my life," he said, walking into our house, finding me curled up on the living room sofa after one especially bad episode. "We're made in heaven."

"But it doesn't feel like heaven when you act that way toward me," I said, unable to meet his eyes. I looked out the window at sunlight glittering on the Sound.

"I don't mean to," he said. "I'm thinking about the scumbag I'm prosecuting, who stabbed a woman to death and left her body in a pile of garbage. Or last month—the mother who let her boyfriend beat and burn her son, refused to speak out against him until one day the beating went too far and the boy died."

I just kept staring outside.

"Can't you try to understand?" he asked, an unusually plaintive tone in his voice—conciliatory, asking for forgiveness. It got my attention.

"I know you see the worst in life," I said. "When you come home, I've wanted you to feel the best in life. Our love. I try to give that to you, but . . . then something happens inside you. I'm never even sure what causes it, and you act like you hate me."

"I could never hate you."

"Just like you could never hit me, or at least that's what you say. But you know what, Griffin? Your anger and the things you say to me hurt worse than fists. My heart aches so much right now . . ."

"No, Claire, please don't tell me that. I can't stand to know I've made you feel this way. Will you let me try, give me another chance?"

he asked, taking my hands, pulling me gently off the couch. He put his arms around me. My body was stiff, defensive.

"I want to, but it keeps happening," I said, my voice cracking.

"Oh God, I can't bear to know I make you cry," he said. "Claire, I promise, I will try so hard."

"That's not saying you won't do it again."

"You have to give me another chance. You're the best woman I've ever known, nothing like the others."

"What others?"

When he didn't reply at first, I took my chance: "Griffin, I think we should go to counseling."

Dead silence for a minute. He dropped his arms, stepped back. "I can't," he said. "I'm in a position where I can't show weakness. Claire, I have to be tough, so the police and detectives respect me, so the defense lawyers are afraid of me. You know, other state's attorneys have cops who laugh at them, don't respect them. But not me. My cops go to the mat for me. They want to make me happy and bring me everything they've got—they're loyal. That could change if they saw me as weak."

"But therapy is private. Doctor-patient confidentiality," I said.

"I know you believe that, but people talk. Word gets around. If there's one thing I know from my work, no secret can be kept forever. People, doctors included, gossip. When they have a high-profile client, they love to talk. I can't do it."

He made some sense, but his words made me feel helpless. Twelve months into the marriage, I was losing hope. And as I said before, every time I relented, went back, I chipped away a little more of myself—but it would take more time for me to realize it.

That day, I said, "When you said I'm the best woman you know, not like the others . . ."

"You are," he said.

"Who are the others?"

He sighed. "Margot, of course. You know what a nightmare it became with her."

He had told me, but as his second wife, I knew there was another side to the story. Even if the choice to start drinking was hers, I could understand how despair over Griffin's rages might have fueled her alcoholism. I'd found a photo of her one time, tucked between books in the children's library. They loved and missed her so much. Sometimes I wanted to track her down, ask what had happened to make her leave.

"And my mother," he said.

"Your mother?" I asked. I was eager to hear more; he hardly spoke about her or of his family at all.

"She was the great lady of Catamount Bluff," he said. "She wore pearls every day, even while swimming in the Sound. She gave parties that people still talk about, volunteered at the Art Academy and our church food bank, was on bank and nonprofit boards. Everyone loved her."

"And you?"

"I loved her too. Except when I didn't."

"Why, Griffin?"

"Because when I made her mad, she locked me in the basement. Burned the back of my knees with her cigarette. She would buy my favorite chocolates and bottles of Coca-Cola . . . this might seem trivial, but she would hide them from me, then eat and drink them herself, right in front of me, telling me how delicious they were and if I were a better boy, I could have them too. But she almost never gave me any."

"Griffin, that's horrible," I said.

He nodded his head. "When I was ten she beat me so hard I had to go to the emergency room. I was black and blue, and she told me to lie and say I'd fallen while rock climbing."

"What about your father? Why didn't he protect you?"

Griffin laughed. "No one went against my mother. He found out it was easier to pretend he was Hemingway—go fishing off Bimini or grouse shooting in Scotland or to Paris with his mistress."

"Griffin, I had no idea," I said.

"You're the only one I've ever told," he said, pulling me close again. "I've never trusted anyone this much."

And I took that to heart: grieving the fact my husband had survived an abusive childhood, cherishing his words telling me I was the only one he could talk to, the only one he trusted. It had taken an entire year of marriage to get to the point when he could tell me—and I felt it was the secret decoder ring to his behavior.

Back then I thought that now that I knew, I had something to work with. It would make me more understanding. It would help me avoid his triggers.

What an idiot I was.

Now, lying in my sleeping bag and listening to the person get closer to my cabin, I pushed myself up from the floor and stood ready to defend myself when he entered. I was picturing Griffin. Our last fight, the night before the art opening I never got to attend, had been about Ellen.

"I don't want what happened to Ellen to happen to you," he'd said through gritted teeth.

"Don't worry, it won't," I whispered to myself in the cabin. I was ready to battle for my life.

I heard my name being called. "Claire! Can you hear me?" Then the sound of fabric ripping. "Jesus Christ!"

Someone had just snagged pants or a jacket on thorns in the thicket. I stood very still. More ripping, as if the garment were being torn free from the brambles. Then footsteps retreating, going back in the direction the person had come—toward Catamount Bluff.

I had recognized the voice.

It wasn't Griffin outside my cabin.

It was Conor Reid.

My eyes stung with tears—that's how badly I wanted to call for help. But Griffin's words about "his" cops came back to me: "My cops go to the mat for me. They want to make me happy and bring me everything they've got—they're loyal."

What if Conor was part of Griffin's force? No matter what I wanted to believe, that Conor was good, that he wouldn't finish the job Griffin had started and kill me, I couldn't take the chance.

One thing I knew was that I had to get out of here. That had been too close a call. I didn't know where I would go, but my refuge in the woods was no longer safe.

ONE DAY EARLIER

26

SALLIE

Dear Ford,

I don't know what I did to lead you on. I don't believe I did anything. You are the son of clients of mine, and I thought you were a nice young man. When you came to swim in the Hawkes' pool, I enjoyed our brief conversations.

I will never understand what led you to accost my husband in our driveway, speak such garbage about me in front of our children. Did you intend to destroy my family? Did your fantasy about me—whatever it is—really convince you that I would ever want to be with someone who could do such a cruel thing?

Talking to Dan about "spring break" . . . who even cares what you meant? It just shows how young you are, a college boy who doesn't understand that people grow up, live complicated lives, try their best.

You are deeply troubled. You are delusional. I care nothing for you, but I encourage you to get help, so you don't hurt my family or anyone else again.

Ford, if you ever come close to me, my husband, or especially my children again, you will regret it mightily. The fact your father has a position of power means absolutely nothing to me. You are sick, and yesterday's criminal behavior proved it. The police won't be swayed by a pathetic little boy saying Daddy will keep him out of trouble.

Stay away.

—Sallie Benson

On Thursday morning, the day after Ford told Dan about Edward, Sallie sat at her desk and wrote the letter. When she finished, she stared at it for a long time, deciding what to do. No words on a page could do justice to how she felt, how Ford Chase had bulldozed her family, crushed the spirit out of them.

She had actually been excited about going away for the weekend. The whole family had planned to go shopping after Dan got home from work, let the kids pick out all sorts of treats to have on the boat. As an extra surprise, they were going to go to Barks and Purrs in the mall, to buy a special tiny life jacket for Maggie.

Now the trip was off—or at least it was for Sallie. She felt as if she deserved the hate she saw in Dan's eyes, the devastation in Gwen's and Charlie's. Ford had reeked of alcohol, slurring the disgusting words he said about her, telling Dan about her affair with Edward Hawke.

"What's an affair?" Charlie had asked, sobbing and throwing his arms around her waist—not because he understood what Ford was saying but because he sensed the violence of the moment.

"It's nothing," Sallie said, wanting to block his ears, rush the children into the house. But Dan stopped her, gripping her wrist and tugging hard.

"It means Mommy loves someone else," Dan said. "And she's going to be with him instead of us now."

"Dan, that's not true! Never! Please, let's go inside."

Gwen stood there silently, staring at Sallie.

"Come on, honey, we're going into the house," Sallie said, touching her shoulder.

"It's better they know who you are," Ford said, staring at her. "Right now, while they're so young, instead of spending their lives, all through middle and high school, hoping their mother is the sweet person they want her to be instead of who she really is."

"Get out of my yard," Dan said.

"You're defending her?" Ford asked.

"No, but I'm going to beat the shit out of you if you don't get into your car and drive away. Then I'll call the cops on you for drunk driving and breach of peace."

"Good luck," Ford said. "And by the way, I know what you did too."

"What I did?"

"Yeah. Spring break ring a bell?"

Sallie turned to look at Dan. He was staring at Ford with disbelief.

"Ellen Fielding wasn't the only girl to drown, was she?" Ford asked.

"That's enough," Dan said.

"How much have you told your wife? Maybe that's why she cheated. She knows the kind of guy you are. Right, Sallie?"

She didn't reply.

"Perfect people in a perfect town," Ford said. "Anyway, nice talking to you both. Enjoy life knowing each other's secrets."

Dan seemed frozen with shock as Ford got into his car, backed out of the driveway, and screeched away. Sallie took a step toward Dan, but he shook her off.

"Don't," he said.

"What was he talking about?" Sallie asked. "Spring break?"

"Are you kidding?" Dan asked. "He's a maniac, just stirring up trouble."

"What girl drowned? And who's Ellen Fielding?" Sallie asked.

"You're confronting *me*?" he asked. "After what I just heard?"

She glanced at the children. They were both crying.

"Mommy, Daddy, don't fight!" Gwen said. Charlie clung to Sallie.

"Let's go for a ride, kids," Dan said. "And we'll get ready to go to Block Island. Maybe we'll play mini golf and get an ice cream. Mommy's not going to come. She has other things to do. But we'll have fun, Gwen, Charlie—I promise."

Sallie went inside, up to her room, and lay down on the bed. Ford's words to Dan haunted her, but she told herself he was just being spiteful—as Dan had said, he was a maniac. Certainly under the influence and not mentally well. She heard everyone come home a couple of hours later, but she couldn't go downstairs and face them, not even her children. She smelled hamburgers, Dan cooking dinner.

She didn't sleep all night. Dan slept in the guest room and went downstairs before dawn. She heard the door close quietly. He started his car and drove away. She went downstairs immediately afterward, made coffee, and drank it on the back porch while thinking about what to do next. Her heart seized when she heard the kids get up, but when they came down, she cooked scrambled eggs for breakfast as if nothing had ever happened. Nobody mentioned Ford.

It was Thursday, and they were happy it was the last day of school before the trip to Block Island. Sallie walked them to the end of the driveway at seven thirty, kissed them goodbye, and told them to have a good day at school. They hugged her as they always did, waved from the school bus steps when they climbed aboard.

Writing to Ford had made Sallie feel a little better. She folded the copy and put it into an envelope. She could never confront Ford in person, vicious and vengeful as he had been, but she needed him to know exactly how she felt, to read what she had to say. She didn't know where he lived, whether he had a place of his own, but she knew where to leave it, where he would be sure to get it. And if he was there, she had a question for him.

The route to Catamount Bluff had become familiar, almost second nature. The security guard—Officer Ben Markham today—waved her through. She had been here so often, working on all four houses, the off-duty cops who manned the gate didn't even stop her anymore.

It was seven forty-five, and the sun had just crested the tops of the trees that lined the road. In the distance, beyond the last house, Long Island Sound sparkled in the morning light.

She drove past two clients' properties—the Coffins and Lockwoods. When she passed the Hawkes' driveway, she averted her gaze and couldn't even breathe, couldn't bear the idea of seeing Edward or Sloane. Or Edward *with* Sloane. Pulling into the Chases' turnaround at the end of the road, she gripped her steering wheel and wondered what to do next. She didn't see Ford's black Porsche, but there was an almost identical red one parked by the front steps.

The Catamount Bluff residents received their mail at the small post office halfway down Shore Road to Hubbard's Point. But they had "social chutes"—small tubes nailed to posts in the ground, used by the four families for informal notices and invites among themselves. She started to roll up the envelope, insert it into the chute, when the front door opened. She quickly hid it behind her back.

Alexander, Ford's twin, stepped outside. She had met him a couple of times when she'd worked on the kitchen. He was forgettable compared to his brother—where Ford had the same focused, magnetic energy as his father, Alexander was quiet, easygoing. Ford had made himself known to Sallie from the beginning—hanging out, asking her about herself, drinking more coffee than any kid should drink, just to be in the kitchen. Then, showing off his body while swimming at the Hawkes'. Alexander had seemed so shy that Sallie hadn't gotten to know him at all.

"Hi, Mrs. Benson," Alexander said now, standing at the top of the steps. He already had a slight summer tan, and his fair hair looked streaked by sun and salt. He appeared worried but attempted a smile. "How are you?"

"Fine, Alexander," she said.

"Have you seen Ford today?" he asked.

"Why would you ask me that?" she asked, taken aback.

"Because he told me he was going to see you yesterday, and we haven't seen him since. We're worried."

"No," she said. She felt nervous, awkward. She had hoped to just leave the envelope and escape. She tried to ease it into the back pocket of her jeans but dropped it on the ground.

"Is that for my parents?" Alexander asked, spotting the envelope.

She hesitated. "It's a note for your brother," she said, bending over to snatch it up.

Alexander looked confused. "Why did you write to him?"

"Never mind," she said, starting to back away. "I'll give it to him another time."

"Please tell me," Alexander said, taking a step forward. "Please. I know he was upset when he headed over to you. If you can give me an idea what happened . . ."

"He was very drunk, Alexander," she said. "He shouldn't have been driving."

"Did you try to stop him?" he asked, his voice shaking.

"There wasn't time," she said. "He was angry and just sped away."

Sallie's heart was pounding. Alexander had left the front door open, and Sallie saw Claire standing just inside. She stepped out, put a hand on Alexander's shoulder. He turned slightly to look at her, and she gave him a warm smile.

"Hi, Sallie. Alexander's worried about his brother," Claire said.

"Sallie said he drove away drunk yesterday," Alexander said. "Aren't you worried too?"

"Yes, I am," Claire said.

"She wrote him a note," Alexander said. "I want her to tell us what's in it—she was the last one to see him. It could give me a clue."

"Alexander, that's between Sallie and Ford," Claire said.

Sallie blushed and felt like running away. She remembered what Edward had told her, that Sloane had been with Claire when Ford confronted her. So Claire knew. When Sallie met her eyes, she saw Claire gazing at her with compassion.

"I'm going to leave now," Sallie said. "I hope he comes home soon, Alexander."

"Mrs. Benson, I know he went over to confront you," Alexander said. "He told me. I told him he shouldn't. I don't really know what happened between you—he didn't go into it—but he was pretty mad when he went over to your house."

"He was," Sallie said, and suddenly she was reliving it, seeing Ford's angry face, hearing his vicious words, and she couldn't help it—everything spilled out. "He said terrible things about me in front of my husband and children. My son and daughter heard the whole thing."

"Your *son* heard all that stuff?" Alexander asked.

"Yes. Charlie's only seven. And my daughter is nine."

Alexander buried his face in his hands. Sallie thought he was going to cry.

"That's it," Alexander said. "I'm sure he's hating himself right now—having your kids see. That's why he's gone away."

"What do you mean?" Claire asked.

"That was our life," Alexander said. "Mom and Dad fighting, us hearing terrible stuff about her. If Ford threw that kind of garbage at Charlie, he'd feel like the worst person on earth."

He is, Sallie thought and wondered why Alexander was so focused on Charlie when Gwen had been just as devastated. She couldn't take this anymore, hearing a brother in so much anguish over the person who had done all he could to ruin her life.

"What if he hurts himself?" Alexander asked.

Sallie saw Griffin, dressed for work in a jacket and tie, approach from inside the house. He raised his hand to wave, but she didn't return the greeting. She just turned away, got into her car. She completely understood the impulse toward suicide. When you hurt people so badly, when you see the effect your behavior has had, you might just want out of this life. She thought of the look on Charlie's face—and Gwen's also. If Ford had seen their pain too—and it had affected him—Sallie was glad. She started her car and drove out of Catamount Bluff for the last time.

27

CLAIRE

I watched Sallie speed away. I had seen Ford's wild fury when he had stumbled into my studio and told Sloane about Edward and Sallie. Sloane's pain, the sudden anguish, had nearly knocked her down. I could well imagine Ford acting that same unhinged, violent way, telling Sallie's husband her secret in front of her kids.

"What was that about?" Griffin asked. He had come into the front hall with his cup of coffee, frowned as he watched the trail of dust from Sallie's SUV driving down the unpaved road. I had brought *Fingerbone* from my studio into the house; it was sitting right there on the hall table.

I willed Griffin to glance over and see the shadow box. I had planned to show him after breakfast, when we were alone, and then drop it off at the gallery. But the scene with Sallie changed all that.

"I asked a question," Griffin said, laser focused on Alexander. "What was she here for?"

Alexander and I exchanged a look. There was no good way out here; telling Griffin the truth could flip the mood switch but so could lying. It was odd, I thought. Now that I was mentally on my way to leaving, I didn't really care anymore. Let Griffin flail around in one of his rages—I knew he had taught Ford how to do the same thing, intimidate people with his moods. He had created a son just like himself.

But Alexander wasn't like that, and I wanted to protect him. I watched carefully to see how he was going to handle his father's question. He opened his mouth to speak, then closed it again. I knew his inner struggle so well—it had been my own for so long. Walking on eggshells was our family norm.

"Ford went to Sallie's house yesterday," I said to Griffin.

"For what?" Griffin asked.

"Claire, don't," Alexander said sharply.

"To speak to her husband and make accusations right in front of her children," I said.

Griffin listened to me but didn't react at first. He sipped his coffee. His eyes looked normal. He turned his gaze from me to Alexander.

"Is this true?" he asked.

"I don't know," Alexander said.

"Are you lying to me?" Griffin asked.

"No, Dad. I knew he was upset, but he didn't tell me the whole story."

"Wait," Griffin said. "You didn't know the whole story, but you knew *some* of the story?"

"That's right," Alexander said, sounding nervous.

"You knew that he planned to visit the Bensons and make a scene?" Griffin asked. "You came here at six this morning, worried about your brother, and you knew that the whole time but didn't see fit to tell me?"

"I'm sorry."

"Is there something else you're keeping from me?" Griffin asked.

"Dad," Alexander said. "She asked about the girls, the old girls . . ."

"What old girls?" I asked.

"A case I once worked on," Griffin snapped, before Alexander could reply. "And I shared the details with my sons—because I don't like secrets in the family. Meanwhile, one of my sons is having an affair with a married woman who's fucking one of our neighbors, and the other is raising secret keeping to a high art." He glared at Alexander.

"You knew? About Ford and Sallie?" I asked. Griffin's cell phone buzzed, and without responding, he walked into the kitchen to take the call.

"He knows everything," Alexander said, sounding miserable. "The security guards spy for him. Markham is always looking around. Plus, the men talk at the Last Monday Club. Edward probably bragged about it now that Dan stopped going. I don't know why Ford wants to join that stupid club so much."

"You don't want to join?" I asked, wondering how he would know whether Dan Benson went or not.

Alexander shook his head. "I wouldn't belong to a club that doesn't take women. I wouldn't do that to Emily. We don't want a life like her parents'. Or yours and Dad's." He gave me an apologetic look. "I'm sorry."

"I try not to let you see it," I said.

"Yeah, well, I do see it." He took a deep breath. "Ford is so fucked up. He won't let anyone be on his side—it's like he feels he doesn't deserve it. And now, all I can think of is him seeing that little kid, Sallie's son—" Alexander shook his head hard as if to dislodge the image. "Hurting a little boy just like we were hurt." He lowered his voice. "My father sucks. It's his fault Ford's the way he is."

Griffin came back into the hall. "That was Wade. Ford's been sleeping it off over there, but he's awake now."

It didn't surprise me that Ford would go to the Lockwoods' house. Wade and Leonora were practically grandparents to the boys.

"He could have called," Alexander said.

"Well, we know where he is," Griffin said. "Let him vent to Wade, as long as he doesn't go out of the inner circle. We have to know who to trust in this world. Sallie Benson and her husband are not among them. I'll deal with this later."

Griffin headed back into the kitchen, and Alexander rushed to his car, keys out.

"Where are you going?" I called to Alexander.

"To get Ford," he said. "Dad sounds calm, but he's not. He's going to head to the Lockwoods' in two minutes, I guarantee, and yank Ford out of bed, and who knows what he'll do. I don't want that to happen. Will you stall him, Claire?"

"No," I said.

"What?" Alexander asked.

"Ford brought this on himself, Alexander," I said. "Your brother needs rehab, some kind of intervention, before he hurts someone—or himself. He could have killed someone, driving drunk."

"Please, Claire," Alexander said. "Don't turn on him—you've always been good to us. He's going to need it even more now."

Just then the garage door began to open, and I heard Griffin's car start up. Alexander was so agitated that he fumbled the car keys, dropped them, practically fell as he got into his car.

Alexander started the Porsche, gunned it, and sped through the turnaround. As he entered the Catamount Road tunnel of trees, dark in morning shadow, I saw something dark yellow flash in front of his car. Alexander braked, skidded sideways, and fighting the wheel, crashed into the stone wall.

Griffin and I tore across the driveway. The car's front end had crumpled like an accordion. The airbag had deployed, and Alexander was slumped into it. Griffin yanked at Alexander's door, but it was out of whack from the impact and wouldn't open. We ran to the passenger side—same thing. Griffin grabbed a rock from the old wall and smashed the car window. He reached in and, working the inside handle as I pulled from outside, we got the door open.

Alexander tried to wriggle free of the airbag as Griffin leaned in.

"Jesus," Griffin said.

"I'm sorry, Dad," Alexander said.

"Are you okay?" I asked over Griffin's shoulder.

Alexander didn't answer me—he was staring at his father. "Something ran in front of the car—an animal. A big cat, I think. I didn't want to hit it."

"You swerved to avoid a *cat*?" Griffin asked.

"Yes," Alexander said. His voice broke, and he tried to struggle free of the airbag.

"You crashed a hundred-thousand-dollar car for *a cat*?" Griffin asked. "Next time, Alexander, hit the goddamned animal." He shook his head at me—disgust at Alexander? At me? I heard voices coming from down the road—Wade and Ford were walking toward our house. Griffin stalked over.

Alexander climbed across the front seats; I helped him get out, and he leaned unsteadily against the car.

"Are you okay?" I asked again.

"My chest hurts," he said. "The airbag really got me."

"I'm going to call 911," I said.

"No," he said quickly, grabbing my wrist as I pulled my phone from my pocket. "It's nothing, seriously."

"Alexander, sit down. You're in shock," I said.

But he wouldn't sit. "It's the car that's wrecked, not me." He glanced over at Griffin, who was talking to Wade, as if he thought his father wouldn't approve of an ambulance. Wade had his arm around Ford's shoulders, one hand on Griffin's shoulder. I could see our neighbor was defusing the situation, and I turned back to Alexander.

"I would have done the same thing," I said. "I wouldn't have wanted to hit the animal either."

He didn't reply but sank to sit on the ground, as if standing took too much effort.

I called 911, then sat down beside Alexander to wait for help to arrive. I thought of the big cat Alexander had swerved to avoid and the myth of mountain lions—somewhere in the woods between Catamount Bluff and Hubbard's Point, amber-eyed shadows more sensed than seen.

28

SALLIE

When Sallie got home, Dan's car was in the driveway—he had left work early. She entered the house, found him sitting in the living room. Not reading, not watching TV, just sitting there. Maggie was curled up at his feet, but she bounded to the door to greet Sallie. Sallie scooped her up and held her.

"I want to ask you where you were," he said, "but I don't want to hear the answer. Maybe you were with Edward. Maybe you were with Ford. What I'm most afraid of is that you'll tell me you were with a client."

"I wasn't with anyone," she said. "I went for a drive."

"That's a good excuse too," he said. "Right up there with how you'd always say you were working. When really you were with one of them. Now I want to know, and you'll tell me the truth for once. Where did you take the drive?"

She took a deep breath. "To the Chases' house."

"Griffin Chase?"

"Yes. I wanted to let Ford know what he'd done—how wrong it was to come here."

"Did you see him?"

"No, he wasn't there. Just his brother and parents. I just wanted to set him straight and ask him . . ." She trailed off, regrouped. "Maybe it was a mistake to go at all."

"Yes, it was a mistake for you to go there. You have no idea who Griffin Chase really is." He closed his mouth tight; Sallie thought he looked scared.

"Dan, I'm so sorry," she said.

"One thing we're not going to do is sit here while you apologize. There's no point in that."

"Okay," she said. She stared across the room at Dan, sitting in one of the armchairs flanking the fireplace. His expression was nearly blank, as if he were feeling no emotion at all. "But I have a question for you too," she said. "Who is Ellen Fielding?"

"What's the difference? She has nothing to do with us," he said.

"Maybe she does! Ford mentioned her when he was here. And another girl who drowned."

"A case of Griffin's," he said.

"No," Sallie said. "He made it sound like something long ago—spring break. Was he talking about you? College?"

"Look, don't try to change the subject—you had an affair."

"And you haven't been honest with me! Don't you think that might be part of what's wrong between us?"

"Here's what's going to happen," he said, ignoring her question. "I'm going to get the boat ready for tomorrow. Buy the provisions, get them aboard. You're going to pack for the weekend. Everything the kids will need for three days."

"I was planning to do that anyway," she said. "But I'm not going. I'm sure that will be a relief to you."

"Yes, it would," he said. "It one hundred percent would be a gigantic relief to me. But you *are* going, Sallie. For the kids' sake. Did you see their faces last night? Did you see how destroyed they were?"

"Yes," she said, her eyes filling. She held Maggie even closer. "And I'm so sorry. I can't even begin to tell you how bad I feel."

"That's nice," he said. "But you saying 'sorry' and feeling bad won't help them. That's why we're going on vacation as planned. They're going to see Mommy and Daddy together, being happy and having fun. They've been looking forward to this, and we're not going to take it away from them."

Sallie buried her face in Maggie's fur. She didn't love Dan, but he was a good father; she knew he'd do anything for their children.

"I can't," she said, looking up.

"You will, though. Feel whatever you feel—stay in bed all day today—I don't care. As long as you're up and waiting for the school bus. And as long as we all have dinner together. And tomorrow we will leave for Block Island."

Maggie barked. She wanted to go out, so Sallie put her down and followed her into the kitchen. She opened the back door, and Maggie ran into the yard. Sallie looked around at the flower beds, the swing set, the garden shed—signs of a happy suburban family.

There was no point in arguing with Dan. She'd do everything he asked. The idea of being confined on the *Sallie B* was almost unbearable. She couldn't stand the idea of being so close to Dan—having him look at her with this blank stare.

Or wondering about Ellen Fielding, whoever she was.

Or being with herself.

Or being at all.

29

CLAIRE

Wade and Leonora Lockwood's kindness and good humor got us through those tense moments of Griffin confronting Ford, Alexander wrecking the car, and the aftermath. The ambulance arrived along with a cluster of police cars and volunteer firefighters. Leonora came hurrying over to see what was happening.

I understood why Alexander had resisted my calling 911; once the call went out for an emergency at Griffin Chase's house, all emergency personnel would mobilize. Griffin was so private about family problems that he wouldn't want anyone to see that one of his sons had crashed his car, that the other one was halfway between smashed and hungover.

Griffin started to climb into Ben Markham's car to follow the ambulance to Easterly Hospital. Wade caught him by the arm. "Want company?" he asked.

"I'm fine, Wade," Griffin said.

"After your son crashes a car? I doubt it. I'm coming with you," Wade said. He waved to Leonora, then got into the back seat of the squad car. The EMT vehicles pulled away, and a tow truck hauled off the totaled red Porsche.

Ford, Leonora, and I stood in the turnaround.

"I don't get how Alexander managed to drive into the wall," Ford said.

"He was worried about you," I said. "He was going to the Lockwoods' house to get you."

"Well, obviously I walked home myself," Ford said, glaring at me.

"Ford," Leonora said. "None of that sarcasm, especially to Claire. You need to sober up. Black coffee, two Excedrin, a run along the beach, an ice-cold swim, and a hot shower. Trust me, I know. I've got sixty years of experience helping my husband and his band of merry drinking buddies."

Ford nodded, and Leonora gave him a big hug. Ford disappeared into the house.

"Thanks, Leonora," I said.

"Of course, sweetheart. Actually, coffee sounds good. May I invite myself in for some?" she asked, giving me a big smile. She was tall and just slightly stooped, with bright-blue eyes and pure-white hair pinned up in a French twist. She wore her customary pearls and a bright-yellow-and-pink caftan. In her seventies, she was still stunning.

"I'd love it," I said.

We went into the kitchen, and she leaned against the counter while I measured coffee into the percolator. I knew from years of neighborhood brunches and meetings that Leonora liked cream and sugar. When it was ready, I poured two cups, and Leonora poured a third. She picked up one and started for the back stairs.

"Is that for Ford?" I asked. "Leonora, he can get it himself."

"Dear, let me take it to him, so we can talk alone. I'll be right down."

I heard her footsteps on the floorboards overhead, then muffled voices, and then she returned to the kitchen. She walked in chuckling.

"I shouldn't laugh," she said. "But he is green around the gills. I haven't seen that kind of hangover in quite some time. Frankly, he reminds me of his father. Griffin had a few tough mornings along the way."

"He almost never drinks now," I said.

"Because of Margot," Leonora said. "Griffin saw what booze did to her, and he wanted to be a good influence on the boys. I think he's succeeded with Alexander. Ford's going to need help. Years ago, Wade suggested military school, but he's far too old for that now. And he's too spoiled to join the navy, so I guess it'll have to be a shrink."

"Yes," I said, but I must have sounded doubtful.

"You're worried that Griffin won't go for it? I can see that. His position makes him vulnerable—he's afraid people will talk. Especially with the election coming up."

I didn't reply.

"Griffin talks to Wade," Leonora said. "Not as much as to you, I'm sure. But we're all family." She sipped her coffee, watching me over the rim of the cup. "I'm not sure you knew what you were signing on for, my girl."

"'Signing on for'?"

"The Catamount Bluff madhouse. Too much money has done a real job out here. Wade was born into it, and the only way he escaped being spoiled rotten was by shaping up in the navy. When I first married him, I looked around and saw everyone having cocktails at noon, sneaking in and out of beds all around town. I wanted to go straight home to Maine—the lovely, innocent little lobster village where I grew up."

"But you stayed," I said.

"Yes," she said. "I adore my husband. And I've grown to love it here. When it comes to Catamount Bluff, home is home. Surely you feel it, too, at this point. And I'm sure you know how much we love you. And *trust* you."

"Thank you, Leonora."

"You know, it was Wade who first suggested Griffin run for office. That's how much he believes in him."

195

I didn't reply and tried to keep my expression neutral. I didn't want her to guess what I was thinking about Griffin running for office.

"We know he'll make a marvelous governor," she said. "Dear, may I have more coffee?"

Leonora was so warm; she and Wade had embraced me as one of their own. I stood up to get the coffee pot, to refill our cups. She obviously didn't know the truth about Griffin, would never believe what he was really like.

"A lot of drama here today," she said, holding up her cup while I poured. "Too much."

"It was," I agreed.

"I wish to God that Sallie Benson had never swept into our lives, with all her white paint and white tiles and enchanted white moon gardens. Wrecking a good family."

"You know about Sallie and Edward?"

"Yes, dear. Word gets around. And Ford didn't help, dashing about like an old gossip. But he's in love with her, silly though it may be— and there's nothing like a Chase man in love. Believe me, I saw it with Griffin, with you."

"When we got married?"

"No, before. The first time. When you were just out of college. That summer you got together, I told Wade that Griffin was over-the-moon in love with you. I'm just sorry it didn't last, that it took so long for you to get back together. Margot was a mess." She sipped her coffee, added another teaspoon of sugar. "Of course, it didn't help that Victoria didn't like her."

"Griffin's mother?"

"Yes. She was impossible to please. I bet she would have loved you—being an artist, so talented. So good to Griffin. Between you and me, I think Victoria wanted the woman in Griffin's life to make up for what she couldn't do. I hate to speak ill of the dead, especially in her own kitchen, but she was a cold fish."

"That must have been hard on Griffin."

"It certainly was. She was a woman who never should have had a child. She had her own interests, and she loved her husband, but she neglected Griffin. So did his father. Wade says we were better parents to him than they were. And I'm talking about before his parents died. They were simply not present."

"He was lucky to have you," I said.

"We felt that way about him. No children of our own, so Griffin was it. Wade would make him get up at dawn, go surf casting with him off the beach. They would catch blues and stripers—they would clean them, and I'd cook them. Griffin loved it. He wanted to go after bigger game, so when he was a college senior, we gave him an early graduation present. Wade took him deep-sea fishing."

It warmed my heart to think of Wade giving Griffin something so important—not just a fishing trip but the chance to spend time with a mentor who really cared. Something he had obviously lacked at home.

"He must have loved it," I said, trying to remember Griffin going— it must have been earlier that summer, before he and I got together, and he had never mentioned a trip with the Lockwoods to me.

"Yes, he did," Leonora said. "Wade chartered a sixty-foot sportfishing yacht, and springtime in that latitude that time of year was just perfect. There were still sailfish around, with blue marlin just showing up. Wade and Griffin caught a couple of each, along with bluefin tuna and bonitos."

"Sounds amazing," I said.

"It was, for all of us. I stayed ashore at the resort along with dear friends—my tennis partner, Jenny, and her stepson, Danny, and Griffin's little friend. We'd go to the beach and play tennis all day while Wade and Griffin were out on the boat."

"'Little friend'?" I asked.

"It was very much about Wade and Griffin," Leonora said, as if I hadn't spoken. "He felt very strongly that Griffin needed his full attention—to get him on track for life. Of course, we felt bad that Danny didn't get to go fishing with the men, but we tried to make it up to him. We rented him a dirt bike. He took up windsurfing, had lots of adventures."

"That sounds like a good compromise," I said.

"I think so. At night we'd all have dinner together. The kids would stay out late dancing, and Wade, Jenny, and I would stay in playing backgammon. Nothing like treating three teenagers to a lovely spring break—their last before having to enter the real world and get jobs—and having loads of fun ourselves."

"Spring break?" I asked.

"Yes, right before graduation," Leonora said.

"Where did you take them for spring break, Leonora? Where was the resort and the fishing?" I asked, the back of my neck prickling.

"Mexico. The Caribbean. Wade chartered the boat out of Puerto Juárez."

"Not Cancún?" I asked, feeling relieved.

"Well, just north of there. My husband knows fishing, and he wasn't going to charter through the resort for top dollar. He went to the ferry dock and paid cash."

"So you stayed in Puerto Juárez?" I asked.

"Oh, God no," she said. "It was very, shall we say, 'rustic' back then. We stayed in Cancún."

"Who was Griffin's 'little friend'?" I asked. "The one you mentioned a minute ago?"

"Ellen," she said. "His college girlfriend."

I couldn't move or even breathe.

"That poor girl who died," Leonora said. "You know as well as I—terrible for you, finding her body like that. It nearly destroyed Griffin, dear. He took her death so hard, and I think that is the reason he wasn't ready to settle down with you back then. It tore him up."

"I didn't know he went to Cancún," I said, barely hearing anything she had said after that. "I only knew that Ellen did."

"Dear, it's better to leave some things in the past."

"Did anything bad happen down there, in Mexico?" I asked, trying to keep my voice from shaking. "Everyone said Ellen got depressed after she got back."

She looked away. "We were all rattled that last day at the resort."

"Why?" I asked.

"A girl drowned," she said. "She worked at the hotel—a chambermaid, I think. An American girl, only about twenty years old. We'd all seen her around; she was very friendly. Ellen took it hard—we all did."

My hands were shaking; I had to clasp them under the table so Leonora wouldn't see.

"How did she drown?" I asked.

"I don't know, darling. She went swimming after dark. A riptide, I suppose," Leonora said. "Now, listen to me."

"What is it, Leonora?" I asked.

"These are family secrets," she said. "Griffin told Wade that he has never discussed them with you. Is that true?"

"Yes," I said.

"But did you learn about Cancún from someone else?" she asked.

"Only that Ellen went," I said. "Not Griffin. I'm very surprised to hear it now."

"Griffin has told us that you've been saying things about Ellen's death. That it might not have been an accident."

"It might not have been," I said.

"Two things," she said. "Very important. First, you must stop saying that. It hurts Griffin. Second, do you realize what trouble you could be stirring up for him politically? Wade is very concerned that you might talk about it to outsiders."

"Leonora, why wasn't Ellen's death investigated?" I asked, remembering how Griffin told me he'd been questioned by Police Commissioner Morgan, a friend of the Lockwoods', with Wade present.

"Because we protect our own," she said. She grabbed my hand. At first it felt like a loving gesture, but then she began squeezing harder, until it hurt. I looked into her eyes and saw pure ice. "We are a family, whether related by blood or not. Every family has its secrets. And I expect you to keep ours. Your husband is going to be governor."

I tried to yank my hand away, but she squeezed it tighter.

"Many people have invested in Griffin. He is going to win."

"Leonora, you're hurting me . . ."

She continued, ignoring me. "There is too much at stake for you to be throwing ridiculous accusations about. You have no idea—this movement to elect your husband is so much bigger than you. The boys are on board one hundred percent. We are going to protect Griffin from anyone who threatens this campaign. I need you to understand that."

Tires crunched on the driveway, and I heard the garage door creaking up. Leonora heard it too and smiled. She dropped my hand.

"The boys are back home," she said. Her face was suddenly pleasant again, her tone warm, as if those poisonous words had not just fallen from her mouth.

And the door between the kitchen and garage opened, and Griffin, Wade, and Alexander walked in. I quietly left the room and walked into the hall. I stared down at *Fingerbone*—at everything I had gathered from the tidal pool where the tide had taken Ellen, at the skeletal hand I had created from bare twigs. Leonora's words rang in my ears; the bones in my hand hurt from her grip. I hadn't realized how badly I was shaking.

Leonora's attempt to warn me off had the opposite effect. I wanted to shove the truth of what I planned to do into her face, all of theirs. I lifted the shadow box and started back toward the kitchen.

I heard Wade telling Leonora that the EMTs had listened to Alexander's heart and lungs, and by the time they got to the emergency room, Alexander decided he was completely fine and refused to go inside.

"He decided to just come home," Griffin said. "So he got into Ben's squad car, and here we are."

"You Chase men are too tough," Leonora said. "Alexander, you should have gotten checked out and had X-rays."

"I didn't want to go in the first place," Alexander said. "Claire's the one who called."

"You're lucky to have such a caring stepmother," Wade said.

"He is indeed," Leonora said. "Right, Griffin?"

"Absolutely," Griffin said.

That was my cue. I entered the kitchen and placed my shadow box down on the white marble counter.

"What's that?" Wade asked.

"It's a piece I'm about to deliver to the gallery for my show," I said. "It's dedicated to you, Griffin. Come look, everyone."

They all crossed the room and stared down into the tidal pool I had created. I saw all four of them—Griffin, Alexander, Leonora, and Wade—take in the sight of mussel and crustacean shells. Could Griffin hear the sound of crabs tearing at dead flesh? He stared into the world I had created, at the hand, at the Roman coin I had bought on eBay.

"What an honor to have your wife dedicate a work of art to you!" Wade said. "This is marvelous! Just fantastic."

"Can't you see what it is?" Leonora asked through gritted teeth. "I just told her to keep her ideas to herself and now this. Garbage."

Griffin didn't reply. I watched his face twist.

"It's called *Fingerbone*," I said to my husband. "Can you guess why?"

I knew, even before he lifted his head to look at me, that his green eyes had turned black.

And they had.

SIX DAYS
LATER

30

CONOR

The knife was found by two sixth-grade girls walking down Main Street in Black Hall.

Once Conor got to the scene, he learned that after school lots of kids went to the Starfish Sweet Shop. Janie Farrow and Alison Roberts had bought a bag of strawberry and lime jellybeans to share and were sitting on the curb throwing them up in the air and popping them into their mouths.

One dropped and rolled on the pavement and into a storm drain. The girls had crouched down to look inside. It was dark in there, with a small concrete shelf, then a drop-off into who-knew-where. On the shelf were Alison's green jellybean, some candy wrappers, dry leaves, a weird buoy-looking thing with a key dangling from a chain, and a knife.

Janie stuck her arm inside the opening and pulled the knife out of the drain. She wasn't sure why; she just thought it looked cool. At first Alison thought Janie had cut herself because there was blood on the blade.

Other kids gathered to look at it; then Nancy Fairchild, the owner of the Starfish, came outside to see what was going on. She told the kids to step back and not touch it again, and she called the town police, who notified Conor.

"Well, we might have some physical evidence," Ben Markham said when Conor arrived and led him to the sidewalk in front of the candy store. One look at the Sabatier carving knife and Conor knew it was part of his case.

"Could be from the set on the Chases' kitchen counter," Conor said.

"I figured," Markham said. "Last Friday, walking through the house, you pointed out the knife block, the empty space."

Conor took photos of the knife. He snapped shots of the storm drain. When the techs arrived, they would lift the grate and get better photographs and video, but he wanted some pictures on his phone. He wanted them from this angle, the way the knife had looked when the girls made their discovery.

"But even if it did come from the Chases' house, any intruder could have gotten hold of it," Markham said. "The door between the garage and kitchen is never locked. Say someone was waiting for Claire to open the garage door, overpowered her—he could have easily just walked into the kitchen, grabbed this, and finished attacking her."

"How do you know that door is never locked?" Conor asked.

"I've been moonlighting at the Bluff for twenty years now," Markham said. "I've got keys and alarm codes to all four houses—I check the properties when the families go on vacation. And in that amount of time, you get to know people. Griffin is the best they come. The boys are a little spoiled, but they wouldn't hurt a soul."

Conor didn't reply. Markham was close to Griffin Chase, and he certainly seemed adamant about the perpetrator not being a member of the family. Then he saw Chase's state-issued Chevy Malibu pull up to the curb, and he glared at Markham.

"Seriously? You called him?" Conor asked.

"Out of courtesy," Markham said. "He deserves to know—his wife is still missing."

Griffin got out of the car in his perfectly pressed dark suit and starched white shirt, his red tie. His face looked haggard, as if he had aged five years in these last six days.

"Jesus Christ," he said, staring down at the knife.

Conor watched him. He thought of Claire's question, whether it was possible for a person's green eyes to turn black. Chase's eyes were green.

The forensic truck arrived, and techs began taking photographs, creating a map of the scene. They bagged the knife to send to the lab for fingerprints and DNA testing. The techs printed the drain's grill, then removed it to examine what else was down below.

Conor watched as they photographed, removed, and bagged leaves, pebbles, and chocolate bar wrappers and the floatable key holder made of white foam, key dangling from the chain.

The tech hooked the chain, held it up for Conor to see. He spun the foam buoy around; the letters *SB* had been written in black marker. *Sallie B*?

Conor looked up and down Main Street. He saw green recycling cans at the curb. If someone had dropped a weapon and the key chain down the drain, he could have disposed of additional evidence in other places. He might have split up incriminating items to lessen the chances of getting caught. Garbage collection usually took place on Mondays, recycling on Thursdays. With the holiday, the pickups were delayed by a day.

He was too late to check garbage cans, but the recycling truck had not yet come by. Because the bins were in the street, he knew he was safe to search without a warrant—once trash was out for collection at the curb, it was considered abandoned and thus fair game for the police.

He snapped on a pair of latex gloves and walked down the street opening the hinged lid of each green barrel. A third of the way down the street was the Woodward-Lathrop Gallery. He opened their recycling can. It was full to the top with wine bottles and plastic glasses— probably from Claire's opening last Friday, but it stank like rotting garbage—odd for recycling.

Shoved down beneath the glass and plastic was a heavy black trash bag, lumpy with whatever it contained. On the outside was a rust-colored streak that might have been dried blood.

Conor took photos of the can and its contents, then turned toward the candy store, wanting to get the attention of someone from the forensics team. Griffin Chase was staring at him and started walking over. This was predictable. Conor was going to slam Markham for calling Chase.

"What have you got there?" Chase asked.

"Sir, I'm going to have to ask you to let us do our work."

"You're investigating my wife's disappearance, and it's going to be my case. That's her gallery," he said, pointing at the yellow Victorian house. "I want to see what you've found."

Here comes the shitshow, Conor thought. He was about to cause himself as much grief as he'd ever had in his career. "As of now, this is a crime scene," Conor said. "It's an open investigation that involves your family."

"How fucking dare you?" Chase said, brushing against Conor—but hard, as if he wanted to knock him down.

Conor held him firmly by the shoulders, keeping him away from the recycling bin.

"Mr. Chase," Conor said. "You honestly do not want to interfere with my investigation."

"You'd arrest me?" Chase asked.

"Yes," Conor said.

"I'm going to call Steve Langworthy, then Jim Magnus," Chase said, referring to the state police chief and the chief state's attorney. "And they'll talk to the governor. If this is the way you want to play it, you can deal with the consequences."

"Understood," Conor said. They had a twenty-second stare-down; then Chase turned and walked away with his minion Markham a step behind.

The moment had been invaluable. Chase had shown his capacity for rage. He nodded for Duncan Jones, a local police officer, to establish a perimeter around the site.

This bag could contain leftover cheese and smoked salmon from Friday's opening, but from the blood on the bag, he suspected something a lot worse—evidence connected with Claire's disappearance.

Conor thought of the knife. He ran through his interviews with Ford and Alexander Chase. Alexander had been obsequious, defending and protecting his brother. Ford's hostility had been glaring and so had Dan Benson's. Motive was possible in both cases, but in spite of what Markham had said about ease of access to the Chases' kitchen, would Benson really have had the opportunity—or knowledge—to enter the kitchen and steal a knife?

If someone from outside the family had wanted to attack Claire, they would have come prepared or known that weapons would be available at the house. Benson had said he stayed away from Sallie's business life, but could it be possible he'd accompanied her to the Catamount Bluff houses while she was working on them?

When Conor glanced back at Chase, he saw him deep in conversation with Markham, and again he pondered their relationship. He didn't like not knowing whether Markham was a good cop or too loyal to Chase to be trusted in the investigation.

Conor wanted to tear open the bag, but they needed to dust it first as well as inventory the rest of the garbage can's contents. He would continue searching other recycling bins along the street. He would tell Markham to call the town and have them stop today's collection. Then he'd get his guys to start checking footage from security cameras up and down Main Street.

"Hey, Detective," Jones called, pointing into the can.

Conor looked inside. Wedged beneath where the bottles, glasses, and black trash bag had been was one of Claire's shadow boxes. Conor had seen it at last Friday's opening. And he had seen Griffin Chase walk out of the gallery with it under his arm: *Fingerbone.*

31

TOM

Blue Marine LLC had salvaged the wreck of the *Sallie B*—the parts of the hull that hadn't been destroyed by fire—and towed it to the coast guard pier in Easterly. Tom Reid stood silently staring at what remained of the *Sallie B.*

Conor had sent him a photograph of a floating foam key chain marked *SB*. It had been found with items connected to Conor's case, and Tom needed to know how it intersected with his.

Tom's fellow coast guard investigator, Matthew Hendricks, had been focused on the *Sallie B*'s fuel system. Tom found him in his office at the head of the dock. A diagram of the factory specifications of a brand-new Loring 42 and a map of the interior of the wreck as she was now were tacked to a board behind his desk.

"What have you found?" Tom asked.

"Gas leaked into the bilge," Matt said. "The minute they started the engine, the boat became a ticking time bomb. Either the spark came from the engine or someone turned on the stove. And the boat blew."

"How did the engine look in general?" Tom asked.

"It's clear the owner kept the boat well maintained—the marina faxed over the service records. The engine was serviced a week before departure to get ready for the trip. Pistons and valves are all in good condition. I'm looking at the mechanic's checklist, and I don't see the fuel feed."

"Running time from their slip to the explosion site was about thirty minutes," Tom said. "Wouldn't the boat have exploded within a shorter time period?"

"Unclear," Matthew said. He opened a file on his computer, turned the screen so Tom could view the images.

"This is the starboard bypass fuel feed. And here's the port," Matthew said, and Tom examined a clear photo. "When Benson turned the key, gas flowed through the manifold to the port engine. But see this gap here? The starboard feed was left open—the line is disconnected from the carburetor."

"And fuel dripped into the bilge," Tom said.

"Right. From that point on, the voyage was doomed."

"One spark," Tom said.

"That's all it took."

"So if the engine was in good condition, the boat seaworthy, how did this happen?"

"That's up for grabs," Matthew said.

"Could it be sabotage?" Tom asked.

"Possibly, but it could also be an accident. Since the boat was just serviced, it's possible the mechanic forgot to reconnect the line."

"That would be a pretty significant mistake," Tom said. "West Wind is a good marina. I can't see any of their mechanics being that careless."

"It happens," Matt said.

Tom knew he was right. Not paying attention was one of the most common causes of boating tragedies. But according to Conor, there had been trouble in the Benson marriage.

"When Gauthier first questioned Benson, she said he was barely conscious, slurring his words, but he told her 'they got her.' My brother, Conor, is a detective with the Major Crime Squad, and he wonders if he'd actually said 'I got her.'"

"And what? He blew up his boat and risked the kids just to kill his wife?"

"That would be crazy," Tom said. "But some people are."

"So your brother's working this case? I thought it was Detective Miano."

"They work together," Tom said. "Conor's on another case that might overlap with ours."

"Which one?"

"Missing woman. Claire Beaudry Chase. She knew Sallie, and Conor thinks it's a pretty big coincidence, both of them harmed on the same day."

"That is pretty weird," Matt said. "Glad the cops are taking the human side. I've got the technical part. I'm going to head over to West Wind and talk to Eli Dean and his yard guys, find out if they screwed up. I'm leaning in the direction of it being an accident. If the boatyard is responsible, Benson will have a nice lawsuit on his hands."

"Let me know," Tom said. He thanked Matt, asked him to keep him in the loop. He got into his car and headed toward Shoreline General. When he got to the nursing station on Gwen's floor, he was glad to see that Mariana Russo was on duty.

"How is she?" Tom asked.

"She's making progress," Mariana said. "But then she has setbacks."

"Is she talking?" he asked.

"Very little," she said. "The first she spoke was when you brought her dog to see her. Since then, a few words here and there. Mostly 'yes,' 'no,' simple replies when we ask her if she's hungry, sleepy, things like that. Nothing to do with the accident."

"What about the setback?" Tom asked.

"Seeing her father," Mariana said. "Gwen became almost hysterical the last time he visited, almost as bad as before. And she didn't speak for hours afterward."

The nurse led him down the hall to the sunroom, where they found Gwen sitting in a chair, intently writing in a journal.

"Hello, Gwen," he said.

At the sound of his voice, she looked up and smiled. The thought that crossed Tom's mind was that she looked hopeful.

"I wanted to visit you," he said. "To see how you're doing and tell you Maggie misses you. She's having lots of adventures at our house— we take her down to the beach, and for such a small dog, she's a real champ at jumping driftwood logs."

"She likes to swim," Gwen said in an almost inaudible voice.

"She does? Well, now that I know that, we'll take her swimming," Tom said. He gestured at the chair beside her. "Is it okay if I sit down?" She nodded.

"I thought you might like to see some pictures of her," Tom said. He pulled out his phone, scrolled through to a series he had taken of Maggie: out in the garden with Jackie, playing ball, running on the beach, curled up on an armchair in the living room. "She's really cute, and we're making her at home, but I can tell she can't wait to see you."

"How?" Gwen asked.

"It's just a look dogs get. Same as people. You know how dogs smile? Their tongues hang out, and their eyes look extra-extra-bright? Well, Maggie does smile, but her eyes are only extra-bright, not extra-extra. But they will be when you get home and you can be together."

"Together," Gwen said. "Me and Maggie and Charlie."

Tom's heart stopped. Had she still not been told about her brother? He stared at her, at her smile getting wider and wider, and he couldn't speak.

"You'll be with your dad," he said.

"And Maggie and Charlie," she said. "And Aunt Lydia sometimes."

"Gwen," he began. It wasn't his place to tell her about the search, that they hadn't found him, that Charlie wouldn't be going home.

"You'll rescue him," Gwen said. "Just like you rescued me."

"Gwen, I wish I could, more than anything," he said.

"You will," she said. "He's alive."

Okay, Tom thought. It was a fantasy, and she needed it to keep getting better. It was a survival mechanism. Her psyche was playing a trick to cajole her into recovery.

"You don't believe me?" she asked.

"I didn't say that," Tom said.

"The boat picked him up."

"What boat?"

"A merman was driving it. Like a mermaid but a man. Part fish, with black scales. He took Charlie to a sea castle, to be safe with King Neptune and the Sea Queen."

"When did the merman take him?" Tom asked, playing along with the imaginary scenario she had created.

"In the dark of the night and the dawn of the day," she said. She pushed her journal toward Tom. "See? I drew it. My mom always said to draw things you never want to forget."

Tom studied the open book. There were eight panels of intricate and surprisingly sophisticated drawings laid out like a comic book.

"You're talented," he said.

"My mom taught me. She was a designer, and she liked to draw."

Tom examined the panels. They depicted a cabin cruiser like the *Sallie B* at the dock, a family of four having a meal down below—a dog like Maggie sitting under the table. Then panels of the boat on fire, a girl in the yellow raft, a small boat with two people in it, a boy floundering in the water, and the boy in the stern of a motorboat, waving at the yellow raft. The final frame showed an opulent castle with the boy standing on a balcony and a blackbird perched on the peak of the castle's turret.

"That's Charlie," Gwen said, pointing at the boy. "I wish the merman took me to the sea castle too."

"Why do you say it's a sea castle?" Tom asked.

"Because I saw some pictures of it," she said dreamily. "There were big stone bird statues at the gate and on the roof."

"Okay," Tom said, realizing how fragile she must be to have created such an elaborate rescue scenario for Charlie.

"I called for Charlie to swim to me, so I could get him back in," Gwen said. "He and I were in the little yellow boat together when the explosion came. All of a sudden—fire everywhere and wind began to blow. It blew our yellow raft off the deck—we flew like a plane and landed in the water. We both fell overboard, but I was holding on to the yellow boat. Charlie was farther away."

"You saw him in the water?" Tom asked.

"Oh yes."

Tom tried to find the words to ask if he had been burned or otherwise injured, but Gwen continued.

"He was trying to swim to me, but the raft was drifting, moving over the waves out to sea." Her chin wobbled. "The water was moving so fast. I kept trying to get into the raft, so I could paddle back to him."

"I'm sure you tried hard," Tom said.

"Yes," she said. "I was kicking hard. My arms were tired. That's when I saw Charlie get rescued. The merman was calling my name. He was looking for me, but he couldn't see me because I was in the water. I yelled to him, but he didn't hear. And when I got back onto the raft, I looked for Charlie again. He was in that boat, and it was driving away."

"What boat?" Tom asked.

"The blackbird boat."

"Why do you call it that?" he asked.

"Because that's what it is."

Tom took a deep breath. Her story was getting wilder. Did she need to invent a boat that could fly?

"It's the one that was following us," she said.

"When was it following you?" he asked.

"The whole way from the marina," she said.

"Did anyone else see it?" Tom asked.

"Just Charlie."

Tom was silent for a moment. She seemed to really believe what she was saying.

"Why did you say a merman was driving the boat?" he asked.

"Don't you know what a merman is?" she asked, sounding surprised. "Like a mermaid, only a man. He has magic. He saves people that fall into the sea. He follows boats that might be in trouble." She looked straight at Tom. "Like ours was. He has powers that told him we would need him. Only a magical merman would know it."

"I see," Tom said, and now he was sure: she was escaping into a fantasy world to avoid knowing her brother had drowned, inventing mermen and a flying blackbird boat.

"I want Charlie to come home," she said, two big tears running down her cheeks. "Even if he's happy in the sea castle, he would miss me as much as I miss him. I want my brother. I want my brother. I want him home." She lowered her head and began to weep.

As the sound of her sobs got louder, Tom stepped to the door, called down the hall for Mariana. She and another nurse came running.

"Gwen," he said, taking her hand. "Get well, okay? Maggie needs you."

"And Charlie," she said, sobbing. "He needs me too. Now it's time for you to find Charlie in the castle, like you found me in the raft, and bring him home. He needs to come home."

Tom exchanged a glance with Mariana, who nodded to him—she had heard what Gwen was saying, and he was sure she'd tell the doctor. He gazed at Gwen—so slight and seemingly frail but with the strength to survive overnight on a raft in the cold ocean—and wondered if she would ever truly come back from the experience, whether the trauma would lock her in a world of unreality forever.

It was hard for him to leave her, but he knew she was in good hands. He walked out of the hospital, took deep breaths of fresh air, prayed the best he could for Gwen to be okay, for her to survive this the way she had survived the boat explosion and that long night alone at sea.

32

CLAIRE

My father used to say I could do anything. I could run as fast as the boys at Hubbard's Point, hit a baseball farther, swim out to the big rock without even breathing hard. My parents never tried to urge me into any field of study; when other working-class parents like mine wanted their kids to get practical jobs with regular hours, steady income, and health insurance, my parents wanted me to follow my dreams. That was all they ever asked of me.

I am doing it right now—following my dreams: of life, safety, and escape. It all began with a reverie of truth, that once I learned what happened twenty-five years ago, I knew I couldn't keep my husband's secret anymore.

On the seventh night, I left the cabin. I still felt weak, and I knew I needed to get more food than I'd been able to forage. The moon was out, which made it both easier to find my way and treacherous in terms of who might see me. A warm wind blew up from the cove, rustling the branches overhead.

My sanctuary was about midway between Hubbard's Point and Catamount Bluff, and my heart was pulling me home to the Point—I wanted to see Jackie, have her shelter me. But I wasn't at all sure that I could trust the men in her family, Tom and Conor. Instead, I went the opposite way, toward the Bluff. Griffin would never expect it.

I cut through the woods, along a narrow track. The leaves had popped in the last few days, and the moon cast dappled light on the ground. I heard a distant cry—the big cat? It sounded like a child sobbing, but then it dissipated, and I chalked it up to wind whistling through the trees. A pair of barred owls called in the distance. I wondered if the golden eyes of the mountain lion were tracking me. The thought made me hurry along.

All the houses on Catamount Bluff were dark. I hid in the marsh grass, watching. I thought I saw someone move behind a curtain at the Lockwoods' imposing house, but there were no lights on. It must have been the breeze through the open window. I stared at it for a long time, remembering the venom I'd heard in Leonora's voice the last time we talked.

Other than that rippling curtain, there was no movement, but I knew the security guard would be doing his twice-hourly patrols. I waited for the first pass—a slow cruise up the road from the gate to our house. I tried to see who was driving, but the car was too far away. It circled our turnaround and returned in the direction of the guard shack at the main road.

That gave me half an hour before the car came back.

I skirted our house, staying behind the boulders that dotted our yard from the woods to the beach. My heart was pounding when I drew parallel to my studio. This was the most dangerous part—I'd have to run about twenty yards across the moonlit lawn. Without my watch or cell phone, I could only estimate the time, and I guessed it was nearly midnight. Griffin usually went to bed early and slept soundly; the boys were night owls, but the lights in their old bedrooms were off, and in any case, I couldn't imagine why they would be staying at our house.

I took a deep breath and more limped than ran across the wide expanse, slipping behind my studio on the seaward side. I had left the house without my keys, but I kept one hidden under a stone angel in the herb garden. My hand shook as I slipped the key into the lock.

As soon as I stepped inside, my shoulders dropped with relief. Every inch of this building was me. I smelled paint, solvent, wood glue, seaweed, channeled whelk and mussel shells, driftwood covered with barnacles. The large north windows did not face the moon, but the ambient cool-blue moonlight was enough for me to see.

First thing, I went over to the bookcase. The shelves were full of art books, beautiful editions by American, French, Italian, and German publishers. My collection of nature volumes took up half the space—lots of old books by favorites such as Louis Agassiz Fuertes, William Hamilton Gibson, and Henry David Thoreau. I took down a volume I had hollowed out—a law book, irony intended—and was relieved to see the packet of materials was still there.

I grabbed my satchel, stuffed it with fruit and cheese from the small refrigerator, a can of walnuts, a box of wheat crackers, and a jar of almond butter. I went to the medicine cabinet in the bathroom, grabbed some first-aid supplies. And I wrapped the packet of the journal and letters in a soft cloth and put them into the bag along with a pen and a fresh notebook.

I thought of my phone, in the cup holder of my car in the garage. I wondered if the police had impounded the car as evidence, part of the crime scene. I had a landline—it was an old wall phone, right next to the cabinet that held my supplies. But who would I call? Calling 911 would defeat the purpose—town cops would come, possibly Ben Markham, certainly officers on Griffin's side.

Almost ready to leave, I walked over to my worktable and gazed at my work in progress. I had built the frame, cut sections of thin, fine balsa wood to create the beginnings of the great house. Because it was a commissioned work, I had never intended to display it in my show. I checked between the back of the frame and the false bottom, made sure that the letter was still there. It was.

My laptop was fully charged. I stared at it for a few moments. It could be my lifeline—I could email Jackie or Sloane or Nate. Depending on their response, I could decide whether I could put my life in their hands. At least I could scan the news, find out where the search for me—or my body—was focused.

I opened my laptop, googled the local paper, and saw my face on the front page. I started to read the article, but something else caught my attention: Sallie Benson had been killed in a boating explosion. I felt complete shock and sadness. I had seen her just a day before my attack. I quickly hit print, then did the same for the article about my disappearance. There were links to previous articles; I printed them as well.

One story mentioned that several Facebook pages dedicated to my case had sprung up. I quickly logged on to my account, glanced at my wall full of hundreds of messages. I searched for the pages mentioned in the news story and saw that there were many—all devoted to finding out what had happened to me, emblazoned with photos of me. I opened the first page, then a second and third—saw photos of me and countless comments. I printed as much of the content as I could.

I debated taking the letter with me, but I decided to leave it. If Griffin or his cops caught me and searched my belongings, they would destroy the letter, and the friend who wrote it might be in danger. Better to leave it here for Jackie or Nate—someone who cared about me—to find if I never returned. They would realize it was evidence of what happened to me.

Just as I slid everything else into my satchel, I heard the cry again. Distant but chilling—the mountain lion or a human? Whatever it was, I worried the sound might wake up Griffin and the neighbors, so I quickly shut the lid to my computer and let myself out the door. I slipped the key back under the angel and darted as fast as I could back to the shadowed shelter of the boulders.

I heard the call again, a wail of despair. An auditory illusion made it seem it was coming from inside our house or one of the other houses along the road. The crash of breaking waves echoed against the rocks, distorted the sound, confusing me in terms of direction. I realized it sounded more human than animal, but then it rose in pitch like the cries of a cat.

Thirty minutes had passed, because here came the patrol car. I walked back into the woods, disappearing into the brush and trees. For a moment I wondered if I should have brought the wild animal mixture—my scent would be fresh, and if search or cadaver dogs were brought back to the Bluff, they could easily track me. Then I realized— it wasn't that dumb tin of powder that had been protecting me from being found—it was the cougar itself.

The dogs had smelled the mountain lion, and they wouldn't court danger and death by entering its territory. I headed uphill, across the sacred burial ground, and felt my father with me more than ever. The wind was blowing off the sea, and I caught the scent of salt and seaweed coming from the cove where Ellen's body had come to rest.

I heard the cry one more time, and when I turned, I saw the head-lights of the security car stop halfway down the road. Men's voices drifted through the night—the guard talking to someone else. Someone on the Bluff was awake—and watching?

I thought of Leonora and what she had said to me. How foolish I had been to show *Fingerbone* to that group. There was such an air of *we must protect Griffin*. I was a threat, and protecting him would mean I didn't surface again, that I be kept from telling the truth. Griffin might not even have to order it himself. Everyone knew what he wanted. And they all had vested interests in his election.

I wondered if I'd been glimpsed on one of the neighbors' security cameras, and I ducked into the woods and rushed the rest of the way back to my cabin to make my plans. To decide what I should do next.

SEVEN DAYS
LATER

33

CONOR

The seven rivers and fifteen ponds in and around Black Hall had been dragged in the search for Claire's body. The knife had been tested for prints and DNA—no fingerprints, but the blood was Claire's. The floating foam key chain was confirmed to have come from the *Sallie B.* The key fit the lock on the hatchway leading into the cabin.

The trash bag found in the Woodward-Lathrop Gallery's recycling bin contained bloody rags, a black ski mask, and a pair of black leather gloves. Again, the blood was Claire's. The lab was testing the other items for DNA, but so far nothing had come back.

Black Hall residents had been canvassed; security tapes from alarm companies and video doorbells were being analyzed. An hour into reviewing footage from houses and businesses along Main Street, Conor got lucky. At 5:30 a.m. on the Tuesday after Claire's disappearance, a black pickup had stopped first in front of the Starfish Sweet Shop, then outside the gallery.

It was first light—the sun had not yet fully risen, yet the streetlamps had already gone off. The pickup had tinted windows; it was impossible to see through either side. Although the windshield appeared to be clear, no camera captured a head-on view.

At each stop, the driver got out. He looked tall, dressed all in black, with a baseball cap pulled low over his eyes. At the Starfish, he crouched down to shove something into the drain. At the gallery, he opened the recycling bin and inserted the bulging black garbage bag as well as Claire's shadow box.

Conor ran and reran the footage, looking for identifying characteristics of both the driver and the truck. He enlarged the image of the wheels and tires, and he would show them to Don Vietor, a state police sergeant who specialized in vehicle IDs.

The rear Connecticut license plate was visible in one single frame—as the truck drove away from the gallery. Conor looked up the registration, but no such number existed. The plate was a fake or, more likely, had been altered. The right front bumper and passenger door looked damaged, as if the truck had been in an accident at one time.

Conor spent a long time watching the driver get in and out of the vehicle. His facial features were hidden by the hat, showing Conor that he'd taken trouble to disguise himself. If the discarded items had not been found, police would have had no reason to look at security footage in the center of Black Hall. The streets around the gallery had already been thoroughly searched and canvassed in the two days immediately following Claire's disappearance.

The driver must have thought the drain and gallery bin were perfect places because the police had already checked this stretch of road. That indicated that the perpetrator was local, was most likely following the investigation closely, and had a sense of dark and hostile humor: it must have amused him to dispose of Claire's shadow box in the recycling bin outside the gallery where her work was displayed.

"What are you up to?" Jen asked, walking into Conor's office.

"Watching the tapes again. Give me a fresh take, will you?" Conor asked. "Look at this guy and tell me what you see."

Jen pulled up a chair and watched the monitor. Conor played the clip that had been recorded outside the Starfish shop—the driver getting out of the truck, crouching by the drain, standing up, and getting back in the front seat. Next, he ran the gallery clip—showing the same basic movements with a decent side view of the truck.

"What's that?" she asked, pointing at the passenger door.

Conor leaned closer. "Looks like a piece of duct tape," he said.

"Covering something? An insignia or company name?"

"Good catch, Miano," Conor said.

"Another thing," she said. "The driver moves as if he's stiff. Uncomfortable. Look—there—the way he arches his back."

They were silent, watching the clips again and again. Jen was right about the driver—he stood, arched, touched the lumbar region. Maybe it was just stiffness. What about Griffin Chase, all those hours spent in his desk chair? Who connected with the case had been injured? Dan Benson, during the boat explosion. Or Alexander Chase? Word had gotten around about him smashing up his Porsche. Ford was an athletic kid. And all the men on Catamount Bluff seemed like sports-playing Ivy League types. And Wade was old, kind of creaky.

"We sure it's a guy?" Jen asked.

"Not completely but there's something in the movement that seems . . ."

"Guy-like?" Jen asked, smiling. "Not saying you're sexist, but women can throw out evidence too."

"You're right. But who? Sloane Hawke? I can see her having it in for Sallie Benson but not for Claire. They were close friends."

"Jackie Reid?" Jen asked. "Considering it's the gallery's recycling bin."

"No. Trust me," Conor said.

"There's the Claire–shadow box connection—that's big. And just because she's your sister-in-law doesn't mean you know that she wouldn't . . ."

"I *know*," Conor said. "I just do. Let's move on."

"Okay, understood," Jen said. "The big question is, How do these two cases go together other than superficial ways? It's a small town, lots of acquaintances involved."

"Starting with Ford's feelings for Sallie," Conor said.

"Right, maybe Claire tried to interfere. Told him it was a bad idea to go after Sallie? Even laughed at him? And he killed her."

Conor pondered that. "That could be. Raging hormones, Claire confronts him, and he attacks her in the garage. I can see that. And making the big jump to the explosion not being accidental . . ."

"In spite of coast guard findings . . . ," Jen said.

"Because we think in terms of murder, it's what we do," Conor said. "So if it wasn't an accident, why would he kill Sallie if he loved her?"

"Because she didn't want him. She loved Edward. Ford's ego couldn't take it. And if he couldn't have her, no one else would either," Jen said.

"So unrequited love. And fury at his stepmother. Where would he hide Claire's body?" Conor asked. "No traffic went in or out of Catamount Bluff late that Friday, other than a FedEx truck."

"He took a boat? He bribed a FedEx driver?"

"The driver's clean."

"Boat, then," Jen said. "Or he could have just thrown her into the water. Waited for the outgoing tide."

Conor nodded. There was something haunted about that Catamount Bluff stretch of coast. He thought of Ellen Fielding, of how she had washed up less than a mile from the Chase house, in the cove. The tide and currents had carried her there.

Where had they carried Claire?

He hit play again to watch the clip of the truck in front of the gallery one more time. He squinted, scrutinizing the piece of duct tape. He enlarged the image as much as he could, and he saw the barest arc of something painted in gold from under the top edge of the tape.

"What does that look like to you?" he asked. "Is it part of a letter?"

Jen leaned forward. "I think it is," she said. She grabbed a pen and wrote out the alphabet. "With a curve like that, it could be one of several letters. But see that little rise on the left? Looks like the top of the *R*'s vertical."

It took a moment, but then he nodded. Now that she had put the idea in his mind, he could see the *R*.

"And look at the far end of the tape, just below it. A little squiggle— the tail of a lowercase *g*."

Conor didn't hear that last part because he had focused on the crumpled bumper again. His mind raced back to the day of Claire's disappearance, to the hit-and-run on the Baldwin Bridge. A speeding black pickup truck had clipped the back of a Subaru with enough force to send it smashing through the guardrail, into the safety fence.

Conor checked the incident report. He had arrived at the scene at 3:30 that afternoon. The bridge spanned the Connecticut River, between Black Hall and Hawthorne. A drive from the Chase house to the bridge would take five minutes. That fit smack into the middle of Conor's timeline.

Conor had gone straight from the scene of the accident to the Woodward-Lathrop Gallery, where Claire hadn't shown up for her show.

There were cameras on both ends of the Baldwin Bridge. Conor tapped a code into his computer and brought up the live feeds. Then he typed in the date and approximate time and got footage for 3:20 p.m. through 3:40 p.m. on the Friday of Memorial Day weekend. He knew that troopers had checked this video, but Conor was looking for something else—a getaway from the attack at Catamount Bluff.

At the exact time stamp of 3:23 p.m., he saw the truck smash into the Subaru.

"Whoa," Jen said as they watched the truck strike the car's rear end, spin the vehicle around, and keep going. "What's that?"

"That's our truck," he said.

Conor enlarged the image so he could see the driver head-on through the windshield. His face was not visible, because he was wearing a ski mask. Conor felt a combination of triumph, because this was obviously the same truck seen on the gallery's video of someone dumping evidence from the attacks on Claire and Sallie, and frustration, because the mask hid the driver's face.

"Who are you?" Jen asked out loud.

Conor didn't say anything; he was staring at a taped-over word on the driver's door, wondering what it could be.

34

TOM

Tom picked up the phone to call his brother. "I've got to talk to you," he said when Conor answered.

"I'd like that, too, but I've got these two cases," Conor said.

"This is about the Bensons," Tom said. "I could head to the barracks, or you want to come down to the dock?"

"The dock. I'll take a break," Conor said.

Forty-five minutes later, Tom watched his brother's Ford Interceptor pull through the coast guard pier security gate and park in the lot beside a trailer holding an RIB—a rigid inflatable boat. Tom stepped outside. The day had started out foggy, but the sun had come out, and the mist was beginning to burn off.

Several coast guard vessels were tied at the dock: *Nehantic*, two twenty-seven-foot RIBs, and a USCG Jet Ski. There was a storm at sea, and although the harbor waves were not large or dramatic, the hardware holding the floating docks creaked as they rose and fell on swells pushed in from far out in the ocean.

"Thanks for coming down," Tom said, meeting Conor on the pier.

"Your office is a little nicer than mine," Conor said, gesturing at the harbor and waterfront. Tom led him to a bench at the end of the dock, and they sat. One of the cross-Sound ferries passed by; the high-speed Block Island ferry was just loading up with passengers.

"So what's up?" Conor asked.

"Did Matt Hendricks give you a call?" Tom asked.

"Yes, about the fuel line?" Conor asked.

"Yeah."

"We talked," Conor said. "Jen Miano's lead on the *Sallie B* case, so she had a more extended conversation with him than I did. Our lab is working with him."

"Anyway, here's what I want to run by you," Tom said. "Mermen."

"You mean like mermaids?"

"Yeah but male."

"Weird but okay. Why?"

"The little girl," Tom said. "Gwen Benson. She's started talking a bit. The first few days, nothing at all. But when I went to see her yesterday, she told me that her brother is alive."

Conor bowed his head. When he raised it, Tom saw the compassion in his eyes. His brother knew without being told that Tom was torn up by not having been able to rescue Charlie.

"Wishful thinking?" Conor asked.

"I assume so," Tom said. "But she said some things that I can't get out of my mind."

"Like what?"

Tom nodded. "She said that a boat had been following the *Sallie B* all the way from Hawthorne. She called it the 'blackbird boat.'" He paused. "I asked her why that name, and she didn't really say much."

"Did her parents know whose it was?" Conor asked.

"She said they didn't see it. Only she and Charlie did."

"Where does the merman come in?"

"He was driving the boat."

"This sounds like a kids' book. Do you think she read it somewhere?" Conor asked.

"I don't know," Tom said. "It's so far fetched. The kids had been in that yellow raft, and the blast blew them into the water. They both fell overboard. She said the 'merman' rescued Charlie and was calling her name, as if he wanted to save her too. She said he took Charlie to a sea castle that she had seen before in a picture, and it had stone birds all around it."

"What else did she say about, um, the merman?" Conor asked.

"Nothing," Tom said. "She got upset and started to cry. She was begging me to rescue Charlie—I called the nurse."

"I'm sure that was the right thing to do," Conor said.

"It all struck me as pure fantasy—a way to cope with the nightmare she's living through. But I don't know."

"You can't tell me you're taking the merman seriously," Conor said.

"I don't know, Con. She drew pictures in a book, and I can't stop thinking that they show something that really happened—or that she believes happened."

"Where's the book?" Conor asked.

"At the hospital," Tom said. "She had it with her in the solarium, and she let me look through it, told me what everything meant."

"She trusts you," Conor said. "You rescued her."

"Yeah, I guess," Tom said. He still felt miserable about Charlie. His younger brother must have read it on his face; he reached over and patted him on the back. "Thanks," Tom said.

"Look," Conor said. "You know none of this is real, right?"

"It is to Gwen," Tom said and saw his brother looking at him as if he thought he were crazy.

"I'll call Jen and fill her in," Conor said. "Thanks for the lead."

"Want to see what's left of the boat?" Tom asked. "While you're here?"

"Definitely," Conor said.

Tom led Conor toward the large boathouse. The double sliding doors were open, and even from ten yards away the smell of burned fiberglass and wood was overpowering. As often as Tom viewed the wreck, he was shocked that anyone had survived it.

"Wow," Conor said.

"I know," Tom said.

The two brothers stood in the doorway, slowly made their way around the hull. A large hole had been blown in the starboard side, and the burn pattern showed flames had leaped up to deck level, destroying the superstructure: the cabin and the flying bridge.

"With a hole that size, she would have sunk in minutes," Tom said.

"There's almost nothing left," Conor said. "How did anyone get off in time?" Conor asked. "Dan, Gwen? Charlie, if Gwen really did see him in the water?"

They stood there for a few more minutes, solemnly gazing at the boat, looking for any small detail that might provide answers. Tom's thoughts were racing, unable to get Gwen's story out of his mind. He figured that Conor must think he was crazy, but then his brother turned to him.

"I want to see that book of her drawings," Conor said. "Will you come to the hospital with me, ask her if she'll show me?"

"Yes," Tom said. "When?"

"How about now?" Conor said.

The brothers got into Conor's sedan and went straight to Shoreline General—just a few miles away from the coast guard pier. But when they got to the nurse's station on Gwen's floor, a nurse Tom had never met before told them that Gwen had been discharged.

"When?" Tom asked.

"This morning."

"I thought she was supposed to be here at least a few more days," Tom said.

"That I'm not at liberty to discuss," the nurse said. "You'll have to speak to her father or get his permission to talk to her doctor."

"Did her father pick her up?" Tom asked.

"Again," the nurse said. "You'll have to—"

"We get it," Conor said. "Come on, Tom."

They walked out of the hospital, and Tom felt his heart sinking. "I have a bad feeling about the whole thing," he said. "They told me Gwen cried when her father entered the room. Maybe just because seeing him reminded her of what happened but Con—I don't think so. I think she was scared. I half expect to hear that a guy covered in black scales took her away."

Conor called his old partner, Jen Miano, and asked her about Gwen. He spoke for a minute, hung up, and turned to Tom.

"She's at home. Her father picked her up. She's resting in bed," Conor said.

"Jen just took his word for it?"

"No. She was there earlier—went over to continue questioning. He had just arrived home with Gwen; she saw him walk her to her room."

"Okay," Tom said, still feeling uneasy. "I guess I'd better get Maggie over to her soon."

"Yeah," Conor said. "Man, I would like to see that book. I'd say let's go now, but Jen said Gwen's been through enough for today."

The two brothers stood in the hospital parking lot, deep in thought. Tom wouldn't have been surprised to know his brother's thoughts mirrored his own: a little girl in a yellow boat, her brother spirited away by mermen, and a boat that followed vessels about to sink.

EIGHT DAYS
LATER

35

CLAIRE

I woke at dawn, a week and a day after the attack, clear light coming through the window of my cabin. Filtered by the trees, it bathed the pine walls, turned them golden rose, made me feel calm. Nature always did that for me—no matter how tough or confusing life could be, sunrise and the smell of salt air lifted my spirits. I had brought a lot to read from my studio, and I had a busy day ahead of me, but for just then, I lay still, trying to remember a dream.

No, not a dream, a memory, and the quality of light had brought it on: our honeymoon in Italy. We stayed in an ancient villa in Gaiole in Chianti, overlooking the valley to Montegrossi Castle at the top of the hill. Our villa was a thousand years old, with a tower built in 1021 of foot-thick stone, and being there made me feel we could last forever too.

Every morning we'd wake up to rose-gold sunlight slanting through narrow windows. I can feel Griffin's arms around me now. We lay on rumpled white sheets, holding each other, feeling the bliss of finally being married. We packed our days full of hikes, the occasional visit to medieval churches and small museums, but mostly we ate and drank wine and returned to our bed in the tower.

The villa was surrounded by vineyards and olive orchards, and one moonlit night we walked downhill to Badia a Coltibuono, an eleventh-century monastery turned hotel and restaurant that produced its own wine and olive oil. The road was dusty and the olive leaves silver green in the moonlight. We held hands the whole way, ate a Tuscan feast of lemon risotto and *dolceforte* wild boar in the refurbished stables, and ordered a case of their extraordinary Chianti Classico Riserva to be shipped back to Catamount Bluff.

But in the mornings, we would lie together in the early light, hearing sounds of the countryside, with nothing on our minds but each other, and that was what I remembered most. That was what I thought our marriage would be.

When I finally felt able to get up and move around the cabin, I wolfed down food I had brought from my studio and got to work. I had a makeshift desk of two apple crates my dad and I had used to transport food and books from home, and I spread out journals, clippings, and documents I had brought from my studio.

I had saved years' worth of newspaper articles about Griffin's cases and about a month's worth of pieces and editorial letters regarding his campaign for governor. He would be running as an independent, but he was supported by Republicans and Democrats alike. People cited his caring, the compassion he showed to victims and their families, his desire for true justice—not the trumped-up kind designed merely to win convictions.

"State's Attorney Chase is the people's lawyer," wrote Virgil Richards in the *Connecticut Journal*. "He champions the truth rather than prosecuting for headlines. He wants justice for the victims, not personal glory."

A cover story in the Sunday magazine section was titled "The Prince of Caring," with a photo of Griffin standing in front of the imposing granite courthouse, feet spread, arms folded across his chest, jaw jutting out, as if he were guarding the court, marking it as his domain. I looked at that photo and saw arrogance, but I know it was widely thought to portray him as the guardian of righteousness, a protector of victims, determined to bring punishment to the bad guys.

Buried amid the press full of glowing accolades was one editorial by Sean Murphy in the *Easterly Times*, published April 12:

Follow the Money That Leads to Chase

State's Attorney Griffin Chase is enjoying a meteoric rise in the world of Connecticut politics. After nearly two decades of prosecuting cases in Easterly County, his decision to run for governor is not surprising. Talk to anyone around the courthouse and you hear praise and accolades. His charm is legendary; even members of the defense bar speak highly of him.

So why am I hearing whisperings around town about Chase's backers? Chase refuses to accept corporate-PAC money. He can fund his own campaign with his family wealth and that of his friends. He was raised in the exclusive gated shoreline compound of Catamount Bluff. In fact, he still lives there among equally wealthy neighbors Wade Lockwood, Neil Coffin, and Edward Hawke. All are outspoken supporters of Chase.

Wade Lockwood's holdings include approximately 30 percent of the Easterly waterfront. Last year he donated the section known as Lockwood's Harborfront to the city, for use as a public park. He and his wife, Leonora, have funded gardens, a playground, a boathouse, and the planting of one hundred trees.

While sections of Lockwood's waterfront property have been improved, several abandoned warehouses and an unused pier remain. Lockwood's Maritime Gateway project, a mixed-use proposal of condos and a marina, has been perpetually stalled by state environmental and land-use regulations.

Edward Hawke is an attorney with law offices in Lockwood's renovated warehouse complex. In 2018, Hawke successfully defended Maxwell Coffin of the Coffin Group, a family-held company with extensive holdings in the western United States, following an oil spill in Alaska's William Twigg Bay. Maxwell Coffin and his brother, Neil, as well as Edward Hawke, are investors in Maritime Gateway.

An anonymous source informs me that Griffin Chase, Wade Lockwood, Edward Hawke, Maxwell Coffin, and Neil Coffin are members of the Last Monday Club. The all-male club is exclusive; the membership list is secret.

Lockwood, Hawke, and both Coffins have each made substantial donations to the Chase for Governor campaign. Each has something to gain from a friend being elected to the state's highest office. The multimillion-dollar Maritime Gateway project may be at stake. Additionally, the Coffin Group has begun lobbying to resurrect a long-rejected proposal for a natural gas pipeline beneath Long Island Sound. A friendly governor could benefit those plans.

Sean Murphy, the reporter, had a reputation for muckraking, trying to find trouble where there was none. I'd cut out the editorial because I was surprised he would even know of the Last Monday Club's existence and I wondered who the "anonymous source" had been. I'd planned on sharing the piece with Leonora and Sloane but had never gotten around to it.

I turned to the social media printouts. Total strangers had created Facebook groups dedicated to my case; I scanned pages of comments on *WHERE IS CLAIRE BEAUDRY CHASE?* I recognized a few names of acquaintances from town and the past: a girl from my class at RISD, my hairdresser in Black Hall, a student of my father's. But most were unknown to me, amateur sleuths trying to solve my disappearance.

Kiley M: In an effort to learn more about Claire, I am thinking of starting a podcast. Could interview people who know her and possibly gain clues to what happened.

Lexie Wein: Podcast GREAT idea! Would Claire have staged a scene, throw her own blood around. Maybe need to secretly disappear.

Josh Crandall: This is a valid theory.

SuzanneBR: Do NOT say she would stage this herself! This is a Claire support group!

Lexie Wein: This is a discussion group. We should be able to express ideas!

Kiley M: As administrator of this group I have to weigh in. Yes, we are supporting Claire, but to do so, we have to consider all possibilities.

Lexie Wein: She is an artist. Creative. Could have figured out a way to escape her life.

Marisa Albro: Escape from what? She's got a perfect life. Gorgeous home, great hubby, fame, career.

Kiley M: No one knows what goes on behind closed doors. Let's brainstorm who I can get for my podcast. We'll find her!

Lexie Wein: If Claire staged scene she must have intended to throw suspicion on her husband. Trouble in paradise?

Michelle Costas: What about her first husband? Where was he?

Josh Crandall: Worth looking into. Possible lover.

Kiley M: Interesting. So hubby #1 kidnapped/killed her?

Lexie Wein: More like ran away with.

SuzanneBR: I think she is dead, God bless her. Some convict her hubby put away came back to get even. Or fam of convict. Anyone know how to find list of people GC put in prison?

Josh Crandall: Easy to search court records. But still going with idea she staged escape.

Marisa Albro: No way no way no way.

SuzanneBR: Claire's artwork touches my soul.

Fenwick388: Anyone notice the not-so-slight coincidence that another local woman met tragedy this week?

Marisa Albro: OMG yes—Sallie Benson.

Josh Crandall: A coincidence, so what?

Fenwick388: While you're searching court records, Josh, why don't you check out the history between Griffin Chase and Dan Benson.

RaenEC: What are you saying, Fenwick388?

Fenwick388: GC did it. Prince of Caring—BS!! Prince of Darkness more like it. He is a narcissistic sociopath. Trust me, I know a lot about him.

Lexie Wein: Did what?

Fenwick388: Killed Claire. And maybe had something to do with Sallie. He hates women. Including me.

Michelle Costas: WTF? He's a champion for victims, especially women in DV cases.

Fenwick388: He wears a mask.

Lexie Wein: Never heard anything bad about GC. You're being very irresponsible, and you'd better hope LE isn't reading this. You could be in trouble for slander.

SuzanneBR: Who's "LE"?

*Kiley M: Law enforcement. Cops, investigators from Major Crime.
They often follow groups like these. Even get clues from us sometimes ha ha.
Let's solve the case for them.*

*Josh Crandall: GC is in total grief and insane with worry for his wife.
And a great prosecutor for the state of Connecticut. Guar-an-fucking-tee
she'll be found safe. Could even be a publicity stunt for her art show.*

Fenwick388: He did it.

Josh Crandall: Who the hell are you?

*RaenEC: He definitely didn't do it! I know him personally. He is a great
man. So stop lying and spreading BS, Fenwick388.*

It brought me up short to see that RaenEC's profile picture was
of Alexander's girlfriend, Emily Coffin—no doubt the *EC* part of her
screen name. She looked beautiful and yachty, just as she did in real life.
I wasn't surprised that she would be defending Griffin; she was young
and naive and no doubt saw what he wanted her to see.

I wished I had my computer and a fake profile, so I could write to
Fenwick388. This person was clearly someone with lots of anger toward
Griffin—and who had seen his dark side. She said she knew he hated
women, including her.

And who was Josh Crandall? The name didn't sound familiar, but
he certainly seemed invested in the idea that I had staged the scene for
my own disappearance.

I was amazed at the photos that appeared in various posts—my high
school yearbook picture, a candid shot of Griffin and me at our wedding,
a photo of me grinning in my rowboat, oars resting on my knees, and
several pictures of me walking into the Woodward-Lathrop Gallery.

Those last pictures made the hair on the back of my neck stand
up. They were recent: I recognized the jeans and T-shirt I had worn last
week, before my show was scheduled to open, when I delivered the last
of my work. The photographer had captured me going to and from my

car, Jackie greeting me at the door, me entering the gallery. Nothing inside the gallery—the photographer had wanted to stay unseen by me. But he or she had been there, watching.

Every single one of the pictures was posted by Fenwick388.

She had called Griffin a narcissistic sociopath. She knew a lot about him. She had mentioned Griffin's connection to Dan Benson. And I knew that I had to locate her as soon as possible.

36

TOM

Tom told himself that he wasn't acting under any official capacity, so when it was time to take Maggie over to the Bensons' house, it seemed just fine to Tom that Jackie came along. She had gotten attached to the little dog—they both had. Tom knew that Conor had tried to make arrangements to see Gwen's drawings. But so far, the timing hadn't worked. The fact that Conor wasn't pushing harder told Tom he thought Gwen's story was pure fantasy. And it probably was.

Tom called Dan in advance to let them know they were on the way, and he had said that he was meeting with the insurance adjustor, but Gwen was home with her aunt Lydia. Tom parked his truck in the Bensons' driveway, and he and Jackie—holding the dog—walked up the sidewalk.

"Beautiful gardens," Jackie murmured, looking at the beds lining the walk, the roses climbing a trellis beside the front door. "And they already miss Sallie."

Tom saw what she meant—some were wilting and needed to be watered, and weeds had started sprouting up between the bushes. He rang the bell and waited a few minutes before footsteps sounded inside the house.

The woman who answered the door had short white-blonde hair and bright-blue eyes and had to be Sallie's sister—the resemblance to photos he had seen of Sallie was striking.

"Hi, you must be Tom Reid," she said, shaking his hand. "Dan said you'd be coming. I'm Lydia Clarke. Gwen's aunt."

"Good to meet you," Tom said. "This is my wife, Jackie."

The two women smiled at each other and said hello. Clearly recognizing Lydia, Maggie wriggled in Jackie's arms.

"Thank you for what you did," Lydia said, stepping toward Tom. "For saving my niece."

"She's incredible," Tom said. "It was her strength and will to live that kept her going." He remembered how cold the water temperature was that night, how she could have died of hypothermia.

"How is she doing?" Jackie asked.

"You can imagine," Lydia said. "We're still in shock, especially Gwen. My sister was my best friend. I don't have kids—Gwen is the daughter I never had, and I'm trying to do my best for her—and for Sallie."

"I am so sorry about your sister," Jackie said. "And your nephew."

"Thank you," Lydia said. "Gwen knows her mother died, but she can't let herself believe that Charlie did too."

Suddenly the dog began to whimper and squirm in her arms, and Tom saw Gwen coming through the front hallway. Jackie put Maggie down, and she ran straight into Gwen's arms. The little girl crouched on the marble floor, face buried in Maggie's fur. Her head and hands were still bandaged, but the gauze wasn't as thick as it had been in the hospital.

"Thank you for bringing her to me," Gwen said, finally looking up.

"She missed you," Jackie said. "But we loved having her with us. It won't be the same without her."

"She's like that," Gwen said. "She makes everyone happier when she's around."

"Would you like to come in?" Lydia asked. "Have some iced tea?"

"That would be wonderful," Jackie said. She followed Lydia into the kitchen, and Tom hung back in the hallway. He crouched on his heels beside Gwen and Maggie.

"She's happy to be home," he said, watching them play together.

"This is the only place she's ever known," Gwen said, with an air of tragedy belying her age. "And it won't feel the same to her at all. Because it doesn't feel the same to me and Aunt Lydia."

"It doesn't?"

Gwen shook her head. "Because they're gone."

"Your mother and Charlie. I'm sorry, Gwen."

"Nothing will ever bring my mom back," she said. "Aunt Lydia is so sad. I try to help her, and she helps me." Then she glanced up at Tom. She seemed to be waiting for him to say something. "Have you looked for him? My brother?"

"Gwen," he began.

"I know he's somewhere in the world," she said. "Not lost in the ocean. Remember, the sea castle?"

"I do," he said.

"Why aren't you looking there?"

"Well, I don't know where to find it," he said. "Do you still draw those pictures you showed me?"

"Yes, and lots more," she said.

"You know," he said. "Jackie, my wife, works with artists. She loves seeing paintings and drawings. Do you think you could show her your book?"

"I don't like to show anybody," she said.

"But you showed me," he said. "And it gave me a lot to think about."

Gwen bowed her head, pressed her face into her Yorkie's neck for a few seconds. "Jackie took good care of Maggie," Gwen said, her voice muffled.

"She did," Tom said.

"Well, because of that, okay," she said. She stood up and walked into the living room, Maggie at her heels. She climbed onto a sofa and reached between the arm and the seat cushion, pulled out her notebook.

Jackie and Lydia entered the room. Gwen turned the pages, and Jackie drifted over to stand beside her, looking down at each picture. The pencil sketches were detailed, and Gwen had colored some of them.

"These are beautiful," Jackie said. "You're a good artist."

"Thank you," Gwen said shyly. She looked up at Tom. "Want to see one of the new pictures?"

"Definitely," he said.

Gwen turned the pages until she came to a drawing of a large stone house with a turret on one side and a crenellated tower on the other. It resembled the one she had shown Tom at the hospital but with much more detail. Dark gargoyles shaped like birds lined the parapet gutters and cornice moldings. There were pine trees on both sides of the house and a garden in front.

Tom felt startled by a moment of recognition and felt that he had seen this place before. Could it have come from an illustration in a children's book, something he had read in his childhood? And that Gwen had read in hers?

A small boy stood on the roof, his arms outstretched. A king and queen sat in regal chairs on the rocky ground on either side of the palace's entrance. Swirls of blue filled the sky above, and fish swam through clouds.

"What are these lines in the sky?" Jackie asked. "They're really intriguing."

"That's the ocean, not the sky. They're waves," Gwen said. "The fish are swimming all around, like birds. The birds"—she glanced up at Tom to make sure he saw the blackbird gargoyles—"are like fish. And they"—she pointed at two sturdy black-clad guards—"are the mermen."

Lydia walked over, set the tray of glasses of iced tea on the coffee table in front of the sofa.

"Is it okay if I look too?" Lydia asked.

"Yes," Gwen said.

Tom watched the way aunt and niece gazed at each other, the way Lydia sat beside Gwen and put her arm protectively around her. Gwen leaned her head against her aunt's shoulder for a minute, then pointed at the page.

"It's about Charlie," Gwen said. "It's how we're going to find him."

"Oh, honey," Lydia said, sounding helpless.

"He's alive, Aunt Lydia," Gwen said. "Dad doesn't believe me. He says Charlie is at peace with Mom. But he's out there! You have to know that with me, so we stay hopeful and keep looking."

"Gwen, did you tell me that this castle was in a picture that you'd seen before?" Tom asked.

"Yes," she said.

"In a book?"

"No, a photo. With men wearing monkey suits."

Tom must have looked confused, because Lydia laughed. "That's what Dan calls his tuxedo."

"So," Tom said, pointing to the black-clad mermen. "Are these guys wearing monkey suits too?"

"Yes," she said. "They're all going to dance. Charlie too. It's a happy place, the sea castle. Flowers and boats and birds. That is why it's okay he stays there until you find him."

"Where are those pictures now?" Tom asked.

She shrugged. "Around someplace, I guess. I haven't seen them in a long time."

"But it was here in your house?" he asked.

When Gwen didn't answer, Jackie spoke. "You did a really good drawing of the mermen," she said. "They look almost like seals because they're so smooth."

"*Mnnn*," Gwen said.

"Is that because they swim in the water?" Jackie asked.

"Of course," she said. "They love the sea."

"How many were there?" Tom asked.

"Two," she said. "One leaned over to get Charlie, and one called my name." She paused. "One might have been a mermaid."

"A woman?" Jackie said.

"Maybe. I don't know. I want to show you one more thing," Gwen said.

She turned a page to a drawing Tom hadn't seen before. It depicted the interior of a castle with long draperies on tall windows, regal furniture, and a little boy wearing a crown, sitting on a jewel-encrusted throne. Beside him was a table covered with cakes. In the background was a line drawing of a hag holding a broom. She had matted hair, slit eyes, and sharp teeth; her body was hollow—unlike the boy's. Tom wondered if she was supposed to be a ghost. Gwen had drawn a black slash behind her, as if she were emerging from darkness.

"How extraordinary," Jackie said. "There's so much detail. You're a good artist, Gwen."

"Thank you," Gwen said.

"Jackie's right," Tom said. "You are really good. Gwen, would you mind if I took a photo or two of your drawings?"

"You can," Gwen said, and Tom snapped a few shots.

Jackie pointed at the gargoyles. "They look scary."

"They are big crows," Gwen said. "They have hooked beaks and sharp claws, and they eat animals."

"Gwen, who is the lady with the broom?" Jackie said.

"A bad person," Gwen said.

"Why is she there?" Jackie asked. "She looks evil."

"She is," Gwen said. "Once I heard Daddy talking to someone. I don't know who. He was on the phone with his speaker going. The other person said she ruined everything and she has to go. That they wouldn't have to do it if she wasn't going to tear it all apart."

"Tear what apart?" Tom asked.

Gwen shrugged.

"Were they talking about your *mother*?" Lydia asked, her voice shaking.

"No, another lady."

"What is the darkness behind her?" Jackie asked.

"A shadow. Where she lives in secret. They can't see her."

"How sad that she lives in a shadow," Jackie said. "They said that?"

Gwen nodded. "Yes."

"Is she a ghost?" Tom asked. "The way you drew her, her body looks hollow."

"Not a ghost, she's just clear."

"Why clear?" Tom asked.

"That's her name. Clear," Gwen said. "They said Clear ruined everything."

"What an odd name," Lydia said, holding Gwen tighter.

"Wait," Jackie said. "Could it have been 'Claire'? Do you think they might have said *Claire*?"

Gwen looked up, eyes meeting Jackie's, then Tom's. She didn't reply.

"And she lives in a shadow," Jackie said.

"Shadow box," Tom said, and Gwen nodded.

37

CONOR

"Whoa," Conor said on the phone to his brother after Tom had spent five minutes on a stream-of-consciousness rant that sounded more like a tortured dream sequence than anything resembling reality.

"Didn't you hear me?" Tom asked. "She said 'Clear,' but I'm sure she meant 'Claire'—Jackie thought so too. Dan was on the phone with someone, and he said 'she ruined everything' and 'she has to go.'"

"Gwen was hallucinating," Conor said. "I've already said that, and you know it too. There's no way a merman followed the *Sallie B* and rescued Charlie to take him to some enchanted mansion where a scary lady lives in a shadow."

"She must have heard them say 'shadow box,'" Tom said as if Conor hadn't spoken.

Conor took a deep breath. He heard the strain in his brother's voice and understood; Tom had been first on the scene of a horrible explosion, rescued the Bensons' daughter but hadn't found their son. Conor knew well the feeling of guilt when he couldn't solve a case, provide answers to a family.

"Aren't you listening to me?" Tom asked. "You sounded damned interested about her sketchbook, enough to go to the hospital with me. And now you can't even be bothered to check it out?"

"Take a deep breath," Conor said.

Tom did and let out a big exhale of frustration.

Conor was sitting at his desk at the barracks, staring at photos on his wall: of Claire Beaudry Chase, the garage where her blood had been found, and the evidence retrieved from the storm drain and gallery recycling can on Black Hall's Main Street. He thought he had let Tom know he believed the theory had arisen to assuage guilt and grief; he had assumed his brother would have come around to realizing that by now.

"I think someone sabotaged the boat and took Charlie," Tom said.

"It doesn't track," Conor said, trying to be patient. "Jen is working your case hard, and your own guy told her fuel had leaked into the bilge, and that's what caused the boat to blow up. It's an accident, pure and simple."

"There are too many things that *do* track," Tom said. "The name— Clear or Claire. And shadow—that has to refer to her work, shadow boxes, right? And the fact she was going to ruin everything." He paused.

"And you think Dan was talking about Claire when he said 'they got her,'" Conor said.

Tom cleared his throat. "Look, Jackie is really upset," he said. "Claire was—is—her friend. She thinks this means something. We both do. Will you at least pass it on to Jen Miano? Did you even tell her about the sketchbook?"

"Of course I did."

"Listen," Tom said. "I took some photos of Gwen's drawings. Okay if I text them to you? At least take a look?"

"Sure," Conor said.

"Thanks," Tom said in a subdued tone.

"Hey, meet me for a drink later, okay?" Conor asked. His worry was sharper now, knowing how a feeling of responsibility and failure in a case could lead to despair, and he wanted to lay eyes on Tom.

"Not today," Tom said. "I'm on duty."

"Be careful," Conor said.

"You too," Tom said.

Conor hung up. A few seconds later, his cell phone buzzed. Tom's photos had come through. Conor stared at them, taking his time. Gwen had drawn detailed pictures of a castle, complete with gargoyles, crows, and black-clad guards. He saw the ones she'd done of "Clear," the sea witch. The images didn't change Conor's mind, make him think that Gwen's drawings were anything more than a traumatized girl's attempt to keep her brother alive in her mind.

He put his phone in his pocket and went to look for Jen. He wondered how he was going to show her the photos and tell her what Tom had said without making his brother sound bonkers.

NINE DAYS
LATER

38

CLAIRE

Everything felt new and unfamiliar. Moving around by daylight, something everyone took for granted, felt wild and dangerous. I didn't have a disguise, and it was impossible to think I wouldn't be recognized—Hubbard's Point was a private beach within the small town of Black Hall; I lived and shopped and had so many friends here, and for the people I didn't know, my photo was all over the news.

I had regained some strength over the last days, and I had a plan. I needed a computer. I felt I had tempted fate enough by returning home once, so I walked through the woods in the opposite direction, away from Catamount Bluff, until I came out at the top of the hill overlooking Hubbard's Point.

It was seven a.m., early enough in the day that people were not yet sitting on the beach. The tide was out, so I ran along the hard sand at the water's edge to the footbridge crossing the creek and up the steep, narrow stone stairs that led to Jackie's cottage. My heart was pounding as I walked through the hillside thick with coastal scrub, white oaks, and sassafras. The small gray-shingled house was perched on the rock ledge just above. I stood quietly, listening for sounds of the family talking, having breakfast. Nothing.

I poked my head over the crest of the hill to see if there were cars parked along the stone wall—none were there. Tom often left for work before dawn. Hunter worked the early shift as a trooper, and her younger sister, Riley, was a lifeguard at the town beach. The gallery opened at noon on Sundays; although it was too early for Jackie to be opening up, she often went running at the high school sports fields before work. I badly yearned to see her and talk to her, but I wasn't ready to be seen—not even by her.

The house had an outdoor shower enclosed by latticework entwined with ivy and honeysuckle vines. Just behind it was a door, green paint fading from sea wind and salt air, that led to the cellar. I pulled it open, wincing as the hinges creaked. I held my breath, listening for footsteps up above, any sign that someone had heard me, but all was silent. The wooden frame was swollen from humidity, and the latch was stiff; the door didn't quite close behind me—I'd make sure to shut it tight when I left.

Here was a difference between the posh comforts of Catamount Bluff houses and the salty simplicity of Hubbard's Point: the bluff houses had sturdy foundations with wine cellars and, at least in the Chases' case, a temperature-controlled room for storing antiques and fine art. Jackie's cottage was built directly on a granite ledge. The cellar held crabbing buckets, nets, and fishing rods. A rickety ladder led to a trapdoor that opened into the kitchen.

I stood very still for a long time, listening. I heard no one walking around upstairs. Once I was mostly sure no one was home, I climbed up, inched the hatch open, peered around, and hoisted myself into the kitchen. *Congratulations, Claire,* I thought. *You've just broken into your best friend's house.* And I was about to do worse.

The family room was just off the kitchen, and an Apple desktop was set up on a drop-leaf table. I sat down and clicked the mouse. I was relieved to find the computer wasn't password protected, so I went to Safari and brought up Facebook. It was opened to Jackie's account. I logged out, but instead of going to my own page, I created a new username: Anne Crawford. It was meaningful to me alone—Anne was my middle name and Crawford, the name the English settlers had forced on Tantummaheag.

I needed a profile picture. I scrolled through Jackie's photos and, hoping she'd forgive me, chose one of the two of us—photographed from behind, standing at the water's edge, looking toward the horizon. Since our faces weren't visible, it seemed a safe bet. For the cover photo, I uploaded a shot of a sunset, taken from this very spot—Jackie's house—facing the beach and the woods beyond.

I immediately went to the WHERE IS CLAIRE BEAUDRY CHASE? group and requested to join it. Within a few minutes I received a message from Kiley M, the administrator: *Hello! I have a concern. You have zero friends. Are you a bot?*

No, I wrote back. *I'm a person.*

With no friends?

I just joined Facebook. Haven't had the chance to friend people yet.

Well, I have to ask the question: Why do you want to be in this group? And why join it before you even find friends?

The case interests me. I want to know what happened to Claire. It struck me, as I wrote those words, that nothing could be truer.

Okay, you can join. But we are a serious group—we're here for Claire. No self-promotion, no bashing on Claire or other members.

Why would people bash Claire?

Haters in this world. In groups like this, even her attacker could be trolling us and we wouldn't know. We are very careful, and if we sense anything like that, we report to law enforcement.

Like her husband?

We won't bother him, he's got enough going on. But state police, def. So behave yourself!

I will, thanks.

Two minutes later I got my first friend request—Kiley M. I accepted.

My next step was searching out Fenwick388. I found the profile by looking through Kiley's friends. Her profile was set to private, but because we had Kiley M as a mutual friend, I was able to look through her photos. I found the ones she had posted of me, taken last week as I walked in and out of the gallery.

I scrolled through her albums, looking for clues of who she was, people we knew in common. There were several scenic shots of southeastern Connecticut, so I assumed she was local. She had one album labeled *Danger*, and it was filled with photos taken in and around the courthouse, including several of Griffin.

Another album titled *Links between C and S* took my breath away.

Every shot pertained to my life or Sallie Benson's. There were Ford and Alexander at the yacht club; Griffin and me dancing at the governor's inaugural ball; Griffin and several members of the Last Monday Club—including Wade Lockwood, Edward Hawke, and Neil Coffin— the four members, counting Griffin, who lived at Catamount Bluff; me guest lecturing a seminar at Connecticut College. I tried to tell if they were stock photos or if Fenwick388 had taken them herself—I couldn't be sure.

But the ones of Sallie were all publicity shots for her design business, probably pulled from her website: Sallie in a showroom smiling and holding up fabric swatches, at her desk piled high with sample books, in an *Architectural Digest* feature, and on a dock with her husband and kids, all waving at the camera.

The last photo was of a newspaper article about Daniel Benson and how domestic violence charges against him had been dropped by Griffin Chase. Beneath it, Fenwick388 had written *two sociopaths*.

My hands shook, hovering over the keyboard. I wanted to message Fenwick388 about her photos, but what I really needed was to talk to her. I didn't have my cell phone—and couldn't use it anyway—and I had no way to get to a store to get a prepaid phone.

The Reids still had a landline. Many of us who lived along the shoreline still did, because of how often coastal storms knocked out the power. I knew Jackie's number by heart. I wrote a private message to Fenwick388.

Hello. I saw your posts on the WHERE IS CLAIRE BEAUDRY CHASE group page, and I am curious about a few things and might have some information in return. If you are interested in speaking, I will be at this number for the next hour.

I gave her Jackie's number, sent her a friend request, then settled back to wait and stare at the phone. That's when I saw the note in Jackie's handwriting tacked to a bulletin board above the desk:

Clear=Claire?

Scary lady who lives in the shadows=shadow box?

Mermen???

Lost boy in enchanted castle . . .

Scary crows.

Gargoyles?

I frowned, trying to make any sense at all about what the words might mean. I grabbed a sheet of paper and had just started copying the note, writing the first three lines to look at later, when the house phone rang. My heart skittered as I answered.

"Hello?" I said.

"Hello," the voice said. "May I speak to Anne?"

"This is Anne."

"This is Fenwick388," she said. "What did you want to tell me?"

"Actually, I was hoping you could tell me what you know about Claire's case. I saw the photos on your page, and I read what you said about Griffin Chase. I was wondering what made you call him a sociopath . . ."

The line was silent for a moment.

"Are you a reporter?" she asked.

"No."

"What's your interest in the case?"

"I'm local," I said. "I know Claire's artwork. And I read about her husband in the paper."

Again, silence.

"Please tell me why you called him that," I said, pressing. "And why you have so many personal pictures of Claire. Like the ones of her entering the gallery last week. In the Facebook group you mention the courthouse. Do you know Griffin from there?"

"There and other places," she said.

I concentrated on her voice. Did it sound familiar? Had I met this woman? Were we friends?

"Why do you think there's a link between what happened to Claire and what happened to Sallie Benson?" I asked.

"I'm in the process of putting that together."

"Are you a cop?" I asked.

She laughed. "Far from it. Look, it's been nice talking to you, but I've got to go."

I knew I had to tell her something to grab her attention and keep her talking, so I could find out exactly how she was connected to my husband and to what had happened to me.

"He does hate women," I said. "You're right."

"Excuse me?"

"Griffin Chase. You're right about him."

"Yes, I am," she said slowly. "But how do you know that?"

"By the way he treats his wife when he thinks no one can see." I swallowed hard. "And because of something he did a long time ago. To a young woman."

She didn't say anything for so long that I thought she had hung up.

"You're talking about Ellen, aren't you?" she asked finally.

"Yes," I said, shocked to hear her name. "Did you know her?"

"Only briefly but I know why he killed her. It's because of something he did in Cancún. To my best friend. And Ellen saw. He couldn't let her tell."

"Oh my God," I whispered.

"Meet me," she said. "Or I'll come to you, right now. Just tell me where you are."

"Do you know Hubbard's Point?" I asked. And then I told her about the path at the end of the beach.

39

JACKIE

Jackie had planned to get to work early to do some bookkeeping and send out invoices for pieces bought from Claire's nearly sold-out show. On her way to the gallery, she stopped at the high school track and ran three miles. Her work clothes were in the station wagon or so she thought. When she finished her last lap, sweating and out of breath, looking forward to getting to the gallery and taking a shower in the upstairs apartment, and got to the car, she glanced into the back seat and didn't see her duffel bag.

"Oh, great," she said out loud. She'd left the bag containing her black pants, white button-down shirt, and loafers at home—she could picture it on the stone wall just outside the kitchen door, where she had placed it while she'd run back inside to make sure she'd turned off the coffee.

She had—of course. But she'd forgotten the bag.

She turned left out of the high school parking lot and drove back through town—past the gallery, the Congregational Church, and the two narrow rivers and wide salt marshes on her way home.

Jackie had never suffered from depression—she was naturally upbeat, basically hopeful and steady. Even when her first husband had done his acting out and she'd left him, even when the girls had sailed off on an adventure and made her worry, she had hung in there, tough and determined that things would turn out right. The girls were expert sailors, and she had had complete confidence that they would find safe harbor—and they had.

But with Claire missing, and all that blood in her garage, Jackie was in a constant state of anxiety. It was the not knowing that drove her most crazy. She couldn't stop thinking about where Claire might be, what she could be going through. Was someone holding her hostage? Was it one of those horrific scenarios where a woman was held captive in a basement or an isolated house or a warehouse? She lay awake at night, her racing thoughts as bad as any nightmare she had ever had.

The papers were full of articles and commentary; although the police had not released every detail, there were leaks and rumors, including the possibility—posited by a retired forensics expert—that Claire had lost too much blood to have survived the attack. Had she been murdered, her body taken away by the killer and thrown into a swamp or a forest or a deep ocean canyon, where she might never be found? And Jackie would never know what happened to her.

As she drove under the train trestle that marked the entrance to Hubbard's Point, Jackie's heart ached even more. She and Claire had spent their entire childhoods here, and every inch of the place reminded her of her friend. She parked in the road in front of her house and ran up the hill. There was her duffel bag. She grabbed it and heard banging.

The sound was coming from the side of the cottage, and when she went to investigate, she saw the cellar door swinging open and shut in the June breeze. That was odd—the family always closed it tight. When she glanced inside, she saw a glint of light at the edge of the kitchen hatchway—the hatch hadn't been properly shut either.

No one ever entered this way—the hatch dated back to the thirties, when the house had been built, a way into the cellar in case a hurricane or bad nor'easter made it unsafe to go outside or to stay upstairs with the danger of high winds sending the big trees crashing down.

She climbed the ladder, entered the kitchen, and looked around. The kitchen looked normal, just as she had left it earlier that morning. It flashed through her mind that an intruder might be in the house, but she sensed that she was alone. Had Claire known someone was in the garage waiting to hurt her? The thought terrified her.

Maybe she should call the police, say the hatch was open and someone might have broken in. She could ring Hunter—or Conor. She had left her cell phone in the car, so she hurried into the family room and closed the door behind her.

She lifted the landline's receiver and was about to dial when she spotted a paper on the desk. It was an exact copy of the note she had made for herself—the phrases about the Benson case and the strange echoes of Clear/Claire and the shadow lady/shadow box. Her heart was beating so fast she had to sit down.

Her elbow bumped the mousepad, and it woke up the computer. She stared at the screen, at an unfamiliar Facebook profile. Someone named Anne Crawford had logged in on her computer. Anne's profile picture was of Jackie and Claire; Tom had taken it from behind, when they were staring at the sun setting over the golden sea, when they hadn't known he was there.

Jackie stared at Anne's last name. She thought back to when she and Claire were children and Claire's father would take them hiking through the narrow hidden trails in the nature preserve at the end of the beach. She remembered how he would fall silent when they reached the crest of a rocky hill, the site of a burial ground, a tribe of Pequots whose leader was Tantummaheag. And the white settlers had changed his name to "Crawford"—the same name as that of a local sea captain.

Jackie saw that Anne had two friends: Kylie M and Fenwick388. She noticed a messenger notification and read everything that Anne and Fenwick388 had written to each other. The whole exchange had to do with Claire.

It can't be her, Jackie thought. *Can it?* Seeing the name *Crawford* seemed like such a sign. It was a link to Hubbard's Point, the woods at the end of the beach, and Tantummaheag. It killed Jackie to think that Claire might be out there, communicating with strangers on Facebook, and not letting Jackie know where she was.

Jackie sent herself a friend request from Anne. Then she opened her own Facebook page and accepted. Now Anne had three friends: Kylie M, Fenwick388, and Jackie R. Jackie sat back in the desk chair, closed her eyes, and thought about her new Facebook friend.

Jackie stared at the paper that Anne had left behind. She lifted the note to examine it more closely, and tears filled her eyes. Anne's handwriting was Claire's. Claire was alive, still on this earth. Jackie sat very still for a long time.

Then she knew where she had to go.

40

CLAIRE

Maybe I had just made the biggest mistake of my life—agreeing to meet a woman from the internet claiming to have information that seemed almost impossible to believe. But I knew I couldn't stay in my cabin forever, and if I wanted to save myself, I had to hear her story.

A few more people had arrived at the beach, set up their chairs and umbrellas, but I'd borrowed one of Tom's USCG caps and a big towel from Jackie's cupboard, and I walked along the seawall at the top of the sand with my head down and the towel draped around my shoulders. I made it to the path without being noticed.

There were so many better places to meet a stranger, but without a car, my choices were limited. I didn't want to lead Fenwick388 toward my cabin, so I'd directed her to veer right toward the granite bench at the edge of the marsh, instead of into the woods.

I waited in a pine glade so thick and shadowed that the morning sun couldn't pierce the boughs. I was invisible, yet I had a perfect view of the bench overlooking the salt pond and narrow creeks winding through the wide green marsh. This was the site of many joyful crab- bing expeditions—from my own childhood and that of most Hubbard's

Point kids. We'd tie a fish head to a string and pull out buckets of blue shells.

Birders also loved this spot. It was a great place to view shorebirds. During fall and spring migration, warblers passed through in great numbers, and it was common to see people with spotting scopes on tripods dotted throughout the reeds. Right now, the coast was clear.

I remembered one spring with Nate. I had always loved the work of Roger Tory Peterson, the great artist and ornithologist who had lived just a few miles north. When Nate and I were first married, he gave me a pair of vintage Zeiss 7 × 42s—the same binoculars Peterson had used. They weighed a ton compared to more modern optics, but they were razor sharp, bright, with a wide field of view.

We had settled in right here, among the pines, watching a pair of common loons. Brilliant black-and-white birds with red eyes and the ability to dive and stay under for long stretches, they lived up to twenty-five years.

"They mate for life, you know," Nate said.

"People say that about all avian species," I said. "Swans, cardinals, egrets . . ."

"Because it's true," he said, letting his binoculars hang from the strap around his neck, pulling me close.

"You just want it to be," I said. "Because you're such a romantic."

"You're not?" he asked.

I didn't answer, and he kissed me, eased me down onto the blanket of pine needles. The trees were so thick we knew no one would see us, so we undressed each other and made love, and as I was holding him tight, I closed my eyes and knew I wanted more than anything to believe that love lasted forever.

Sometimes I asked myself why I'd left Nate. He was so good, so kind, and so right for me, and I think that was the problem. Losing my parents had set me adrift in ways my mind couldn't comprehend;

I had stopped believing things, especially those that mattered most, could endure.

Now, waiting for Fenwick388, whatever that stood for, I was on high alert. Ever since the attack, I had felt as if I'd been turned inside out, as if all my nerve endings were on the outside. I watched the beach—the direction from which she would come—and saw it was filling up with people. It was a bright, warm June day, and a lot of kids were already out of school. Their whoops and cries of happiness as they ran in and out of the water made a type of background music.

When I looked back, toward the path, I saw a woman hurrying along in my direction. She had shoulder-length blonde hair and killer cheekbones, and she wore wide-legged pants reminiscent of a '40s movie star. I didn't recognize her—but given the timing, I knew she had to be Fenwick388. As she got closer, I felt my body tense and shrank deeper into the pine shadows. This was it, make or break: once she saw me, someone would know my secret—that I was alive, that I was right here.

She arrived at the stone bench, just fifteen yards away from me. She turned in a full circle, alert and obviously looking for someone. I could see that we were about the same age. My heart was beating so fast that I felt the pulse pounding in my neck as if I had sprinted a mile. My mouth was dry.

"Anne?" she called. Then louder: "Anne!"

I almost didn't move. What made me think I could trust this stranger from Facebook more than I could Jackie or Conor? Even now, thinking it could be a trap, I stepped out of the pines, into the bright sunlight.

"Fenwick388?" I asked.

Her mouth dropped open, and she took two slow steps toward me. "Oh my God," she said. "Claire."

41

CONOR

Wade Lockwood had called Conor to say that he wanted to meet—not at his Catamount Bluff home but at his office in Easterly. When Conor had asked what it was about, Lockwood had said only "Claire," preferring to save the rest until their meeting.

Conor was early, so he went through the Dunkin' drive-through and drove along the Easterly semirugged waterfront. He passed brick buildings dating to the 1800s. The ground floors of some housed bars and cafés, with apartments on the second and third floors. Others were abandoned. The sign on a long-shuttered stereo store was faded from sun and salt air. An old vaudeville theater with ornate columns and cornices had been boarded up as long as Conor could remember.

When he got to Lockwood's Harborfront, he parked along the seawall and drank his black coffee. In contrast with the quiet downtown area, this property—newly donated to become a park—was bustling. Wade had developed large tracts of the Easterly waterfront, and this had been one of his last untouched parcels. Until recently, a dilapidated mill, factory, and three rickety piers had filled the space. The land had been in the Lockwood family for two centuries, and it told the story of decline of manufacturing in coastal Connecticut. The Lockwoods had not just survived but thrived on investments and by buying and selling waterfront property.

Bulldozers and backhoes had graded the earth and dug holes for large root balls of already tall trees. An architectural firm had built an ornate Victorian-looking boathouse-restaurant where, eventually, people could have meals and rent sea kayaks. Landscapers were busy laying down turf, planting the expensively enormous trees, creating flower beds, and positioning benches.

At the far end of the park was an area enclosed by a tall anchor fence. Conor knew that some construction sites had temporary enclosures where they parked the heavy equipment at night, but he saw no vehicles. The ground was bare; no turf had been planted. He wondered what it was for.

A Friends of Lockwood's Harborfront nonprofit had been established, but Conor knew that Wade and Leonora Lockwood were paying for most of this. He checked his watch, finished his coffee, and drove around the park's perimeter, taking a long look at the fenced-in dirt as he passed. The area was about as big as the infield of a ballpark. Maybe that's what was planned—a playing field. He drove into the lot behind a renovated brick building and parked his car.

The lobby was sleek, with marble floors and tall windows overlooking the harbor, as if it belonged in a glass tower in Boston instead of here in gritty Easterly. Conor went to the directory and saw that the office of Edward Hawke, attorney at law, was on the third floor and Lockwood Ltd. was on the fourth—the top floor.

Conor took the elevator and stepped into a wide-open modern space. *Lockwood Ltd.* was etched in glass behind a desk, where a young woman with long blonde hair sat at a computer terminal. Conor glanced around. In the waiting area were pale-beige leather armless sofas and chairs that tilted back in a way that didn't look comfortable. The decor was far from old-world Catamount Bluff, not what Conor would have expected.

"You must be Detective Reid," the woman said, smiling. Her hair was down to her elbows. She looked about college age.

"Yes," Conor said. "I'm here to see Wade Lockwood."

"He's expecting you," she said, leading him down a long corridor lined on both sides with closed doors. At the end was an office at least as large as the reception area, done in the same spare, contemporary style. The room had one wall of glass and a view across Easterly and out to Fishers Island. Lockwood sat at a desk facing the door, with his back to the window, and he stood when Conor entered.

"Detective," he said. "Thank you for coming."

"Well, I'm interested in what you have to tell me," Conor said.

"Yes, of course. Can Priscilla get you some coffee? Tea?"

Conor shook his head. "Thanks anyway," he said.

Lockwood gave a nod, dismissing the young woman. He was tall but stooped, with snow-white hair and still bright-blue eyes. The office might've been cutting edge, but his blue blazer, red-and-blue-striped tie, and pressed gray flannels were pure old-boy network. He gestured for Conor to take a seat in one of the leather chairs opposite the desk.

The sun, behind Lockwood, was in Conor's eyes, making it hard to read Lockwood's expression. The furniture placement was obviously designed to put visitors at a disadvantage.

"So, Mr. Lockwood, what did you want to tell me?" Conor asked.

"A man who gets right down to business!" Lockwood said. "No small talk, no 'what a great view.' I like that."

"Well, you do have a great view," Conor said.

"Thank you," Lockwood said. "I grew up with it. My grandfather had his office right here—it looked a little different, as you can imagine. I used to visit him and my father after that. I'd look out at the sea, and all I wanted to do was sail away on it. I joined the navy, wanting to see the world and leave the grime of Easterly behind, and guess what? This place pulled me back like a magnet."

"I can see why," Conor said. "Now, you mentioned Claire."

"Yes," Lockwood said. "What is the status of the case?"

"We're following leads," Conor said.

"Another way of saying you have no idea where she is."

"Where do you think she is, Mr. Lockwood?"

"I'm worried," he said. He sighed and leaned back in his chair. "About her and about the rest of the family."

"You're close to them?" Conor asked.

"Yes. Griffin's the son I never had. The boys are like my own grandchildren. Losing Claire has devastated them. Griffin has a good poker face—has to for his job. But he's beside himself."

"How is their marriage?" Conor asked.

"No marriage is perfect," Lockwood said. "From the outside, those two are very different. Griffin is a hard-driving prosecutor, and Claire is a sensitive artist, the soul of nature. Seemingly opposite ends of the political spectrum—he's conservative; she's liberal. But I'll tell you, I never saw two people more in love. He was wild for her—Leonora and I tried to get him to slow down back when they first got together . . ."

"Why was that?" Conor asked.

"His money," Lockwood said, his tone flat. "That might sound crass, but it's reality. There were plenty of women along the way who saw the big house, the boats, the address. We wanted him to have a life like ours—real love, equal footing."

"But he was wild for Claire," Conor said.

Lockwood nodded. "Yes. He'd lost his college girlfriend—another tragedy. Ellen Fielding."

"Claire found her body," Conor said.

"Yes, she and Griffin were together on the beach. Horrible for both of them. That was really what sealed it for Leonora and me—the way Claire was there for him. He had been through so much already; we were worried about him. She shored him up."

"Since you knew him so well, and you and your wife were like parents to him, you must have known Ellen too."

"We absolutely did."

"And . . ."

"Unstable. People said she might have committed suicide. That didn't seem far fetched to us."

"What makes you say she was unstable?"

"Oh, she was unhappy. Overly sensitive. She was clingy with Griffin until suddenly she decided she wanted to break up, right after graduation. We asked him why, and he had no idea. Poor kid."

"Sounds tough," Conor said.

"Well, yes," Lockwood said. "And her drowning, just awful. I was in the navy, and I know how terrible accidents on the water can happen in an instant—a slip on a wet deck or, in Ellen's case, on the rocks. Horrible accident."

Conor's antenna went up. Terrible accident, horrible accident. The old man was driving home his point.

"There was a silver lining, though—he got together with Claire," Lockwood said.

Conor stared at Lockwood, wondering why he'd been summoned to his office. The rich really were different; this old man looked at women and saw gold diggers. He liked Claire because she had shored up Griffin—as if that were her purpose on earth, to heal a wounded man. And he had called Conor and asked for a meeting—why? To give helpful information or try to learn what the police knew?

"Do you think Griffin would have hurt Claire?" Conor asked, staring at him hard.

"Good Lord, no!" Lockwood said. "Haven't you heard what I've been saying? He is devastated."

"Is that why you called me here? To make sure I understand that?"

"I thought you'd be smart enough to figure that out on your own," Lockwood said. "I merely wanted to let you know Leonora and I want to help your investigation the best we can. We want this case solved."

"Okay," Conor said. "Now I have a question. How does Claire's disappearance affect Griffin's run for office? You're a big supporter of his, aren't you?"

"I resent that tone, but yes. I support him. I donate to his campaign. And nothing changes; to Griffin, a life of public service comes second only to family. I can't tell you how much I admire that trait of his."

"Another question," Conor said. "Back to Ellen for a minute. You said she was clingy."

"Yes. Hanging all over him."

"Where did you see her do that?"

"Oh, I don't know. It's ancient history," Lockwood said, scowling.

Conor could see he regretted having brought it up. He thought about a fact he'd seen in the Ellen Fielding file; Griffin had been questioned by none other than Tuck Morgan, the police commissioner—a very unusual circumstance—in the presence of a family friend. And the investigation had been shut down before it even began. Could that friend have been Lockwood?

"Tell me, Mr. Lockwood. Are you still in touch with former Commissioner Morgan?" Conor asked.

"Tuck? Yes, of course," Lockwood said. "Great guy, a longtime friend . . ." Then he stopped himself and narrowed his eyes, staring at Conor as if he'd just figured out he'd been tricked.

Lockwood's phone buzzed, and he answered. He listened a moment, then stood and offered Conor his hand, dismissing him.

"I have another meeting," he said. "Please don't hesitate to call if I can help. And I would appreciate your letting me know if there's progress on the case."

"We don't discuss open investigations, Mr. Lockwood," Conor said.

"Know this," Lockwood said, his tone suddenly sharp and cold. "I will do anything I can to help Griffin. If you go after him, you'll be making a mistake."

"I'll keep that in mind," Conor said, staring the old man down.

Lockwood stared back, his features immobile: a block of granite who had just threatened a detective.

In the lobby Conor saw three men standing by the window. Two from Catamount Bluff—Edward Hawke and Neil Coffin. The other was someone Conor knew only from news stories and from seeing him around the courthouse during his trial: Maxwell Coffin, Neil's brother.

All were political supporters of Griffin Chase. And, like Chase and Lockwood, members of the Last Monday Club. Neil Coffin nodded to Conor as he walked past, but Hawke and Maxwell Coffin turned away.

42

JACKIE

The burial ground.

Jackie's mind raced, turning over everything she had seen on her own desk, in her own house: Claire's handwriting, the Facebook page for Anne Crawford. That name alone told her so much. It brought back memories of childhood, of all the times she and Claire had wandered the woods at the end of the beach. Claire had been so close to her dad; he had taught them about the sachem Tantummaheag, and Jackie thought she knew where Claire would hide.

The Pequots had lived on this eastern part of the Connecticut shoreline, Mr. Beaudry had told them. In summer, the Algonquian-speaking tribe would fish in Long Island Sound, find crabs and shellfish in the marsh, and raise corn and squash in the fields. Each winter they would move into longhouses in the dense forest north of Black Hall, sheltered from storms and the cold sea wind.

By the 1740s, English settlements were growing, and the colonists pressured the Pequots to give up their land and ways of life. Many tribal members were driven away. Those who stayed found it more difficult to maintain their traditions; even their graveyards were destroyed by development. The bodies of Pequots buried at Half-Moon Beach, east of Black Hall, were moved to a town cemetery. Throughout the region, many Pequot graves were bulldozed and not even acknowledged.

Claire's dad talked about the tragedy of what had been done to the tribes. In 1637, the English captain, John Mason, led a massacre on a Pequot village in Mystic, killing over five hundred men, women, and children.

Archeological digs uncovered grave shafts pointing southwest, where bodies were buried in the fetal position, on their right sides. Their bones told a story, Mr. Beaudry had told Claire and Jackie. When the skeletons were examined, they discovered ribs scarred by tuberculosis and evidence of other diseases brought across the Atlantic by the English settlers.

"This is the cemetery of Tantummaheag's tribe," Mr. Beaudry had said to the girls, pointing at the hilltop clearing.

"Crawford," Claire had said. "Why did the settlers call him that?"

"They called him 'Uncle Crawford.' It was disrespectful," Mr. Beaudry said. "Erasing his culture."

"Will anyone ever disturb the graves?" Jackie asked, heartbroken at the very idea.

"No," he said. "Never. People did—other cemeteries at other times—it was sacrilegious and evil. But it will never happen here. I'd die before I let it."

It was late afternoon, and the sun was moving across the sky. He'd told the girls to look over the treetops toward the Sound, where the sun was getting ready to set, creating a path of gold on the water's surface.

"The grave shafts point that way," he said. "Because Tantummaheag believed that the spirit travels southwest when it left the body."

Anne Crawford, Jackie thought, running along the beach. She felt her own spirit rise, heading toward the sacred place. She passed friends and neighbors with umbrellas and blankets set up along the water's edge, barely seeing them. She hurried as if life depended on it—because maybe Claire's life did. Claire, who had taken the name bestowed on a great man by people who wanted to control him. Jackie thought of Griffin, how he had dominated Claire, and she saw the dark humor in her friend's choice.

The sun glinted off the wide blue bay. She squinted, wishing she'd worn a cap to shade her eyes. The brightness nearly blinded her, and she slowed down. The hill path was just up ahead. Once she skirted the marsh and ducked into the trees, she'd be okay. She saw two women walking fast from the stone bench toward the parking lot.

One of them was tall and glamorous looking, striding along with a purpose. The other was familiar and beloved, petite but strong looking, and she was wearing Tom's blue salt-stained coast guard cap. Jackie would know her anywhere, and she lost her breath.

They had a head start, and by the time Jackie caught up, the other woman was unlocking a silver Renault. Jackie nearly threw herself into Claire's arms, but she stopped when Claire's eyes met hers: their expression was just this side of terrified. Her face and neck were bruised, and her hands were covered with cuts.

"Claire?" Jackie said.

"Quick, get in the car," Claire said, sounding panicked, and Jackie scrambled into the back seat.

"What's going on?" Jackie asked, watching Claire, up front, duck down as the other woman drove them through Hubbard's Point, under the trestle, and onto Shore Road.

"You didn't say you were bringing someone," the woman said, glancing down at Claire.

"It wasn't planned," Claire said. "But Jackie is my best friend."

"Claire," Jackie said, reaching forward to squeeze her shoulder. "Where have you been? I've been out of my mind. We *all* have been."

"There's a lot to tell you," Claire said.

"Where are we going?" Jackie asked. "What's going on?"

"This is Fenwick388," Claire said. "We just met."

"*Fenwick388* is my screen name. I'm Spencer Graham Fenwick."

Jackie glanced at Claire and saw a glimmer of recognition in her eyes.

"We're going to my place," Spencer said. "Claire will be safe there, and we can talk."

"Claire, why don't we just call Conor?" Jackie asked. "Let's do that now, have him meet us somewhere now."

"We can't do that," Claire said. "Not till I know whose side he's on."

"Whose *side* he's on?" Jackie asked. "There's only one side—*yours*. He's searching for you—he's in charge of your case!"

"That's the point," Spencer said. "Because cops and prosecutors work closely together. He might be feeding information to Griffin."

"He's my brother-in-law!" Jackie said.

"I know, Jackie," Claire said. "But I just can't be sure yet."

"Then what about me?" Jackie asked. "Am I on the wrong side too? Why didn't you call *me* for help?"

"I'm so sorry," Claire said, turning around to look into Jackie's eyes, reaching back to take her hand. "Jackie, I love you. I'm sorry it's been this way. But we're together now. I'm so glad you're here."

"So am I," Jackie said, squeezing her hand hard, not wanting to let go.

"The point is that Claire is safe, she's here now, and we have to make a plan," Spencer said as she drove east.

"Did Griffin do this to you?" Jackie asked, looking at the bruises on Claire's face and neck and the cuts on her wrists and hands.

"I think so," Claire said. "But he wore a mask. He wouldn't let me see his face. That's what's making me crazy, Jackie. It's why I've stayed hidden, didn't even call you. I don't know anything for sure."

As Spencer drove them through seaside towns that Jackie had known her whole life, along streets that were as familiar to her as her own road, she felt she had entered a foreign landscape, unknown and unfriendly, a place she had never been before.

It took a long time, driving on back roads instead of the highway, all the way to Charlestown, Rhode Island. Spencer turned right off Route 1, heading toward the sea, past a sign that said OCEAN STATE SEASIDE HAVEN. A sandy driveway ran through a coastal forest of scrub pines, past a row of identical one-story cottages. She parked the Renault beside the last one, leaned over Claire to take a notebook from the glove compartment, then slammed it shut.

Jackie and Claire followed her to the front door, and Spencer unlocked it. Inside was a single room containing a double bed, a couch and an armchair, a coffee table, and an efficiency kitchen. Two generic seascapes and the kind of corny signs sold in summer town gift shops— THE BEACH IS THATAWAY! and THE WORST DAY OF FISHING IS BETTER THAN THE BEST DAY OF WORK!—hung on the walls.

"Have a seat," Spencer said. "I'll make some tea. Claire, you must be hungry."

"Don't worry about that," Claire said, sitting beside Jackie on the sofa. Claire stared at Spencer, riveted. "I know who you are," she said.

Spencer gazed at Claire with a smile, a compassionate expression. "You do? Most of my work is fairly underground."

"I've read a lot about domestic violence over the years," Claire said. "Your clients post on Reddit. On the dark web, too, I suppose. You help victims get away."

"I never call them 'victims,'" Spencer said. "They are so strong. They have gone through hell—a hell they entered out of pure love. Abusers are weak. They trap women who have gigantic hearts, who want to help these poor, sad wounded birds."

"That's what I think too," Claire said, nodding. "I've always believed we have big shoulders."

"Absolutely. The abusers know that, and they take pleasure in breaking their partners down. It's part of their fun. Plus, they get all that love, all that attention."

"Spencer," Jackie said, feeling spun around by the back-and-forth. "Obviously, Claire knows what you do, but I don't. I'm sorry."

"I have a foundation," Spencer said. "I help women escape from abusive relationships."

"The Spencer Graham Fenwick Foundation," Claire said.

"Yes," Spencer said. "My name comes from the women in my family. *Spencer* and *Graham* were the surnames my mother and her mother were born with. They taught me so much—both by what they could and could not do in life. I could have named my foundation for Marnie—I thought of that—but I wanted to honor the women in my family."

"Marnie?" Claire asked.

"Yes," Spencer said, gazing at Claire with eyes full of sorrow. "She was my best friend."

"I want to know about her," Claire said. "And please tell me what you know about Griffin."

Spencer nodded. "First, I never expected it would be you—I thought I was meeting someone named Anne. I thought 'Anne' and I would pool our knowledge about Claire's case—you going missing, all that blood in your garage, Griffin's involvement. See, I have a story about Griffin too. But it's really a story about Marnie." She set the notebook down on the low table in front of them. Jackie could see that it was bulging with news clippings and loose sheets of paper.

"Tell us," Claire said.

Jackie watched Spencer sink back in the armchair, close her eyes, and take a deep breath. She seemed to be willing herself to relive the worst moment in her life. And then she began to talk.

43

CLAIRE

I was riveted, listening to Spencer, a woman I had read about, who had seemed more like a phantom of the internet than an actual person.

"Marnie Telford was my best friend," Spencer said. "From the time we were in sixth grade. You know how sometimes people outgrow each other as they get older? We were the opposite. We got closer."

"Like us," I said, glancing at Jackie.

"I wish Marnie and I had the chance to say that now. But we didn't. She left this world too soon. It all began—and ended—on a trip we took when we were juniors in college."

"To Cancún," I said and felt my stomach flipping. Was this it? Was I about to hear the story that would explain it all?

"Yes," Spencer said.

At first it had been a thrill. It was their first time really on their own—away from college, out from under their parents' supervision, making their own money. Working at Las Ventanas Resort, the luxury pink hotel on its own private beach, had been a dream. It was too high end for the usual spring break crowd, but there were plenty of young people on vacation with their parents.

"Or, in the case of Griffin, some family friends," Spencer said.

"Wade and Leonora Lockwood," I said.

"Yes, they were the hosts. A friend of Mrs. Lockwood's was along and her stepson, Dan. Plus, Griffin and his girlfriend, Ellen. The group seemed like typical guests. Superrich, there for the fishing and beaching and lots of cocktails. Marnie and I were chambermaids by day, cocktail waitresses by night—we were working extra shifts to save up money."

"And you served them?" I asked.

Spencer nodded. "At first we were just the hired help, but Griffin, Ellen, and Dan were our age, and we began to be kind of friendly."

"You joined them for dinner or something?" Jackie asked.

"No," Spencer said. "That wouldn't have gone over with the Lockwoods. You have to picture this place. Five stars, right on the beach, but with a restaurant where people 'dressed' for dinner. The guests either knew each other from yacht clubs or business deals or Yale—or they'd read about each other in the *Wall Street Journal* or *Town and Country*. Drawing the wagons tight so no riffraff, like hotel employees, could get in."

"You're not riffraff," Jackie said.

Spencer smiled. "Our parents were Washington people—they would have gotten along just fine with the resort crowd—but they weren't there. To people like the Lockwoods, Marnie and I were just the hired help."

"But Griffin saw you differently?" I asked.

"I'm not sure how he saw us. It started with Ellen. She caught us after lunch one day, when we were just finishing our shifts, and invited us to hang out with them that night. On a beach a few miles from the hotels, one that we knew pretty well, where we sometimes went to get away from the resort people."

Spencer and Marnie had said yes, excited to escape the hotel for a few hours. Marnie thought Dan was cute, scruffy, and easygoing compared to perfectly preppy Griffin.

The girls wore sundresses and sandals, glad to leave their Ventanas uniforms behind. Ellen seemed nice, and she said she was relieved to have other girls around. But Spencer had noticed something: the way Ellen kept looking at Griffin, with deference, as if trying to read signals from him.

"I felt weird almost as soon as we got into the car. It was a Jeep—the Lockwoods had rented it to go off-road, exploring the Yucatan. Griffin drove and Ellen sat up front; Dan was in back, between Marnie and me. He was sweating—I could feel it through his clothes, like he was nervous about what was about to happen—and Ellen kept glancing over at Griffin, talking to him in a low voice."

"What *was* about to happen?" Jackie asked.

I listened to Spencer describe the ride: the radio was on as they left the bright lights and bustle of the hotel zone. The foliage along the roadside was thick, dark green in the headlights. The sounds of tree frogs and Yucatan night birds came through the open windows. They drank Coronas; when Griffin finished one, he hurled the empty bottle at a street sign. They heard the glass smash.

Griffin turned off the main road, and they bounced along a rutted track, trees growing so close they scraped the sides of the Jeep. Eventually they broke into a clearing at Playa Mariposa, the calm Caribbean a black mirror reflecting the stars, spreading into infinity.

"Ellen said she thought there'd be more people here," Spencer said. "She sounded nervous. Marnie told her it was safe and we went there all the time—just to get away from the resort crowds. Only locals knew about it. And kids who work at the hotels."

"You'd gone there before?" I asked.

"Yes," she said. "And it started off as a good time, but there was a strange vibe between Griffin and Dan."

Something about the way Griffin spoke to Dan made Spencer think the two boys weren't really friends, that Griffin, in fact, looked down on him, was embarrassed by him. After a season at the resort, she couldn't miss the differences in status—who in the party had the most money, who was in charge, who was the diva, who called the shots.

Ellen spread out a blanket—Spencer knew she'd taken it from the room—and the boys brought a cooler and a canvas bag down to the water's edge. Dan took a small CD player out of the bag and turned on the music. There was an offshore breeze keeping most of the insects away, and they were lucky it hadn't rained lately. Dry weather kept the mosquitos away.

Dan handed out more Coronas, and Griffin opened a bottle of tequila with a silver label. He had brought a lime, and he cupped it in the palm of his hand and cut it into slices with a bone-handled knife.

They began trading stories about colleges and hometowns, life in New England and inside the Capital Beltway, and the inevitable do-you-knows. Spencer's freshman-year roommate had gone to the same boarding school as Ellen's cousin; Marnie's stepbrother had been wait-listed at Wesleyan—where both Griffin and Ellen went—but wound up at Trinity. Dan's family used to go to Washington, DC, every spring vacation to visit his aunt, and it turned out she lived on the same Georgetown block as Marnie.

While Spencer listened to Dan and Marnie talk about Q Street and waiting in line for ice cream at Thomas Sweet, Griffin poured another round of shots and handed them around. The music mix was good. He reached for Spencer's hand, but she glanced at Ellen and pulled it away. Wasn't Ellen his girlfriend? Everyone but Ellen began to dance; Ellen sat on the blanket, watching. Griffin put his arm around Marnie and began to slow dance with her.

"Griffin told us he wanted to walk down by the water, take a swim," Spencer said. "I told him no, there were sharks after dark. He kept saying he wanted to, and Dan joined in. Ellen didn't say anything. Marnie really liked them, I could tell, and she said we could at least get our feet wet."

So they all walked to the tide line, teasing the waves. The water hit their bare feet, exploding into a million bright stars—bioluminescent marine organisms that glowed at night. Spencer and Marnie had seen it happen every time they went down there for beach parties; the phenomenon always shocked and delighted kids on vacation from the north. The five of them held hands, dancing in the shallow water, kicking great sprays of water that showered them all in tiny saltwater stars.

"Dan, Marnie, and I were standing in the water, but Griffin and Ellen walked away, having an argument. That's when I began to feel dizzy from the tequila," Spencer said.

She went back to the blanket to lie down. She looked up at the sky. She said it was so dark there, without hotel or city lights, that the stars seemed to shower down around her, brushing her shoulders as they fell onto the sand.

The sound of the waves on the sand was rhythmic and beautiful, and she remembered thinking that *this* was why she and Marnie wanted to travel, to have magical nights like this, where everything came together in one peaceful, exciting, spontaneous, exotic moment. She knew she'd be hungover for her breakfast shift in the morning, but as soon as she could, she would start an article about the perfect beach party on a Yucatan night.

The beach began to spin; it felt like more than the alcohol, as if she'd been drugged. She closed her eyes and passed out for a few minutes. Or longer. She woke to the feeling of sweaty heat and the pressure of someone's leg across hers. She wriggled to get out, but an arm held her down. Marnie was on her back beside her, thrashing beneath Griffin. Dan was holding Spencer down, his face close to hers. She tossed her head back and forth to keep him from kissing her.

She screamed and yanked her hands free, shoving his shoulders as hard as she could, punching his face. He grunted and hit her back, stunning her. Drunk as he was, he fumbled his way back. He tugged at the waistband of her panties, couldn't manage to pull them down.

Dan was breathing heavily, telling her to hold still. She vomited into his face, and he jumped away, swearing.

Marnie was lying beneath Griffin, and he was holding her down, arms pinned to her side. Spencer saw Griffin's naked buttocks, jeans down to his ankles. His chest pressed against Marnie's face, but Spencer heard her muffled cries.

"He was raping her," Spencer said. "I jumped on his back, smashing him with my fists as hard as I could, screaming for him to leave her alone."

He roared at her, flinging her away. He reached up to rub his head where she'd yanked his hair. In that second Marnie rolled out from under him and began running down the beach. She disappeared into the darkness, but Spencer heard splashing and tore after her. She couldn't catch up. By the time she reached the tide line, she saw Marnie diving into the sea.

"I dived in myself," Spencer said. "But she was swimming so fast. I yelled for Ellen to help me, but she was up at the Jeep, looking the other way."

"What about Dan?" I asked.

"He sat next to Griffin on the blanket as if nothing had happened. I was twenty yards offshore when Marnie disappeared—there was nothing but black water."

There was not even a ribbon of blue-green fire to show where she had been.

"I dived for her. Over and over, screaming her name," Spencer said, closing her eyes and seeming to go very far inward.

No one spoke for a few minutes. I watched Spencer slowly, steadily, gather herself. The window was open, and a warm breeze blew through her Rhode Island cottage in the pines. She wiped her eyes.

"I never saw Marnie again," she said. "Her body washed up two days later."

"I'm so sorry, Spencer," I said.

"Thank you," she said. "I'll never get over losing her that way. I kept thinking, What could I have done differently, to help her, to save her? If I hadn't drunk so much, or if I'd figured out they were drugging us. If I'd caught up with her before she'd jumped into the water . . . if I'd had better instincts about Griffin."

"You saw what he wanted you to see," I said, picturing him at that age—at any age. "Charming, fun . . ."

"And he had a girlfriend," Jackie said. "So you would never have thought he'd be dangerous to you."

"What happened?" I asked. "After you called Ellen to help you?"

"Nothing," Spencer said. "I heard Griffin say, 'Let her go swimming if she wants.' For some reason, that sobered me up. I realized if I stayed in the water searching for Marnie, I might not come back."

"What did Ellen do?" I asked.

"She and the boys left me there. They went back to the hotel. As they drove away, I screamed for Ellen to send help. It took forever, but finally some police—so-called police—arrived."

"They weren't?"

"They were resort security," Spencer said. "They had uniforms on, drove a car with a flashing light on top. I was too messed up to realize at first. They came running down the beach, wrapped me up in a blanket, and tried to get me to leave—without even going in to *try* to find Marnie. No rescue squad—nothing."

"What about Griffin and Dan?" I asked. "And Ellen? What did they say?"

"They left the resort that night," Spencer said. "Their whole party. The Lockwoods checked out and returned to Connecticut."

"Wasn't there an inquest?" Jackie asked.

Spencer shook her head. "We'd been drinking. Everyone said Marnie's death was an accidental drowning—and it was, in the sense that nobody held her under. But she'd been terrified—she ran into the water to get away from Griffin. When I told them that he had raped her, that Dan had tried to rape me, they never even investigated." She took a deep breath. "To them, we were just a bunch of kids partying, having fun."

"Did anyone even examine you? Or Marnie . . . after she was found?"

"No. We were just chambermaids, and they were paying customers— no one was going to ask questions."

"The Lockwoods paid them off," I said.

"Of course they did," Spencer said.

My skin was crawling as I thought of the vile thing Griffin had done to Marnie. My husband had raped a young woman. And Ellen had watched and done nothing. Dan Benson, now grieving for his wife, had assaulted Spencer. And the Lockwoods—my friends, Leonora and Wade—had whisked the boys away that same night, as if they had never even been there at all.

"Why did Griffin say to let you go swimming if you wanted?" Jackie asked.

"Isn't it obvious?" Spencer asked. She stared at Jackie, then at me. I felt the blood rushing through my body.

"It is," I said.

"I was inconvenient," she said.

"He hoped you'd drown too," Jackie said.

"Yes. Because if I had, there would be no one left outside their circle to tell the story," Spencer said.

"Did you ever tell anyone?" I asked. "After that night?"

"For a long time, no," she said. "I quit work—went home to my parents. All they knew was that Marnie drowned. That I was trauma- tized. I wrote her parents saying how sorry I was—they wrote back tell- ing me it wasn't my fault, that horrible accidents happened. The story, with our friends, became that Marnie was a daredevil, lived on the edge, took one risk too many. And I never contradicted them."

"You never told about the rape?" I asked.

"What was the point? She was gone, they had to mourn her, and I didn't see the point of telling them what Griffin did. What she went through. No one down there believed me—there was no proof, and no one was going to make Griffin pay. All I wanted to do was forget." She paused. "I did a good job of that. Took a long time to go back to college. Found very effective ways to keep from thinking about what happened. But then I knew."

"Knew what?" Jackie asked.

"That I had to help women who'd faced men like Griffin. I finished college, went to law school. But that wasn't enough. I was only able to represent one woman at a time, so I established a foundation that can do much more."

"I know you fund clinics and go after abusers in court," I said. "But how do you raise the money?"

"I used part of what I inherited from my grandmother," Spencer said. "She would have liked nothing more than to help this cause. We have a network of journalists that publicize specific stories, and those reports bring in donors."

I nodded, taking that in. I felt a surge of energy, knowing that I wanted to be involved in this. I was already using my experience to tell my story—and Ellen's—through shadow boxes like *Fingerbone*. But I wanted to do more.

"When I read about you," Spencer said to me, "I knew it was time to focus on Griffin. He has such entitlement—prosecuting criminals when he's worse than any of them. And now, running for governor. He got away with Marnie's death for so long. I couldn't let him get away with yours."

"And you want to stop him," I said.

"So do you, right?"

"Yes," I said. "I didn't know about you and Marnie. But I know about Ellen."

"He killed her because she knew. She was the only one besides me. Once I started the foundation, I worried he might come after me, but I'm very careful. My house is in the name of my trust; he'd never find it," Spencer said.

"I'm glad," I said. Spencer radiated strength and savvy; I knew she didn't underestimate Griffin. "What about Dan? He was right there and knows everything. Isn't he in danger?"

"Dan was part of it," Spencer said. "They had it on each other. Mutually assured destruction if one of them told." She paused, gazed hard into my eyes. "So he tried to kill you because you know about Ellen," she said.

"I didn't see his face. He wore a mask and gloves."

"If he was going to kill you, why would he care whether you knew it was him or not? He's so arrogant that I would think he'd want you to know," Spencer said.

I thought about that, as I had every day since I'd been attacked. "He's a monster but a very particular type of monster," I said. "He has to be thought of as the good guy, even as he's pulling the wings off dragonflies."

"Claire, if not Griffin, who did this to you?" Jackie asked, holding my hand.

"It was Griffin," Spencer said. "It had to be."

I thought so, too, but I wasn't completely sure.

And I thought about how Wade Lockwood had helped to bury the story about Marnie and protect Griffin, just as he did later that same year, after Griffin had killed Ellen, and Wade made sure there was no investigation.

I wondered what he was doing right now, spinning what had happened to me, steering all suspicion away from Griffin Chase, the son he never had.

44

CONOR

Conor drove toward the southeastern corner of Connecticut to meet two men with a strange story to tell.

One month before Claire Beaudry Chase went missing, Lance Staver and Jim Dufour, members of the Ravenscrag Sportsmen's Preserve, hiked the three-hundred-acre club property, training their German short-haired pointer puppies to become superb hunting dogs, when they came upon a disturbed area—a pile of dead leaves.

Upon investigation, they found that the leaves had been heaped on top of a sheet of plywood. They kicked aside the plywood and discovered a hole in the ground. It was six feet long, three feet deep, and two feet wide. Four bags of quicklime were piled on a white plastic tarp at the bottom of the hole.

"Totally a human grave," Staver said.

"Yeah, wonder which member is killing his wife?" Dufour asked, and the two men laughed. They figured one of the club officers had dug the hole to dispose of animal carcasses. Once a deer was field dressed, the meat removed, there was the problem of the body—left in the meadows, it rotted, attracting predators like coyotes and bobcats, hawks and ravens.

None of that would be a problem, except lately a few members with small children had complained about the smell and about the dangers of being on the club grounds when critters with big teeth were out there ready to pounce, which to Staver and Dufour was bullshit. If you didn't like wildlife and the food chain, join a country club, not a sporting club.

They forgot about the hole until Claire Beaudry Chase's disappearance hit the news, was on TV and in the local papers every day, and they remembered how a group from the Black Hall–New London area, where the missing lady was from, had rented out the property for an outing during the wild turkey hunting season, and they began to wonder.

Conor was following up on their call. The day had dawned foggy, and at ten a.m., the mist had just started burning off. By the time he got to North Stonington, where the club was located, the sky was bright blue and the day was hot.

Jim Dufour was short and round with a fringe of hair that looked like a monk's tonsure. Lance Staver was stocky but fit; he wore a T-shirt that said *NAVY SEAL TEAM 6* and had an American flag tattoo on one forearm and a howling wolf on the other.

"Call me crazy," Dufour said as the three of them set out on a trail behind the club building—a white farmhouse with a wide porch and two chimneys—"but this thing's got human grave written all over it."

"When did you first find it?" Conor asked.

"Round about April, maybe midmonth," Staver said.

"And you didn't report it then?" Conor asked.

"Truth is, we didn't think much of it until we read about the Chase woman," Staver said.

"And we started thinking, What if she's here?" Dufour said with an exaggerated shiver. "That's why we called you."

"Good that you did," Conor said.

They crossed a meadow full of tall grass. At the far side was a thick wood, and they skirted the trees until they came to a pond. Staver explained how the pond was stocked with trout every spring and how the club released game birds every fall.

"Something for everyone," he said.

Conor was sweating and took off his blazer, slinging it over his shoulder. Staver glanced at him, nodded with approval. "Smart move, you got long sleeves under there. This is a nasty year for ticks." Conor didn't mention Staver's T-shirt or the fact he was wearing camo shorts.

"We're getting close," Dufour said. "Now, you see those humps of brush and leaves?" He pointed at three piles between the woods and the water. "People think we're just out here killing animals, and we are, but truth is, we are also into conservation. The eastern cottontail population has been declining in recent years. Too much development, habitat displaced by a bunch more houses and stores. So we build these brush piles to give the rabbits somewhere to live."

"And we don't shoot them," Staver said. "We only go after the non-endangered. But the thing is, all these piles of twigs and branches and leaves are just things we take for granted out here. Whoever piled them up was probably trying to make it look like just another bunny site."

"But it wasn't," Dufour said. "You could tell a person did it to cover that hole in the ground."

"And what made you put it together with Claire Beaudry Chase?" Conor asked.

"Well, on account of the fact that group of lawyers and whatnot from down Black Hall way were here for a turkey shoot in March."

"Lawyers?" Conor asked. But the two men stopped short before they answered, and so did he.

"Huh," Staver said. "Looks different."

"Completely different," Dufour said.

"That's where the plywood was," Staver said, pointing at a patch of ground, bare dirt sunken down about a foot, compared to the level grass-covered area around it. "It was covering a deep pit, we're talking a good three feet, but half of it's been filled in."

"Damn it to hell, someone put someone in that grave." Dufour took a step toward the spot, but Conor stopped him.

"I'm going to ask you to not go any closer," Conor said.

It was a potential crime scene, so he took photos with his iPhone and called his office to ask for the Major Crime Squad van to be dispatched. While waiting for the forensics team to arrive, Conor took Staver's and Dufour's statements.

They sat in the clubhouse on leather chairs beside a large fieldstone fireplace. One entire wall was covered with antlers with brass plates identifying the species and the member who'd bagged it. There were several vintage black-and-white photos of men in tuxedos, a sepia-toned close-up of a Model T Ford, and two out-of-focus shots of what appeared to be the same car on a snowy road and in front of a massive Gothic stone building.

"Whose car is that?" Conor asked, leaning closer.

"One of the founders," Staver said. "Zebediah Coffin. This land belonged to his family—that picture in the snow was taken here, on the road to the club. Back then they farmed the property."

"Well, *they* didn't," Dufour said. "The Coffins hired some poor slobs to milk the cows. They lived in that place." He pointed at the photo of the stone building.

"Nearby?" Conor asked.

"Down on the water," Staver said. "Same name as this place—the rich ones have to name all their property. The oldest Coffin brother still owns it."

"He and his wife stay there when they're not at their other places," Dufour said. "San Francisco, Saint Bart's, Colorado. When they're not home, the caretakers look after the house. We got plenty of founders' heirs here. Should be thankful to them, right? Having the foresight to start this club?"

Another wall contained trout and bass mounted on wooden plaques. There were several framed slogans, incongruously embroidered with silk thread, including IF YOU'RE NOT SHOOTING, YOU SHOULD BE LOADING; I'D RATHER BE JUDGED BY 12 THAN CARRIED BY 6; IF YOU

CARRY A GUN PEOPLE CALL YOU PARANOID; NONSENSE! IF YOU CARRY A GUN WHAT DO YOU HAVE TO BE PARANOID ABOUT?

Conor stared at the signs. He had seen similar sayings before, most recently on the study wall in the home of a family where the six-year-old son had found the loaded pistol in his father's desk drawer and blown a hole through the chest of his three-year-old sister while playing hide-and-seek.

"Second Amendment," Staver said, following Conor's gaze. "Gun wisdom. Those were made by one of our female members."

"Guns don't kill people," Dufour said. "People kill people."

And six-year-olds kill three-year-olds, Conor thought.

"Can you narrow down the date you first saw that hole in the ground?" Conor asked.

"Let me check," Staver said, scrolling through the calendar on his phone. "It was a weekend. I remember Jimmy and I were checking the cottontail dens, and I had to make it quick because it was my turn with the kids, but my ex was jerking me around, saying I couldn't get them till five because of a birthday party. But I can't remember whose birthday. One of their cousins, I think."

"That's right," Dufour said. "You were pissed."

"Got it," Staver said, looking up. "April fifth."

"Okay," Conor said, writing it down. "And when did that group of lawyers come here?"

"That we'd have to check with Al on—he's our membership officer, and he takes care of renting the place out now and then. But he's not in today," Staver said. "And they weren't just lawyers. Businessmen, too, and whatnot. White-collar types."

"Can you get Al's number for me?" Conor asked.

"Got it right here," Staver said and read it off.

"You mentioned Black Hall. That's where they were from?"

"Somewhere around there," Dufour said. "That's how Stavie and me put it together with the Chase woman."

"What was the name of that club?"

"Jeez, that escapes me," Staver said. "Wasn't one I'd ever heard of, but it had a ring to it. I liked it, I remember that."

"One of them had to be a member here, or know a member, because we're not open to the public," Dufour said.

"And everyone had to have the proper licenses and permits," Staver said. "Al would have made sure of that."

"Got it," Conor said. "Think I can get the membership list from Al?"

"Hell, we can do better than that," Staver said, pushing himself out of the deep chair. "We've got it right here." He walked over to a bulletin board, removed a sheet of paper, and handed it to Conor. "We're a small club. We keep membership down, on account of we don't want to overhunt or overfish our property. It's part of our charter. The founders planned it that way."

Conor scanned the list of about thirty names. He stopped at *Wade Lockwood.*

"Could Lockwood have been the member who brought that group here?" Conor asked.

"Could've been," Staver said. "Great guy. He loves this place, definitely brings guests, likes to show it off."

Farther down the list was another familiar name: *Neil Coffin.*

"How about him?" Conor asked, pointing.

"He keeps to himself more than Wade," Staver said. "He and his brother, Max, usually come here together."

"They are your basic Ravenscrag royalty," Dufour said. "Zebediah's great-great-grandsons. Their family goes back to the Mayflower or thereabouts, brought their muskets right over from England. They needed a hunt club, didn't they? So old Zeb and a bunch of his buddies founded this one." He chuckled.

"Neil's wife is a California yoga type," Dufour said. "She comes to the Christmas party and pisses all over the slogans and trophies. She has a stick up her ass. My wife is like, *you don't like it, honey, you don't have to be here. We respect the way you live your life, you respect ours. But you* know, we can't actually say anything to her, on account of her being a Coffin. Like I said, they're royalty here."

"Right, because they're descendants of Zeb," Conor said.

"Day of the week!" Staver said.

"Excuse me?" Conor asked.

"The name of their club. It was Saturday something."

"Not Saturday," Dufour said. "That would have made sense, a little excitement on the weekend. Monday, it was. Who celebrates a Monday?"

"The Last Monday Club?" Conor asked.

"Bingo," Staver said. "That's it."

The Major Crime Squad arrived. Conor thanked Staver and Dufour for their statements, told them he would be in touch if he needed anything further. Then he asked them to unlock the chain across a dirt road that led toward the fishing pond. Conor rode in the van, directing the driver to the half-filled-in grave-shaped hole.

The team set up a perimeter and began to search the tall grass and the damp earth around the pond. The techs in their protective white jumpsuits excavated the hole slowly, sifting through the relatively soft, recently tossed-in dirt with all the care of an archaeological dig.

When they got to the bottom, where the earth was hard and damp, they found no body. The bags of lime had been removed, but the tarp was there, spread flat on the cold ground. As Conor stared at the plastic, he thought he saw footprints and knelt down for a closer look. Indeed, there were shoe impressions in a film of dirt and a calcified-appearing white substance. The soles of the shoes had left a distinctive repeating wave pattern—fine and intricate parallel lines.

Conor took his own photos, then gestured for the techs to photograph, measure, and take samples. He had the feeling he knew what would come back: Top-Siders and limestone. His brother wore boat shoes with that precise wavy pattern—the cuts in the rubber soles were designed to grip slippery and wet decks, to keep the wearer from sliding overboard.

And limestone tended to harden, just like cement. Even the dampness of the earth couldn't keep that from happening. People thought the use of quicklime sped the decomposition of bodies, but in fact, it tended to preserve them. It prevented putrefaction, the rotten smell that attracts insects and animals. In that sense, Staver and Dufour could be correct—that this hole had been dug to hold the carcasses and spoils of the hunt.

But Conor didn't think so.

The plastic tarp had been spread so smoothly, and a trickle or more of quicklime had spilled from bags the two men had seen. A boater—someone who wore Top-Siders—had stood in this hole, preparing it as a grave. All this time, it had been waiting for a body.

Claire's, he thought. Here was the connection again: he thought of the boating shoes and pictured the foam key chain found in the storm drain with items linked to her disappearance. It had come from the *Sallie B.*

Dan Benson was a member of the Last Monday Club. Conor wondered if he had been along with the others who had descended upon the Ravenscrag Sportsmen's Preserve for a turkey hunt in March. He might have scouted a deserted location, a disposal site. Two dead wives. Had Griffin and Dan conspired to kill Claire and Sallie? Had Griffin coerced Dan into killing Claire? And in return, had Dan contrived for Griffin, or someone connected to him, to destroy the *Sallie B* with his wife on board?

Conor thought of Wade Lockwood. The man who loved Griffin Chase like a son, who had warned Conor to leave Chase alone. How was the timing of all this connected to Chase's run for governor? Having a dead wife made him sympathetic, as long as he wasn't a suspect.

Conor pulled out his cell phone and dialed Jen. They had to apply for a warrant to search Dan Benson's house, office, cars, and the wreck of his boat to see if he had a pair of Top-Siders caked with quicklime. They would search for DNA, weapons, GPS coordinates, and anything else connecting him to the disappearance of Claire Beaudry Chase.

45

TOM

Tom was trying to get hold of Jackie, but when he called both the gallery and her mobile phone, it went straight to voice mail. He texted her, and after three hours, he didn't receive a reply. That was unusual, and it made him wonder, but he wasn't exactly worried. He headed across the parking lot, past the van, three state police cars, and Conor's unmarked vehicle, to the boat shed, where what was left of the *Sallie B* was stored on a cradle.

The building was cool compared to the hot weather outside, and it still smelled strongly of smoke. He walked toward the hull, looking up at the charred and gaping hole just below the waterline, hearing the chatter of officers getting ready to do their work. His head investigator, Matthew Hendricks, stood amid the detectives and troopers.

The Major Crime Squad had gone over and over the boat, but late yesterday Conor had called to say they would be back to search again. As Tom approached, he saw his brother standing at the *Sallie B*'s stern, reading a sheaf of papers.

"What have you got there?" Tom asked.

"A copy of the search warrant," Conor said, looking up. "We already served it to your commandant, but here's one for you too."

Tom took the papers and read the first page.

SEARCH AND SEIZURE WARRANT / STATE OF CONNECTICUT SUPERIOR COURT

To search the Sallie B, a 42-foot Loring motor yacht (color white, registered to Daniel and Sallie Benson, which is currently stored at the United States Coast Guard Pier B in Easterly, CT).

For property described in the foregoing affidavit and application, to wit:

Blood, saliva, physiological fluids, secretions, and genetic material, hair, fibers, fingerprints, palm prints, footprints, shoe prints, dirt, dust, and soil, paint samples, chemical samples, and items that may contain traces thereof; hatchets, axes, knives, and other sharp-force instruments and cutting tools, shovels and other digging equipment, blunt-force instruments, glass and plastic fragments, marks of tools used to gain access to locked premises or containers; cellular telephones and electronic communication devices, to include SIM cards, computers, and electronic storage media, digital imaging devices; infotainment system/vehicle electronics/GPS navigation devices; photographs or handwritten notes by, to, or from the victims, and male/female clothing and/or footwear; traces or bags of quicklime. The evidence will be collected and submitted to the Connecticut Department of Emergency Services and Public Protection Forensic Science Laboratory and/or other qualified law enforcement facility for physical examination, scientific testing, and forensic analysis.

"What are you hoping to find?" Tom asked. "Other than everything." He tapped the search warrant.

"Shoes, basically."

"All this for shoes?"

"Deck shoes," Conor said, pointing at Tom's feet. "With ridged soles. Like yours."

"And the rest of what's in the warrant? 'Infotainment system'?" Tom asked.

"The Bensons have SiriusXM radios in each of their cars and on the boat, and the systems come with location services. Someone might turn off a cell phone or GPS but forget about their radio."

"Don't you already know the *Sallie B*'s cruise track?"

"We're checking for anything we might have missed."

"Is Benson under arrest?" Tom asked.

"No, not yet."

"Will he be?" Tom asked, thinking of Gwen and how that would affect her.

"Depends on what we find. Possibly, though. Jen has teams on the way to his office and the Benson home right now."

The house, Tom thought. It was nearly three thirty p.m., and unless she was still at school, Gwen would be there.

"Is it okay if I head over?" Tom asked. "To check on Gwen?"

"That would be great, actually," Conor said. "I hate what she must be going through, and how much worse it will be if her father was involved."

Tom drove straight to the house. Jen Miano hadn't arrived yet. He parked on the street, not wanting to get boxed in by police vehicles. As he walked up the front sidewalk, he caught sight of Lydia Clarke and Gwen working in the garden on the side of the house. Maggie barked and raced toward him.

"Hey, little one," he said, picking her up. The Yorkshire terrier squirmed in his arms and licked his face, and he had no doubt that she remembered her time with him and Jackie.

"Hello there," Lydia said, surrounded by garden tools and flats of annuals—snapdragons, zinnias, cosmos, and other flowers like the ones Jackie bought to fill their window boxes.

"Hi, Tom," Gwen said, doing her best to smile but unable to hide the sadness in her eyes.

"Look at that garden," Tom said. "It's really pretty."

"Mom usually plants these," Gwen said. "They're her favorite summer flowers."

"Well, they're beautiful," Tom said.

"She would like them," Gwen said.

"I'm sure she would," Tom said. He listened for police cars, tried to catch Lydia's eye. She noticed and brushed the dirt off her hands, stood up.

"How about if I get us some lemonade?" she asked.

"I'm going to keep planting," Gwen said. "This garden is going to be for Mom and Charlie. And when he comes home, he will help water it."

Tom and Lydia walked around the corner of the house.

"The police are coming to search," Tom said. "I'm surprised they're not here by now. You should get Gwen out of here."

"Search for what?" Lydia asked.

"They have a long list."

"Is this about what happened to Sallie?" Lydia asked.

"Partly," he said.

"Good," she said.

"What do you mean?"

Lydia leaned forward to glance at Gwen and make sure she was out of earshot.

"Something's going on with Dan," she said. "He barely pays attention to Gwen; he never mentions Sallie, and when I bring her up, he looks angry. And he's on his phone all the time—texting or talking. He's definitely hiding something. I just don't know if it's related to what happened to Sallie."

"Have you told my brother?" Tom asked. "Or Detective Miano?"

A frown clouded Lydia's face. "No," she said. "Because I'm not sure of anything. And because of Gwen. I don't want to tell the police anything about Dan unless I'm sure. It would just make things worse for her."

"Well, let's get her out of here now, so she doesn't have to see a bunch of cops going through her house."

"I should stay, shouldn't I?" she asked. "To be home when they arrive?"

"You don't have to," he said.

She shook her head. "I feel as if I do, for Sallie. I don't want a bunch of strangers tromping through her house."

"They will anyway," Tom said. "I think it's more important that you look after Gwen."

"She trusts you," Lydia said. "Do you have time? Can you take her? She loves the beach, if you could just go for a walk or ice cream or . . ."

"No problem," Tom said. Lydia ran to get Maggie's leash and a sun hat for her niece, and Gwen was so comfortable with Tom that she didn't even question the plans.

"Are we going to see Jackie?" Gwen asked when they backed out of the driveway.

"She was busy this morning," he said, "but let's give her a call and see if she wants to meet us."

He was just making the call when they passed the first cop car heading in the opposite direction on the Bensons' street. Then another, six altogether. He looked over at Gwen, but she didn't seem to notice the vehicles. Jackie answered the phone, her voice coming over the truck's speakers just as Tom thought he was going to have to hear another message.

"Hey," he said. "Where've you been?"

"There's a lot to tell you," she said. Her tone of voice told him it was big, that she was bursting to tell him. "You won't believe this, and you can't tell Conor yet. I'm with . . ."

"Jackie, Gwen's in the car with me," he said quickly, so she wouldn't reveal anything the child shouldn't hear.

"Oh," Jackie said. "Hi, Gwen."

"Hi, Jackie," Gwen said.

308

"We're going to take a walk on the beach," Tom said. "Want to come?"

"I can't right now," Jackie said. "But how about if I meet you later— we can go to Paradise for fried clams. How does that sound, Gwen?"

Gwen nodded. "Good," she said.

Both Tom and Jackie were silent for a moment. He wanted her to tell him what was going on, but he sensed she was holding back because of Gwen.

"Jackie, just tell me, Are you okay?"

"Tom," Jackie said. "You can't imagine how okay. I can't wait to see you. Meanwhile, have fun by the water. Gwen, do you like to find sea glass?"

"Oh yes. I love it."

"I know a good place," Jackie said. "In Stonington, the small beach near the lighthouse museum. Especially when the tide's out."

"It'll be low tide in an hour," Tom said. He liked Stonington, a small town with a lot of big old houses, an unfortunately shrinking fishing fleet, and a favorite restaurant in the midst of a boatyard. He passed Stonington by water nearly every time he went out on patrol.

"That sounds great," Jackie said. "Have fun!"

"Thanks," Tom said. "You too. Whatever it is you're up to."

"We will," Jackie said.

Tom heard the smile in her voice, and it made him chuckle. He disconnected, glanced at Gwen to make sure she was okay, and began to drive east.

46

CONOR

The police executed the search warrants at Dan Benson's office and home, the separate building that served as a garage, and his vehicles. Benson was at neither location. There was also an urgent feeling among the team, excitement building, because it felt as if the case were about to break.

Conor and Jen had combined their resources in what the press had started calling the "task force," even though the department had not given it an official name. The goal now was to find Claire if she was alive or locate her body if she was not.

When Conor Reid arrived at the Benson home, he saw two satellite TV trucks parked up the road. In high-profile cases like this, the media staked out homes of victims and suspects, and obviously the word had spread about the search. Two state police officers, including Hunter, had been stationed at the head of the Bensons' driveway to keep the public out.

The reporters called out questions. Conor waved as he walked past. He had a good relationship with most of them, had done interviews with many after Beth Lathrop's murder and the subsequent trial of her killer, but there would be no statements until today's search was completed, if then.

Conor entered the house by the front door. Lydia Clarke was sitting in the living room, a copy of the search warrant in hand. She was thin, with white-blonde hair; a framed photo of Sallie, arms around Gwen and Charlie, was on the bookcase behind her, and Conor felt his heart tug to notice how alike the sisters looked.

"Detective," she said, rising and shaking his hand.

"Sorry for the intrusion, Ms. Clarke," he said.

"Don't be, and call me Lydia. Your brother took Gwen away, so she wouldn't have to see this. That's all I care about," she said.

Conor nodded. When he had given Tom a heads-up, he'd figured that might happen. "Can you tell me where your brother-in-law is right now?"

"No idea," she said. "Dan and I aren't close. He doesn't tell me where he's going or when he'll be back."

"Does he have a place in the house where he goes on his own? An office, maybe?"

"Down in the basement," she said.

"Can you show me?" Conor asked.

"Sure," she said. She led him through the first floor, past police officers intent on their search. The basement door was just off the kitchen. Downstairs, Dan had a tool bench, an ornate carved-oak desk, a billiard table, and two vintage pinball machines. There was a floor-to-ceiling bookcase filled with books. A built-in wall unit served as a bar, and there were two closed doors, behind which were a large closet and a bathroom.

Conor looked in the closet and bathroom. He walked over to the leather desk chair and examined it. He opened the desk drawers and looked inside each one. The shallow top drawer stretched the width of the desk and was haphazardly filled with pens, pencils, paper clips, and other office supplies.

The next drawer contained piles of envelopes held together with rubber bands. Conor riffled through them; they appeared to be mostly bills. The forensic accountants could go through them.

In the same drawer, he found several hardbound annual reports, going back a few years, for the Last Monday Club and for the Ravenscrag

Sportsmen's Preserve. He chose the current year for each and opened to the membership lists. He set the lists side by side, cross-checking one club against the other. Maxwell Coffin was president of both.

He knew that Max and Neil were brothers. Another Catamount Bluff connection. Conor used his iPhone to shoot pictures of each list of officers.

Tucked into the Last Monday Club book was a handwritten note. Conor read the lines:

Exhibit starts at 5—GC accounted for all afternoon, will be at gallery by 5.
CBC—4–4:30 optimal.
Site prepared in advance and disposal MUST BE completed by 7. Investigation will have started at CB by then.

Conor knew he was looking at a timeline of the Friday Claire disappeared. It was a script for killing her, disposing of her, and providing an alibi for Griffin—GC. He wondered whose handwriting it was and bagged the note.

Finally, he opened the bottom drawer and found it stacked with brown leather-bound photo albums. As he removed them, he wondered why they were here and not on the bookshelves or otherwise out where the family could look through them.

"That's where they went," Lydia said, watching from the doorway.

"What do you mean?" Conor asked.

"Oh, Sallie and Dan were very big on keeping photo albums. There must be hundreds of photos in there." She paused. "The kids love looking through them, especially Gwen. I suppose it's the same with all children, wanting to know everything about their families."

Conor looked through the one on top of the pile and saw that the pictures were from a different decade. The styles were all wrong for current times, and he recognized a much younger Dan Benson on the beach with a ponytail. He was wearing cutoffs as a bathing suit; beside him was Griffin Chase with long hair, Ray-Ban sunglasses, and the same cocky expression he had today. Between them was a girl beaming and giving a peace sign; he recognized her as Ellen Fielding.

Flipping through the album, Conor saw more photos of the trio as well as other familiar faces—Wade and Leonora Lockwood. On a sportfishing yacht, sipping cocktails under a thatched beach hut, on the beach, at a dinner table. Clearly on vacation, somewhere tropical. One picture of the hotel showed a Mexican flag.

As Conor glanced through the other albums, he saw that Lydia was right—the family had taken many photos, especially of the kids. The timeline progressed from Sallie and Dan's wedding, to the births of Gwen and Charlie, and through their childhoods—building sand-castles, playing Little League, in costumes for school plays and concerts, opening Christmas presents, Gwen outside a church in a white dress and veil to receive her First Communion.

The last album, at the bottom of the drawer, had an insignia embossed on the green leather cover: it was the same one Conor had seen on Griffin's and Edward's shirts, an imposing blackbird with outstretched wings and words in Latin beneath: *Corvus Corax*. When Conor began looking through the pages and saw the pictures inside, he caught his breath.

They were of the sea castle.

He thought of the photos his brother had sent him; a shiver ran down his spine. Gwen had drawn this exact scene. Two men in tuxedos stood on the balcony of a big stone mansion at the water's edge. The mermen. One was Griffin; the other was Dan. Gargoyles hulked behind them.

Now he put it together. This was the same house depicted in the gallery of photos at the sporting preserve, the one Staver had said shared a name with the hunt club: Ravenscrag. And now the crest on the men's shirts and the front of this album made sense; it wasn't just a black-bird—it was a raven.

The album was devoted to the house and the people within it. From cars in the courtyard, Conor could tell the pictures were from the present day, but there was an old-world flavor to the scenes depicted. Formal portraits of men in black tie, group shots that seemed to have been taken during a ball, men and women dancing to an orchestra.

He recognized Wade and Leonora Lockwood, Edward and Sloane Hawke, Neil and Abigail Coffin, Maxwell Coffin and a woman he didn't recognize, Dan and Sallie Benson, and Griffin and Claire Chase. In one, the two couples—the Chases and Bensons—were standing together.

And Dan had said he'd never met Claire.

The last photos were of young people. Children of the members, perhaps, Conor thought. The Old Guard would want new blood so their traditions and way of life could continue. Ford and Alexander Chase were in half the shots. Some showed them dressed formally at the same dances as their father and Claire, but in others they were more casual, with kids their own age. On the tennis court, having a picnic, sailing at the dock.

A series of three pictures caught Griffin's attention: Ford, Alexander, and Emily Coffin in a small powerboat. The hull was white, and ravens were stenciled on the side.

The blackbird boat that Gwen had seen following the *Sallie B.*

Conor slid the photos out of the album's clear sleeve to get a better look. In one shot, taken from behind, he saw the name of the boat and the home port emblazoned on the transom:

RAEN
STONINGTON, CT

And in a close-up of Emily, he saw that same word, *Raen*, printed in black letters on her white T-shirt.

Lydia had been standing beside him, paging through one of the earlier albums. She stopped to look at the photos Conor was holding.

"Pretty girl," she said.

"Do you know her?" he asked.

"No, she's the daughter of friends of Dan and Sallie. I was curious, though. Once Sallie showed me the photos in that book, pointed out the house, and said it was one of the biggest in Connecticut. I asked her about the word on the girl's T-shirt, and Sallie said it meant *raven* in Scots."

Conor watched as Lydia closed the album and pointed at the insignia. "*Corvus Corax* is Latin for *raven*," she said. "I asked her what the significance was. She said that the raven is one of the smartest birds, entirely black to blend into the night. There's a legend, dating back to medieval times, that England could never be conquered as long as there were ravens at the Tower of London."

"Okay," Conor said, skeptical but also noting that this crew of men really did live in another world. Their rules were different, and legends counted more than laws.

"Sallie said that, to this day, there are ravens at the Tower of London. They're fed by the Ravenmaster of the Yeoman Warders. Sounds like a fairy tale, doesn't it?" Lydia paused. "It bothered me to see Sallie surrounded by people like Dan's friends."

"Why?" Conor asked.

"Whatever the literary legends are—in Britain, in mythology—to Dan's friends, the ravens are here to protect the group's wealth. They see themselves as important, deserving privilege, getting to do what they want."

"Who in particular?" Conor asked.

"Griffin Chase," she said without hesitation. "He's their great hope for the future. He's going to bring civility and structure back to society." She snorted. "They might tell themselves that, but what they really want is for him to let them develop every inch of the shoreline and fill their pockets. She said that Dan once told her they'd kill for him."

"For Griffin?" Conor asked.

"Yes," Lydia said. "She said Dan said it like a joke. I'm not sure she took it that way, though."

Conor pictured the grave in the middle of the Ravenscrag Sportsmen's Preserve and, again, wondered if they had dug it for Claire. She was the wife who knew too much. He thought of those missing bags of quicklime.

"Lydia, your sister was obviously a great gardener. Was that something she and Dan would do together?"

"No," she said. "Sallie was the one with a green thumb. I was in awe of her. It's all I can do to plant a few annuals. I'm only doing it for Gwen. Dan did have a way with landscaping, though. He was going to plant some rhododendrons and a dogwood tree, but he hasn't gotten around to it."

"Did you ever see bags of lime among Sallie's garden supplies?" he asked.

"I don't think so. Why?"

"Where did Sallie keep her garden things?" he asked, sidestepping the question.

"In a bin on the terrace," she said.

Conor was about to ask her to take him to the bin when something occurred to him. "When did you first find out Dan was going to plant that tree?"

"Sallie told me a few days before she died. It bugged her because he had the ground all ready for planting, tilled and dug. She said it had been that way for a month, they were past the prime time to get the tree and bushes into the ground, and she was afraid the kids would fall into the hole."

"The hole?" he asked. "Where is it?"

"Right beside the garage, out back," she said.

"I didn't notice it when we came in."

"Come to think of it, neither did I," Lydia said.

Conor hurried out the door, around the side of the building. He saw it right away: a rectangular plot of freshly disturbed earth, the exact shape as the one he'd seen at the hunting preserve.

"This is weird," she said. "It was a big old hole just yesterday. Why did he fill it in instead of planting the rhododendrons?"

"Let's go back to the house," Conor said. After she went inside, he found Jen with a bunch of forensic techs in Tyvek overalls. "Get your shovels," he said to them and led them back to the recently filled-in grave-shaped hole. He felt sick, wondering if they were about to uncover Claire's body, dusty with white quicklime.

"You okay?" Jen asked.

He shook his head. "I want to find her but not like this . . ."

"I know, Conor," she said. Then, "What fucking balls it would take to bury her right behind his house."

The police erected portable tents to prevent onlookers and media drones from seeing what they were doing. When the techs began to dig, Conor pulled Jen aside and showed her one of the photos of Ravenscrag.

"This is the place Gwen drew," he said.

"Where she thinks the mermen took Charlie," Jen said.

"Let's start calling departments along the shoreline, ask who knows where this house is. It's not exactly discreet—it's got to be a landmark to people who live near it," Conor said. His stomach flipped; he was standing here with Jen Miano, talking in a calm voice while listening to shovels scooping and throwing dirt. The sound was rhythmic and solemn.

He and Jen stood still and silent. His thoughts were for Claire. It took another few minutes before the sound of digging stopped.

"Detectives," one of the techs said, beckoning them over.

Conor's heart skipped as he approached the hole and steeled himself to look into the face of Claire Beaudry Chase.

"Holy shit," Jen said.

And Conor agreed but didn't speak as he stared down at the body of Dan Benson, a bullet hole in his head.

47

CLAIRE

Spencer drove us back to Hubbard's Point and dropped us off at Jackie's house. Telling us about Marnie had taken everything she had, and she wanted to spend the rest of the day alone.

When we got to Jackie's, Tom was out. I actually wished he were there; I was ready to come out of the shadows, and I wanted to tell both Tom and Conor what had happened, what I knew. Jackie handed me a clean towel, and I went upstairs to take a shower. I stripped off my old clothes—so rancid Jackie just threw them away—and stood under the stream of hot water for the longest time, loving the feeling of being clean, not wanting the shower to end. When I got out, I put on a pair of Jackie's khaki shorts and a blue Vineyard Vines T-shirt and went into her kitchen.

Jackie had made us tuna fish sandwiches, and we ate them with potato chips and iced tea, just as we had when we were kids, and no meal had ever tasted so good. While we ate, Jackie filled me in on the news—articles about me that had been in the newspapers and stories that had appeared on channels 3 and 8.

"I don't know how you stayed hidden so long," she said. "Your face is everywhere. There was a story about you in *People*."

"Oh, great. All these years of making art, and now I'm known for being missing."

Jackie laughed. "Well, it's working. The gallery has been getting calls from all over, lots of people stopping by."

I thought about the gallery, how I had been attacked the day my show opened. How nervous and excited I had felt—not just because of the anticipation of my exhibition opening, the trepidation of hearing the opinions of critics and collectors about my latest work—but because of Griffin. Because I had just shown him my shadow box—*the* shadow box, the one that mattered.

"What happened the night of the opening?" I asked.

"It was successful," Jackie said. "It nearly sold out."

"Remember the piece I delivered late that afternoon?" I asked.

"Of course. *Fingerbone*."

"Did you know what it was about?" I asked.

"I knew it had to do with Ellen," she said. "With you finding her body in the tide pool."

"I don't have proof," I said. "But I know Griffin killed her."

She sat silently, looking into my eyes. "He bought it, you know. *Fingerbone*."

"He did?" I asked, feeling a chill run through my body.

"Yes," Jackie said. "He took it home that same night. But it wound up in the garbage outside the gallery. Other things had been discarded up the street. Kids found them, including a knife that Conor connected to your attack. The cops searched the whole neighborhood. Either someone stole the shadow box from Griffin, or he threw it out himself."

I tried to picture it: Griffin heading into town, stuffing art and weapons into trash bins. "What else did the kids find, besides the knife?" I asked.

"There was a key chain. The Styrofoam kind boaters use and it came from the *Sallie B*."

So there was a connection between Sallie and me—it made sense. Spencer's story was the missing part of the puzzle—the Dan factor.

"This is all about timing," I said quietly.

"Timing for what?"

"Griffin's campaign," I said. "He had too much to lose—I was going to leave him. It's been hard enough having suspicions about Ellen all these years. I couldn't let him run for governor knowing he's a murderer. He always knew I suspected—I just didn't know why he'd done it until yesterday."

"Because of what happened in Cancún," Jackie said. "Ellen knew."

"And so did Dan, and he must have told Sallie," I said. "So now, getting closer to the election, they murdered her. And nearly killed me. Because I knew too."

"Griffin and Dan? But what about the kids," Jackie asked. "How could they have let them be collateral damage? Charlie is dead, and Gwen is beyond traumatized. She's with Tom right now. He just told me on the phone."

"I want to meet her," I said, feeling numb. "We're the two survivors. What can I do to help her?"

Jackie took a deep breath. "I don't know. She's troubled, and how can she not be? And how can she live with her father—if he really did that to Sallie? She has this elaborate fantasy that Charlie is being held in a castle by the sea. She did these incredibly intricate drawings of a mansion with turrets and towers and scary crow gargoyles."

"Do you have the drawings?" I asked.

"Not the originals," Jackie said. "But Tom took photos and sent them to my phone. Hold on." She began scrolling through texts, and when she found the right one, she showed the shots to me. I saw the castle, the crags and cornices, the turret, the gargoyles with thick black beaks and folded wings, the men standing on the balcony.

"Wait," I said. "They're not scary crows. They're ravens."

"What are you talking about?"

"It's not an imaginary place," I said. "It's a real house."

"How do you know, Claire?"

"Because I've been there. A fundraiser for Griffin. Emily's father—Maxwell Coffin, one of Griffin's supporters—owns it. It's an absolutely insane, over-the-top replica of the 'ancestral estate,' as they put it, in Scotland. You can't see it from the road—it's on acres of land, up a long driveway. On the outskirts of Stonington."

"That's bizarre," Jackie said, looking shocked. "Tom's taking Gwen to the lighthouse in Stonington now. How do you know the owners?"

"I don't, really. Max is Neil's older brother. We've met a few times, but that's it. He and his wife commissioned me to do a shadow box of their house. Of Ravenscrag."

I was practically shaking, remembering that night—and the letter that followed. I pictured the Gothic Revival mansion, the crenelated towers, the walls lined with English sporting art and austere nineteenth-century family portraits. The curved marble staircase was lined with photos taken in the early part of the twentieth century, people at black-tie affairs and in country-gentleman garb holding guns and posed with white-and-brown spaniels.

It was a very dressy affair, full of pomp. Max's wife, Evans, had worn a mauve satin gown with a jeweled bodice, and the two of them had walked me down to the seawall, where the waves broke on the rocks below, sending spray upward, so I could look back at the mansion and start imagining the shadow box I would create.

Evans stared at me while Max talked about my great talent, how he had been an admirer ever since Griffin first told him about my work. Extraordinary, he had called it. Mysterious, storytelling, soulful. I kept glancing at Evans, and initially I thought she was upset that her husband was paying so much attention to me.

But the expression in her eyes told me something else—imploring, warning, as if she were telling me to beware. But of what? I certainly knew about dangerous husbands, but what would I possibly have to fear from hers? I wasn't to find out until weeks later, when the letter came.

Abigail and Neil Coffin were there, of course, as well as some of our other Catamount Bluff neighbors—they often attended Griffin's fundraisers. Griffin and I had driven over with Wade and Leonora Lockwood.

Alexander and Ford lived in the guest cottage, available to housesit when the family went to stay at any of their other houses, in St. Barts, Vail, and San Francisco. Ford was absent that night, but Alexander and Emily were helping to bartend. Max was the first to sign a big check to the campaign to elect Griffin Chase as governor of Connecticut.

Abigail, Sloane, and I had stuck together. I had been grateful to Abigail for giving us a tour of the house; I couldn't stand the sound of Griffin's voice cajoling the crowd, while I knew who he was, what he had done. It had been eating me up for so long, and I knew I was coming to the end of my time with him.

I remembered joking with Sloane Hawke that she had finally met her match in terms of the preppiest girl's name ever, that Abigail's sister-in-law, Evans Coffin, had her beat. I had thought Evans might join us, even show us the rooms, but she stayed in the salon, listening to my husband. As I walked past her, she gave me that same look: be careful. At least that's how I read it.

And it turned out that I had read her right.

Abigail identified most of the staid characters in the family portraits, and she said the men with guns had been photographed at the family's hunting preserve just a few miles north.

"The one where the guys still go to hunt?" Sloane had asked as we entered the book-lined study.

"Yep," Abigail said. "That's the place. Named after this house. Or the other way around. I always forget. Neil and Max's grandfather liked consistency and reminding everyone of the, ahem, ancestral pile in the western highlands." We all chuckled.

I looked around at the taxidermy—dead animals and birds, especially ravens, hawks, and owls, gathering dust on shelves around the room. But that wasn't the memory that took my breath away: next to a raven with wings outstretched was a row of Nate's books. Ten volumes by my ex-husband, Nate Browning. I glanced inside one and saw an inscription in Nate's hand: *To Max, who knows what matters. NB.*

"Worlds collide," Abigail said, leaning closer. "These people read books by your first husband and are trying to elect your second husband. And trust me, Max won't let you alone until you make that shadow box for him."

I chuckled, but inside I was shaken; Nate was academic and non-political, a scholar who spent his time in the field or at his desk—when he took a stand politically, he was single issue, voting for the candidate who vowed to fight climate change. To Nate, *that* was what mattered. Did Max agree with him?

Griffin was a political animal who pretended to care about conservation. He certainly did fight to protect the land around his home, but across the state was another story. He would never put the environment first, certainly not at the expense of business, of attracting large corporations into the state. That's what the gathering was about—to drum up support for him and his agenda. I assumed Max would be in line with Griffin's way of thinking, not Nate's.

"Why would Gwen be drawing a picture of that house?" Jackie asked now.

"I don't know," I said, still stuck on the memory of seeing Nate's books there. I remember thinking that I would tell him, that we'd have a laugh about it—political high rollers interested in his poetic research. And I would tell him about the raven gargoyles, the absurd grandeur of a fifteen-thousand-square-foot Scottish castle in a New England town of sea captains' houses and candy-colored fishermen's cottages, how the Coffins had wanted me to replicate it in a shadow box.

And how I had started to do just that, because it was so over-the-top Gothic, surrounded by hedges and English gardens, straight out of one of those dreams that verges on nightmare. My husband was the only reason I had gone to Ravenscrag: a den of vipers gathered together to raise a fortune to elect Griffin Chase.

"Claire, I know you've felt safer staying hidden, but we have to call Conor. And I want to call Tom. They both need to know you're okay and to hear about this place. We've all thought Gwen has been fantasizing but maybe . . ."

"It's real," I said. My mind was racing, recalling the piece I had started, the notes I had made based on that talk with Max Coffin, and the secret I had hidden beneath the frame.

"I believe you," she said. "We have to call Tom and Conor right away."

"Can I use your computer first? I have to send an email."

"Sure," she said. "Someone's going to be very surprised to hear from you." We walked to the desk, to the same laptop I'd used to contact Spencer, and I logged in to my Gmail account. I ignored the hundreds of emails and wrote one to Nate: I'm alive. I never would have guessed you were one of them. Never. Were you in on the plan? Did you know they were going to kill me? Not you, Nate. Why did you have to be part of it?

My eyes were wet when I hit send. Of all the people in my life, I would have expected that Nate would be true-blue forever. It felt brave to use my voice, but this was just the beginning. I had a lot more to say to many more people. I felt my strength full force—it was back, and I was going to use it. First thing, I needed to get that letter.

"Jackie, you call Tom and Conor, okay?" I asked. "I have to go to my studio. There's evidence there. Now that I know Ravenscrag is involved, I need to get it. It's the link."

"That's crazy, Claire," she said. "You can't go back there on your own, not after what happened to you."

"No one will see me," I said. "I'll go through the path along the beach. Besides, you'll know where I am. That makes me feel safe."

"Conor will want to interview you . . ."

"You can tell him where I am too. He can find me at the Bluff—I'll tell him everything right there. I'm doing the right thing, Jackie. I'm taking care of my own life, and I promise you, I'm going to bring these guys down. Especially Griffin."

Jackie didn't want to let me go, but she knew I was determined. She wanted to drive me, but I said no. I needed to walk down the path through the trees, past the spot where Ellen had died. I would need all my strength for this—and it came from the woods, the tide pools, the marsh, and the burial ground. It came from the big cat and the spirit of my father and the knowledge I had, finally, about what Griffin had done.

And so I kissed my friend and left to go to Catamount Bluff for what I hoped would be the last time.

48

TOM

By the time they got off the highway in Mystic, the fog that had been hovering just offshore began billowing in. The foghorns were low and mournful, and when Tom glanced across the front seat at Gwen, he saw her sinking down, as if the weather and accompanying mood were taking the air out of her.

It had gotten damp and chilly, so Tom decided a walk on the beach might not be the best for Gwen; she was still fragile and recovering. Besides, the idea was nagging him that he had seen something important, connected to Gwen's drawings, while passing by these points of land on patrol. They drove east toward Stonington along Route 1. The water was on the right, behind the shops and houses. Low hills were interspersed with salt marshes and rocky coves.

"Are we going to the lighthouse?" Gwen asked.

"Yes, we are," he said. "But I thought it might be too soggy for the beach."

"I love beach walks in the fog," she said. "And the rain. Mom did too. Any weather at all."

Tom smiled over at her. "People after my own heart," he said. "I'm the same. The sea and the beach, no matter what."

She nodded, then resumed looking out the window. Tom scanned both sides of the road as he drove. It was habit for him; on patrol he kept a loose gaze, taking everything in. He never knew when he might spot someone in distress or a fisherman pulling lobster pots that belonged to someone else or debris in the water. Jackie and her daughters teased him about it, said he was only halfway present when he was in the car or on the sailboat with them, that the other half was saving lives that didn't even need saving yet.

This stretch of road was full of big estates, most of them behind hedges or down long driveways. The rich paid extra for privacy—large pieces of property protected them from prying eyes. He was cruising slowly, craning to see a glimpse of the houses among the trees, when he spotted the stone columns.

Tall and imposing, on either side of a paved driveway that wound through oak trees up a boulder-strewn hill, the columns were topped by ravens with their wings spread wide. On the left post, a slab of granite was carved with the house name: *Ravenscrag*.

He had slowed almost to a stop, to get a better look, when Gwen noticed the birds on the columns.

"Tom, that's them!" she said. "The exact same! They're in Daddy's pictures! This is where the mermen took Charlie. Drive in there, we have to get him."

"Let's call my brother first," Tom said. "You know he's a policeman, and—"

"No, we have to go there right now!"

He hesitated. What if they were wrong, and this was just another Stonington estate? They could drive up, take a look at the house, and leave. If someone stopped him, there was always the "wrong turn" defense. On the other hand, what if Charlie really *was* there? What would he do then?

Tom dialed his brother as he drove up the hill. At the top of the rise, the house came into view. It stopped him dead: previously, he had only seen this structure—it could only be called a castle—from the seaward side. Massive, built of fieldstone, it had two square towers and a turret. Gargoyles—birds of prey—hunched all along the roofline.

"The sea castle!" Gwen cried—and it was. Tom recognized it from her drawings. Conor answered the call.

"What's up?" Conor asked.

"Look, I can't talk right now," Tom said, stopping behind a Mercedes SUV parked under an ancient maple. "I just pulled into this wicked-crazy place, and I've got to turn around and get out—I'll call you as soon as I'm back on the road. You're going to want to get over here."

Gwen opened the truck door. Tom tried to grab for her, but she was moving fast and called back to him, "Charlie's in there! I'm going to go get him."

"Hang on," Tom said to Conor, jumping out of the car to chase Gwen. He caught up to her and grabbed her. "We're going to get help, Gwen. Come with me now."

"No," she cried. "He's here. Charlie!"

The front door opened, and a young man wearing a ball cap stepped out. Tom's heart skipped—he had seen the kid's picture in the paper. He was one of Griffin Chase's twin sons.

"Can I help you?" the kid asked. A young woman poked her head out from behind him. She had her hands on the shoulders of a small boy. Tom couldn't believe his eyes—it was Charlie. Gwen had been right the whole time.

"Charlie!" Gwen shouted, tearing toward the house. She threw herself at her brother, holding him in a tight hug, pulling him away from the woman. Tom was right behind Gwen, his eyes on the two adults. Adrenaline pumped through his body.

"Gwen, Charlie," he said carefully. "We're going now. Come with me."

Gwen raised her eyes to him—she was full of joy. It almost made him smile. She clutched Charlie's hand, walking toward Tom. Tom let them go ahead, glancing behind him at the front door. Only the woman was there.

"Alexander, stop them!" she called.

Tom and the kids made it to the truck.

"I've got this, Emily," Alexander Chase said, and Tom saw him lift a gun, a Sig Sauer semiautomatic, the same model Conor carried. Tom thought of his own service gun, in the safe at home.

"You're the merman and the mermaid," Gwen said, staring at Alexander and Emily. "You followed us in your boat and saved Charlie."

"That's right," Emily said. "I'm glad you know that. And we're going to take care of you now."

"But we have to go home. Our Daddy's waiting for us."

Alexander made a frustrated sound. "Jesus Christ," he said.

"Shut up," Emily said to him.

"Come on, Gwen, Charlie," Tom said, never taking his eyes off the gun. He heard his brother's voice on the phone in the truck, calling his name, the line still connected.

"Don't listen to him, Charlie," Emily said, taking a step forward. "Let's show your sister around. All the cool rooms and the tower and the swimming pool . . ."

"I know you're nice, but we're going with Tom," Gwen said, arms clasped around her brother.

"They're not nice," Charlie said, starting to cry. "They were following us to Block Island. To shoot Daddy when he got off the boat. But Ford did instead. The one who came to our house that day, when Mommy and Daddy started yelling."

"Stop talking," Alexander said.

"I heard you, though." Charlie wept. "I heard you say it. You said he would tell on your father and your father would lose and you said he shot Daddy."

Tom assessed Alexander. He was tall, looked soft and slightly heavy, and his hand was shaking. He wasn't comfortable holding the weapon. Tom calculated—would the kid actually shoot them?

"You shot Daddy? Did you kill our *mom?*" Gwen asked.

"No," Emily said in a sweet, cajoling tone. "We had no idea the boat was going to blow up. It was a horrible accident. We would never have wanted you to be hurt."

"Em, please? Stop," the young man said, glancing at her and pointing at Tom.

"What's the difference?" she asked. "Who cares what he hears? You know what you have to do."

"You don't have to do anything," Tom said, in as reasonable a tone of voice as he could manage. "You've done no harm so far. You saved Charlie. He wouldn't have made it without you. The explosion was an accident. No matter what Ford may have done, you haven't shot anyone . . ." He had his arms around Gwen and Charlie.

"Get away from them," the young woman said.

"You're not in trouble," Tom said. "You don't want to hurt us, I know that. You saved Charlie. That's the kind of kids you are. We're going to leave now."

He scooped Charlie up into his arms, guiding Gwen toward his truck. He kept his eyes on the pistol, his heart thumping. The man's arm dropped to his side, and he lowered his head—he wasn't going to shoot. Tom opened the door, pushed both of the children inside.

"You idiot," Emily said, grabbing Alexander's arm. "You can't let them go. After everything? What are our fathers going to say?"

Tom climbed into the driver's seat. The truck was still running, the phone still on speaker, and he heard Conor's voice coming over the speaker: "I heard everything. Get the hell out of there."

"Roger," Tom said. "Leaving Ravenscrag now." He jammed the truck into reverse and spun the wheel to turn around, tires screeching on the driveway pavement. He looked in the rearview mirror and saw Emily tug the gun from Alexander's hand and come stalking toward the truck, arm extended.

"Go, Tom, hurry!" Gwen cried, watching her.

Tom shifted into drive and hit the gas, and the young woman fired. He felt the punch in his shoulder as the glass in the driver's side window shattered and hot blood pouring from the hole in his shoulder, and the last thing he heard was his brother's voice saying his name over the phone, repeating it, yelling it, drowned out by the shrieks of Gwen and Charlie.

49

CONOR

Conor heard the unmistakable gut-twisting sound of a gunshot, and his brother stopped talking. The line was still open. The children were screaming, a boy and a girl. Now a sharp female voice:

"Come with me, both of you. Right now," she said.

"I want to go home!" Charlie said, sobbing.

"You killed Tom!" Gwen yelled.

"It's your fault, Gwen," the woman said. "I told you and Charlie to come with me. Look what you made me do."

"Tom!" Gwen cried.

"Come with us now," a man's voice said. "Come on, Gwen, you're safe here. You want to be with your brother, right? We'll take care of you and figure this out."

"Charlie, run away from them! We have to get help for Tom!"

Conor heard a loud smack, as if someone had just been hit, then both children sobbing.

"Is this really happening?" the woman asked. "Now we're stuck with *two* brats? This was not in the plan!"

"Look, we've done our part," the man said. "I proved myself to Dad. And so have you."

"The difference is, I never needed to! My parents respect me. At least till now! Is my family supposed to keep these brats forever? Why did the boat have to explode? Fucking unforeseen nightmare—their damn mother should still be alive to take care of them."

"What do we do now?" the man asked.

Since Ravenscrag was owned by Max Coffin, the woman had to be Emily, Alexander's girlfriend.

"Proved myself to Dad," the man had said a moment ago. What kind of dad made a kid prove himself by shooting someone? *Griffin Chase*, Conor thought, so if the woman was Emily, this must be Alexander.

"Let's just get the kids inside and call for help," the man said.

"Call the police?" the woman asked. "Are you kidding me?"

"No, call *him*—my dad will know what to do," the man said.

Conor had already sent dispatch a text message to send police and an ambulance to Ravenscrag in Stonington. Tom could be dying. Conor sped onto the highway, listening to every word, every inflection of the voices on the phone. He pressed harder on the gas.

"Tom," Gwen said, her voice shaking. "Tom needs to go to the hospital . . ."

"I can*not* take this anymore," the woman said.

Gwen started to scream, then Charlie did, the shrieks receding, as if they were being dragged away. Conor listened intently. He heard some scraping and fumbling, as if one of the two captors had stayed behind with Tom's truck. He heard gurgling, as if his brother were choking on blood, trying to breathe.

"Shit," the man said. "You're still alive?"

Conor knew this was his chance.

"Listen to me, Mr. Chase," Conor barked. "This is the state police. Do not hang up."

"What the fuck?" the man asked.

"Alexander, I am going to give you some very careful instructions," Conor said. "I know where you are, and I am on my way. So is an ambulance, so are local police, and Tom Reid had better be alive and on his way to the hospital when I get there."

Silence.

"I hear him breathing right now," Conor said. "If anything happens to him, the charge is murder. I don't know who shot him—you or Emily. But he's your responsibility right now. You got that? He dies, you're his murderer."

No answer.

"Did you hear me?" Conor asked. "You and Emily Coffin had better make sure those kids and my brother are safe. Understand?"

"Shit," the man said. Conor heard the phone jostle, then disconnect.

Conor called dispatch to get precise directions to Ravenscrag. He was told it was just off Route 1, east of the borough, no street number, the drive flanked by two stone posts with ravens on top. She transmitted the GPS coordinates to his phone.

"Send every available unit," Conor told her. "Get Life Star in the air right now. There's at least one gunshot wound, adult male. Emily Coffin and one of the Chase sons are holding the two Benson children, Gwen and Charlie." He swallowed hard. "The gunshot victim is my brother, Tom."

"You got it, Detective Reid," the dispatcher said. "We are all with you, every one of us."

"Thanks," Conor managed to say.

He sped toward Stonington. His mind was spinning, the shock of talking to Tom, hearing the shot, then hearing that horrific sound—how many times had Conor heard it in his life, at crime scenes, the death rattle of victims choking on their own blood? How much time did Tom have?

He tried to picture Tom—his older brother who had always been there for him, who had protected him when they were young, the ferociously tough Coast Guard Commander Thomas Reid—dying alone in his truck.

Conor stayed in the left lane, siren screaming, passing cars that pulled over to get out of his way, and when he hit a bottleneck at the Waterford junction of I-95 and I-395, he split the lanes in two and drove down the middle.

By the time he took the exit to Stonington Borough, he heard sirens and looked up to see the Life Star helicopter hovering overhead. Had it already picked up Tom, ready to fly to Yale New Haven, the closest level-1 trauma center?

No, it was landing now. Conor could barely breathe. He followed the chopper, heard the thwap-thwap of the rotors as he tore through the stone gates, up the hill toward the monstrosity of a house he'd seen in the photos of Dan Benson and at the sportsmen's preserve.

The mansion's turnaround was full of local and state police vehicles and two ambulances, lights still flashing. Personnel, including tactical units in riot gear, swarmed the front entrance. The helicopter was landing in an open section of lawn just south of the house. Tom's truck was parked on the edge of the driveway, both driver's-side doors open. Conor jumped out of his own car and ran to his brother's.

The driver's seat was a bucket of blood. It had seeped into the leather seat, coursed down the door side, puddled on the floor mat. Tom was not there. A trail of blood—not drops but thick, smeared swaths of it led from the driveway into a bayberry thicket—as if Tom had dragged himself into the bushes.

Conor strode over, both afraid he would find Tom and afraid he wouldn't: and he didn't. He spotted a torn scrap of blue fabric snagged on a low branch and a blood-covered Rolex watch with the stainless-steel band broken. The watch was facedown in the mud, and Conor thought he saw letters etched into the back of the case.

Conor knew, as if his brother were right here to tell him, that the watch belonged to Tom's attacker, that Tom had ripped it off his wrist in a violent struggle. The thought of his brother being strong enough to fight gave Conor a shot of hope.

He left the evidence in place and walked toward the door of the house. The SWAT officers were exiting the front door, which meant that they had cleared the premises and most likely found no one inside—no one alive, at least.

"Anyone in there?" Conor asked Trooper Rich Sibley, standing by the door.

"No, sir," Sibley said. "Trooper Allen reviewed security camera footage, and it looks as if two vehicles left the garage twenty and twenty-five minutes ago. We don't have a description of the suspects or the plates. And the camera filmed in black-and-white, so we don't have vehicle colors."

"What about Tom Reid?" Conor asked.

"No sign of him," Sibley said. "He is top priority. Along with the children."

"Thanks," Conor said. He considered the possibilities that his brother had been abducted, along with Gwen and Charlie, or that he had escaped. He knew the troopers would have broadcast a bulletin over the state police radio. The dispatcher at the barracks would inform the CTIC—Connecticut Intelligence Center—which, in turn, would alert all law enforcement agencies in the state. Because it was an assumed kidnapping, the NCIC—National Crime Information Center, run by the FBI—would send a teletype notifying law enforcement nationwide.

Conor walked over to the Major Crime Squad van. Maria Stewart was the forensics chief in charge of this sector of the state. Conor had known her since he was just starting out as a young trooper and she was already making her mark as a forensic scientist. They had worked together on many cases. He found her inside the van, dressing in white coveralls and booties.

"Hey, Conor," she said.

"Hi, Maria."

"I just heard about Tom. What's his condition?"

"No idea. He didn't sound good on the phone. There's a lot of blood loss, and he's not here."

"Every force in the state is on this, Conor. I promise."

"Hey, Detective! EMTs! Over here!" a forensic tech called.

Conor raced across the drive and beat the ambulance personnel by a few seconds. A shallow gully stretched the length of a hedgerow, and Tom lay in it. A starburst of blood bloomed on his left shoulder, but his eyes were open, and he nodded when he saw Conor.

Conor jumped in beside him, took off his jacket, and pressed it into the wound.

"Tom? Stay with me, okay?"

"They had Charlie—and they took Gwen. The girl shot me. I was so close to getting the kids out of here," Tom said.

It killed Conor to see his brother's eyes fill with tears. Tom squeezed them tight, his mouth clamped shut as if holding the pain inside.

"Sir, let us take care of him," one of the EMTs said.

"I'm staying with him," Conor said.

"No. Go find Charlie and Gwen," Tom said, slurring his words. "That's what you do—get them, make sure they're okay. The dog . . . they'll want to see Maggie. It will make them feel better, just ask Jackie, she'll tell you about Maggie . . ." Tom's voice trailed off.

Leaving his brother's side was the hardest thing Conor had ever done. He watched the emergency workers take vital signs, pack the wound, move Tom onto a stretcher.

Conor watched the EMTs load Tom into the Life Star helicopter, shut the doors, and take off. Conor swallowed past the lump in his throat. He stood still, looking up until the helicopter disappeared from view. Then he got into his car, hit the siren, and sped toward the highway, in the direction of Catamount Bluff.

50

CLAIRE

I took the steep path at the end of Hubbard's Point Beach and zig-zagged into the trees. I had lived in these woods during the days after my attack. I had salved my wounds and bathed in Long Island Sound. I had counted on the ghost of my father and the cries of the mountain lion to keep me safe. Protection came in many forms. My love of nature and my father, and their love for me, had made me strong and brave, and I had survived.

I passed the rocky cove where my part of the mystery had begun twenty-five years ago, that summer night when I found Ellen's body. I could still see the gold of her bracelet glinting in the starlight.

Had Ellen worn that bracelet in Cancún? Had the Roman coin, dangling from the heavy links, captured the ocean's bioluminescence, the sea fire, the night she had been a witness to Griffin raping Marnie Telford? Spencer's description of that hour on the beach seared in my brain, and it gave me even more courage, strengthened my will to con-tinue down the path to Catamount Bluff.

I emerged from the woods into the clearing—the open property that ran between the houses and the edge of the trees. I smelled honey-suckle and roses; all the gardens were in bloom. Instead of ducking for cover, I held my head high and strode toward my studio. Waves broke on the rocks, their sound mingling with that of a lawn mower working somewhere down the road.

It was late afternoon, but the sun was still high. We were approaching the longest day of the year. I wondered who was at the Bluff, who might be looking out the window. If they saw me, would they think I had risen from the dead? Wade and Leonora were probably home, ready to start their cocktail hour.

I didn't care who saw me. Jackie knew I was here, and I was ready for this to end.

Crossing the lawn, I heard a car pulling into our driveway, doors opening and slamming, and distant voices. My back stiffened and my heart pounded—habitual fear. I ran to my studio and stepped inside.

I looked out the window toward the house. No sign of anyone outdoors and no one was coming toward my studio, so I figured I hadn't yet been seen. Good, it would give me time; besides, I felt reassured by the almost certain knowledge that Conor would be on his way here as soon as he spoke to Jackie.

My studio was tidy. It wasn't always this way—when in the midst of a project, I lost track of space and spread my materials out all over the place. But having finished my work for the exhibition, I had cleared nearly every surface. The exception was the rustic farmhouse table in the corner—the table itself bought at a flea market in the Berkshires when Griffin and I were first married.

We had gone cross-country skiing, were staying at an old inn just north of Stockbridge. The trails had been beautiful—fields covered with fresh powder on top of a deep packed base, lined with tall pines and spruce, limbs heavy with snow. If there were a manual for romantic winter weekends, this one—at least the first night—would have its own chapter. A fire in our bedroom fireplace, snow falling outside, the coziness of an 1890 inn. Griffin had bought me a first-edition book of poems by Emily Dickinson. She had lived in Amherst, just an hour east.

"Thank you, I love it," I said, holding the book. Not just because I adored poems but because he had been so thoughtful, had brought me an unexpected gift. I'd been on edge, walking on eggshells with him to avoid setting off his moods, and the weekend was a healing balm. No stress. No anger.

"Let me read one to you," he said.

"Should I choose it?" I asked.

"No, let me."

We were lying on the rug in front of the fireplace, snuggled up with down bed pillows and comforter, firelight reflecting on the ceiling above us.

"Here's one," he said and read one of her most exuberant:

> "Wild nights—Wild nights
> Were I with thee
> Wild nights should be . . ."

I laughed and held him tight, loving the spirit of the poem, the energy and emotion he put into reading it. We joked about having our own wild night, and our passion kept us up so late that we slept through breakfast and didn't start skiing until nearly noon.

On the way home, we stopped at the Long Brook flea market, wanting to buy something to always remind us of the weekend and our wild night. I had thought it would be something for us to share, but as soon as he saw the table—old scarred maple, held together with wooden pegs—he said I had to have it.

"For your studio," he said. "So you can spend all day working and thinking of me."

"I always think of you," I said.

"But this will be different," he said, putting his arm around me. "This table will hold your supplies. Your boxy things."

"Shadow boxes," I said.

"Right," he said, chuckling—and that laugh was my signal that it was all about to change. "Shadow boxes, sorry. Sounds like something kids make in art class. Anyway, this table will hold all the weird little things you pick up. It'll support them, hold them up, the way I do for you."

"Well, we do that for each other," I said. I didn't know if he was referring to money—he certainly had more than I did, but I sold my art, earned a living.

"Don't pretend it's equal," he said. We were standing at the checkout; he had his credit card ready.

"Which part?" I asked.

"Support," he said. "I'm giving you all I have."

"And I'm not doing that for you?"

"You could be more understanding," he said, his jaw set and his eyes darkening. I knew I had a choice—I could fight him on his statement, stand up for myself and say it was hard to be understanding of someone who flew off the handle so easily. But instead I took his hand, squeezed it, and forced myself to smile. I chose to believe that the weekend was a new start.

I tried not to think of Nate—easygoing, even-tempered Nate, the husband I had taken for granted and had left. I told myself that Griffin had been through so much in his childhood, had gone through a bad time with Margot, and that it was up to me to be patient while he learned how to love me. Yes, I was in the running to be a new age saint.

We loaded the table into the back of the Jeep. When we got home to Catamount Bluff, Wade Lockwood met us on the road; he helped Griffin carry my new worktable into the studio, setting it down in this very spot where I now stood. I hadn't moved it since.

It held the materials I had started to gather to build the shadow box for Max Coffin. I had sketched Ravenscrag from memory—from the walk I'd taken with Evans and Max to the seawall, when I'd looked back at the house and noticed all the bizarre features.

My drawing was still on the spiral-bound sketchpad. I had collected a basket of black feathers—whether they came from crows, grackles, red-winged blackbirds, or ravens, I wasn't sure.

I had already built the frame. It was fourteen-by-sixteen inches, four inches deep. I had cut basic shapes from balsa wood—the outline of the house, the crenellations of the towers—and glued them into place within the frame, ready to be adorned with other elements. Even with the anxiety of being home, the artist in me was pleased to see I had succeeded in giving the impression of Ravenscrag.

I counted on the fact that Griffin was so deeply uninterested in my work that he wouldn't have disturbed this shadow box, and I was right about that. I lifted the false bottom and saw the envelope inside. This is what I had come for.

I pulled out the letter from Evans. It was written in blue ink on pale-blue stationery, in small, tight handwriting, and had arrived days before I was attacked. Finally, I had learned what she had been trying to tell me that night at Griffin's fundraiser.

> Dear Claire,
>
> I am writing this by hand because Max reads my email, checks the call logs on my phone.
>
> You know the Last Monday Club has twenty members. But within it is a much smaller group—my husband, his brother, Wade, and Griffin. Over the last two months those men have split from the club and come here to Ravenscrag. It is more private, and they need privacy as they strategize your husband's election campaign. Alexander and Ford were at the last meeting.
>
> They are the most powerful men in Connecticut, and they are counting on Griffin to eviscerate the laws and protections that hold their companies in check.

They are counting on him, as governor, to deliver more riches, more power, to them all.

I have heard them talking. They believe that you have "something on him" that could prevent his election. You pose a threat to him—to them.

Perhaps my imagination is too vivid. Perhaps the danger to you is mostly in my head, but I strongly believe it's greater than that, and you are not the only one. Dan Benson, another member of the club but not of the inner circle, "has something" on Griffin as well, and he also needs to be careful . . .

I heard footsteps and voices, so I quickly tucked the letter back into the envelope and looked out the window. Alexander and Emily were walking toward the beach with two children—I immediately recognized them from news stories: Gwen and Charlie Benson. I knew Gwen had been rescued, but I'd thought Charlie was dead. Like me, he had come back to life.

My emotions went wild—I wanted to grab the children, get them away from here. I hesitated for just a moment. I always believed that Alexander was kind. I'd seen him being gentle, not like Ford. Was it possible he and Emily had the children's best interests at heart? *No,* I thought. He was just better able to hide his evil, like his father. He'd been at the meeting, part of the group targeting Dan and me. I had to save Gwen and Charlie.

I shoved the letter into my pocket, then took a deep breath. I stepped outside my studio door, ready to call to Alexander and pretend I still thought he was good. Hide the fact that I knew everything.

"Claire," Griffin said quietly.

I wheeled around. The sound of his voice made my fists clench, ready to defend myself and fight him off. He was standing right there, ten feet away, in the shadow of the privet hedge.

"I wondered what happened to you," he said.

"I escaped," I said, staring into his green eyes.

"That's unfortunate," he said.

"I'll scream," I said, pointing at Alexander and Emily and the children.

"It won't matter," he said. "My sons will always help me."

We had an audience—the four of them standing still, watching us. Would Griffin kill me right in front of them? I glanced at his hands; he didn't seem to have a weapon.

"I didn't expect you to be here," he said in an almost confessional tone. "I was planning to meet the children and get them set up."

"The Benson children?" I asked.

"Yes," he said. "Their mother's death was a terrible accident. Who could ever have guessed? Only Dan was supposed to die. A quick shot to his head after they docked at Block Island. And you were supposed to go, too, of course."

"Why?"

"Because neither of you could be trusted to keep your mouths shut. To be discreet and loyal. You couldn't forget Ellen."

"And Marnie," I said. "She deserves to be remembered too."

"You see? You're obsessed, how would you even know that? I never told you. I suppose there's someone else out there who wants to take me down. You're going to tell me who that is," he said. "Jackie—you've talked to her about it?" Griffin asked.

I thought of Jackie and Spencer, clenched my jaw and felt a trickle of cold sweat run down my back, knowing I had to warn and protect them.

"I was young and . . . overactive," Griffin said. "People make mistakes, but they deserve to be forgiven, especially when they're in a life of public service. Let's go inside, so you can tell me who else you've told," he said. I stared at his eyes. They were the barometer of his rage, and they were still green.

"What about Gwen and Charlie?" I asked quickly. "You said you're going to get them set up?"

"Of course," he said. "They are innocent, and now they're orphans."

"You killed Dan?"

"Ford did. I told you, my sons will always help me." He stared hard at me. "You're worrying about the Benson children. Don't. I know what it's like to suffer as a child, to be badly treated, abandoned. I could never do that to them. They will be fine."

"Where are you going to send them?" I asked, horrified by yet another of Griffin's machinations, playing with lives, discarding them when they threatened or had no further use.

"We have friends," he said. "Who will take care of them. You don't have to worry, Claire. They will have everything they could ever need or want."

"Except their parents."

He laughed. "Listen to you, talking about family. How ironic." His eyes narrowed. "You were going to abandon us, weren't you, Claire? I felt it—I could almost read your mind. You knew my political plans— how critical this election year is to my future. A separation, divorce, and whatever garbage you planned to publicize about Ellen would ruin me. It would destroy our future."

"*Our* future?" I asked.

"Not yours and mine," he said. "My sons' and friends'. My true friends."

"The inner circle?" I asked. "The men? So you can make them richer, share the power?"

"Get inside," he said, grabbing my shoulder with one hand, shoving me toward the door. At the same moment, he gestured to Alexander and yelled, "Take them out of here *now!*"

The children began to cry, and the girl dashed ahead. Emily lurched after her, grabbed her, distracting Alexander and Griffin.

I wrenched myself out of his grip and started to run. I thought of how Griffin had ambushed me in the garage that Friday—and it was him, I was sure now—I had felt that same grip on my arm, smelled his sweat rank with hate and violence.

I heard a boat engine putting along, just down the bluff. Was it here to take the children away? To be flown out of the country? If I could just beat Griffin to the rickety stairs, I could grab the kids away from Alexander. As I started to run, I rounded the end of the stone wall and saw Wade Lockwood hurrying from his house, blocking my way to the beach.

Griffin grabbed me from behind, holding my arms so tight I felt he might rip them out of the sockets. "You shouldn't have come back," he whispered.

Griffin put his hands around my neck and began to strangle me. I wrenched away, tried to run, and in that one instant before he caught me again, I looked into his eyes, and they were black. He grabbed me again.

"Stop," Wade shouted. "Not here."

"What the hell, old man?" Griffin asked, dropping his hands. I rubbed my throat and saw Ford walking down the hill with Leonora.

"Wade," Leonora said. "Have you lost your mind? You let her go and all is lost. Do you want victory in November or not?"

"I didn't say let her go. Just not here. I don't want this on Catamount Bluff," Wade said. "Take her somewhere else."

"I'll take her somewhere, Dad," Ford said. "You shouldn't be involved anyway. We'll protect you."

"Good boy," Leonora said. "Griffin, let's get the children out of here."

I was ready to run, but Ford and Wade grabbed me, tried to force me to the ground. I kicked and screamed, and Ford clamped his hand over my mouth. I bit him as hard as I could, and he wrenched away.

"Goddamn you!" Griffin shouted and tackled me.

I fought him with everything I had, scratched his face and kneed him so hard in the groin that he bellowed and rolled off me. I knelt on top of him, gasping for breath. I grabbed his neck with both hands and squeezed with all my might, the way he'd done to me. His cheeks were raked and bloody from my fingernails. He was moaning from the kick in the balls, his eyes nearly rolled back into his head with agony, but I pressed my thumbs into his Adam's apple and made him look at me.

"You murderer," I said. "Your life is destroyed, you know that? And women brought you down."

Ford grabbed my hair and tried to pull me off Griffin, but I had the force of a wildcat in me. I banged him in the face with my elbow; bone met bone, and I heard his nose break. He grunted in pain, but I felt and heard an inhuman roar boil out of me, drowning out his pathetic cry. Sirens wailed, the sound coming from Shore Road, getting louder as the vehicles sped into Catamount Bluff.

"Griffin," I said, finally letting go of his neck. I stood up and towered over him. "I want you to realize that this is the moment everything changes for you. Right this very second. You're over. And I'm here to watch it happen."

Griffin scrambled to his feet. Leonora had called to Alexander and Emily, and they were carrying the screaming children up the hill toward the house. Wade and Ford headed to the Lockwoods' house; Griffin followed them, limping. They didn't even wait for him.

Our peaceful bluff hummed with noise. I heard that boat engine idling in the Sound, and now the police cars were so close that I heard their tires crunching on the driveway. The two children clutched each other, crying. At the sound of the sirens, the adults had abandoned them in the middle of the lawn.

I went to the children, crouched down beside them, put my arms around them.

"My name is Claire," I said, my voice hoarse from Griffin's hands around my neck. "Are you Gwen and Charlie?"

Gwen nodded, eyes wide with terror.

I glanced toward the main house and saw a dozen state and Black Hall police officers and other emergency personnel streaming onto the property. Conor Reid spotted us.

"Claire," Conor said, running over.

"They killed Daddy! And they tried to kill her!" Gwen said.

I hugged her as she wept into my shoulder. I felt her shaking with grief and horror.

"Is it true?" I mouthed, looking at Conor. He nodded, and I could see the emotion in his eyes.

"Gwen," Conor said after a few moments, crouching beside us. "I'm going to take you and Charlie to your Aunt Lydia. She is going to be so happy to see you."

"You look like Tom," Charlie said.

"Yep," Conor said. "He's my big brother."

"They shot him," Charlie said.

"He's going to be okay," Conor said. "Jackie's at the hospital with him right now."

"Bring Maggie to him," Gwen said, lifting her face from my shoulder, shuddering as she tried to stop her sobs. "She will help him get well. She always makes him smile. We'll share her with him."

I held Gwen's and Charlie's hands, and we walked with Conor around the big house I had lived in with Griffin, past the old barn where he'd nearly killed me the first time. The turnaround was full of emergency vehicles. I saw Ben Markham put handcuffs on Griffin. I left the children with Conor and walked over to stand in front of Ben and Griffin. Griffin glared at me, his pupils fully dilated, his eyes gleaming black.

"Thank God you're okay, Claire," Ben said.

"I'm better than okay," I said, never taking my gaze off Griffin.

"Get me away from her, Ben," Griffin said.

"Seems she has something to say to you," Ben said. "So you're gonna listen."

"Prison," I said to Griffin in a quiet voice. "I wonder what that will be like for you. I hope when you get to the lockup today, you'll think about what I said back there on the lawn. I hope you'll remember, then and forever, the moment it all changed. And I hope that when you close your eyes, you'll see us. Me, Ellen, Marnie, Spencer, all of us. That's my wish for you, Griffin."

Then I nodded at Ben, letting him know I was done, and he opened the door to his police car and locked Griffin into the caged back seat.

Other officers surrounded Ford, Alexander, Emily, and the Lockwoods. Conor walked toward me with Gwen and Charlie. A female EMT came over and knelt down beside the children, gently asking them if they were hurt.

"I want you to get checked out too," Conor said to me.

"What about the kids?"

"I'll drive them to Shoreline General. And we'll call their Aunt Lydia," he said. "She'll meet us there. She doesn't even know about Charlie yet. You don't have to worry, Claire. She's their guardian now. She's ready for this."

"I hope so," I said, thinking of all they had lost, what they were about to face. Then, I suddenly thought of Jackie, of how she had supported me, been there for me, and how I had hurt her by hiding out so long. "Did Jackie call you?" I asked. "To tell you I had come back here?"

"It was a race," Conor said. "Between Jackie and your other friend."

"Excuse me?"

"Spencer Graham Fenwick," he said. "She gave me a quick rundown about Griffin, and she told me to watch out for you. She was afraid he'd try again."

"Spencer did it," I said. "Without her, there'd be no justice. She gave me the key to why he did it all."

I closed my eyes, thinking of the sisterhood: all of us who had been affected by Griffin's violence. I wasn't sure when Spencer planned to leave Charlestown. I knew she had important work to do, but I hoped she would stay for a while at least. We had so much more to talk about. I wanted to learn all she knew about monsters—men like Griffin. I hoped that maybe I would be able to help somehow. Justice was its own art, shining light into the shadows, complex yet ultimately as simple as can be: bringing balance, making things right. Helping women know that their experience, no matter how horrific, was their strength. It showed them that they were their own superheroes.

"There's someone else," I said. "Evans Coffin—Max's wife. You've got to get to her, protect her. She gave me this." I reached into my pocket, handed Conor the letter. "You'll understand when you read it. Her husband and his brother were in on this too."

Conor nodded. "We'll pick them up," he said.

"Just make sure Evans and Spencer are safe. Griffin and his friends are after everyone who knows."

"I will," he said. "Spencer is coming to the barracks, and I'm going to take her statement. And I'll read the letter and go see Evans." He gazed at me for a long moment. "You'd better call Jackie."

"I will," I said, smiling.

"Yeah," he said. "You've got a team rooting for you, that's for sure. No one was going to let up."

"Thanks, Conor," I said.

Then I saw him lift his gaze, looking past me toward the beach. It was only then that I realized the sound of the boat engine had stopped. And when I turned around, I saw the skiff's owner hurrying toward me, huffing and puffing like any other self-respecting scientist with a big belly.

"Nate," I said.

"You're alive, you're alive," he said, grabbing me hard, rocking me back and forth in a massive hug. "Do you know what I've been thinking? The world went so dark for a while because there was no Claire. I thought I'd never see you again."

I leaned into him, letting him hold me, my heart pounding as I tried to make sense of what I had believed when I saw those books and what I felt now.

"What was that email about?" he asked, holding me at arm's length. "What did you think I was part of?"

"I saw your books at Ravenscrag," I said.

"What's that?"

"It's a house. Owned by Maxwell Coffin."

He squinted his blue eyes tight, as if trying to remember the name. When he opened them, I saw his big smile and the burst of sun lines around his eyes. "Evans's husband," he said.

"You know Evans?"

"Yes," he said. "She's a great environmentalist. Came to one of my lectures and gave me a big donation to help fund that last expedition to the Bering Sea."

"Then why did you sign the books to Max instead of her?" I asked.

"Because he's a die-hard industrialist who'd like to develop every protected place on the planet. She thought that if I signed the books in a positive way, he might have a change of heart."

"I'm guessing that's not likely," I said.

"I wasn't holding my breath," he said. "Come on, let me drive you to the hospital." He touched my neck, the raw spot where the rope had chafed and burned, and then he leaned forward to kiss it.

Conor heard what Nate had said, and he nodded.

"I'll check in with you a little later," he said. "I'll get your statement then."

"Thank you," I said. Officer Peggy McCabe had handcuffed Emily Coffin and Alexander Chase; other officers had cuffed Ford, Wade, and Leonora.

Conor opened the back door of his Ford police car, letting Gwen and Charlie climb inside, then buckling the seat belts around the kids. I watched them drive away from Catamount Bluff.

I looked at Nate. "We're stuck here," I said.

"No, we're not," he said.

"It's a long walk out of Catamount Bluff."

"I thought we'd go by boat," he said. "It's a beautiful day."

I loved that idea. We held hands, my ex-husband and I, and walked through afternoon shadows past the house and barn and studio, across the lawn. Halfway to the weather-beaten beach stairs, I stopped still, listening.

"Did you hear that?" I asked. I swore I heard the big cat cry, way off in the distance.

Nate looked at me with an expression in his eyes that might have been skepticism. But his smile grew wide, letting me know it was wonder.

"I did," he said.

"I didn't imagine it?" I asked.

"Nope," he said. "You've got a mountain lion in those woods."

"I always knew it," I said. And I whispered, "Thank you, I love you forever."

Whether to the cat or my father or the ghost of Ellen Fielding, I wasn't sure, but I knew that the kids and I were safe, that Griffin and the others had been arrested, and I could hear the music of the sea, of the beach, of the woods that had saved my life.

And when Nate squeezed my hand and said to me, "I heard that," I realized he might have thought that I'd been whispering to him. And that was fine with me. Because in the deepest way possible and every way that counted, it was true.

ACKNOWLEDGMENTS

I am so grateful to Liz Pearsons, my amazing editor at Thomas & Mercer. Much gratitude to Charlotte Herscher, my developmental editor, Shasti O'Leary Soudant, my cover designer, and my entire T&M team, including Sarah Shaw, Laura Barrett, Alicia Lea, Susan Stokes, Brittany Russell, and Lindsey Bragg. And epic thanks to Gracie Doyle.

Boundless gratitude to my agent and close friend, Andrea Cirillo. A big thank-you to everyone at the Jane Rotrosen Agency: Jane Berkey, Meg Ruley, Chris Prestia, Annelise Robey, Christina Hogrebe, Rebecca Scherer, Amy Tannenbaum, Jessica Errera, Kathy Schneider, Sabrina Prestia, Hannah Rody-Wright, Julianne Tinari, Donald Cleary, Michael Conroy, Ellen Tischler, Hannah Strouth, and of course, the legend himself, Don Cleary.

Many thanks to my dear friend and film agent, Ron Bernstein.

Cynthia McFadden is a brilliant journalist. When I wrote about abuse of people and abuse of power in this novel, I thought of how Cynthia goes after the story and brings the truth to light. I'm thankful for her inspiring work.

I am thankful to Colette Harron for her wonderful heart. And she knows all the magical houses . . .

Andrew Griswold, director of EcoTravel for the Connecticut Audubon Society, is a great friend and one of the best birders and naturalists I know. Although it is claimed that Connecticut's last mountain lions went extinct in the late 1800s, there have been many reported sightings since then; in 2011, one was killed by a car on the Wilbur Cross Parkway. I thank Andy for discussing my fictional cat's habitat with me.

My thanks to Teri Lewis for her countless kindnesses as a friend and assistant and for her sweetness to the cats when I can't be with them.

I am grateful to Sergeant Robert Derry of the Connecticut State Police for his stories and accounts of law enforcement on the highways and byways of Connecticut.

Thank you to my exuberant and creative social media manager, Patrick Carson.

Lifelong thanks to William Twigg Crawford for keeping an eye on the sky and always letting me know the wind speed at Ledge Light.

Gratitude to Katherine Verano and Melissa Zaitchik of Safe Futures. Their support has been invaluable. Safe Futures serves those impacted by domestic violence, sexual assault, stalking, and trafficking in southeastern Connecticut. Please reach out to them or the National Domestic Violence Hotline if you or someone you know needs help.

I adore and am forever grateful to my sister Maureen Rice Onorato and brother-in-law, Olivier Onorato. We speak every night, no matter what. They take me sailing on *Merci*, lead me through Saint-André-de-Cubzac and Saint-Émilion, share tales of their cat, Georgie, and the white-breasted nuthatches nesting in the bluebird house, and make me laugh nearly every time we talk. There's nothing better than going through life with the people you love, and for me, that list begins with Maureen and Olivier.

ABOUT THE AUTHOR

Photo © by Kristina Loggia

Luanne Rice is the *New York Times* bestselling author of thirty-five novels that have been translated into twenty-five languages. In 2002, Connecticut College awarded Rice an honorary degree, and she also received an honorary doctorate from the University of Saint Joseph. In June 2014, she received the 2014 Connecticut Governor's Arts Award for excellence as a literary artist.

Several of Rice's novels have been adapted for television, including *Crazy in Love,* for TNT; *Blue Moon,* for CBS; *Follow the Stars Home* and *Silver Bells,* for the Hallmark Hall of Fame; and *Beach Girls,* for Lifetime.

Rice is a creative affiliate of the Safina Center, an organization that brings together scientists, artists, and writers to inspire a deeper connection with nature—especially the sea. Rice is an avid environmentalist and advocate for families affected by domestic violence. She lives on the Connecticut Shoreline.

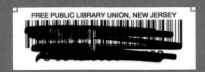